LILY'S LITTLE FLOWER SHOP

LISA DARCY

BLOODHOUND
— BOOKS —

Print ISBN 978-1-913942-53-3

To my dearest friend, Louise, florist and fashionista extraordinaire. I miss you every day.

CHAPTER 1

Lily

My standard skinny latte in hand, I power walked into my office building and caught the elevator to the eighteenth floor. Though today's routine was much the same as any other day, my hands were clammy and a knot of discomfort built inside me. I switched on my computer and squinted at my Fitbit. Seven forty am. I liked to be one of the first in, especially on a Friday; clear the decks for the weekend.

'Hey! Beat ya.' Taylor, my best friend and super-cute lipstick lesbian (her words, not mine), sat down on my desk and crossed her legs. A tall, slim redhead with huge blue eyes, Taylor was always upbeat. 'Nervous?'

I swivelled in my chair. 'A little.' I paused. 'A lot, actually.'

As a sales manager for AustIn, one of Australia's five largest insurance companies, my job was as dull as it sounded, but it paid well. For eight years, I'd been catching the metaphorical lift to the top, always stopping two floors short. I was up for

Operations Manager, a national position overseeing the ten sales managers and their teams. Whispers said I was a sure thing, but I never got my hopes up until the contract was signed.

'Don't look now, but your rival's smirking by the coffee machine.'

I looked over my shoulder. Glenn Kelly, mid-thirties, tall and smug, wearing a cheap navy suit and brown brogues. Holding court with his squad.

In a company scandal twelve months earlier, Glenn had celebrated signing a new client by taking him and several male staffers to a seedy strip club. The CEO, Alastair Briggs, brushed it aside as a 'juvenile indiscretion' with a boys-will-be-boys sigh. Since then, Glenn had arranged several more dubious celebrations at company expense.

I shook my head and glanced back at Taylor. 'Snake.'

'No one has your expertise, Lil. The champers is chilling. We'll be celebrating soon. Yeeha!'

For the next hour, I kept my head down, calling overseas clients who needed more than a routine email. One hour rolled into two and by eleven, I still hadn't had a shoulder tap or call beckoning me to Alastair's office. The inside of my mouth was raw from chewing so hard.

I put off going to the bathroom all morning, until I couldn't stand it any longer.

When I arrived back at my desk, I'd missed a call. A voicemail from upstairs requested my immediate presence on the twentieth floor. I smoothed down my blue silk shirt, raked fingers through my hair, freshened my lipstick and stepped into the hall. Adrenalin pumping, I pushed the elevator button and distracted myself by guessing which of the four lifts would make it to the eighteenth floor first.

Number one as it happened.

'Nice,' I said to a delivery guy seemingly engulfed by a

massive bouquet of colourful blooms. The sight swept me in a wave of nostalgia for my mostly happy teenage years working in a florist shop. Simpler times.

A couple of minutes later, I entered Alastair's office and shook his hand. 'Good morning.' My stomach muscles tensed.

'Lily, sit down.' He beamed, gesturing to one of the chairs in front of his desk. 'Firstly, I'd like to say how impressed the board is with your professionalism and expertise. Client feedback is outstanding. As usual.'

Okay... I took a seat, cautiously optimistic.

'Truth is, Lily,' he continued, 'the company feels you'd be wasted in senior management.'

Here it comes...

'The OM's job will be mainly admin, running the show from the inside. Minimal client contact.' Alastair took a breath. 'That's why we're giving the job to Glenn.'

KA-BOOM!

Glenn, the most unprofessional man I had ever worked with. Glenn, the man who took clients out lap dancing. Glenn!

'But this is what I've been working towards,' I said, trying to remain in control. 'I'm more qualified than Glenn.'

'The board feels Glenn is a better fit. I went into bat for you and gave it my best shot, but my hands were tied. They feel he's more suited to an administration role.'

'The board consists of nine middle-aged white men and three women—'

'And five of them wanted you for the role—'

I shook my head. Unbelievable.

'You understand, don't you?'

I understood all right. Don't let Glenn near people. His antics were out of control, but the company felt he was too valuable to discipline and risk losing. Alastair had poached Glenn from a rival company, and he'd bought several million-dollar clients with him. I stood up, keeping my breathing regular. In. Out. In. Out.

'I'm the better fit,' I said.

'There'll be more opportunities down the road. Don't think of this as a dead end.'

But that's exactly what I thought. This was the worst scenario I could have imagined. Today was all or nothing.

I moved for the door, barely able to put one foot in front of the other. Out in the hall I pressed the elevator button not caring which bloody lift arrived, so long as it was now. I took a deep breath, determined not to fall apart and lose face in front of my colleagues.

Taylor was waiting in my office with a bottle of Moët. 'Congratulat—' She stopped when she saw my expression. 'What happened?'

'The board and Glenn-fucking-Kelly, that's what,' I said, fighting back tears.

Moments later, the man himself poked his head into my office. Thank God it was only his head. 'No hard feelings?'

I smiled weakly. 'Not at all. Congratulations.'

'Thanks, Lil, and don't worry, I'll be a fair and righteous commander.' He winked and gave me a lascivious smile.

Fair and righteous commander? What did that mean? The man had no morals. He'd screw anyone, literally and figuratively, to get what he wanted.

There wasn't much more to say. Taylor wanted to take me out to lunch, but I couldn't stomach food. I couldn't stomach the office either, what with Glenn strutting around taking congratulations from everybody. Operations Manager? More like Official Moron.

I switched off my computer, grabbed my bag and walked out. I didn't make a big deal about it. I didn't flounce or storm. I remained composed.

'Anna, I'm heading out to kill myself,' I told my assistant. Okay, I didn't actually say that. 'Anna, I'm heading out for the rest of the day.'

She didn't need to know I was heading to the nearest bottle shop and then home.

❧

Seven hours later, Matt, my handsome boyfriend with evening stubble, dark wavy hair and a six-pack courtesy of Anytime Fitness, strolled in my front door. 'Where have you been? I've been calling all afternoon.'

'Pluto.'

He stared at me. 'You all right? You look terrible.'

I burst into tears. 'I've had a shit day.'

He took me into his arms. 'The promotion?'

I nodded.

'Hey, I've got some great news that'll cheer you up. Guess?'

'Matt, I really don't feel like—'

'Okay, spoilsport, I'll tell you. I got it!' Matt beamed.

I had no idea what he was talking about.

'The transfer! It's come earlier than expected.'

I shrugged. 'What transfer?'

'The transfer I put in for ages ago. I told you about it. We're moving to Singapore!' He held up a bottle of Bollinger. Where had he been hiding it?

I slumped on the sofa and dried my eyes. 'That's great.' But really, I felt like he'd kicked me in the stomach.

'I know you were hoping to move up a rung—'

'A rung? I was expecting to get the fucking promotion, Matt! But the board gave the job to fucking Glenn. He's got as much skill as a goldfish, but he has a penis—'

'Lil!'

'What? It's true. I have a vagina so clearly that rules me out of the boys' club. It's the second promotion I've missed out on in six months. Not to mention an extra fifty grand.'

'Sorry, I understand. That's horrible for you.' Matt hugged me. Then he picked up the champagne, popped the cork and retrieved two flutes from a side cabinet. 'Look at it this way. Now, you're free to come to Singapore with me like we planned.'

I got to my feet, legs trembling. 'We never planned—'

'Okay,' he said, pouring the bubbly. 'But we did talk about it. It was going to come up sooner or later. It happens to be sooner. To tell you the truth, part of me is a little relieved you missed out today.'

'What?' I shook with anger. I was touched he wanted me by his side but pissed that he just assumed I'd go along. I'd been to Singapore several times – overcrowded and then there was the weather. I had enough difficulty coping with Sydney's humidity.

'I know it's selfish,' he said, 'but now you're free to come with me.'

'Right, and what exactly would I do over there?'

Matt handed me a glass. 'Cheers, babe.' He went to clink his glass with mine.

I couldn't do it. I turned away, gulped and sneezed.

'You don't have to work. You can spend your time eating out, shopping, socialising.'

I felt like bashing my head against the wall. Or maybe Matt's. 'Why would I want to give up my career and do nothing all day, as your hanger-on, without my own identity? Besides, I don't know anyone in Singapore, so who would I socialise with?'

'Woah! Where's all this coming from?'

'*Where's all this coming from?* I've been working towards this promotion for years. It's not just another rung on some imaginary ladder,' I said, tense and taut. 'What would you have done had I got the promotion?'

Matt looked taken aback. 'What do you mean?'

'If I'd been made Operations Manager, would you have given up Singapore to stay here with me?'

He hesitated before placing his hands on mine. 'We don't have to worry about that now. The decision's been made for us.'

'For you, maybe.'

'Sorry. I know you're bummed but take it as a sign. For us. Our future.'

I rubbed Matt's arm, trying to be happy for him.

We finished our drinks and walked up the road to our favourite Vietnamese restaurant. The temperature was still over thirty degrees. The promised thunderstorm hadn't broken, and the air was oppressively humid. I had a splitting headache and felt nauseous.

At the end of a short meal of rice paper rolls and spicy noodle soup, I asked Matt if he'd mind going back to his apartment. I needed sleep and I didn't want to share my bed.

'But we're supposed to be celebrating. Come on,' he said, taking my arm and dragging me down the street towards my house. 'I won't bite. Much.'

The last thing I wanted was for Matt to bite me, but I was too worn out to argue. Inside, I saw Trouble, my pet rabbit, sprawled out on the sofa. I scooped him up. 'For a rabbit, you act a lot like a dog.' I put him in his hutch with a carrot and grain, and then Matt and I went to bed.

We had sex but, as enthusiastic and attentive as Matt was, I just went through the motions.

Later, although I needed to sleep, I lay awake for hours wondering what to do. Matt slept peacefully, as he always did after sex. Celebratory fucking, he'd called it. Celebratory for him. He snuffled and snuggled into me, so close it was claustrophobic. I could barely breathe. I pushed him away.

I glanced at the beside clock. 3am. My mind raced.

Everything had changed in the past sixteen hours. I didn't want to move to Singapore, but did that mean I didn't love Matt? That our relationship was over? We'd been together three years but hadn't made the leap to co-habitating. We certainly hadn't talked about marriage, children, and a combined mortgage. I had my mortgage. He had his. I held part of me back, maybe because there were certain conversation topics with Matt that were off limits. Maybe because I couldn't truly be myself with him. I quickly shooed those thoughts away. Matt and I were compatible. We both had an aversion to cooking, green tea and vegans. We were physically compatible. And, Matt accepted Trouble as his own.

Matt was a good man. But what would he have done, had I got the promotion? I rolled over with my back to him and stared into the silent darkness. My brain refused sleep.

What about my job? My career? Could I bear to work under Glenn knowing that everyone knew I wanted that role? But if I left the company, where would I go? The job market was flat. There weren't many options out there.

CHAPTER 2

I must have woken up crying because Matt had his arms around me, kissing my neck and whispering, 'You didn't get the promotion you wanted. You're pissed. It's perfect timing, don't you think?'

I nodded and fell back asleep, too exhausted to argue.

In the vague recesses of my mind, I thought I heard the phone ring, then talking and laughing. In a mess of tangled sheets, I opened one eye and saw Matt holding the landline. I really needed to get rid of that thing. The only people who rang it were marketeers and my mother.

Shit! Mother!

I sat up. It was eight on Saturday morning. Matt was talking to Mum. Who else would call this early on a weekend? No doubt she'd already put a load of washing on, vacuumed, watered the garden and cooked bacon and eggs for Dad.

He glanced over at me. 'The princess is finally awake Mrs M. I'll put her on.' He handed me the phone.

'Mum,' I said, wiping the sleep from my eyes.

'Darling, Matt's been telling me the great news about

Singapore. I'll miss you, but what an amazing opportunity for you both.'

'My career's here in Sydney.'

'Lily! You're as stubborn as your father. And Iris for that matter. It's her birthday, by the way.'

'I know, Mum.' I took a deep breath. 'I have to go. Talk to you later.'

'Don't leave it too long. We still need to discuss Christmas.'

Joy. Christmas was less than three weeks away.

I hung up, gobsmacked. 'Matt, you shouldn't have said anything. You know what Mum's like.'

'I do. I told her about Singapore because I hoped she might convince you to come with me.'

Matt had no idea. Neither did Mum. They didn't get how much my independence meant to me.

'You're coming with me, aren't you?' Matt said, stroking my thigh, impatient for an answer.

'I don't know if I'm ready... I need a shower.'

I scrubbed my hair a little too roughly. Then vigorously combed through the conditioner. What the hell was wrong with Matt, believing I'd drop everything to live with him in Singapore? He'd relegated me to the little woman whose only activities, for the foreseeable future, would be shopping and socialising. And presumably having a lot of sex. It might be an exciting prospect for some, but not for me.

I didn't know what to do next, but I definitely needed time out. The city air seemed overwhelming. I needed to escape the claustrophobia that had engulfed me. Taking off to the south coast to visit Iris for her birthday seemed the perfect solution.

When I walked out of the bathroom, Matt was waiting expectantly. 'How about we eat out this morning? There's this new café—'

'Matt, it's my Aunty Iris's birthday. I haven't seen her in forever, and a drive might help clear my head.'

'Great. I'll come with you.'

'I'd rather go alone.'

Matt hesitated. 'But I have Jem's buck's party tonight, and tomorrow, the work golf tournament.' He squeezed my shoulder. 'I won't see you all weekend.'

'By the sound of it, you wouldn't anyway. Monday night?' We always spent Monday night together, usually at my house.

He sighed and stared at his hands. 'If you really want to go alone...'

Ten minutes later, after phoning Iris to arrange lunch, I jumped in my car. I blasted the radio so loud I could block the noise in my head. I drove south, and soon, the city, time and traffic disappeared.

Two hours later, I turned off the Princes Highway into Clearwater, way ahead of schedule. I wound down the windows and breathed in the fresh sea air. How I'd missed that. It smelt so clean after Sydney's smoky haze. I was early for lunch and even had time to buy her a gift. Flowers?

Memories of her flower shop flooded back. As a teenager, I'd regularly visited in the school holidays to help out. I loved the happy atmosphere, the camaraderie of the locals, and Iris's full-on, caring approach with every customer she met. She seemed to know everything about every flower. When I was younger, I wanted to be like her, a massive ball of energy and fun.

I parked the car, climbed out and stared at the view. With the ocean on one side and mountains on the other, this place was idyllic. I didn't come down nearly enough – and every time I did, I asked myself why I didn't visit more often. I wandered around, enjoying the relaxed country coast vibe, people chatting in cafés, the ocean sounds, and surfers with bleached blond hair sauntering to the beach with their boards. What more could a girl ask for?

Well, a flower shop for one. I scouted the village twice in search of flowers. Out of luck, I ventured into the deli and bought chocolates instead. Then I found the café where Iris and I were meeting.

'Lily-Pily!' Iris boomed as I walked through the doorway. She stood from her chair and waved madly. Wearing a bright orange caftan and a fluoro green and red head scarf, silver, sparkly nails completed her look. 'Sweetie!' She grabbed me in a huge bear hug and covered me in kisses. 'Who's my favourite niece?'

I smiled. 'Me, as I'm your only one. You look divine. Happy, happy birthday.'

'It's the festive season,' she chortled. 'I should hope I look divine.'

I gave her the chocolates. 'Sorry, I wanted to buy you flowers.'

We sat down. 'The less said about birthdays the better. Thank you for the choccies though.'

'I was surprised you were free. I expected you to be out celebrating—'

'Bowls Christmas lunch. Practically everyone I know is going.' Iris made a face. 'I don't do bowls, no matter how much bubbly is on offer.'

Across the table, I placed my hand over hers. 'Fabulous! A win for me.'

'Me too. Now, tell me all your news. Your mother says you're off to Singapore in the new year. How did that happen? Cute Matt talk you into it?'

'Wishful thinking on Mum's part. I'm not going to Singapore.' I slammed my hand on the table harder than I meant to and the waitress, who looked no more than twelve, who'd stepped up beside me, flinched. 'Sorry,' I said, glancing at her. 'Mothers.'

After we ordered, Iris asked, 'So what's happening?'

I told her about being passed over for a promotion, how Matt was being transferred to Singapore and that I had no idea what my next move was to be. 'I feel trapped.'

'Darling,' she pointed a full fork of lettuce at me, 'you need to follow your own dreams. Not your mother's. Not Matt's. Not mine. Yours!'

Easy for Iris to say. She'd done exactly what she wanted, regardless of the consequences. Like refusing not one, but two marriage proposals from men who were considered 'good stock' and opening a business by herself at a time when a woman's place was definitely in the home. She'd owned a successful flower shop for thirty years, ten kilometres inland from Clearwater, until retiring eight years ago.

'The question is,' Iris said, 'what do you want from your life? You say you don't want to work with this Glenn creature, or run away with Matt to be a kept woman, so what does Lily Mason want to do, besides spend sunny Saturdays visiting her favourite aunt?'

'I don't know. But I'm fed up. I don't think I can stay at AustIn. Me busting the proverbial gut climbing the so-called fucking corporate ladder, has been for nothing.'

Iris reached across the table and took my hand. 'Please. Tell me what you really think.'

'All I've done since uni is work. Hard. And get the odd jay-walking fine for rushing across the road to work. I guess I wanted to tick all the boxes. Relationship, career, financial security, a home. A mortgage, at least ... There has to be something more.'

'Marriage? Babies—'

'No,' I said a little too loudly. Memories of a sixteen-year-old

Lily rushed back. I squeezed my eyes closed and settled my breathing.

'Sorry, Lil. I shouldn't have mentioned—'

I waved her words away. 'It was a long time ago.'

She nodded. 'Don't look back, sweetheart. Forward, Lils. Always forward. No good ever comes from dwelling on the past.'

'You're right.' Iris was generally always spot on.

'Why not consider Singapore? It might be good for you and Matt. A fresh start.'

'I don't want to go. I don't like Singapore and the thought of living in a city apartment...'

'You're a career girl and took a knock yesterday—'

'It's more than a knock, Iris.'

'Why don't you explore the possibilities of what a move overseas could offer you? Have you really given it serious thought?'

'Why do I have to defend myself? I love blue skies and the beach. But the crowds. The hassle. There's no parking. Sure, it's a popular tourist destination but I don't want to live in the midst of it.' I sat back and ran my fingers through my hair. 'To be honest I've even had enough of bloody Sydney.'

'Woah. Take it easy, girl. Somebody needs a break. And sometimes you don't realise you need a break until something like this happens.'

'Yeah, corporate life was fine while I thought I was advancing, but if that's not happening, why put up with it? I want something for myself. I've been going non-stop for eight years and have barely had time to breathe. Maybe it's time to take a step back. Smell the roses, that sort of thing. I wouldn't mind a change of pace. I always thought I'd open my own business one day, but that never happened.'

'Lily!' Iris spoke so loudly I almost fell off my chair. 'You're only thirty! Plenty of time.'

'Thirty-one, actually.' And feeling seventy.

'Of course. That one year makes all the difference. Okay, old girl, let's go for a stroll about town. You can keep telling me about your woes while we walk.'

I paid the bill and as we stepped outside, I heard familiar chimes. I pointed. 'Look! The ice-cream van's coming down the street.' In summers spent with Iris we'd drive into Clearwater after she closed the shop and we'd eat fish and chips at the beach before treating ourselves to a vanilla soft serve.

'Tourist season has hit,' she scoffed.

'I love it.'

Aunty Iris linked her arm with mine. 'Sentimental for the old days?'

I sighed. A double-edged sword. Some memories I wanted to permanently erase but mostly, I wanted to keep them close. 'Clearwater's a slice of heaven. Can't beat that ocean view.'

'Slice of heaven, perhaps, but noisy. But then I've lived here for forty years.' She paused. 'Maybe I'm just tired.'

'You! Tired? Never!'

Iris didn't actually live in Clearwater. She lived on acreage inland, fifteen minutes from Clearwater. Her nearest neighbours were half a kilometre away. Iris liked it that way. She'd lived alone since her partner Mike died years earlier.

'Would you look at that!' she said, stopping in front of the vacated butcher shop. 'Old man Christof has quit. He's been saying he would for the last ten years. Finally, true to his word.' She tapped a fingernail on the window. 'The floor plan reminds me of my old flower shop. Looks like a massive cold room at the side there.'

'Now who's feeling sentimental?' I peered inside. 'A pity there's no florist in Clearwater.'

'None in the surrounding towns either now. Mine was one of the last. It's a tough business.'

'I loved spending my holidays helping you out.'

'Good times, sweetheart, for the most part.' She kissed my forehead. 'For the most part.'

'Do you ever wonder—'

'No and neither should you. I do, however, remember you doing your floristry certificate before you got high and mighty and decided you wanted to study business and make squillions of dollars.' She squeezed my arm. 'Which you have.'

'Yeah, along with getting caught up in the corporate world, a mortgage and kale smoothies.'

'War cabbage! 'Twas once the fashion that everyone wanted to be gluten intolerant. There'll be a new fad next week.'

We wandered down the street to the end of the shops and crossed over to walk back to our cars. Iris stopped outside the real estate agent. She'd loved looking in these windows ever since I could remember. 'A gal can dream, can't she?' was one of her favoured mantras.

The *For Lease* sign struck me straight away. 'The butcher's shop's for rent.'

Iris smiled and walked in, making a beeline for a woman of similar vintage to herself. 'Trish.'

The woman turned round and beamed. She had thick white bobbed hair and a huge smile. I liked her immediately.

She held out her hand. 'Yes, Trish Foster.'

'Iris Ingram. You sold me my house many moons ago.'

'Of course.' Trish shook Iris's hand. 'What did you do with the old shed?'

'It's still standing, full of loved but broken furniture, books I can't part with and a family of fat possums.' Iris gestured to me. 'This is my gorgeous niece, Lily. We were wondering what the story is with Christof's shop. Finally had enough, hey?'

'Afraid so. With the new supermarket, he couldn't compete. Or rather, he didn't want to. Decided his time would be better spent with his grandchildren up Port Macquarie way.' Trish spoke in a throaty drawl, like she'd been smoking since she was fourteen.

'So, it's vacant?' Iris said, turning to me. 'Could you see yourself owning a little café or maybe a gallery, Lil?'

I smiled. 'And not having a single care in my make-believe world? Sure.' How could anyone possibly have career or romance woes living in paradise?

'I'll show you inside if you like,' Trish said. 'Give me a moment to lock up here.'

'We're being nosy,' I said. I didn't want to waste her time.

'Nonsense,' Iris chimed in. 'Trish, we'd love to take a gander.'

Five minutes later, the three of us stood inside the butcher's shop trying not to gag. It was smelly, small and cold. The shop had housed butchers since 1904 and though the guy vacating had cleaned it, he'd done a lousy job. The place reeked of blood, guts, and meat.

Shop, cold room storage and a toilet downstairs, leading to a rear pebbled courtyard. Upstairs housed a compact, two-bedroom flat with a sunny balcony, that held two cane chairs and a sturdy round table, big enough for dinner, drinks, whatever ... I sat down in one of the chairs and squinted at the uninterrupted view of the ocean.

'Imagine having a flower shop downstairs and living up here,' Iris said to no one in particular. 'I would've adored it.'

'Clearwater could do with a bloody good florist,' said Trish, walking back downstairs.

Outside on the street, I peered upstairs at the balcony while we waited for her to lock up.

'What do you reckon?' Iris asked.

'About?'

'A little adventure down south?'

My heart skipped a beat.

Trish joined us and handed me her business card. 'Nice to meet you, Lily, and lovely to see you again, Iris. Don't be strangers.'

I put the card in my bag and glared at Iris. 'Utter madness!'

'Come on,' she replied. 'Can't we at least have a bit of fun with your mum? She'll go crazy at the thought of this.'

'Iris! She already thinks you're a bad influence.'

She winked. 'Bossy older siblings always think that.'

During the two-hour drive back to Sydney, I fantasised about owning a flower shop in Clearwater. The town had changed over the years. Many more apartments, that's for sure; a massive new skatepark next to the redesigned playground; and a new supermarket that had replaced the corner store. Not the sleepy backwater it had been fifteen years earlier when I was visiting with Iris every few days.

But me? A florist? Alone? Crazy. Still, my fantasy lingered. Me, surrounded by colourful blooms. Happy. Smiling. Stress free. Me, not worrying about deadlines and sales targets and pushy chauvinistic bosses. Me, my own boss. Drinking kale juices ... or not.

Who was I kidding? I imagined my mother's reaction. She'd have a fit. I didn't want her to have a heart attack on my account.

Plus, there was Matt. He was ambitious and while he was sometimes dismissive of my needs, I knew he didn't mean it. He was just insensitive. I worked harder because he worked harder. He was never over at my place before seven at night, so I was rarely home much before then either. I'd been motivated before I met Matt, but he was the one who'd ignited the flame and urged me not to settle. Most of the time, I couldn't imagine us not being together. We were a team. We relied on each other.

Matt was my rock. My insensitive and ambitious rock, but still mine. That's why I'd been shocked he was so blasé when I told him about Glenn getting the promotion ahead of me. But I wasn't going to dwell on it. I'd missed him today and kind of wished he'd taken the trip with me.

I rang him. 'Hey. What's happening?'

'Hanging with the lads. You still bummed?'

'Yes.' My voice was a little louder than intended.

'Don't sweat the small stuff, Lil.'

'Small stuff? How can you say that? I deserved that job.'

'I know, but it's not personal. It's just business. You have to play the game.'

Stung like a slap on sunburnt skin, my good mood evaporated. They had all let me down – the system, the company and my own boyfriend. I knew where I stood, smack bang in the middle of shit.

'What?' I asked after a while. 'Hang out at strip clubs and lap dancing bars? Is that what you expect me to do? It's easy for you to talk about playing the game. You're a man. Men always win at this game. I'll talk to you later.'

I imagined us not together. It was scarily easy to do.

CHAPTER 3

On the bus Monday morning, everyone wore earphones as usual, listening to music, playing games, and checking out Tinder. The temperature? Twenty-eight degrees with a top of thirty-seven forecast. It was going to be a stinker. Most faces looked hot, irritable and sweaty. Maybe because of Tinder, most likely because of the weather.

An advertisement on the wall panel above one of the windows showed a pristine sandy beach, rolling waves and cloudless blue sky. *Escape to the south coast where the sun shines, sand sparkles and the beach beckons. What are you waiting for?* It seemed directly aimed at me.

What are you waiting for? My job, that's what. I had a job to do. A job I was very good at. Even if I was pissed off.

Coffee in hand, I was seated at my desk by seven forty-five. As I sorted through emails, a new one arrived from Alastair to Glenn, copying me and the rest of the team. I read it and read it again. Several accounts were to be reshuffled. Mainly mine. Effective immediately.

As the new Operations Manager, Glenn Kelly would prefer a more hands-on role than the previous OM. Glenn will speak with you individually to ensure the smooth and efficient transfer of information … I am sure you will agree that this new direction is fresh and exciting and in the best interests of the company…

Blah, blah, fucking blah.

Of my twelve accounts, three provided the majority of my bonuses. Taking them away effectively meant cutting my salary by a third. I stared at the email a bit longer, tapping my fingers on my desk.

Fight or flight?

At a minute past eight, I cleared out my personal belongings. A framed photo of Trouble swimming in the bath, one of Matt and me from a Christmas party two years earlier, a motley African violet, some hair clips and my spare travel card. Not much to show for eight years. Everything but the plant fitted in my bag. I took a deep breath and walked out, handbag and plant in one hand, half-drunk coffee in the other.

While I waited for the lift, guessing which one would arrive first, Taylor stepped out of elevator three and eyed me suspiciously. 'What's going on?'

I shrugged, determined to remain calm. 'Taking some time off.'

'You okay?' Taylor looked bemused.

'Talk to you later.' I handed her my plant and stepped into the lift.

Out on the street, I fished Trish's card out of my bag and phoned her. She answered after two rings.

'It's Lily Mason calling. Is the butcher shop still for rent?'

'Lily, how nice to hear from you so soon. Sure is.'

'Good, I'll take it.' I'd sort out the details later.

After I'd hung up, Taylor rang. 'At the risk of repeating myself, what's going on?'

'I'm quitting, getting drunk, moving to the beach and opening a flower shop.'

'Yeah, okay. What's really going on? Glenn pissing you off already?'

'You wouldn't be laughing if you had to report to him.'

'No, I wouldn't. I'll stick with Human Resources, thanks. So, what's up?'

'I told you.'

'A flower shop, just like that?'

'It would appear so.'

An hour later, after another coffee and a big breakfast of avocado and tomato on sourdough, I returned to the office, got an audience with Alastair, and resigned.

'I understand your position, Lily—'

I rolled my eyes. 'On Friday, you said nothing would change. For crying out loud, Alastair, I've lost viable accounts and it's only...' I made a point of checking my Fitbit '...Nine-fifteen. Monday morning.'

'I wish you'd reconsider.'

'Why? I've lost a third of my business and he has zero respect for his female colleagues.'

Alastair stared at me. 'I give you my word I'll be keeping close tabs on him.'

'Your word doesn't mean much, given our previous conversation. Besides, I don't want to work under Glenn.' I took a moment to calm down and breathe. 'Give me a reason to stay. Tell me you'll let me keep my accounts.'

He said nothing.

I knew it. 'I rest my case.'

Thankfully, Alastair let me take my entitlements. Accounts took all of fifteen minutes to present me with my final pay statement. I was home just after ten thirty.

'Aunty Iris,' I said, when she answered her phone. 'I've done it.'

'Done what, darl?'

'Resigned. I've spoken with Trish. The butcher's shop is mine.'

'Pardon?'

'I'm opening a florist shop.'

'Wow, you move fast when you set your mind to something.'

I hesitated. 'Do you think I've done the wrong thing?'

'Good heavens, no! Lily-Pily, I knew the corporate world couldn't hold you captive forever. You and I are simpatico. We're flower girls ... we need to be free with our blooms.'

'Er, yes. I guess.'

'Just know that unlike finance and business, running a flower shop will never make you millions. But you'll be rewarded in so many ways you'd never expect.'

She'd said much the same to me when I'd enrolled for the floristry diploma. At the time, her words led me to choose a career in finance. This time, I wouldn't be swayed. 'Better to live the dream and be poor than to never give it a go.'

'That's the spirit, my girl. And at Clearwater! A mere fifteen minutes' drive from me. You are one lucky lady. I can be at your beck and call when I'm not scouring the flea markets, playing bingo or napping. Now then,' she said, suddenly serious, 'what did your mother say? I can almost hear her screams from here.'

'Let's keep this conversation secret until the lease is signed. But all going well, I'll be moving down early January.'

Two hours later, Trish emailed me the preliminary contract, which included terms and conditions, the dimensions of the shop, renter expectations and the owner and real estate agent obligations. Straightforward.

My heart screamed 'YES', but my business head wasn't so sure. I'd always been so careful ... there was an option to sign for six or twelve months. I closed my eyes. This was my chance. Blinking, I signed for twelve months.

Holy Fuck!

I'd avoided Matt all weekend. Perhaps *avoided* was too strong a word. We spoke and texted, but I hadn't seen him since Saturday morning. He knew I was pissed off but didn't know I was about to completely uproot my life. The sooner I could tell him and clear the air, the better. Or so I hoped. We needed a proper conversation and Monday date night was the time. I heated up a beef lasagne from the local deli, made a green salad, opened a bottle of Shiraz, and waited for Matt to arrive.

Seven o'clock came and went. Sick of tapping my fingers and talking to Trouble, I poured myself a glass.

A text came through at seven twenty.

Sorry, babe. Still in a meeting. Should be there by nine. Please wait up. X

I drained a second glass and picked at a piece of lasagne while Trouble ate my salad. At nine, I covered what I hadn't eaten with plastic wrap and put it in the fridge. I placed the leftover wine on a side bench, put Trouble in his hutch and went to bed. So much for having a heart to heart.

Sometime later, Matt crept into the bedroom. 'Hey,' he whispered, climbing in beside me.

'We need to talk,' I said, sitting up, instantly awake.

'Can it wait till morning? I'm knackered.'

I took a deep breath and lay back down. We were both shattered. Yes, our talk could wait till morning.

Ten minutes later, after thrashing about and getting even more agitated, I poked him in the ribs. 'I've quit my job and I'm opening a flower shop on the coast.'

'Ha.' He patted my head, half asleep. 'Good one, Lil.'

❧

At five am, my alarm beeped. I hit the snooze button.

Matt reached over. 'Was I dreaming last night when you said something about flowers?'

'You still haven't said what you would've done, had I got the promotion.'

'Does it matter?'

'To me? Yes.'

Matt shook his head. 'I don't know. This transfer is a promotion. It means a lot to me.'

I nodded. 'As did mine, to me. So, I've been doing some thinking. I'm like one of those mice in a spinning wheel, running all the time, exhausted, but never moving forward. Just going around in circles.'

'I'm confused.'

'I'm not happy. I haven't been properly fulfilled for a while but I've been too busy and worn out to notice.' I rubbed my tired face. 'So,' I yawned, 'I've taken out a lease on the old butcher shop in Clearwater.'

Matt was awake now. He took his hand in mine. 'Please tell me you haven't really done this?'

'I've left the company. I couldn't stay after what happened. There's no way I can report to Glenn. He's a misogynist.'

'How could you make that decision without me?'

'Pardon? You made a decision to relocate to Singapore without me.'

'It's not the same.' He dropped my hand. 'My choice includes you. I was thinking about our future.'

'No. You're thinking about *your* future. I'm thinking about mine.'

He climbed out of bed, clearly annoyed. 'What does this mean for us?'

I got out of bed too. 'There's still an *us*, Matty. But I need to do something for myself.'

'I want you to come to Singapore with me.'

I shook my head. 'I can't.'

'You on the coast? You'll be bored and lonely.'

I shrugged. 'Maybe.'

'And we'll be apart.' He was frowning. 'Why can't you at least give Singapore a go? You could get a job there. How about working for a multinational based in Asia?'

'I can't. A working visa would take months. Besides the company would have to sponsor me.'

'There are charities crying out for volunteers. I'm sure you could work with animals. You've always wanted to do that—'

'In Australia!'

'Freelance from home then?'

'What home? I'm sorry but it's not what I want to do.'

'And opening a florist's is?'

'Yes.'

'I don't believe you. When is all this happening?'

'January.'

He shook his head. 'Madness. You'll be fed up in a couple of months, missing me terribly and longing to join me in Singapore.'

'Maybe.' I loved Matt, but events over the past few days had forced me to confront uncomfortable facts. I didn't want to live in Singapore. I didn't want to report to Glenn. I needed to focus on my ambitions, my dreams, and I was under no illusion it would be easy.

CHAPTER 4

Over the next couple of days, I finalised exit details at work. I drove down to Clearwater to inspect the shop again, and to sign the contract.

The shop still stank. Its grimy grey walls were not exactly welcoming. I had serious doubts it could be transformed into a pretty flower shop. It did have beautiful wooden floors though, underneath the ancient lino. The upstairs apartment had been well kept. All it needed was a fresh coat of paint. Even the bathroom was in good nick. As for the veranda and view, it was unbeatable. I loved it. When I stared out at the ocean, I felt calm.

And the business? I'd managed client accounts worth over a million dollars. Plus, Aunty Iris would help. She loved me ... I was strong, confident and capable.

Except when it came to telling Mum and Dad. Mum in particular. I thought it best to deliver the news in person. I drove back to Sydney, parked in their driveway, steadied my shaking hands and exhaled. Before I'd even stepped out of my car, Mum was standing at the front door.

Gary (named after Gary Cooper), our ancient poodle, was yapping beside me as I walked towards her. 'Hey, fella,' I said, bending down to pat him. He was blind in one eye, practically bald and hobbled around on three legs.

Inside, I explained the situation.

After several tense moments, Mum demanded, 'Are you having a nervous breakdown?'

I shook my head. 'I'm thinking clearly for the first time in months.'

'Really, Lily? Because this is the first I've heard of it. Since when did you want to move to the coast and sell flowers?' She paused. 'Retail!'

'It's what I want to do.'

I waited for her to clutch her chest. Instead, she held up her hands and wiggled her fingers. 'I suppose you want to end up with arthritis in your fingers, like Iris. It was a mistake letting you spend all those formative years with that woman.'

'Mum!'

'What? She's eccentric. The caftans, the make-up, the jewellery. You have beautiful hands, Lily. City hands.'

I pushed my hands into my jeans' back pockets. She watched me intently, with that all-knowing, all-seeing look on her face. It annoyed the hell out of me.

Dad turned to her. 'Lily's an adult, Daisy. She can do what she wants.'

'Thanks, Dad,' I said, hugging him.

'Even if we don't necessarily agree with her.'

I released him, scowling.

'And what about your poor father,' protested Mum. 'This is going to inflame his gout no end.'

Dad shook his head. 'Daisy!'

'Well, it is, Owen.'

I was in despair. 'Sorry, but it's what I want to do—'

'After two days' consideration?' Mum rolled her eyes. 'It takes me longer than that to decide on trying a new brand of dishwashing liquid.'

'Give it a rest, love.' Dad had never been good with confrontation.

'If you're sure, Lily.' Mum banged cups down on the kitchen bench. She, clearly, was *not* sure. I knew this because two minutes later, after pouring the tea, she started up again. 'I can't believe you're doing this. You don't know the first thing about flowers.'

Which was a bit of an insult, given all the time I'd spent in Iris's flower shop over the years. What Mum really wanted was for me to move to Singapore with Matt.

'And what about your house? You're just going to up and leave?'

'I'll rent it out. The inner city is crying out for rental properties and the rent will pay my mortgage. I've thought it all through. Besides, that's exactly what I'd have done if I moved to Singapore.'

'Pftt. He won't wait for you forever,' she sniffed, no doubt pining for grandchildren who were slipping further out of reach.

'I haven't asked him to. He's a free agent.'

'You'll live to regret this, Lily. Mark my words.'

One of my mother's favourite sayings, *Mark my words*. What? Out of ten? One hundred?

&

I found Christmas stressful at the best of times, but combined with quitting my job, clearing out my house and Matt heading overseas, it was even more exhausting than usual. But sleep wasn't an option, and before I knew it, it was January second and Matt was leaving.

'You're being incredibly selfish,' he said the night before his departure. 'And fiscally irresponsible. This isn't you.'

Keeping my anger in check, I replied, 'I'm good. My cottage has been rented.' The local real estate agent had found renters within days of signing me, and I was confident the couple with the baby and the cat would love the house as much as I did. They were beginning a new chapter in their lives, and so was I.

'I can't believe you're not coming with me.'

'I'd always regret not giving it a go if I didn't at least try.'

'What about giving us a go?'

'I don't want to live in the box you're trying to contain me in, Matt.'

'So I'm not good enough for you?'

My thoughts returned to a conversation we'd had early in our relationship. *No, Matt, I'll never be good enough for you.* 'You're ignoring the point. I don't want what you want.'

'Won't you miss me?'

We went around in circles, not listening to each other and becoming more agitated and frustrated.

The next morning at the airport, Matt held me tight. 'I thought I'd be able to persuade you.'

'We'll be fine.' I was trying to be brave, but my breath caught, unsure when we'd see each other again. Would it be months ... or longer? 'You're only a few hours away and we'll talk all the time. You'll be so busy you won't even miss me.'

'I'll miss you every day, Lil. You're my best friend. I was really hoping...' Matt trailed off.

I released him and wiped my eyes. 'Call me when you land.'

We kissed again and hugged one more time. Finally, he walked through the departure gate. At the last moment, he turned and waved awkwardly.

Then he was gone.

A couple of days later, the full removal truck turned out of my inner-city street and headed for my new home in Clearwater.

Most of my possessions, except for Trouble, my laptop, essential toiletries and a change of clothes, were in that van. Swiping away tears, I took one last look at my little cottage. I would definitely miss the garden. Some of the agapanthuses were still in bloom, and the crepe myrtle had just started flowering in vibrant shades of pink. I wouldn't miss the noise though and not being able to park within walking distance of my home.

I climbed into my car and looked at Trouble in his carry-all on the front passenger seat. 'Ready, buddy?' He twitched, then twitched again.

Taking a deep breath, I started the engine, took my foot off the brake and accelerated. Onward and upward.

New year. New life.

When I arrived in Clearwater, Trish greeted me. 'Welcome to your new home.' She handed me the keys. 'I'm so glad you didn't change your mind.'

I banished all sad thoughts and niggling doubts. 'Thank you. I'm really excited.'

Fumbling, I opened the front door and stifled a gag as the meat stench hit me. But I smiled. 'Home!'

Together, we unpacked my car and carried Trouble and a few plastic bags upstairs. I took in the million-dollar view.

'I hope you'll be very happy here, Lily,' Trish said, as she placed my bags on the kitchen bench.

After she left, I waited for the removalists, who arrived half an hour later. By the time they left, my little flat was crammed with furniture. I should have offloaded more of it before I came. My new bedroom and living area were fitted out much as my cottage had been. The other bed, a couple of side tables and two bookshelves were crammed into the second bedroom, along with at least a dozen boxes. It looked like a junk shop. To make the place feel a little like home, I put my favourite photos on one side table and my collection of snow globes from around the world, on another. The Eiffel Tower from Mum and Dad, and the Empire State Building courtesy of Taylor, were two of my favourites. I also had one from Hamilton Island where Matt and I had holidayed a couple of times. They were dust collectors, but I loved them. What next, a teaspoon collection? I didn't shrug at the possibility.

I stared at the four boxes stacked on the kitchen floor. The sooner I unpacked them, the sooner I could relax. But the biggest job was waiting for me downstairs. I'd promised myself that Lily's Little Flower Shop would open in mid-January, less than two weeks away.

After returning from the local supermarket with every cleaning product available, I set about scrubbing ... and then scrubbed and cleaned some more. I smelt like meat, ammonia and sweat.

I collapsed into bed at midnight. Thankfully, the removalists had assembled the bed. I'd hastily thrown on a flat sheet but was unable to deal with finding a fitted one. Trouble didn't seem troubled at all. His hutch was still his hutch.

I woke at daybreak, every limb aching but keen to get back into it. After eating a banana and feeding Trouble, I headed back downstairs and got on with cleaning. My hair was piled on top of my head, and my shirt and shorts were damp and covered in grime.

'Hey,' a voice boomed behind me.

I was so focused on scrubbing the cold room, I almost slipped.

'Sorry. Didn't mean to startle you. I'm Ben. Ben Ravenstone.' He held out his hand.

I smiled. 'Lily, but I don't think you want to shake my hand.'

We both glanced at my grotty wet gloves.

'Perhaps not. Welcome to the neighbourhood. How are you finding everything?' Ben was tall, tanned, smiley faced, dressed for the beach, Bondi or Clearwater.

'Yeah. Good,' I said, conscious of my dishevelled appearance and the shop odours.

'Early days,' he replied. 'I have a small vineyard and restaurant down the road a bit. Maybe we can do some contra deals from time to time.'

'Sounds great. I'd never say no to a deal involving wine.'

'Good to know. I'm not in town often. I'm mainly based in Adelaide, but next time I'm back, I'll be sure to pop in. Good luck.'

No sooner had he left than another local dropped by.

'Andy,' he said by way of introduction. 'I've got the framing shop a couple of doors down.'

I smiled. 'Lily.'

He laughed. 'Like the flower?'

'That's the one.'

Andy was tall, like my previous visitor, maybe six foot, average build, wide, open grin, with scruffy sandy hair and an even scruffier beard.

'Don't want to hold you up, but if there's anything you need or want to know, just ask.'

'Thanks, I will.' He gave me his number and left. I wiped my gloved hands on my shorts, swept a few stray hairs from my face and got back to scrubbing.

By the end of the day, in addition to Ben and Andy, I'd met the travel agent, Sally, the baker, and the hairdresser, Zena. They were all eager to find out what was going on. I appreciated their enthusiasm but was exhausted from having to repeat my story over and over.

'Lily ... from Sydney. Yes, a sea change. Yes, a florist. It *is* funny that my name's Lily and I'm opening a flower shop.'

'Ah, Clearwater could do with a florist...'

'A good one, mind you, but without those exorbitant city prices...'

'We don't want anything too fancy...'

'Oohh, I hope it will be exotic, like the ones in the city...'

And my personal favourite. 'I'll take a bunch of flowers and a kilo of sausages, thanks,' followed by raucous laughter.

The next day, people wandered in and out like they had all the time in the world to chat and watch paint dry. I had offers of help, food and company. The locals seemed genuinely amused to have someone new to play with. I wasn't used to so much attention, especially from strangers.

I didn't want to appear rude, but these interruptions every few minutes were putting me way behind schedule. I'd met more people in Clearwater in two days than I'd met in two years in my street in Sydney. How would I remember their names and occupations? Name tags wouldn't go astray.

That night, I posted up sheets of newspaper to cover the front windows and door for privacy. I wanted Lily's Little Flower Shop reveal to be ... BIG! And it wasn't going to be if the locals kept popping in to watch me scrub walls.

Over a shared salad dinner with Trouble, I lay on the floor and wrote a list. As well as cleaning and painting, I had to get extra shelving and signage, place the counter/workbench, order business cards, advertising ... and every muscle in my body ached, unused to physical labour. My brain though, fired, operating on pure caffeine.

After I'd set up my Facebook page, Instagram and a minimalist website (I'd flood it with photos of the shop, flowers, and hopefully testimonials, soon enough), I sat on my veranda nursing a glass of wine and staring out to sea. There was so much more to do. Still, I was excited. I couldn't wait to see Lily's Little Flower Shop painted on the front door, and overwhelmed as I was, my grin couldn't have been wider.

I glanced inside to where Trouble was hopping between several unopened boxes and unpacked clutter that filled the available floor space. I figured we could get away with living in a mess; we weren't expecting visitors anytime soon.

This was so different to the life I'd lived the last eight years working for a corporation – the city, suits, high heels, travel. At the time, I thought I'd been blessed with the whole package. But I wasn't quite. I took a moment. Would it be a drag, living and working in the same place? I shook my head. Not in the short term. For the foreseeable future, the flower shop would be my priority.

Feeling a little homesick after a glass of wine, I sent Taylor an email.

Pop Quiz: What does seaside air do to humans?

You don't know, do you, Taylor? Well, for a start, people talk slower down here … a lot more slowly. BTW, have met a few locals who seem to like me. I will fit in. (That's my mantra — I will fit in.)

You'll be thrilled to know I've finally gotten rid of the meat smell in the shop and my flat — though I still can't eat the stuff. Think I'll go vego for the time being. It hasn't done Trouble any harm. Yes, Trouble is settling in well. (Thanks for asking! Not! I thought you cared about the fluffy one?)

Truth, though, I really miss you. I miss Sydney and I almost miss the office gossip and chaos. I miss Matt and pork dumplings … agh. I'm raving. It's such a big change. Please visit soon.

Exhausted. Send news. L x

CHAPTER 5

Andy

On Tuesday morning, Andy stood in his shop examining his handiwork, a framed family portrait, before calling Barry at the newsagency.

'Just made the midday deadline, Barry. I'm sure Paula will be thrilled.'

'Let's hope so,' Barry replied. 'I'll pick it up before her party.'

Satisfied that he'd cleared his backlog, Andy sat down and started sketching Lily's shop front or what he imagined her new shopfront would look like. As he squeezed paint from tubes on to his palette, he chuckled at the memory of walking past her shop that morning to find Mrs Beattie's nose pressed firmly up against the newspaper-covered windows.

'Morning, Mrs Beattie.'

'Andy, why do you think they've gone and done this,' she said, drawing herself back.

'I guess Lily wants the new shop to be a surprise.'

Lily was catching on fast. The neighbourhood thrived on newcomers and their stories.

Back to his painting. Vibrant colours, buckets of red roses, purple hydrangeas and, of course, pink and white lilies. He'd paint her door green. If he liked it enough, he'd give it to her as a shop-warming present. As he settled in, his phoned pinged. He ignored it. No doubt a client texting him with their framing order. After several more pings in rapid succession, he picked it up.

'Bloody Edie.' He shuddered. Why did his ex-wife keep harassing him? He deleted the messages after reading the first.

He shook the images of Edie and their life together from his head and locked his shop up early so he could attend his weekly group session with his long-time therapist, Joanne.

※

'Who wants to kick off today's meeting?' she asked once everyone had sat down with cups of tea and biscuits. 'Andy, you look concerned.'

'Concerned is one word for it.' Andy knew he could be honest here. Most people had been coming to this session on and off for years. 'Edie's back at her old tricks, texting, harassing.'

'Go on.'

'The usual. I'm scum, don't deserve to live, need to be locked up. Should never have been allowed out of hospital.'

Heads nodded. In sympathy, Andy hoped.

'And how do those words make you feel?'

'I try not to read them obviously, but sometimes, like today, I couldn't help it and when I did, I felt worthless. Shit.'

'Got a new number, has she?'

Andy nodded.

'You've blocked it?'

He nodded again. Andy had blocked Edie's number more times than he could remember, but she'd just bought another cheap pre-paid and the texts flew again.

'When you're feeling overwhelmed, take a break,' said Joanne calmly. 'This goes for all of you. These times are difficult but try to remove yourself from the situation. In your case, Andy, walk along the beach or do a mountain hike. Walking releases endorphins.'

'I know, but sometimes thoughts crowd in and I feel at a loss. Incapacitated. And then I think about how Edie drove me over the edge, and I ended up in hospital.' He touched the scars on his arm and hand.

'And do you remember what you decided in hospital all those years ago when we first met?'

'That I couldn't go back.'

'Back to Edie?' Joanne prompted.

He bowed his head. 'Our marriage was poisonous. I had to face up to issues that had been circulating for months, possibly years.'

'And you did. Keep reminding yourself how far you've come. You're a different person now. Until Edie moves on, she'll continue to harass you, with hang-up calls and abusive text messages. You did well today, by blocking her number and coming here this afternoon to talk about it.'

'But why?' said Andy. 'Why does she continue to torment me? It's over. Has been for years.'

Joanne was silent.

'Why?' Andy pleaded.

'You know why,' said Joanne confidently. 'Edie was in control of her relationship with you and then all of a sudden, she wasn't. You stood your ground, removed yourself from a toxic relationship and divorced her. She wasn't in charge anymore.'

Joanne took a breath. 'Edie grew up in a family where she had no voice. A sick mother; a controlling father. She wants to play her father's role, Andy, not her mother's.'

Later that night, Andy repeated Joanne's words as he stared at his prints and canvases. He could get lost for hours in his art, whether it be the beach, the waves and skyline with the hills in the distance; or in the bush, on one of his regular hikes, gums and scraggly natives. Just being outside helped ease his mind.

Joanne was right. He was doing well, considering the circumstances, and the next day, he'd take a long beach walk before work.

CHAPTER 6

Lily

Several days later, I'd finished the cleaning grunt work, installed my ready-made shelving and bench/front desk, and painted every wooden surface off-white. When I say *me*, I mean the two painters that Trish had recommended, painted every wooden surface off-white. They transformed the building.

With the shop's opening in a little over thirty hours, Aunty Iris picked me up at 3.30am and we set off for the Sydney flower markets.

'This is so exciting,' I said as we motored up the highway.

'It is rather,' she replied. 'But I wish you'd let me help you these past weeks. I haven't even seen you.'

'I wanted to do it myself. Besides, I didn't want you getting filthy and tired and resenting me.'

Iris grinned. 'Glad you felt that way.'

We arrived at the markets just after five. There were flowers as far as the eye could see, and people, so many people. 'This is

... incredible.' I clasped my hands together to stop them from shaking.

Iris patted my shoulder. 'Better get used to it, darl. This is your life now.' She breathed in deeply. 'Intoxicating, isn't it? The fragrance, buzzing trolleys full of beautiful blooms. Memories.'

And loud! Noisy banter between the growers filled the air, as they laughed and drank coffee. 'They seem happy,' I replied.

'These people are a special breed, often part of generations of flower growers. Hard-working. They start at 2am or earlier. They genuinely love flowers, and in my experience, do it for the love not the money.'

'Lily!' The voice was instantly recognisable.

Iris clutched my arm. 'Tell me again, why you felt the need to invite your mother?'

'Mum,' I said, walking up and kissing her. 'Thanks for coming. I appreciate it.'

Mum sniffed. 'It's very early.'

I nodded.

'Let's get on with it then,' said Iris, all business.

We followed Iris as she deliberated, compared blooms and contemplated what would sell in Clearwater.

'I rather like these.' Mum picked up miniature pineapples and examined them before replacing them. 'These are nice,' she said, moments later, pointing to a bunch of red gladioli.

'Daisy!' Iris said, sounding irritated. 'It's not about you. Lily needs to think about her customers.'

'But I am a customer, Iris.' Mum paused. 'The flowers here are so cheap. I don't know how florists get away with charging so much. Highway robbery, if you ask me.'

'Sister, dearest, we're at the markets. To make any sort of profit, Lily will need to charge at least three times as much.'

Mum twitched. 'That's outrageous.'

A headache loomed. Watching Mum and Aunty Iris bicker

took me back to my childhood. Whenever they got together, they argued. If anything, it had gotten worse over the years. I don't know how their parents coped. I would have abandoned them to the streets at a young age.

Mum counted the number of roses in each bunch. 'Some of these have only ten flowers.'

Iris nodded. 'Flowers are sold in bunches of ten, not twelve. That way, when a customer wants a dozen, it means breaking up a second bunch at additional cost.'

Mum was not impressed. 'Outrageous!' Obviously, her word of the day.

'Tony!' Iris shouted, moving away from Mum. 'You still here?'

'Iris, lovely lady,' the man boomed. 'I'll be here until they drag me out in a box.' He hugged her. 'It's been a while. Still looking as glamorous as ever.'

'Always the charmer.'

'What gives?' he asked. 'Getting back in the game?'

'Nah. I've earnt my freedom, but my niece, Lily,' she pointed to me, 'is following in my footsteps.'

Mum groaned. 'More's the pity.'

Iris rolled her eyes. 'Meet Lily and my older sister, Daisy.'

Ninety minutes later, Iris's station wagon was full to the brim. Would my Mini be up to the task? I had to do this run at least twice a week.

'Please come home soon,' Mum said, when I kissed her goodbye.

'You'll find me here twice a week, if you ever fancy an early morning coffee,' I said. From next week, I'd be going to the markets every Tuesday and Friday morning, but in preparation for my grand opening, Iris and I agreed it was better to come a day earlier.

'Your mother means well,' Iris said as we set off to the coast.

'But let's limit her excursions to the markets. Miniature pineapples? Really!'

❦

Back in Clearwater, Iris and I unloaded the flowers as locals peered in through the gaps in the newspapers covering my windows. Armful after armful of blooms were loaded into the cold room – dahlias, gardenias, kangaroo paw ... I was getting confused.

'Are these peonies?' I asked, holding pretty pink and purple flowers.

Iris shook her head with a sigh. 'They're lisianthus, commonly known as the poor man's rose.' She pointed to other flowers in a nearby bundle. 'Those are peonies.' She sat at my workbench and began writing labels.

Meanwhile, I busied myself stripping the leaves off stems and putting them in attractive display buckets.

'Heaven help me if customers switch nametags for a lark. I'll be fucked.'

By eleven, Iris was knackered, so I sent her on her way. But not before she shared some parting words of wisdom. 'Nervous?'

'Terrified.'

'Don't be. Everyone will love you. Florists need to be friendly, approachable and sincere. You have all those qualities and many more, Lil. You'll be fine.'

'Really?' I wasn't convinced.

'A final word of advice,' Iris said in her most serious voice. 'Customers will want your help with anything from soils and plant nutrition, to light and temperature control. You should know the proper methods of handling cut flowers, and, of course, show some creative and artistic flair to come up with innovative arrangements.'

44

Dear Lord! 'As if I'm not worried enough.'

Iris maintained her serious face for several more seconds, then chortled. 'Don't worry, just messing with you. I bluffed my way through thirty years. You can do the same. People will tell you their life story and treat you like a counsellor. Now, before I leave,' she reached into her tote bag, 'I have a gift for you.'

She handed over a package. I ripped the paper off to find a bright pink apron with the words, Lily's Little Flower Shop embroidered in black on the front.

'I love it. Thank you so much.' Tears streamed down my cheeks as I hugged her tight.

'Are you sure you don't want me to stay?' she asked.

I shook my head. 'You've done more than enough. I'll muddle through. It's a brave new world.'

For the remainder of the day, I prepared bunches, bouquets and posies – Australian natives, purple kale flowers, lilies, chrysanthemums and carnations, all ready for my grand opening. After putting them in their assigned buckets, I carefully placed them in the cold room.

I filled small silver buckets with gift cards, ribbons, ornaments and packets of water purifiers, and popped them on my bench. But what to do with the gardening clogs I'd impulsively bought online? What was I thinking? I had nowhere to display the twenty pairs I'd bought. This was a flower shop, not a nursery. I'd really have to overcome my online shopping urge.

Shattered, I headed upstairs late and set my alarm for six.

Shattered maybe, but I couldn't sleep.

My phone pinged – a text message from Matt.

Congrats on your grand opening tomorrow! I'd send flowers but ha, ha, you probably have enough. Love ya, babe. Me. Xxx

Afterwards, casually stalking his company's website, I noticed several photos of Matt smiling brightly with his arms around women. He'd always been a touchy-feely person, but still, it rankled. I lay in the darkness waiting for the kookaburras to herald the sunrise for what seemed like forever.

Up before the alarm, I paced, worrying and chewing my nails. What to wear? When I'd unpacked my clothes, I soon realised that my look was all wrong. My clothing was too stiff and formal for the relaxed beach vibe of Clearwater. I was used to wearing heels, my hair neatly styled, or on the days when I was rushed, tied up in a loose professional bun. Here, I needed a complete change. For the past two weeks I'd worn tattered old gym gear.

A couple of days earlier, I'd considered checking out the surf shop, which was staffed by impossibly beautiful seventeen-year-olds. The racks of floaty dresses and flat sandals beckoned. But I couldn't do it. Sooner or later, I'd have to brave it, because I'd look ridiculous in my corporate uniform of navy pinstriped pencil skirts and cream silk blouses or tailored black pants and button-down shirts. Way too stitched up.

Today, I chose a plain black T-shirt, black skirt and black runners, then put on my pink apron. I was so excited, I could barely breathe.

At eight, Iris rang. 'Lily-Pily, your big day has finally arrived. All set?'

'Yep. Can't wait.'

'Sure you don't want me to swing by?'

'I'll manage.'

'That's the spirit. Knock 'em dead. Call if you need me, but not between twelve and three. It's bridge day at the club. I just know I'm going to win. You're my lucky charm, Lils.'

Iris rang off and I got on with taking flowers out of the cold room and positioning them around the room. With flora filling every available space, the shop was transformed – colour and fragrance filled the air. The tiled cream walls gleamed fresh and sparkling, while wicker baskets and dried Australian natives hung from the ceiling's many butcher hooks to add drama.

My little flower shop. Happy, happy, happy.

Just before ten, I placed a couple of flowering hydrangea, African violets and buckets of lilies at the front door. I positioned my chalkboard on the pavement. *Clearwater Beach is blooming. Come inside and say hello.* Smiley face. I ripped off the paper covering the windows and the door, kissed Trouble on his nose, opened a Red Bull, hung my *open* sign on the inside of the door and waited.

And waited.

Living and working in the city, I'd been conditioned to think fast, work fast, and talk fast. All the time. Everyone rushed, cutting people off mid-conversation, finishing sentences for colleagues and doing that rapid rolling hand movement to hurry people's conversation along. Sure, it was incredibly rude, but most people in my office did the same. It was contagious.

I cleaned my teeth in the shower, gulped coffee and texted whilst walking ... multi-tasking to save time, so I'd have moments for other, more important things. On the rare occasions I actually took a break, I had no time to wait for lights to change before dashing into traffic, narrowly avoiding getting mown down by a bus I just didn't see. Hence several jay-walking fines.

Who'd have thought that two hours south of Sydney, there'd be such a massive shift ... from the way people dressed, to the way they spoke, walked and lived. Everything was slower in Clearwater. The previous afternoon, at the chemist to buy Nurofen+ and multivitamins (headaches and not eating properly), I champed at the bit to get back to the shop, while the customers in front of me yakked to the pharmacist, seemingly with all the time in the world.

I'd forgotten how to breathe and observe. I'd forgotten how to sit quietly and just ... be. Now I had a while. But I wasn't sure that was a good thing. I'd been open an hour and no one had walked in. Not even a local asking where they could buy chicken wings or mince.

My mind went into overdrive. Maybe Mum was right. This was a huge mistake.

At last, Trish popped in. 'The shop looks fabulous. I love it. You've brightened up the streetscape. The colours are simply stunning.'

'Thank you,' I said, as an elderly lady walked through the door.

Trish winked, and said, 'Good morning, Mrs Beattie,' and was out the door with a 'Best of luck. See you soon.'

'Good morning,' I said brightly to the woman.

She smiled, gazing around the shop. 'Good morning, dear. Don't you look pretty ... and all these flowers.'

'Organised chaos, I like to call it,' I said when she almost tripped over a bucket of hot-pink roses. I glanced up at my antique wall clock. Seventeen minutes after eleven. 'You're my very first customer. Other than Trish. I've been open for business exactly one hour and seventeen minutes.'

'You and your husband have come down from the city, I hear.'

'Just me. Me and my rabbit, Trouble.' I pointed to Trouble who was perched on a step ladder between buckets of gerberas, oriental lilies and green foliage.

'Ooh,' she said, walking over to pat him. 'My grandchildren have pet rabbits.' She stepped back and looked at me. 'No husband then?'

'Just me.'

She clicked her tongue. 'That's a shame. A woman needs a strong man beside her, guiding her, especially nowadays.' She peered around. 'You're doing all this by yourself?'

I beamed. 'Yes, I am.'

She looked bewildered. 'Aren't you lonely?'

I shook my head. Could this woman stop talking? I was struggling with demons of my own. I didn't need another person adding to them. This was me. My fresh start and I was determined to make a go of it, despite what had happened all those years earlier.

'Could I interest you in some roses or lilies?' I gestured towards a bucket. Or maybe an invitation to join the twenty-first century?

I didn't even realise I was tapping my foot until I looked down and noticed it moving. Really, what difference did it make if she took ten minutes or an hour to decide? I had nowhere else to be, and neither, apparently, did she. It's not like I was rushed with customers or the phone was ringing off the hook.

As she browsed, I read through the paperwork I still had to complete. I must have filled out over twenty forms to do with the shop in the past few weeks. While I was busy ticking boxes, she accidentally knocked over flowers and almost fell over Trouble, who had hopped from the step ladder to the floor and was nibbling stray hay.

'I'm so sorry.' I scooped up Trouble and locked him in his daytime hutch, which had the clogs piled on its roof.

The woman picked out a bunch of purple hydrangeas.

'Stunning,' I said, thankful she'd found something to her liking. I wrapped them firstly in soft pink tissue paper, then in hessian cloth and clear cellophane, finishing off with a bright pink ribbon.

As she was leaving, she said, 'I'm sure we'll find a nice young gentleman to take care of you.'

I wanted to protest but thought better of it. I'd made my first sale and it gave me a warm glow.

A short time later, customers started trailing in. Husbands buying flowers for their wives, young men buying gifts for their girlfriends, sticky beaks just 'having a look'. I fumbled through as best I could, wrapping flowers, making almost pretty bows from brightly coloured ribbons and wishing everyone 'a very happy start to the weekend'. I smiled until my jaw ached. It was hard work being so upbeat.

I did fine until a customer came in, asking for *helianthus annuus*.

I shook my head, bewildered. 'I'm not sure we have those.' I'd like to think he wasn't purposely trying to trick me. But really?

The smarty pants pointed the sunflowers right in front of him. 'Gotcha.'

Still, I couldn't complain. He bought three bunches.

Eight hours after I'd opened, I closed the front door. Relief. I'd survived my first day. All by myself. And I'd actually earned money. Doing some quick calculations, I realised I hadn't made a profit, but still, I had sold over half the flowers I'd bought at the markets and my chest swelled.

CHAPTER 7

I was carting buckets of flowers into the cold room when Andy, the framing guy, knocked on the door.

'Evening,' he said. 'Care for a drink?' He held up a bottle of Moët.

I smiled and closed the cold-room door. Completely knackered, I longed to climb into bed, but, 'Could I ever. I'd never say no to Moët!'

Moments later, Zena, the hairdresser, walked in holding a bottle of wine. 'Congratulations! You made it through your first day,' she said, acknowledging Andy with a smile. 'Let's have a drink and I'll tell you what you've let yourself in for.'

Two minutes later, Andy poured three wine glasses of bubbly.

'I don't have champagne flutes,' I apologised.

Zena waved me away with a dye-stained hand. 'Close enough is good enough. Here's cheers!' She looked about my age and like a hairdresser – shoulder length, psychedelic pink hair with blonde streaks – pale skin, green eyes, great smile. Sexy. Effervescent.

'To Lily,' said Andy, who was older than us, maybe mid-thirties and single. I only knew he was single because he'd told me earlier that week when I first met him, but not in an 'Are you single too? Great, let's sleep together' way. A bit eccentric, he probably wore cardigans in winter.

'To Lily's Little Flower Shop.' Zena giggled. 'Did you venture into flower sales because of your name or vice versa?'

'Long story. Bit of both, I guess.'

'And who's this funky fellow?' She pointed to the hutch.

I opened the latch so he was free to hop about. 'This is Trouble.'

Andy watched him intently. 'Looks like he could get up to mischief. Will he be a regular companion?'

'Hope so. As long as he doesn't get freaked by customers, or eat my potential profits, I'll keep bringing him downstairs. He's good company.'

Andy beamed. 'In, say, a way a dog isn't?'

'Dogs can frighten people, especially kids.' I kissed Trouble on his nose. 'Rabbits are harmless.'

Zena took a drink. 'Me likey. Makes a change from the butcher's shop.'

I wrinkled my nose. 'Can you still smell meat?'

Zena shook her head.

'Just a little,' said Andy. 'But it's been a stinking hot day.'

I almost laughed. Yes, it was mid-January but given the sea breeze, the temperature couldn't have been more than twenty-five degrees. Unlike Sydney, which was sweltering through its fourth day of mid-thirties and eighty per cent humidity.

'So, what *is* the Lily story?' Zena asked, topping up our drinks.

'Born and bred in Sydney, tired of the city and corporate life.'

'And you thought moving to the seaside would make a good change?' Andy asked.

I shrugged.

'You could have gone to New York or London,' said Zena, 'but you chose the south coast?'

'I went with the flow and the flow drifted here.'

Andy nodded. 'Know exactly what you mean.'

He hummed a tune I didn't recognise, then noticed Zena and me watching. 'Was I humming out loud?'

We nodded.

He shrugged. 'Too much time alone.'

As I said, eccentric.

'So, how long have you been a florist?' asked Zena.

I glanced at the clock on the wall. 'About eight and a half hours.'

Zena laughed. 'Okay...'

'I did a course years ago, but sort of got caught up with other stuff.'

Andy raised his eyebrows. 'Life intervened?'

'Something like that.'

'Well,' said Andy, 'we're thrilled you've settled here. You and your shop are the talk of the town.'

'Sounds ominous.' I sat on a wooden work stool alongside my new friends.

'Ominous has got nothing on Clearwater, let me tell you,' said Zena. 'Some of the people—'

'Let's not frighten the newbie, hey, Zena? Plenty of time for that.'

Zena looked like she wanted to say something more but as her lips started moving, she caught herself and nixed it. I was going to have to wait to see if Clearwater rivalled Midsomer for murders.

Andy took a breath. 'The locals can be harsh with newcomers. I still consider myself new even though I've lived in the area eight years.'

'You didn't grow up here?' I sipped my champagne.

He shook his head. 'I settled on the coast because it's more interesting here than in Melbourne where I grew up. I get to know the writers, artists, all the creative types. It suits my way of thinking.'

Zena rolled her eyes. 'Surrounded by simple, down-to-earth arty types who feel free to express themselves.'

'Like you, Zeen, with your pink hair,' he shot back.

She laughed. 'I try. Actually, Lily, Andy's a pretty good artist.'

'I noticed the easel and paints in your shop,' I said.

'If I couldn't paint, my days would be very long, especially in the winter when trade is slow. But when I become immersed in a project, the hours fly by.'

'So, winter ... I'll keep that in mind.'

'Wish I could say the same,' said Zena. 'My salon's always busy. Too hectic sometimes.'

Despite having known her a short time, I was completely taken with Zena. 'Love your hair.'

Zena flicked it nonchalantly. 'Thanks. You too can have hair like mine. This week, pink. Next week? Who knows? It's only hair and I'm a hairdresser. How can I inspire clients to experiment if I turn up every day with boring brown?' She glanced at Andy and then me. 'No offence.'

'No, I agree.' And I did. I wasn't working in a corporate environment anymore. I could have any damn hair I chose. My own hair was naturally auburn with no real style. As my mother frequently told me, it was getting straggly. She'd die if I showed up with pink or blue hair ... in fact, any colour that wasn't a shade of brown. I swallowed some champagne, thankful I couldn't see the careless ponytail behind me. The more I looked at it, the more I liked Zena's hair.

'Where are you from?' I asked her.

'Norfolk Island.'

'Really?'

'Yep. Born and bred. But not inbred.' She paused. 'Sorry it's a Norfolk joke. I left the island after high school and did hairdressing at TAFE.'

'They have a high school on Norfolk Island?'

'Yes, and electricity too.'

Ha! All I knew about Norfolk Island was that Colleen McCullough had lived there and something about convicts and a mutiny on the Bounty.

'So, hairdressing?' I prompted.

'Yeah,' said Zena. 'I figured it could take me anywhere in the world. Growing up isolated, I always dreamed of living in the city. When I was at school, the Gold Coast seemed so glamorous, so I moved to Brisbane. But when I got there, it was overwhelming. As soon as I got a chance to leave with my then boyfriend, I did. And here I am.' She sipped her drink. 'Rent's cheap and I cut hair on the side in return for favours.'

Andy smirked. 'Just like Norfolk?'

Zena glanced at me. 'He's winding us both up. He knows I mean food and magazine favours. I'm totally comfortable with the barter system. I could do you a weekly wash and blow-dry in exchange for an arrangement.'

I nodded.

'Wait till you get to know the café and restaurant owners,' Zena continued. 'If you're willing to supply flowers, you'll be drowning in cappuccinos, chocolate cake and lasagne.'

Excellent. I could get used to this kind of swap. Though where would I find the time to have a regular wash and blow-dry?

Zena blinked. 'I've been here four years. A seventh of my life.'

That made Zena three years younger than me.

'One day I'd like to see the world, the Eiffel Tower, Big Ben, the Statue of Liberty...' Zena broke into a happy glazed smile. 'But for now, I want to be here.'

'Sounds good,' I agreed.

'There's no pressure, no expectations...'

'I wouldn't be so sure of that,' said Andy, lobbing back into the conversation.

'For me, it's a hell of a lot easier navigating life here than in the city.' She paused. 'Or on the island.'

Zena noticed me glancing at her ensemble of a loose-fitting black velvet dress, forest green wrap and Doc Martens.

She bowed. 'You like? It's called charity shop chic.'

I laughed. 'You're underselling yourself.' My eyes widened when she discarded her wrap.

'Look out.' Andy put down his glass with a flourish. 'Lily's noticed your friend.'

Zena patted her arm. 'I was inspired by *The Girl With The Dragon Tattoo*, so I got one.'

'What did you think of the book?' Andy asked.

Zena looked at him blankly.

'You didn't even read it, did you?' Andy smiled.

'Well, no, I didn't read the books on principle. I don't want to read about murder, rape and torture. I can read all that online.'

'Pink hair and tattoos,' I said. 'I like it.'

Zena smiled. 'Thanks. What about you?'

'Nothing. Nada. I don't even have pierced ears.'

Zena shrugged. 'You've got good skin for a tatt, but yeah, I don't have any piercings either. Who'd do that? The pain.' She flinched. 'The pain.'

'Kill the pain you feel,' said Andy.

'INXS,' Andy and I said together and laughed.

'Keep the heart.'

Zena stared. 'You guys are weird.'

Half an hour later, Zena and Andy left, and I got back to

storing flowers in the cold room and sweeping the floor. I turned off the front shop lights, picked up Trouble, and dragged my legs upstairs. Lily's Little Flower Shop was officially up and running. Tired as I was, I felt fulfilled. My new life in Clearwater. What a beauty. All undulating rises, dips and views. The ocean setting was unbeatable. The sound of the waves crashing on the sand was pretty special too. I would force myself to relax and take the move in my stride, living each day as it came.

CHAPTER 8

'Hello,' I said when Andy bounded through the door late Saturday morning.

'I planned to take a long walk. But tripped over a few buckets out the front and thought I'd stop in.'

'Occupational hazard. I've done it a few times.'

'Locals haven't bought all your flowers yet?'

'Not quite, but it's been non-stop.' I brushed hair from my eyes.

'Excellent.' Andy picked up Trouble. 'Got long ears, hasn't he.'

'He's a rabbit.' I took a moment. 'I've got a question.'

He put Trouble down. 'Sounds serious. Shoot.'

'Hope you don't think I'm being out of line here, but I'm on a huge learning curve and...'

'And?'

'A guy came in to order flowers for his wife's birthday on Monday...'

'So far, so good.'

'Yeah, but he also wanted flowers delivered to someone else

the same day and the thing is...' I shook my head. 'It doesn't matter.'

Andy raised his eyebrows. 'You're saying this guy ordered two bunches of flowers – one for his wife and one for his mother? Sister?'

'Something like that.'

'It's probably nothing like that.' He grinned. 'Just because this is a small community, doesn't mean we don't have big city dramas and tensions. We've got it all here in Clearwater.'

'I'm beginning to think you might be right.'

'There's no *think* about it. I know we do.' Andy smiled. 'Trish knows all the gossip.' He glanced at the door. 'Speak of the devil.'

'What have I missed?' she asked, walking in. 'How'd your first day go yesterday, Lily? Were the natives kind?'

'Absolutely.'

'Andy, you're looking a bit devilish yourself. What have you been up to?'

Andy chuckled. 'Me? Lily was just asking about some of the locals and I told her that if she wants info, you're her go-to person.'

'Andy, I don't gossip.'

'I know you don't, but you still know everything. Who's doing whom, who's had a falling out. That sort of thing.'

She nodded and raised her eyebrows.

Andy and I watched Trish expectantly.

She sighed. 'Okay, but no names. Fallouts happen for two reasons. First: lovers stop their affair, and then bitch about each other.'

'Sounds reasonable,' I said.

'Yeah,' said Andy. 'Like Brad, the jeweller, and baker Sally.'

'Andy!' Trish glared.

'What? It's common knowledge.'

I deadheaded a couple of yellow daisies. 'Baker Sally?'

Andy shrugged. 'Everyone calls her that. No idea why.'

Trish laughed. 'Back in the day, there were two Sallys in town. It started as a joke. Sally would introduce herself as baker Sally, so people knew which Sally was calling. The other Sally's long gone, but the name baker Sally stuck.'

'Okay.' I was intrigued. 'And the second reason?'

Trish whistled. 'Ah! Usually concerns gardens, trees, nature.'

'Really?'

'Cutting back. Pruning one's hedges. That behaviour doesn't sit well in this community. They're all tree huggers. I'm not fanatical, but I know how to toe the line. My livelihood depends on happy customers and I try to avoid offending anyone.'

'I'll keep that in mind.'

'Living in a small town means that to keep a secret, any secret,' said Trish, 'you have to be discreet. Keep your mouth shut and the secrets to yourself.'

Following Trish's advice, I kept my mouth shut and scooped up Trouble who'd been nibbling at my sandshoe laces.

'Andy?' said Trish finally. 'Have you finished stretching my canvas?'

I laughed.

'Sounds more fun than it is,' he quipped. 'Yes. I'll drop it by this afternoon. And on that note,' Andy said, 'I'd better scoot back. No time for a walk now, Sergeant Trish.'

'I'll come with you,' Trish beamed. 'But before I go, Lily, do you need anything?'

I shook my head. 'I'm good. Excited about spending the night unpacking boxes, boxes and more boxes. With Trouble's help, of course.'

'Good luck with that. Life is short. I'll call in again soon. Take care.'

With that, Andy and Trish disappeared out the door.

CHAPTER 9

Tuesday morning, after a visit to the market, I got straight to work on the flower arrangements for Trish, baker Sally, as well as a couple of bouquets for a patient at the local hospital. All the research I'd done, along with Iris's wisdom, led me to believe that Mondays and Tuesdays would be the slowest days of the week. So far, so good. The previous day had been slow, and today, by eleven, I'd only had two walk-ins.

I focused on the positives: being my own boss, not wearing a suit, and being surrounded by gorgeous flowers. Sure, I couldn't remember the scientific names from my course, but I was studying all things floral every spare moment and hoping the info would eventually come back to me. Despite the intense learning curve, I felt alive. Alive, but tired. That would pass.

Another good thing? I was so busy, my mind spinning with everything I had to manage, I had little time to think about Matt and what he was getting up to in Singapore. As for my demons? I was too tired to think about them. In my head, I said that, but they were always lurking. Mistakes. Decisions I'd made. I had to deal with them, but not just now.

I opened a can of Red Bull and browsed my emails, including one from Taylor.

```
RE pop quiz, what makes city folk think
they can move to the beach, snap their
fingers and fit right in?
    Jokes, poppet. I know you'll be tight
with the yokels — and you have buddies
already? You're flying. Glad to hear meat
stink has vanished and that Trouble isn't
troubled by move. Still can't believe you
are a florist … it's so NOT YOU!
    What's news? Nothing.
    Strategy meeting at ten like every
friggin' Monday morning. You know the
drill. The sales team talk in circles
about meeting their targets and gloat
about how well they're doing despite the
economic downturn. Creepy, jerky, fuckwit
Glenn is enjoying being top dog. Still
making sexist remarks and generally being
an obnoxious C. I don't think he has a
clue what he's doing. Catch ya later, T X
```

I gulped my Red Bull. I missed Taylor, but ugh, I was happy to be rid of Glenn. I glanced towards the front door, willing customers to stampede.

Trish breezed in a few minutes later. 'Greetings. How's your first Tuesday going?'

'Fine, I think.' I offered her a stool and she sat down. 'Can I get you a tea? Red Bull?'

'No, love. Just popped in to say hello. I thought you might be feeling homesick.'

'I don't miss my old job, or the city for that matter, but I do miss Mum and Dad.'

'That's only natural. I'm sure they miss you too. I miss my kids. My son's interstate most of the time and my daughter lives in Sydney.'

I sighed. 'I'm an only child.'

'Me too.' Trish beamed.

'My mother takes it as a personal slight that I moved away.'

'Mothers can be like that,' Trish agreed. 'Hopefully, she'll come down soon and I can meet her. If she's anything like Iris, I bet she's a hoot.'

I rolled my eyes.

'What? They don't get along?'

'I'm sure they love each other but,' I took a moment to word my next line, 'chalk and cheese. Iris is outgoing. Flamboyant. Mum is ... I love my mother. It's just she can be hard going at times. Iris has always been so much more laid-back.'

Trish patted my shoulder. 'She can afford to be. She's like the doting grandma who gets to return the child. But I tell you what, my two, they're twins ... talk about rivalry. The jealousy, the fights. My daughter always thought that Ken, that's their father, doted on my son. But that wasn't the case at all.' Trish paused. 'I was heartbroken when Ken died. The kids were so young, not even teenagers. I think it affected the three of us more than we care to admit.' She blinked as if thinking back in time. 'I was so busy dealing with my own grief. My son coped better.' She smiled. 'He had soccer, basketball, running. My daughter? Not so much. She thought I was ignoring her.' Trish took a breath. 'I wasn't. I was sad. It wasn't something I could snap out of.'

'I'm so sorry.'

She stood up, wiping away many tears. 'I often wonder how life might have turned out, had Ken ... look at me, babbling like an old woman.'

'Not at all. I can imagine it's been very difficult for you.'

Trish brightened. 'I have my memories. And now, I best leave you to it. Call me anytime.'

'Actually, can you recommend a good local accountant? I'd like to talk with someone about the business.'

'Sure can.' She fossicked around in her bag and, pulled out a card. 'Henry Goodes, above Andy's framing shop. Great bloke. Genuine. I'll call him now if you like.'

I nodded. Now was as good a time as any. Trish phoned, and after exchanging a few words, handed me her phone. I spoke briefly with Henry and we arranged to meet in his office the following morning at eight thirty.

Trish walked to the door, turned, then said, 'Please talk to me if you have concerns. Even to chat.'

I felt the same ... talk to me.

❧

Henry shook my hand when I entered his office. An Aboriginal flag and photos of elders and, presumably, family and friends, cluttered his windowsill and a side cabinet.

'I haven't had the pleasure of visiting your shop,' he said, 'but from the outside, it looks a lot more inviting than Christof's butchery.'

I grinned. 'Thanks.'

'If he ever comes back to town, don't tell him that I told you.' He smiled genuinely. 'Take a seat and tell me all about Lily's Little Flower Shop. Cute name by the way.' Henry's voice was encouraging and full of warmth. Late thirties, jet black hair, a firm handshake and a wide smile.

After giving him a quick lowdown, I handed over the paperwork I'd accumulated since starting.

He read over my scratchings while I fidgeted in my chair and gazed out the window. I'd never get complacent about the view.

'It looks like you're undercharging.'

I winced. 'It's a country town.'

He nodded. 'I know. People here don't expect to pay city prices, but we still run businesses, Lily. All of us. Andy, Trish, you, me. My mob's been here forever, and it took my dad till he was almost sixty to charge people what he was worth.'

'What did he do?'

'Master carpenter. Still is.'

I nodded.

'We all have overheads. Electricity, rent ... it doesn't come cheap. If you keep going the way you are ... well, I hope you have a lot of savings.'

'I've ploughed most of them into my house in Sydney, cottage really. And of course, for the shop, stock and fittings.'

'Property? Great. Sensible.'

'Thanks. Renters are paying my mortgage, so I don't have to worry about that side of things.'

'Good to hear.' He cocked his head to one side and hesitated before speaking. 'This is a business, Lily, and you need to treat it as such. I like what you've done re your initial Facebook page, Instagram and company website. But for these to be effective, you need to constantly update them. You can't post status updates once every three weeks. Consistency's the key.'

I twitched in my chair.

'You might want to think about whether you need all of these platforms? Are they helping or hindering? Perhaps you could choose one form of social media and concentrate on managing it effectively.'

'I like posting photos on Instagram and I think I should keep the website.'

He nodded, and continued reading my figures, before

speaking again. 'The tourist season is just about over. Not to be a downer, but you need to have a business plan to cope with the inevitable slow in trade.'

'That's why I'm talking to you.'

'I'll look at your overheads and plan for the weekly income you need for the business to work. Sound reasonable?'

I scratched at my neck: anxiety rash. 'Yes.'

Henry continued reading, then gasped.

'What?'

'You took out a full-page advertisement in the *Coastal Review* for three thousand dollars?'

I frowned. 'Where I come from, advertising's a must.'

'Ads are fine if you earn that money back in revenue, but let's face it, you're going to have to sell a lot of flowers to recoup *that* outlay.'

'Yeah. My aunt was appalled. She says that the best advertisement is a few extra flowers in each bunch.'

'Sounds like a wise lady. No more advertising for now, hey? Three grand is a fifth of the cost of a van.'

'A van?'

He took a breath. 'Let's talk about your car. A blue Mini, isn't it?'

I pulled a face. 'Yes. Cute. Compact. Solid, reliable—'

'And great for inner-city driving and parking. But even with my limited floristry knowledge, I can see it's impractical. Seriously, you need a van. A small one maybe, but a van or station wagon.'

'I guess.' I'd never envisioned myself driving a van. 'I love my Mini.'

Henry laughed. 'It'll be cost effective.'

'A tax deduction?'

'Of course.' He looked back down at my figures. 'Lily, I hate to say it but if you don't stick to a solid financial plan, you'll be out of business in two months.'

Henry and I covered a lot of ground during our meeting. I felt rudely nude, but also worn out. Henry got me thinking. My flower shop was a business. And I really did need to make money. A profit. There was little cash flow. Thank God for the village contra deals. I was living on free cappuccinos and the occasional Greek salad. I'd also picked up a few weekly standing orders, one from Barry, the newsagent, baker Sally, and another from Trish.

In the city, I never gave a second thought to spending money, whether I was eating out, catching Ubers, or buying clothes. But there, I earnt a great salary. Now I was going backwards, I missed my city income more and more. A regular paycheck. Sick pay. Holiday pay. Working for a corporate giant had its advantages. At the time, I took them for granted. At least my Sydney cottage was rented out.

I left Henry, convinced I needed to do two things: look into buying a van and raise my flower prices. I wasn't happy about either. But I wasn't sure what else I could do. I worked sixteen-hour shifts and the shop was open seven days. I couldn't hold customers at gunpoint and demand they buy my most expensive bouquets.

Besides, I didn't have a back-up plan – Lily's Little Flower Shop had to be a success. This is what I wanted. No ifs or buts. But what if I failed? Could I sell my Sydney cottage? The house I'd made my home? The gardens. The thriving inner-city vibe. I shivered. If I sold it and blew my money in Clearwater, what then? Would I ever be able to go back? Selling the cottage was more than likely a one-way street.

❦

Thankfully, business surged that day. People flew in and the phone rang off the hook. It only took someone to have a baby, birthday or anniversary, for me to realise I hadn't ordered enough flowers to fill the incoming orders.

I didn't get the flower mix right at the markets. A baby girl had been born and most of the townspeople wanted pink, yellow or white flowers for little Freya, two point three kilos, and her mother, Jessica (weight unknown). With my limited supply, I created five individual arrangements featuring pixie carnations, daisies, gerberas, and roses, in various shades of pink and cream. I hoped my customers were happy. I certainly was.

But my once-beautifully manicured nails were broken and dirty and my palms had calluses, like the rough hands of a middle-aged farmer. Mum's words about getting arthritis in my fingers rang in my ears. I wanted to shout *Be quiet!* Plus, I had scratches and sores on my arms from where branches and thorns had stabbed me.

I spied Trouble munching on some greenery. 'What are you staring at?'

His head shook, making his ears flop to either side. He steadied himself, peered at me and hopped under the table.

'Safest place for you,' I called after him.

CHAPTER 10

Aunty Iris walked into the shop an hour later. 'Sweetie, your shop is darling. Beautiful. Like I imagined. How's everything?'

'Okay.'

She grabbed me by the shoulders, bangles jangling. 'Said with such conviction.'

'There was a birth I hadn't counted on. Several people came in wanting pink flowers and these,' I pointed to several bouquets on my crowded bench, 'are also for the new mum. I underordered.'

'Don't fret. As you get to know the locals, you'll hear of impending births, weddings, that sort of thing.' Iris inspected the bouquets. 'Well done.'

'Really?'

Iris nodded. 'Really.'

'I'll need to close earlier today to deliver them.' Five of the ten arrangements were going to Jessica at the local hospital maternity ward, but the others were scattered within a twenty-kilometre radius. 'Maybe I've made a mistake—'

'About the mis-ordering, agreeing to deliver—'

'Everything. The shop—'

'Nonsense! Ever since pre-school, you go about your life counting your mistakes. Why not instead count life by the adventures you've had? Some good. Some not so good? All brave! This shop is *not* a mistake. Once you get on your feet, hire a uni student to make the deliveries. You can probably handle them yourself at this stage, but you'll need help on big ticket days like Christmas, Mother's Day and Valentine's. Speaking of which, Valentine's Day will test you.'

I sighed. 'Thanks for the tip.'

'Tell you what,' Iris said, happily. 'Give me those deliveries. I've missed seeing newborns.'

'You're a lifesaver.'

'I know!'

After Iris left, a familiar-looking guy walked in. 'Ben, isn't it?'

He smiled. 'Good memory. How are you enjoying Clearwater so far?'

'Loving it. The locals have been very welcoming.'

'Good to hear.' He picked up a pair of clogs from Trouble's hutch. 'Interesting.' And put them down again. 'I like what you've done with the place. Damn sight better than the butcher shop.'

'Thanks.' I stared down at the clogs on my feet, garden green. I was trying to lead by example, but they weren't really practical for the shop. I'd almost tripped several times. Win some, lose some. I got back to my paperwork so Ben could continue his inspection unfettered.

I was still feeling my way with customers. I didn't want to rush at them and gush ... I hated it when shop assistants pounced on me the second I walked in, but I also didn't want to appear standoffish or rude.

Moments later, I rushed and gushed. 'Can I help?'

He picked up some white arum lilies. 'I'm after something white. White with greenery.'

'Classy.' That is, I meant to say 'classy', but my voice morphed into some alien twang and it came out as 'clarsee', which sounded anything but. I showed him the range of white and cream lilies, roses, hydrangea and dahlia.

'Great, I'll take them.'

I held an armful of flowers. 'All of them?'

He nodded. 'Why not?' Then handed me his platinum Visa card.

I acted casual as I chatted, prepared the flowers. Multitasking at its finest. My fingers were all thumbs, tripping over each other. In the past, when I'd bought flowers and watched the florist whipping them into a stunning arrangement in three minutes flat, they'd made it look ridiculously easy. So simple. But as I'd learnt way back in my course, there was an art to it. It was coming back to me, but I was out of practise. Trimming the stems (always at an angle, forty-five degrees was best), dethorning the roses, and arranging them so that the bunch looked even, not cluttered or squashed. Thankfully, while I was fumbling, his phone rang. I had a few seconds to get organised. I really needed to speed up the process.

After I'd arranged the flowers with some green foliage, I wrapped them simply with green tissue paper and clear cellophane. They looked great. I was pleased. I took a quick photo with my iPhone for an Instagram post and did cost calculations in my head.

He was still on the phone, so I wrote the price down on a piece of paper and held it up. He nodded, then keyed in his pin number into the EFTPOS machine. I couldn't help noticing his brown tussled hair and strong jawline. And his strong hands, not chubby and squat. Clean fingernails too.

I glanced at the whirring machine. And looked again.

Instead of charging him eighty-five dollars, I'd charged him eight hundred and fifty.

'They look great,' he said, after he'd finished his conversation and stuck the phone in his back pocket.

'Yeah, but I'm so sorry,' I said, gulping. 'I've overcharged you.'

He shrugged. 'How much?'

I grimaced. 'Seven hundred and sixty-five dollars.'

'That's a lot of flowers.'

'If you give me your card again, I'll fix it.'

'Really? You want my credit card again? How can I trust you?' But he was smiling.

'I'm so sorry. I hope you're not in a hurry.'

'Well...' He stared into space for a moment. 'No. Take your time.'

Again, I asked him to punch in his pin number and again, he obliged. 'I think we've got it sorted now, Ben, but please check your statement.'

He took back his card and pointed to a corner of the ceiling. 'Water damage. You might want to get that fixed before it gets any worse.'

'Thanks. I only had it patched and painted a couple of weeks ago. I'll add it to the list.'

'There's a list?'

'It's an old building. Things go wrong.'

'Make sure you talk to your real estate agent about it.' He winked and picked up the flowers. 'Thanks again.'

He left, and I glanced down at my black T-shirt and skirt uniform. I really needed to visit that surf shop.

After closing, I sat on my veranda gazing out across the park towards the ocean. I was the luckiest woman on the planet. I also had no food. I did have a six pack of Red Bull and a view. And a rabbit. But I was tired, and with exhaustion came melancholy. Would it always be this arduous?

I padded to the back window, which overlooked a rear lane. It was so quiet. Just one walker with a dog; Alsatian, by the looks. I didn't see many of those in the city. There was also the odd bit of highway noise, but it was muted, distant.

❧

In bed, I couldn't get comfortable. My brain fired. What if I wasn't meant to be a florist? Maybe my destiny *was* in corporate life?

I'd received several short emails and photos from Matt. He'd been gone just three weeks and was making the most of his overseas adventure, coping with the heat, sipping Tiger beer, riding scooters. I shook my head. Business Matt negotiating the traffic and pedestrians in Singapore on a scooter? I'd seen the photos but still couldn't quite believe it. He said he missed me and the feeling was mutual, so why hadn't I mentioned him to Andy and Zena at drinks the other night?

Matt popped into my head at the oddest times, like when I'd see an ad for Bunnings, his favourite hardware shop, or when I ate a mango, his favourite fruit. I guess that was what you did when you'd been together as long as Matt and I had. He'd been my blokey best friend as well as my lover.

I got out of bed, found my laptop, slipped back under the sheet and switched it on to send Matt an email. I struggled to find the words, because I didn't know what to say or what he wanted to hear. Why was it so difficult to communicate with someone I'd spent three years with? Maybe at the back of my mind, I questioned the point.

As I was composing the words in my head, I saw he'd beaten me to it.

Lil,

How's life in the sun? Still can't picture you as a laid-back beach chick. Singapore? Mad, chaotic. Never dull. Miss you. How's that rascally rabbit?
Me x

I sat back in bed, patting Trouble. Matt was in Singapore but might as well be living on the moon. We weren't about to see each other anytime in the near future.

Should I have gone to Singapore, put Matt's needs ahead of mine? The truth was, I'd never seriously contemplated moving there. I just didn't want to be someone's appendage.

Someone's, or specifically Matt's?

Either way, I wanted to do something for myself.

But do I love him?

Of course, I love him. We were together three years.

But we're not together now?

I sighed. No. We're not.

I wanted to stay positive, not dwell on adjustment issues, so I ignored the urge to tell him everything. Instead, I kept it simple, like he had.

Hey Matty,
Life's good and you're right. I'm definitely NOT a laid-back beach chick – not yet anyway. But am working on it. Clearwater has its own brand of mad chaos. Huge learning curve. Crazy in fact. Have met some lovely locals.
Rascally rabbit is curled up beside me, pulling at cotton on my T-shirt as I type this. I miss you too.
Me x

I pictured Matt and me at the beach. Us on holidays at Hamilton Island, Hawaii and Fiji. I loved the simple things we did together, going to the movies, eating at our local Thai, fruit and vegetable shopping. Bloody hell. I missed him. And the sex. I knew his body so well – knew exactly how to make the hairs on his arms and other parts of his body stand on end. I missed his touch, his smell, and I missed the way his body fitted so well with mine.

I punished myself by glorifying the good days and not thinking about the average days. Deep down I knew that sooner or later the rubber band holding us together would snap. If I couldn't talk to Matt about one of the most private and traumatic times of my life, then how could we truly be together and honest with each other? No holds barred?

CHAPTER 11

*Z*ena strolled into the shop on Sunday morning, Lily's Little Flower Shop's tenth opening. 'Greetings. How's everything?'

'Mayhem, but I'm getting used to it.'

'You still haven't been in for a wash and blow-dry and yet you've delivered me a stunning bouquet. I can fit you in anytime, you say the word. Promise I won't accidentally dye your hair blue.' She made a point of crossing her fingers.

'Good to know. Red Bull?'

She nodded. 'Please. I could use a boost.'

I retrieved one from the cold room and handed it to her. I'd only had one extended conversation with Zena when she'd come over on opening night but she seemed in no hurry to leave. 'Everything okay?' I asked her.

'Yeah. Boyfriend shit.'

'Ah, I know all about that.'

Zena raised her eyebrows. 'Do tell.'

'Short story, I missed out on a promotion just as my boyfriend Matt got a transfer to Singapore. He expected I'd go with him and basically be a kept woman. I snapped, came down here to visit my aunt and the next thing you know, I'd quit my job, moved, opened a flower shop and Matt's overseas. You?'

'My boyfriend Nate and I are on and off. I'm too weak to end it permanently, but I know he's not good for me. What I really want is to make my salon the best on the south coast. I want to be the "go-to" hairdresser, for style, cut and colour. Today, Clearwater; tomorrow, Australia!' Zena sighed. 'But Nate keeps pulling me back in and I get distracted.'

I sat on my stool listening.

'I want to prove my parents wrong. I want to make it here. I refused to stay on Norfolk and marry a local, which is what they expected.'

'Really?'

Zena nodded. 'Or at least after completing my hairdressing apprenticeship, go back and set up a business on Norfolk. I've been in Clearwater four years and they've never been to visit. They came over when I was living in Brisbane. Reluctantly.'

'It's not the same, but my parents, Mum in particular, was gutted when I didn't move to Singapore with Matt, so when I quit my job anyway and moved down here ... well, they couldn't understand it. But so far, I love it.'

'So do I. Sure, the Clearwater community annoys me sometimes, what with locals knowing what you're up to, where you've been and who you're screwing, but this is my home now. I feel safe here.'

I nodded. 'I'm lucky. My aunt lives nearby and she's a huge help. And I understand what you mean about your salon. I feel the same way about this.' I extended my arms dramatically. 'More than anything, I want it to be a success, which is why I don't care that I work twelve-hour days, more on market days. I'm prepared to put in the miles.'

Zena stood. 'Touché! Thanks for letting me vent. I'm really

glad you moved here, Lily. We should have drinks after work every Friday night.'

'I'd like that. You and Andy, and Trish, of course, have made me feel very welcome.'

Zena smiled. 'Good, and now, I'm going home to kick Nate out. Again! Then I'm taking a six-month relationship hiatus. No dates until July. At least. My sole focus will be on the salon.'

'Good for you.'

'Yep, by July, I'll have my act together and know exactly what I'm after in a relationship. And be desperate to shag anyone who crosses my path.' She giggled. 'In the meantime, I really need to change the locks.'

CHAPTER 12

I t was early February and Lily's Little Flower Shop had been operating for two weeks. I was doing okay.

Since my overcharging mishap, I'd become proficient with the EFTPOS machine and had overcome several more hurdles, not least of which was freezing several hundred dollars' worth of flowers in the cold room. I'd now mastered the Fahrenheit thermostat and was getting used to rising early for my regular trips to the flower market. Then there was the flower arranging, preparing gift baskets, delivering flowers, ordering more paper, vials and goodness knows what else. I barely had time to feed myself and Trouble, or dwell on my precarious financial situation.

Just after ten, the phone rang. 'Good morning, Lily's Little Flower Shop. How may I help you?'

'Yeah, I ordered flowers for my girlfriend yesterday and haven't heard from her. Did you deliver them?'

I got out my order book and checked his details.

'Yes, Mr Walton, I delivered to that address at six fifteen last night and left them on her veranda as instructed.'

He sighed loudly. 'She hasn't called.'

'Maybe you could call her?'

'I might just do that,' he said, clearly irritated. 'I can't believe she wouldn't tell me she received them.'

I felt like telling him that perhaps she didn't want to talk to him. There were lots of reasons why recipients didn't immediately acknowledge flower deliveries. Either they were busy grieving, trying to get over an illness, or caring for a newborn. Possibly they were make-up flowers sent after a fight and the partner was still angry. Or despite the beautiful bouquet, this girlfriend wasn't ready to forgive and move on.

As I recalled, her house didn't have a doorbell, so after knocking several times, I'd left the flowers propped up against the front door. It amazed me how many people didn't have doorbells. Or house numbers ... and then there were the people who had ferocious barking dogs. No wonder posties got fed up.

I swept the floor, but before I could empty the bin in the huge garden waste disposal behind the shop, I needed to lock the front door. Whenever I wanted to use the bathroom or empty the bins, I had to lock the shop for five or more minutes. Before setting up, I hadn't considered the logistics of being alone. When I used to help Iris, there were always at least two of us. I didn't think twice about visiting the bathroom or disappearing to the local café for ten minutes. These days, buying a coffee was a major production, let alone going to the bank and grocery shopping.

'Valentine's Day soon,' Trish said as she strode through the door before I'd had a chance to lock it. 'Excited?'

'Nervous,' I replied.

'Hope you've got some help. I'm sure it will be a huge day for you.'

I nodded. Maybe it was time to drag Taylor down the coast for a couple of days.

'You look worried,' Trish continued. 'Everything okay?'

'I have a few maintenance issues.' After Ben mentioned the damaged ceiling, I added it to my growing list – a dodgy toilet flush, a hall light bulb that kept blowing and a drainage issue with the sink.

She looked horrified. 'Why didn't you tell me sooner? What's the problem?'

I foraged for the scrap of paper I'd written on and handed it to her.

She was quiet a moment before saying, 'All easy fixes. Leave this with me.' She folded the paper and stuffed it into her handbag.

❧

The next morning, I visited the local car dealership and instantly fell in love with a second-hand, red, low-mileage van. After negotiating a trade-in, I purchased it on the spot, and three days before Valentine's, I collected it and waved goodbye to my beloved Mini.

As soon as I drove the van back to the shop, I sent Taylor a text and snazzy photo:

Guess what? My faithful old Mini has gone but am sure Verna the van and I will get along just fine. Xxx

Taylor rang me immediately. 'Verna?'

'I bought a red van called Verna. She's adorable.'

She whistled down the line. 'You're really serious about this gig, aren't you?'

'Hell yeah,' I cackled. 'I love, totally love living on the coast—'

'I sense a "but" coming.'

'Nah, it's just full-on, seven days a week and given that I'm already a borderline insomniac, I'm working in a daze, on autopilot. A couple of times I've arrived at the flower markets at six am wondering how I got there.

'Lil, you went from being a corporate workaholic, managing a team of twenty-five, with a long-term boyfriend and excellent job prospects to ... and I'm not being harsh here, Lil, just honest, quitting your job, having no underlings. Except Trouble ... how is the beast?'

'Perfect, as always.'

'Good to hear. And Matt? You haven't spoken about him much.'

I sighed. 'I don't know what's happening with him.'

Taylor barely paused for breath. 'And another thing, you haven't given yourself time to grieve and process your old career or Matt moving overseas. Instead, you've pushed headlong into your next project. You always need to be busy, busy, busy! Have you ever thought about slowing down and stopping to "smell the roses"? Ha! Good one, Taylor.'

I was used to grieving. I'd been doing it since I was a teen, which is why I needed to keep busy. 'I have grieved and processed, thank you very much. I don't need to dwell. Onward and upward.'

'Still, you must be knackered ... surely you're going to crash soon?'

'Thanks for the vote of confidence.'

'You know what I mean.'

'Reminiscing only makes you sad and bitter. And lonely! Happily, I have no time to be lonely. Too buggered. And I have an endless stream of locals popping by to shoot the breeze.'

'Ugh.'

'Yeah, am trying not to get impatient.' I chewed the inside of my lip. 'Valentine's in a few days.'

'Don't remind me. My well is as dry as the Sahara. Give me a shout if you need a hand.'

§♠

The day before Valentine's, I woke in a hot sweat, heart pounding. Maybe I was worried about sales, or maybe I was feeling unloved and lonely. Waking up on Valentine's Day without someone to cuddle zapped my energy. It was 3.30am. I needed to get to the markets. Instead, I picked up my phone and read a message from Matt.

Imagining you in an apron and scarf, picking flowers in a field somewhere. Love, Me x

Matt was trying to be cute or charming, but I bristled. His message showed a complete lack of understanding about what I did. The morning I'd woken up beside him hoping I was getting the promotion seemed a lifetime ago.

I was about to hit delete when he phoned.

'Hey, sexy. So, are you wearing an apron?'

'It's three thirty in the morning, so, no.'

'Shame. I miss you.' He sounded a bit drunk. 'What *are* you wearing? A lacy black bra—'

'A black T-shirt.'

Matt sighed. 'I bet your boobs look magnificent. I'm imagining them cupped in my hands, stroking them, kissing, nipping your nipples.' He laughed. 'Nipping—'

'Stop.'

He hesitated. 'I was trying to get you in the mood.'

'For phone sex?'

He didn't reply.

'I don't want pretend sex, I want physical sex with you, Matt. Real intimacy.'

'Well, I'm not in Clearwater if you haven't noticed.'

'I've noticed, Matt. Look, I'm tired. I've got a busy few days ahead of me. Can we talk later?'

'Sure. Whatever. I was trying to tell you that I miss you.'

'Yeah,' I said quietly. 'I miss you too.'

I hung up, wondering how long we'd be able to keep the relationship going.

On my first trip to the flower markets in my new – well, second-hand – van, I missed my old car, but Verna handled the long drive more smoothly than the Mini and it had a much better sound system. I parked, got out of the van and took a deep breath, list firmly in hand. Inside, the atmosphere was Frenzied. Yes, capital F.

'Whatever quantity you're thinking of buying, double it,' was the popular refrain of the morning. I had over thirty orders to fill. I hoped to get another twenty, as well as a few walk-ins.

'Roses keep. But if you can't fulfil a sweetheart's order for two-dozen long-stemmed blood-red roses, your life won't be worth living,' said Tony, offering me his 'very best price' for roses. 'Tomorrow, you'll have no time to breathe.'

The sellers kept repeating the same words.

'You've been warned. Double your estimate and double it again.'

'Make sure you have extra staff,' said another.

'Extra staff? There's only me.'

A couple of sellers and florists looked at each other and laughed.

'Honey,' said an older renowned Wollongong florist. 'Time for a reality check. Call in your favours. You're going to need all the help you can get.'

I twitched. No doubt this was the best time to own a flower shop! At least that's what Aunty Iris seemed to think. But she'd also warned me that Valentine's Day would be one of the busiest days of the year. Pity she wouldn't be here to help me. She'd told me when I first opened the shop that she'd planned a cruise to the Whitsundays with Mavis, her widowed neighbour. After I'd doubled and re-doubled my quantities again, I drove like a maniac to Clearwater. I could do this.

By eleven, I needed help. Orders were piling in via the phone, email and fax, and I needed someone to deliver the following day's orders while I served in the shop.

I rang Trish. 'Don't suppose you know a student with a driving licence who'd like a day's work tomorrow?'

'Leave it with me. I'll see what I can do.'

Ninety-five per cent of the orders came from men who 'ummed' and 'ahhed' and didn't know what flowers they wanted or how much money they wanted to spend. When they finally decided (generally, ninety-nine dollars for one dozen long-stemmed red roses, including delivery), they didn't know what to say on the card, so they 'ummed' and 'ahhed' some more. Meanwhile, the bips of the next call sounded on the line.

Everyone wanted their loved one's flowers delivered at 9am. Plus, everyone's loved one seemed to have an exotic double-barrelled name. Not that I begrudged anyone having an exotic name; they were just difficult to spell.

Fifteen minutes later, Trish called back. 'I've got a charming young man, Damien, to help you out.' I could hear the smile in her voice.

Yay for Trish and her contacts.

A hell of a lot of men left it until after two o'clock to order flowers, while still demanding they be delivered first thing in the morning to an office they had no address for.

I'd underestimated how long it'd take to prepare the flowers and deliver them. Every man and a few women within a fifty-kilometre radius, were ordering from Lily's Little Flower Shop.

Overwhelmed, I rang Taylor. 'Help.'

'Proceed.'

'Valentine's Day and I have seriously overestimated my ability to deliver.'

'So, you called your good buddy, problem-solver-extraordinaire? I knew it. I'm also smart. I'm not expecting any flowers tomorrow, so I may as well come down and soak up other people's love.'

'Thank you! Thank you! Thank you!'

I'd been up since forever, had drunk four cans of Red Bull and was wired, exhausted and wrung out. At least I had my university student, Damien, lined up for an 8am start. That just left dethorning the roses, placing them in vials or bouquets and writing out all the cards ... dozens and dozens and dozens of cards. Taylor and I would be up all night, preparing orders. No exaggeration. I hadn't warned her about this.

By 4pm, the phone calls still hadn't subsided. I eyed the door, desperate to close, but the stream of walk-ins continued. I'd have thought the gesture romantic, if I had time to think.

Taylor bowled in as I was closing the front door at six thirty.

'Lily!' she shouted. 'Love, love, love it. Let me look at everything. So cute. Love the butcher hooks. Oh, and all the pretty baskets. Wow! The colours. Oh my God,' she barely paused for breath, 'it's amazing. Let's not even talk about the view. Your shop is stunning.' She clapped her hands.

'Thanks. Now, if you could pop out the front and promote my stunning wares— on second thoughts, don't. I have my hands full.'

'Truly, Lil,' she said, taking it all in. 'The shop's gorgeous. Well done, you.'

'Don't congratulate me yet. The night is young, and we've got a lot of orders to fill.'

'No worries.' She lifted up a huge drink cooler I hadn't noticed, the kind that could hold an entire picnic. 'Give me ten minutes to plonk my stuff down, whip up an antipasto platter and open the champagne.'

'Champagne,' I repeated slowly. 'I'm not sure...'

'Come on, it'll be fun. Now then, where's my favourite Trouble maker?'

Just as she said the words, Trouble popped his head around the side of a basket full of pink and cream miniature roses.

Taylor squealed. 'There's my boy!' She picked him up and rubbed her nose against his. 'Come on, Lil, get the glasses out. A woman's not a camel. Do I have to do everything?'

'Okay, okay.' I turned on the answering machine, retrieved two glasses from the shelf, and Taylor poured the bubbly and laid out the olives, goat's cheese, salami and other assorted goodies. She also threw some lettuce in Trouble's bowl. 'There you go, gorgeous.'

'If I just have one to relax,' I said, sorting through the orders, 'we'll fill these in no time.'

Taylor raised her glass. 'I bags writing the love messages on the cards.'

'Should be straightforward. Most guys were too embarrassed to tell me their romantic message, so on the whole they're simple "I love you"s.'

'Sweet!'

Minutes later, Zena came by. As usual, she looked amazing, dressed in a funky hot-pink cord dress, fringed with multicoloured pom-poms.

'Love your style,' Taylor told her. 'Could you give Lil a few tips?'

Zena smiled and looked me up and down. 'She's a tough one.'

I'd just finished pouring Zena a drink when Andy walked in.

'Looks like you have everything under control,' he said,

spying our drinks, food and piles of orders laid out on the bench.

'Looks can be deceiving.' I introduced him to Taylor.

'So many orders,' said Taylor. 'You weren't kidding about us being up all night.'

I handed Andy a drink. 'Second biggest flower day of the year according to today's papers.'

'And the towns around here haven't had a flower shop in forever,' added Zena, 'so I assume all the women will be expecting flowers because their husbands and boyfriends have gotten away with not giving them for years.'

'What's the biggest day?' Taylor asked.

'Mother's Day,' Zena and I said at the same time, then laughed.

'Can I do anything to help, Lil?' Zena offered.

'Taylor and I have it covered.'

Taylor looked up. 'We hope.'

Zena and Andy finished their drinks and left us to it.

'So,' said Taylor, as we worked our way through the orders and our bottle of champagne. 'What's happening with lover boy?'

I looked at her, momentarily confused. 'Matt? Nothing. I don't know. How can we sustain it when we don't know when we're seeing each other again?'

'Really?'

'Sometimes I flip-flop, but seriously, it's a matter of time.'

Taylor sipped her wine and put her head to one side. 'You could always fly to Singapore and surprise him. See if the spark's still firing.'

'Yeah, right.' I speared a rose at her. 'One, I don't have time. Two, we're...' I paused. 'It's too hard. And three, I hate surprises. Getting and giving them. You know that.'

Taylor smiled. 'Ah, the *Surprise*.'

Surprises of any kind aren't much chop. Oh, I used to like them back when I was young and innocent. Dad bringing home chocolates for Friday night treats. Mum picking me up after school on a whim to take me shopping. Those were good surprises. I thought I'd always be a fan. Until I was sixteen, and then again in my early twenties when I paid my boyfriend an impromptu visit.

I'd been dating Richard for six months and decided to surprise him after his regular Saturday golf game. I knew where the spare key to his flat was hidden – in a broken pot, home to a long-dead cactus. I let myself in, put wine in the fridge, arranged the cheese, olives and biscuits expertly on a plate and waited, knowing he was due any minute. When I heard his car pull up, I readied myself to jump out and yell 'surprise', in my sexiest underwear.

Except he wasn't alone. He was with a mutual friend.

I gave them the benefit of the doubt. She'd been having issues with her boyfriend and needed to talk. I hurriedly threw on some clothes, but something stopped me from walking into the lounge room to join them. Instead I took a peek. They were practically having sex up against the wall.

I froze, but when he pushed his hand up under her skirt and she moaned 'fuck me, fuck me now', I couldn't hold back. I walked in, said something like 'cheese and crackers anyone?' and kept walking straight out the front door.

I shook my head. I was done with surprises.

'Good old cheatin' Richo,' Taylor said as we continued dethorning rose stems.

By midnight, we'd knocked off three quarters of the orders. 'We could turn in and get up early to finish them,' I suggested when I noticed Taylor yawning.

She shook her head. 'Nah. Let's get them over and done with.'

CHAPTER 13

We finally finished a little before 2am and headed upstairs, my adrenalin pumping. I dozed on and off till 6am and then got up, showered and scrubbed, ready to face the onslaught.

Leaving Taylor to sleep, I went downstairs, opened the door and placed baskets of roses on the pavement. Then I wrote on my chalkboard: *A flower cannot blossom without sunshine, and man cannot live without love.* Max Muller.

Damien arrived promptly and was on the road by eight twenty-five. So far, so good.

I was so busy in the cold room I didn't realise Taylor had slipped out and returned until she presented me with a latte and chocolate croissant. 'Happy Valentine's Day!'

'And to you,' I said clinking my paper cup with hers. 'Let the madness begin.'

'I thought we went through all that last night?'

'We did. Round two is about to start.'

She laughed. 'Bring it on.'

'Or should I say, has started.' I bit into my croissant. 'A guy just came in wanting a single red rose delivered to his girlfriend's work, on the hour, every hour. What a pain in the ass.'

'What did you say?'

'That we'd do our best. She's a nineteen-year-old who works at the surf shop a few doors down. It's doable. I'm charging him for it though.'

'He's probably a uni student. How romantic.'

I rolled my eyes. 'Yes, it's romantic, but no, he's an insurance agent from Kiama and almost twice her age. I got the full story in under five minutes.'

Taylor rolled her eyes. 'Right. Charge him through the snout.'

We were still laughing when several gawky teenage boys from the local high school ambled in, each wanting to buy a single rose to take to school. I was so overcome with their sweetness, I charged them cost price.

'You'll never make any money if you keep doing that,' said Taylor, after they'd left.

'They're fourteen. It would've taken lots of courage to walk in.'

We spent the morning fielding orders, making bouquets and generally being run off our feet.

'Ever considered going into the flower business?' I asked Taylor as I watched her expertly arrange a dozen roses and wrap them. 'You have more flair than I do, that's for sure.'

She shooed me away. 'Lil, refill the buckets out the front. We need more roses, more colour!'

At midday, Ben, the guy I'd overcharged weeks back, sauntered through the door. I felt a slight shiver when he smiled.

'Hey,' I said.

He peered around. 'Everything looks so good.'

He was obviously looking for flowers to give to a girlfriend. Or wife.

Taylor poked her head out of the cold room. 'Hello, good-looking.'

I almost died. 'Don't mind her. She's delusional. Been sitting in the freezer too long.'

'Taylor Glover.' She held out her hand to shake Ben's. 'Damn glad to meet you.'

Taylor was such a flirt. I shook my head. No. Just no.

'You too.' Ben smiled.

'What can we do to help?' Taylor flicked her hair. 'Come in here to charm us with your scintillating conversation?'

She looked drop-dead gorgeous. Red hair falling across her face. Simple denim shorts, white T-shirt. Effortlessly cool. I was sweating, hair scraped back in a high ponytail, wearing grubby gym gear and yet, I hadn't seen the inside of a gym since I'd moved here. I could barely look at Ben.

'Taylor!' I shouted.

'I wish,' said Ben. 'But it's a busy day at the winery.'

Taylor raised her eyebrows. 'Winery?'

'Yeah, you'll have to come out for a tasting.'

'We'd love to.' Taylor grinned.

'Chained to the shop, I'm afraid,' I quickly added.

Taylor snorted.

'I know the feeling,' Ben agreed. 'I'm only supposed to be visiting from Adelaide but have got caught up with the day-to-day running of the place. Which is why I'm here. We're giving roses to all the "ladies who lunch" and embarrassingly, we've run out. So,' he said, pointing to the roses outside, 'can I buy say, four dozen?'

Taylor snapped her fingers. 'Your wish is our command.' She walked back inside the cold room and emerged a few moments later with an armload of roses.

'Thanks. I should've ordered them last night but one of my staff lives near a rose farm and said he'd pick them up. He grossly underestimated. And the ones growing in the vineyard aren't a patch on yours.'

'Happens to the best of us,' I said.

Taylor handed him the flowers. 'There you go, sir.'

Ben opened his wallet and handed me several fifties and smiled. 'Safer than EFTPOS.'

I grinned. 'Agreed.'

'See you around and please visit the winery when you have time.' He went to walk out the shop, then turned. 'How did you go with the leaks?'

'Getting sorted.'

'Good to hear.'

'Are you serious?' Taylor said, after Ben had walked out.

'What?'

'Lily Mason! Why aren't you fucking that guy? I tell you, Lils, if I were that way inclined...'

I shook my head. 'Could have fooled me.' But, I didn't have time to chastise her further because more customers streamed through the door.

Half an hour later when I took a moment to breathe, I noticed a text from Matt.

Happy Valentine's, hon. Miss you. Thought about sending you flowers, hee hee, but you know the drill. Hope you're selling a few. Me. xx

I fumed at his smugness and even though I knew he didn't mean it, maybe I'd have liked him to send me flowers.

Thankfully, I didn't have more than another minute to dwell on it. I wouldn't have thought there'd be so many walk-ins, but they kept coming in – people I'd never seen before. And they couldn't all have been tourists; the school holidays had finished over two weeks earlier.

I kept going, drinking Red Bull and working on autopilot. In the thick of it, Taylor amicably chatted as each new customer arrived. She was a godsend. There's no way I could have kept my shit together had she not been here with me. All I wanted was to close up shop and sleep for several days.

❦

We had some brief downtime between two and three o'clock, and I stupidly thought the rush might be over, but then the school boys piled in again, buying roses for their mothers. I almost wept.

'Really, Lil,' said Taylor. 'This is a business. You can't get overly emotional every time someone buys a daisy! Or a rose! There's generally a reason why people buy flowers.'

At six, Zena wandered in with a bottle of wine. 'Room for one more?'

Taylor poured us each a glass and then stood on the pavement handing out single red roses.

'This is great publicity, Lily,' Zena said as we sipped our drinks and watched bemused locals tentatively taking the flowers, worried it was some kind of trap. 'Let's join her.'

Declaring us officially 'done' at 7.30pm, I closed the front door and lay down in the middle of the shop surrounded by the day's detritus. Moments later, Taylor and Zena joined me. We were sitting on the floor laughing when Andy knocked and walked in.

'Hope I'm not interrupting.'

The three of us quickly sat up. 'Of course not,' I said, catching my breath.

'A rose, sir,' said Taylor, standing and handing him one.

Andy blushed as he accepted the rose. He was a sweetie.

'Coming to the pub?' Zena asked as she pulled some stray leaves from her hair.

'Nah,' he replied. 'But you guys have fun.'

Andy left and the three of us marched over to the pub where we drank more, ate salt and pepper squid, and played pool till closing.

⁂

I took the next day off. My first. It was either that or die. At exactly 5.30am, I rolled over, switched off my alarm and went back to sleep. At ten I woke again, as hungover as hell. The previous night flashed before my eyes.

'Oy,' I said, walking into the second bedroom where Taylor was curled up on the bed, snoring. I nudged her foot until she opened one eye. 'Does my memory deceive me or were we actually giving away roses last night?'

'I have the phone numbers to prove it,' she mumbled.

'Hey! Could you two keep it down to a dull roar?' Zena called out.

I peered at her, spread out on the sofa in the lounge room. 'You look uncomfortable.'

'I am. But it was worth it. I haven't had that much fun since forever.'

'Shouldn't you be at work?' I asked.

'Midday start so, yeah, soon.' Zena stood unsteadily. 'No one will notice I'm wearing the same clothes, will they?'

I looked her up and down – a crumpled mess in an electric blue catsuit. Even her pink hair looked forlorn. 'You could wear something of mine.'

It was Zena's turn to look me up and down. 'Thanks, Ms Corporate, but I'll wing it. I have an emergency clothing stash at the salon. I'll have a shower here though.'

Taylor and I watched as Zena stumbled toward the bathroom.

'Yeah,' said Taylor, coming to life. 'You really need to loosen your tie.'

'I'm trying but I've had no time to eat, let alone shop for clothes.'

'Well, today's your lucky day.'

'My first free day in over a month. Do I really need to shop?' I slumped into a chair. 'Don't answer that. Let's not go until I've taken a few Panadol.'

'And drunk some strong coffee.'

'And eaten a bacon and egg burger,' came a muffled voice from the bathroom.

Twenty minutes later, after I'd fed Trouble and inspected the carnage in the shop, the three of us sat in the sunshine at a local café, wearing sunglasses against the light.

'I needed this,' I said, drinking a cappuccino, enjoying the sun's warmth.

'What? A hangover?' replied Zena.

I smiled. 'Could have done without that, but this.' I stared out across the ocean. 'A day to breathe, take in what I've done over the past month. Figure out what's working, what isn't and maybe also answer an email or five.'

'There'll be plenty of time to answer mail later,' said Taylor. 'You seem to have settled in well.'

'Thanks, but I'm still an outsider. Not that the locals haven't been welcoming, but I'm very much the new kid in town.'

Zena nodded. 'I know how you feel. Not that it stops me from nabbing contra deals wherever I can.'

Taylor nodded. 'Don't be so hard on yourself, Lil. It's not like you've had any free time to get to know people. Your days and nights run into each other. It's crazy.'

'I expected business to slow down after the tourists packed up, but I'm just as busy. As for yesterday? Insane!'

'Don't complain,' said Zena. 'You'll get your downtime soon enough.'

'I guess.' I glanced down at the community newsletter, sitting idle on the table. There was information about various classes on offer: tai chi, table tennis, tap dancing, ukulele group. I've wanted to do tap since I was little. I loved the *tapping* on floorboards. It reminded me of romance and joy.

'Zena, wanna learn tap dancing?'

She shook her head. 'Can't. Hung-over.'

'I'll take that as a yes. Starts next Monday night, six o'clock.'

'I'll have to check my schedule.'

'What else are you doing?'

'Sometimes I work late,' Zena wailed.

'Work late the other five nights. You have plenty to choose from. What shoe size are you?'

'Say yes,' Taylor chimed in, and giving a wide smile. 'Lil's not going to accept the other answer. And I'd say a thirty-eight.'

'Thirty-seven,' Zena scowled.

I waved to Andy who was strolling towards us.

'Ladies,' he said, stopping at our table. He turned to Taylor. 'Thank you for my rose.'

Taylor smiled.

'You should have come to the pub with us,' I said.

'Next time,' Andy said and left us to it.

'He's nice.' Taylor peered down the street to see Andy disappear inside his shop.

'You think every man is *nice*,' I said. 'Because you can flirt and know nothing will come of it.'

Zena raised her eyebrows. 'Why?'

'I'm a lesbian.'

'Really? I'd never have guessed.' Zena paused. 'Not that there's anything wrong—'

Taylor laughed. 'It's fine. What about you? Do you have a partner?'

'No. I'm steering clear of men right now. Don't need the angst. This town is tiny. People gossip, and the hairdresser's supposed to listen to gossip, not be the subject of it.'

I puffed out my cheeks. 'It's over with Nate?'

Zena sighed heavily. 'I don't know why I kept giving in to him for so long. I mean, he's nice in a no-hope dope smoker kind of way.'

'But?' Taylor urged.

'He didn't do anything except surf – the waves and the internet. No helping with cooking. No gardening. No washing-up. The final straw came when he stopped showering. He couldn't be bothered cleaning himself, but still expected me to sleep with him. No thanks.'

'Fair enough,' agreed Taylor.

'I finally kicked him out a couple of weeks ago, keen to start afresh and in control. My previous boyfriends were carbon copies of each other. All surfer slackers who occasionally dabbled in paid work. Vince, the sometime painter, Brent, the sometime landscaper, and Ty, the sometime poet.'

'And you thought you could save them,' said Taylor.

'Exactly. Or at least look after them. What's with that?'

Taylor tossed her hair. 'I'm the same.'

'She is,' I agreed.

'At the back of my mind,' said Taylor, taking the ball, 'I know each relationship will end the same way. I'll get frustrated by their inability to establish some kind of financial independence and maturity, and I finish it, vowing never again to fall for the same kind of person.'

Zena nodded. 'Too right. I'm done. Just yesterday, Mrs

Beattie asked me again if I was still seeing Nate and when I said no, again, and jokingly added I was on the hunt, she patted my arm and advised me to "give the blokes a rest awhile, lest you be considered loose, dear". Me! Loose!'

'She didn't!' I almost spat my coffee out.

'Did too. And by *loose*, she clearly meant slut. I'm not a slut. Far from it. A serial monogamist, in fact.'

'So your July promise?' I asked Zena.

'Promise? What promise?' Taylor asked.

'The promise I've made to myself,' replied Zena. 'I'm swearing off men until July.'

'Why July?' Taylor pressed.

Zena laughed. 'I figure by then I'll be ready to jump into the sack with the first guy who gives me the eye. Or woman.'

'Do tell,' Taylor encouraged.

'Don't let my hair fool you.' Zena flicked her locks. 'I've kissed a few girls, and as the song goes, *I liked it*.'

Zena and Taylor clinked coffee mugs and Taylor said, 'Come over to the dark side. You won't regret it.'

I rolled my eyes. 'Oy. Get a room.'

Pulling herself away from Zena, Taylor turned to me. 'What about you?'

'I've kissed a girl.'

'Not that. I'm talking about Matt. Did you hear from him last night?'

I shook my head. 'Nah. Only the text at lunchtime.'

'Why don't you call him? What harm could it do?'

'After the other night, I want a break.' I'd told Taylor about the phone sex debacle. The whole conversation seemed wrong. Not at all intimate. Maybe I'd been too worried about Valentine's to let myself go and have fun, but even today, I wasn't in the mood. It felt off and I was in no rush to speak to Matt again.

Taylor listened, brow furrowed. 'Okay,' she said finally. 'What about Banging Ben?'

'Ben? No.' Despite wearing glasses, I shielded my eyes from the sun with a palm.

'Andy?'

'Taylor. For goodness' sake. Give it a rest.'

Zena raised her eyebrows and turned to Taylor. 'What about you? How's your love life?'

'Non-existent, clearly, given it's VD week and I'm here with you two.' She paused. 'I'm just after great sex. Come to think of it, true love combined with great sex would be ideal.'

Zena and I smiled in agreement.

'Although, there's this girl who sometimes rides the lift with me. Computer animation, fifteenth floor. Bit of a nerd. Her name's Gabrielle. Geeky Gabe.'

'And?' I said, interest sparked.

'She's asked me out.'

'No way,' I said, squealing. 'Why didn't you tell me?'

'I am now.'

An hour later, Taylor and I were sitting in Zena's salon getting washed and blow-dried. My first since before Christmas in Sydney.

'Should be fairly quiet this afternoon,' said Zena, as I watched her doing Taylor's hair. She pointed to the door. 'Spoke too soon. Afternoon, Mrs Beattie. Back so soon?'

'Good afternoon, dear,' the elderly lady replied. 'Did I leave my reading glasses here yesterday?'

Zena shook her head. 'I don't think so.'

'Hi.' I waved.

Mrs Beattie smiled. 'Hello, love. Your shop was very busy yesterday.' She shook her head. 'Zena, can you believe that this young lass doesn't have a husband.' She spoke as if I wasn't there.

Zena shrugged. 'I don't have a husband either.'

'Neither do I,' Taylor piped up.

'What is it with young women today?'

'I'm a lesbian,' said Taylor.

I thought Mrs Beattie was going to keel over. Instead, she said, 'I know a nice young man, clean-cut—'

'Thanks,' I jumped in. 'But I do have a boyfriend. He's overseas at the moment.'

Mrs Beattie shook her head and turned to Zena. 'If you find my glasses, please let me know.'

&

'Taylor, Mrs Beattie will be gossiping all over town,' I said as we wandered around the surf shop. 'Next thing you know, she'll be saying "I met Lily's lady lover at the hairdressers".'

'Good for her,' said Taylor matter of factly, picking out clothes as we wandered along the isles. She had at least ten items.

'That's enough. I'm not trying on all of them.'

Taylor frowned. 'This is the deal. You *are* going to try on everything. You *are* going to parade in front of me and you *are* going to buy at least three items. I don't care what you choose, but we're not leaving empty-handed.'

I scowled. 'See what I mean?' I said, after she forced me to try on a floaty cream sundress.

'You look great, hung-over and all. Wear it.' Taylor glanced around the changing room. 'Buy this one as well.' She pointed to a blue shift dress with a drawstring waist.

'You think?' I wasn't convinced.

'Buy it,' she growled. 'Two down, one to go.'

The third item was a denim jacket. 'How have I managed to get to thirty-one without ever owning a denim jacket?'

As I swirled for Taylor, I felt happy. Really happy. Yes, I bought clothes I couldn't afford, but I'd had a great couple of days, despite being upset with Matt. Valentine's had been exhausting, but spending it with Taylor, and later, Zena, had made it fun. Next, I'd be going to Zena's favourite charity shop down the road.

Taylor was packing to leave when my Sydney real estate agent rang. 'Lily, I'm afraid I've got bad news. Your tenants are moving out.'

'What?' Taylor glared at me and I held up one finger. 'Why? What's the problem?'

'The guy got retrenched. They're moving back to Queensland.'

'They can't break their contract, can they?'

'There's a six-week cooling off period. They make it, just.'

'So.' I paused. 'We need to find new tenants, pronto. Bummer.'

'Yeah.' A short silence followed. 'You're probably going to have to drop your rent.'

'What? Why?'

'There's a glut of rentals on the market.'

'Two months ago you told me business was booming.'

'Two months ago it was, but what with the drought, then the fires. It hasn't been a good summer. They're moving out at the end of the week.'

'So soon? How long do you think it'll take to find new people?'

'I'll do my best. We'll talk in a couple of days.'

I clicked off and threw the phone on the sofa.

'What was that about?' Taylor asked.

'The tenants are moving out of the cottage.'

'That didn't last long.'

'No, it didn't, Captain Obvious.' I rolled my neck to ease the tension. It didn't help. 'Shit. That's all I need. Those tenants were paying off my mortgage.'

'It'll be okay,' she soothed. 'Your cottage is gorgeous, great location too. You'll fill it no worries.'

'Yeah, but I'm in over my head financially.' Since my meeting with Henry, I was more aware of my fragile financial state. I hadn't anticipated buying Verna and the cost had put a serious dent in my meagre savings. Then there was the ever-present fact that I wasn't drawing a salary—

'Maybe we shouldn't have given away those roses,' Taylor said, trying to lighten the mood.

I half smiled.

'I feel bad leaving you,' she said, hugging me tightly.

'So don't go.'

'Not that badly. Are you okay about the house?'

'I have to be. Jake'll find new tenants,' I said through my tears. 'Come back soon. And good luck Tuesday night with Gabe.'

❧

At four o'clock, Trouble and I were sitting in the shop, surrounded by papers, receipts, shopping lists, and empty cans of Red Bull when Ben walked in, bottle of wine in hand.

'This is for you. Thanks for saving me yesterday.'

'I didn't save you.'

'You did, so please accept my gift. The women loved the roses. Besides,' he held up the bottle, 'this is from the winery and if Lily won't come to the winery, the winery will come to Lily.'

I smiled. The last thing I felt like was wine, but I'd force myself. I retrieved two glasses from the back of the shop, and, catching my breath, returned to Ben. He poured the bottle. The label featured a striking silhouette of a black bird on a gold background.

'Ravenstone!' I said. 'I knew I recognised your name. I've bought this at the local Bottle-O. Love the funky label.'

'Yeah, Steve stocks all my wines. And Andy designed the label. This one, and three others.'

'I'm impressed.' I took the glass of Sauvignon Blanc Ben offered.

'Cheers,' he said, clinking his glass with mine.

I sipped my wine self-consciously. 'This is nice.' Was nice the best I could come up with? I couldn't think. My headache was back with a vengeance.

'Here's to many more Valentine's Days at Lily's Little Flower Shop.'

In addition to being tallish and handsome, Ben had charisma. I found myself tongue-tied.

'Did you have a good day?' he asked. 'Business was booming when I was here.'

'Yeah. I think everyone in the district bought flowers.'

He stared at me. 'There's something different about you.'

Possibly the fact that I was hung-over and badly in need of a decent night's sleep.

'You seem more relaxed, settled.'

'That would be the clothes talking.' I was wearing the pale cream sundress Taylor had forced me to buy earlier. 'Taylor took me shopping.'

Ben sipped his drink. 'Looks great. As does your hair.'

I blushed. 'Ah, the hair. I can thank Zena for that.' Zena had put a messy curl through it. 'Tell me about your winery. Sounds like a great business to be in.'

'It is when it's a good season. Drought and torrential rains? Not so much. So far, we're doing okay. We're producing the Sauvignon Blanc that you're drinking now, as well as a Chardonnay and two Shiraz. Starting small, but hoping to include a Pinot Noir next year, and maybe a Cab Sav.'

'How long have you had it?'

'The vineyard was established in 2008. I bought it in 2010 and started production three years ago.'

I took another sip. 'This is going down easily. Have you always been into wine?'

'Yeah. I've lived in the Adelaide Hills for years and have another winery there. Managing the two is getting a bit hectic, especially as this one is taking off. I can't be in two places at once.'

'I've never been to Adelaide.'

'Never been to the City of Churches? It's beautiful, especially where I live in the Mount Lofty Ranges. Though,' he said, gesturing to the surrounds, 'Clearwater's pretty much paradise.'

I nodded. 'I like it so far.'

Ben topped up my glass. 'How about we continue this conversation over dinner tonight?'

I was thrilled and shocked at the same time. But mostly confused. I had a boyfriend. I couldn't go out with Ben. Plus, the news about the house had knocked me. I didn't feel up to a night out. 'Thanks, but I really need to send emails and get the shop sorted for tomorrow. Having the day off today means I'm way behind.'

'Of course. Another time.'

Ben left soon after. I wasn't sure whether he'd asked me as a date or as a friend, but either way, I wasn't about to do anything in haste. I felt Matt's absence like an ache.

I washed the empty glasses and went back to my unread emails. As I scrolled through the inbox, I noticed one from Matt.

```
Flower Girl,
    I    get    the    impression    you're
pissed off.
    Flower   arranging   still   stressing
you out?
    Flower   arranging!   I   can't   say   the
words without laughing.
```

But seriously, what's up?
Did I fuck up that badly the other
night? We should try it again soon. I
need you.
How were VD sales?
Me X

Did he really want to know how I'd been doing? Did he care? I was pissed off that Matt was laughing at my job, *my business*. The ache was definitely subsiding. I shot back:

It's my business. I'm paying bills,
dealing with contractors, suppliers,
clients. Laugh all you want but I'm
really proud of myself and I don't need
your approval.
I'm doing very well, thank you.
Yesterday was the busiest day so far. I
sold loads.
What have YOU been doing?

It was a hasty ill-conceived reply and I regretted it as soon as I pressed send. An hour later, I got this reply:

Woah, Easy Tiger,
Just having fun. You're busy, doing an
amazing job. The photos look incredible.
I bet you're the talk of the town.
What have I been doing? Working long
hours on boring technical stuff, with
boring technical people.
About to head out for drinks with

```
contractors. Wish me luck. These boys
aren't known for taking it easy.
    Love, Me xx
```

I couldn't bring myself to reply. Instead, I faffed around the shop, filing – and I hate filing. Did Matt and I have a future together? I couldn't see it, but I missed him.

A couple of hours later, there was another email from Matt.

```
Hey Sexy,
    Too pissed. At some sleazy Singaporean
bar drinking … drinking what, I have no
idea. Wish you were here to take me
home. X
```

Great! He was getting pissed at a bar and I was spending the night alone with my rabbit.

❧

Later, in bed, my phone pinged. I was surprised to find the text wasn't from Matt.

Don't think I won't ask you out again. Ben. PS: Don't work too hard.

I responded immediately.

With an offer like that, how could I refuse?

Ben: I know! And yet you did.

Me: It was the flowers talking … they have powers, you know.

Ben: Thanks for the tip. In future, I won't listen to them. You want to catch up for dinner sometime?

Me: Maybe. Xx

As soon as I sent the text, I noticed the two kisses, so I sent him another message.

I didn't mean the kisses by the way. It's just what I do.

Ben's response was immediate.

I like what you just do. Xx

If Ben asked me out to dinner, I'd make it clear I had a boyfriend. A boyfriend who lived in Singapore, but a boyfriend, nonetheless. Ben and I could be friends, just like Andy and I were. There was nothing wrong with that. Still, my goosebumps multiplied.

❦

The next day I woke to an email from my real estate agent Jake, confirming our discussion that the tenants would be vacating at the end of the week and suggesting I reduce my rent by six hundred dollars a month.

Six hundred! Fifteen per cent?

'Jake,' I said, phoning him straight away. 'I can't afford to drop the rent that much.' No way could I afford to maintain the cottage and the shop with such a dramatic rent reduction. My calculations were based on me renting out the property at four thousand dollars a month.

'I'm sorry, but that's what comparable homes are renting for. Yours was always at the high end. We got lucky.'

'And yet, they're moving out,' I said, tears in my voice. 'See what you can do.'

He rang off and straight away Mum's number popped up. I'd avoided her long enough. 'Hi, Mum.'

Big sigh on the other end. 'Good. You're alive.'

I grimaced. 'Just. But it's been worth it. Valentine's Day went well ... oh and I've bought a new car. A van. Verna.'

'I thought you were being careful with your spending.'

I groaned. 'I am but my accountant convinced me I needed it. Much more practical than the Mini.' There was no way I was telling her about my tenants leaving.

'I see.' She paused. 'When are you coming home? Your father has gout, you know.'

'I know. How is he?'

'Hobbling. So, home?'

'As soon as I can. Why don't you come down Sunday afternoon? I can close the shop in time for lunch. Iris can come over too.'

'I saw Iris at the markets the other week. That was enough.'

I'll say this about my mother – she's very definite about what she will and won't do.

'So that's a no then?' she said, sounding annoyed when I didn't answer.

'Mum, it's too hard right now. I'm open seven days a week.'

Silence.

'Fine, Lily. Your father and I will come down Sunday afternoon. That's assuming you'll have time to see us.'

'I'll make time, Mum. Promise.'

She rang off, clearly unimpressed.

No sooner had I disconnected when Iris phoned. 'I'm back!'

she thundered. 'How did it go, Lily-Pily? So sorry I couldn't be there to help, but I do have a glorious tan.'

'I bet. The day was great. Tiring. Taylor was a huge help.'

Iris chuckled. 'Good.'

'Heaps of stock left over though. Hopefully I'll sell it all in the next couple of days.'

'What? You can't do that! For starters, everyone in town will know they're leftover VDs, and secondly, they're not fresh. You can't possibly fob off three-day-old flowers.'

'But, normally flowers last—'

'Not when it comes to Valentine's Day. You can't do it. Rule number one: Only sell fresh flowers. Your reputation is at stake.'

I groaned. 'What do I do? Give them away?' I was thinking about the roses Taylor had already given to random strangers.

'You'll think of something.'

I took a moment. 'On an entirely different topic, Mum's coming down next Sunday.'

'About time.'

'You'll come over to see her?'

'I didn't say that.'

'But?'

'If I must.'

After Iris hung up, I sat staring at the leftover flowers. Profit down the drain. Surely, I could get away with selling them. But Iris was right. Customers would know.

I shuddered. I guess my life wasn't so bad, especially compared to those women living in the retirement village. I'd made a delivery there a week earlier for a lady's birthday. Elsie. She'd been so grateful, teary with happiness.

What the hell. I closed the shop, gathered several bouquets and drove two kilometres to the retirement village.

Kristi, the receptionist I'd met on my previous visits, was surprised to see me. 'Don't tell me I've forgotten a resident's

birthday? I have them all marked on the calendar. I never forget.'
She shrugged. 'Okay, maybe once, but I'm always reminded by
mid-morning.' She glanced at the clock on the wall. It was three-
fifteen.

'You haven't forgotten,' I said, placing the bouquets on the
table. 'These are left over from Valentine's Day. I thought you
might like them. Something to brighten everyone's day from
Lily's Little Flower Shop.'

'Oh.' Kristi smiled. 'Thank you so much.'

Just then, three women came flying into reception – flying,
given they would have been in their early eighties.

'Elsie's cheating again.' A roundish lady pointed to the
woman I'd delivered flowers to a week back.

'Who are you calling a cheater?' said another woman.

'What's happened now, Betty?' Kristi looked at me and
sighed. 'Scrabble woes.'

'She uses the rule book all the time to check on two-letter
words.' Betty turned to Elsie. 'Maybe if you didn't get stuck into
the sherry at lunchtime, you'd remember.'

'And maybe if you cut back on the madeira tea cake, Betts,
you'd be slimmer.'

Ouch.

'Hey, hey,' said the third woman, who was wearing bright
pink lipstick, and sporting an immaculate blonde bob. 'That's
enough.'

'I love your lipstick,' I said, trying to defuse the situation.

'You're the flower lady...'

I held out my hand. 'Lily.'

All three frenemies laughed. 'Lily,' they snorted in unison.

'April,' said one. 'And the lipstick's *Orgasm* by NARS. My
granddaughter bought it for me.' The women cackled.

'Come and have a glass of sherry.' Elsie took me by the hand.

'And a Tim Tam,' said Betty, encouragingly.

'Yes,' agreed April. 'And then tell us if "zo" is really a word.'

'Just for a little while,' I said, given I had no choice.

Minutes later, I had a sherry in one hand and the Scrabble rule book in the other.

'Before Lily checks a word, players have to declare it,' said April, assuming control.

'It's been a while since I played Scrabble,' I said, then sipped my drink and spluttered. The liquid was hot and burned my throat. 'Or drunk sherry.'

An hour later, I drove back into town happy. So, I'd lost some revenue. I was still learning. But I'd made notes. Hopefully in a year's time, I'd know my business well enough to order more efficiently. But for now, the lovely residents of Clearwater Retirement Village would have a much brighter dining hall and common room. And I'd made some new friends.

CHAPTER 15

M att rang the next morning. 'Sorry I pissed you off. I was insensitive.'

'I'm not pissed off.' I sounded pissed off.

'You sure you're doing okay? New town, new business, new van?'

'Thanks, Matty,' I said, softening. 'Still learning but Trouble and I are doing all right.' As with my mother, I was determined not to tell Matt about the rental situation in Sydney. He didn't need the ammunition.

'I'm sure you're doing brilliantly.'

'I like your faith in me.'

'Always. And you know, Lil, showing a little vulnerability isn't bad. You can't be superwoman all the time. I miss you.'

I closed my eyes. 'I miss you too.' Matt, Sydney and AustIn seemed like eons ago. 'Who'd have thought we'd be where we are now.'

'It's not forever. We're just doing it hard now.'

'I guess.' I took a breath. 'Seriously, I love owning and operating the business. It's a huge eye-opener, something everyone should do at least once in their lives.'

Silence.

'Of course, my financial situation isn't as robust as I'd like.' Matt still didn't respond, so I continued babbling. 'You should see me driving the van. I miss my Mini but I needed to be practical. Sometimes I feel like Lisa Douglas on *Green Acres*. Without the blonde hair, the farm or the cash flow ... oh and the husband.'

'Babe. Sounds like you're doing it tough. Should I take off some time and help you sort things out?'

I was horrified. 'I don't need a knight in shining armour.'

'Really? Sounds like you do.'

I silently counted to ten.

He changed the subject. 'You'd be having the time of your life if you were here. The food, the nightlife. And the shops are amazing.'

'Shops? What are they again?'

'I'm taking the weekend off and coming over.'

'I can't close the shop.'

'I'm not asking you to. I want to see you in action. Florist extraordinaire. It'll be fun.'

I wasn't convinced but agreed. We needed to see each other to sort out our situation. It was settled. He'd arrive Sunday afternoon and head back to Singapore Tuesday.

Once we ended the conversation, I immediately regretted the arrangement. I had too much going on ... the business, my house in Sydney. I was a shaking mess.

Let's face it, if I was with Matt, swanning around Singapore, I'd be living a much easier life. But I loved Clearwater and my flower shop. I loved the locals' laid-back attitude, their friendly banter (though sometimes it drove me insane), the beach (though I hardly got a chance to go) and the nightlife I was yet to visit.

Late in the day, the newsagent Barry's wife, Paula, stopped in.

Paula was a lurker, the kind of person who stopped by at the end of the day, just to ... well, I didn't know what she wanted but it was rarely to buy flowers.

'Hey, Paula,' I said, putting on a happy face when she walked through the door.

'Hey,' she said, shivering dramatically. 'It's freezing in here.'

I nodded. 'It's a flower shop. If I heat it, the flowers will shrivel and die.'

'I see your prices have gone up,' she said examining several price tags.

I clenched my fists behind me while smiling. 'How can I help you today, Paula?'

'Just browsing.'

Just snooping, like she did most days.

'How are you and young Zena getting along? I hear you're firm and fast friends.'

I nodded. 'Yep. Sure are. It's nice to have a friendly face when you're new in town.'

'And of course, you have the real estate woman.'

'Trish? Yes,' I answered, wondering what her point was. 'Everyone in Clearwater has been very welcoming. I feel like a local.'

Paula walked up to me and placed her hand on my arm. 'Don't kid yourself, dear, becoming a local takes many years.' She eyed me without blinking. 'Many years.'

'I'm sure. Is there something I can help you with today?'

She shrugged. 'I'm after a cheap bunch to take to my sister-in-law's tonight.' She eyed the lilies. 'How much are these?'

'Gorgeous, aren't they? Twenty-five.'

She coughed. 'And these?' She pointed to a made-up bouquet of lisianthas.

'Thirty—'

'Gosh, they're expensive, aren't they.'

'I do have lovely pink and white paper daisies for eight dollars.'

She glanced at the twin buckets and picked up a bunch of each colour, examining them closely. 'Eight for the two, you say?'

'Um, no, eight dollars per bunch.'

'Really?' She took a moment. 'Not that they aren't pretty, Lily. It's just that, how can regular people like me afford them?'

I smiled. 'I guess you could always plant your own seeds, but you'd have to be organised. And patient.'

I wanted to throw her out of my shop. When I'd first opened, I wouldn't have hesitated selling those flowers for four dollars a bunch, but at that price, there's no way I could cover my overheads. I shuddered to think about those first few weeks when I'd overspent and undercharged. Henry's words kept ringing in my ears. *'You're running a business, Lily, not a charity.'*

What if I posted a flow chart on the wall describing the long and expensive process of getting flowers into the shop for sale ... the farmers who plant the seeds in nurseries, nurture, fertilise, water and take care of them while they grow, the farmers who harvest the mature plants, selecting only the best blooms, on-selling them to wholesalers who transport and sell them to flower market suppliers, who then on-sell them to other contract suppliers, who then transport these flowers to flower shops like mine. And voila! Here they were, as fresh and as beautiful as they were in the field two days earlier, except that they were now dirt free and presented stunningly in a freezing environment, ready for customers to take home and admire.

No, I didn't think eight dollars for a bunch of daisies was too much to ask.

'I don't have the time or space to plant seedlings, or to think about planning for them in the future,' Paula said, drawing me from my inner tirade.

I smiled. 'You don't have to. That's why I'm here.'

She exhaled dramatically and examined the flowers again before handing one bunch over. 'I'll take these.'

{❧}

The following Saturday, Andy walked in with a package. 'I have something for you.'

He held a present the size of a huge painting. 'What?'

'A shop-warming present.'

I grabbed it from him and tore off the wrapping. Bingo! A painting of Lily's Little Flower Shop. 'Incredible. The colours, the detail. I love it. Thank you.' The green door! 'I wonder what's happening behind the green door?'

'Shakin' Stevens? Don't know what they're doing but they laugh a lot.'

'Ha.' As I leant the painting against the back of a chair to take a better look, Matt strode in, lunging to wrap his arms around me.

I stepped back. 'I thought you were coming tomorrow.'

'Caught the red eye. Aren't you pleased to see me?'

'Of course, but Saturday is the busiest day of the week.'

Matt spun around taking it all in. 'Mighty fine flower shop. Close up for the rest of the afternoon.' It was more a command than a question.

'Hi.' Andy offered his hand.

'Hey. Matt,' he said before gripping Andy's hand.

I'd forgotten how much space Matt took up in a room. He made himself at home, plonking down his overnight bag and a couple of bottles of duty-free champagne on the bench, before picking up Trouble and kissing his ears. 'How's my favourite fella? Missing your dear old dad?'

Andy grimaced. 'I should get going.'

'Sure, mate.' Matt hardly acknowledged him before holding Trouble at arm's length and turning his body, examining him. 'You've put on weight, boy. The beach agrees with you.'

'Thanks so much for the painting. It's brilliant. I'm really chuffed. How about I hang it here?' I pointed to the wall beside my workbench. 'Everyone will see it as soon as they walk in. Through the flowers, of course.'

Andy managed a smile. 'I'm glad you like it.'

'Matt, what do you think of Andy's painting?'

Matt shrugged. 'Nice. The door isn't green though.'

'I could always paint it,' I said. 'Great idea, Andy.'

The three of us stood silently in the room before Andy spoke. 'I'll get going then. Nice meeting you, Matt. See you later, Lil.'

He walked out the door.

'Lil!' There was a hint of sarcasm in Matt's voice. 'You certainly are getting to know the locals. And you do look *chuffed*.'

'He's a friend.'

Matt put Trouble on the floor and hugged me again. 'I've missed you.'

We kissed. I took in Matt's aftershave, remembering his smell, his feel and touch.

'Can you take an early mark? Maybe show me your new abode, and the beach?' He kissed me again. 'Please?'

I glanced at my watch. It was only one. Matt kissed me. Hesitating no longer, I locked the front door and took him upstairs.

'Nice,' he said, taking in the view of the ocean from my veranda.

'Thanks.' We walked back inside, and I showed him the bathroom and my bedroom. In that order.

'Even nicer.'

I chewed my fingernails. 'Why don't you make yourself comfortable while I finish up downstairs?' There was no doubt I still desired him, but we'd been apart for almost two months. Would we fit together again?

He smiled. 'Don't make me wait too long.'

I scooted downstairs and moved all the flowers into the cold room. Ten minutes later, I was upstairs again, drinking champagne with Matt and catching up.

Matt brushed a stray hair from my face. 'Your hair's longer. I like it. You look different, Lil. Loose.'

'Loose?'

'I mean your hair's out, longer, freer somehow, and you seem more, I don't know, chilled.'

'Well, I'm not wearing a navy business suit and heels, if that's what you mean.'

'Yeah, maybe.' Matt sipped his drink. 'You look relaxed, calmer. This holiday is agreeing with you.'

'Holiday?'

'Adventure, then.'

'Or, as I like to call it, my life.'

'I guess, but it's not like you're going to stay here forever.'

Bristling, I took another sip of champagne.

I'm going to convince you about Singapore. You'll love it there.'

Matt kissed me tentatively and I shifted uncomfortably. 'I'm not moving to Singapore.'

'Shh, we'll talk about it later.'

Some time and more alcohol later, we kissed again.

'You're right,' said Matt. 'The real thing is so much better.'

Suddenly, we were kissing passionately, clothes on the floor, stumbling into my bedroom, rational thoughts abandoned.

Matty's head dipped as he kissed my neck, then his mouth found my left breast, his fingers exploring my inner thighs. I enjoyed the tingling sensations. Kissing, stroking, limbs intertwined. All the familiar feelings and desires flooded back and for the next several hours we lost ourselves in each other. I was relieved. We still fitted together. I loved him.

CHAPTER 16

The next morning, I woke to Matt stroking my breasts and nuzzling my neck. 'Good morning, beautiful,' he murmured in a sleepy, *fuck me* voice.

'Matt.' I pulled away. 'What time is it? The shop...'

'Shoosh,' he said, bringing me close and silencing me with a kiss.

Trying to climb out of bed, Matt grabbed my arm. 'Stay. I haven't seen you in like, forever.'

'It's after nine,' I said firmly, glancing at the bedside digital clock. 'I need to get moving.'

'It's Sunday. Take the day off.' Matt had propped himself up on one arm and was watching me.

I shook my head. 'Can't. People rely on me.'

He pulled the sheets up around him. 'They're only flowers.'

I took a moment. 'Excuse me? Only flowers? I know you're joking, Matt, but seriously.'

He looked at me, bewildered.

'Flowers are there for all the important times. Babies, birthdays, weddings, deaths. Flowers bond people.'

'Okay. Calm down.' He sat up.

'I am calm. But do you really think what I'm doing is frivolous?'

'Well, when you compare it to...'

'What? Business? Finance? Oranges?'

'I didn't say that.'

'I know you didn't. It's implied.'

'Hon,' he said, serious. 'Please, please come back to Singapore with me. You've proven yourself. You have the guts and nouse to start a business. There'll be other opportunities later. But I miss you. I need you to be in Singapore with me and you want it too. I was so touched that you finally showed your helpless side the other day.'

'Pardon?'

'On the phone. I've never heard you sound so vulnerable. I like it. I thought you didn't need me anymore when you let me go to Singapore alone. But seeing your texts and emails, then hearing your voice, well, I knew it was all bluff.'

I shook my head. 'I don't understand.'

'You don't have to, because I do. You're too proud to ask for help. But I love that you need me. I've come to take you away from this mess.'

'Mess?'

'Yes,' he insisted. 'You said so yourself. How worried you were about everything. Why not just admit it isn't working out the way you hoped, and come to Singapore?' He moved to kiss me again, but I pushed him away.

'Matty, look. I don't know how you got that idea. I certainly didn't send out a distress call. I'm sorry if you thought I did. But I didn't. Perhaps you were hearing what you wanted to hear, rather than what I was actually saying. Point is, I'm not giving up on the shop or Clearwater. I've only been here a couple of months.'

'But...' Matt shook his head. 'I love you, and my contract

runs for another year at least. Long-distance relationships don't work.'

'I know,' I said, my voice catching, remembering a recent company website photo I'd seen of Matt hugging women, one in particular, several times. I shooed the memory away. 'I'm staying here. This is where I want to be.'

'Lil, I understand. Look at this place, the ocean, the sun. It's a great spot to take a break from corporate chaos after your embarrassing exit from Austln, but are you really serious about staying here long term?'

Embarrassing? I clenched my fists. 'Yes. I am.'

'Like indefinitely...?'

I didn't hesitate. 'Yes.'

He took both my hands. 'But you love me. I love you. Once you move back to the city, you'll forget all about Clearwater.'

'What city are you talking about?'

'Any city, but for now, Singapore. Look, you said that working seven days a week was wearing you down. Corporate life's not this taxing.'

I pulled back. Yes, the flower shop was hard work, but there was no way I was going back to corporate and working for someone else. Momentarily, I was back in Sydney, wearing a pencil skirt and heels, thinking about the heartache I'd endured in that world – the long hours, the long years, of never putting a foot wrong, years of competing in an unfair playing field where I couldn't cement relationships on the golf course or at strip clubs and was inevitably overlooked at promotion time in favour of a fuckwit with a penis. No thanks.

'You say I'll forget about Clearwater, after I leave here, but I won't because I'm not going anywhere.'

'So where does that leave us?'

'Matty, I love you. You know that.'

'But?'

'I'm never going back to the corporate world. It took leaving to make me realise how much I hated it. And I'm not sure I ever want to live in a city again.' Momentarily, I thought about my inner-city cottage. No tenants. No income. Neglected. Brushing it off, I said, 'I love it here in Clearwater. On the coast. It's my home now. For the foreseeable future at least. I'm working out what I want from life, Matt, and I can't just drop it all and follow you to Singapore. Please try to understand.'

'But what about our future?' He hesitated. 'Don't you want to have a family?'

The one thing we couldn't discuss. 'I have a family.'

'You know what I mean. Children.'

Dumbstruck, I replied, 'I ... of course I do. Just ... just not right now. I need to do something for me.' In truth, I didn't know whether I could fall pregnant let alone have children. It was a topic I refused to talk about with anyone but Iris.

'Is this about that Andy guy?' Matt's tone changed. Sharp. Combative.

Flabbergasted, I just stared.

'Well,' he demanded. 'Is it?'

'Andy's a friend.'

'You two looked pretty cosy when I walked in.'

'You'd know all about that.'

'What the hell does that mean?'

'I've seen your recent company website photos. Doesn't look like you're too starved for companionship.' Fuming, I went on. 'You and some woman, arms wrapped around each other at an awards night.'

'I should have had my arms wrapped around you.'

'Really? That's your defence?'

Matt played his best wounded face. 'She's a mate. I work with her.'

'Whatever. We're done. Let's not make this harder than it has to be.'

'Nothing happened. And I'm so lonely.'

I put up my hand. 'Spare me the *I'm lonely* speech. I've received enough drunken texts to know that's not true.'

'It *is* true.'

'This isn't about you hugging some random wo—'

'She's a colleague! But I get it. You don't want to live with me in Singapore. You want to be here, doing...' Matt sneered and threw his hands in the air, 'this!'

'Yes, as a matter of a fact I do. I'm not your property.'

'I never said you were.'

'You've acted like it often enough.' I turned away. This was becoming nasty. I didn't want it to end like this. Calming myself, I said, 'Ultimately, we want different things.'

'But I want to make it work,' he whispered.

'On your terms. Me moving to Singapore would be a mistake. I wouldn't have any freedom or independence. It wouldn't be equal. I wouldn't be working or earning money.'

'Are you earning any now?'

I couldn't believe what I'd just heard. There was a horrible tense silence. 'That was a low blow.' Tears welled but I refused to let them fall. 'You're unbelievable, Matt. Go back to Asia, to your colleague—'

'Her name is Sami.'

'Okay. Go back to Sami and your amazing ex-pat life.'

'I'm sorry. Sorry I said those things.'

I waved my hand. 'They've been said now. You can't take them back.'

I couldn't breathe. My chest ached. Gasping for air, my heart was breaking for us and for the future we wouldn't have together. Couldn't have together. Because I could never tell him. He'd never understand. The invisible silent wall between us growing thicker with every word. So much we couldn't talk about.

I thought back to a conversation early in our relationship when I desperately wanted to tell him. As I deliberated, news on the TV and internet was raging about the abortion debate. From the beginning, he'd been dismissive. 'Why would anyone in their right mind choose to kill a baby?'

I was horrified. 'Women's bodies. Women's choices,' I'd said, not wanting to take it further.

'So selfish. What about the unborn child?'

'There are many reasons why women have abortions.'

'But I'm not female so I can't have an opinion?'

I'd never be able to tell Matt about my own abortion. He wouldn't understand. Instead, my shame and guilt intensified. I threw myself into climbing an imaginary corporate ladder and buried my feelings of self-loathing. Locked away. Hidden. A secret I only shared with Aunty Iris.

'I'm leaving.'

Was Matt trying to call my bluff? 'Fair enough.' Emotionally wrecked, I was all out of talk and blame.

'Though where I'll stay until Tuesday...'

I couldn't back down now. 'It's over, Matt. You can stay with friends.'

Fifteen minutes later, he got in his car and drove away.

CHAPTER 17

J ust after midday Mum and Dad arrived. The mess upstairs momentarily flashed before my eyes. Then the chaos here in the shop. I'd wanted to present an immaculate shop and apartment but with Matt's arrival and subsequent departure, I'd forgotten about my parents' visit.

'Hello!' I beamed, feeling like anything but beaming, and rushed forward to hug them.

'You forgot we were coming, didn't you, Lily?'

'No, Mum...' I trailed off. No point lying to my mother. She had a sixth sense. 'Sorry. I've been flat out.'

'Yes, you have,' said Iris. 'What with Valentine's Day and all.'

'Where'd you come from?' With four people inside, my little flower shop was full.

'Looking tanned,' said Mum, taking in the tell-tale strap marks on Iris's shoulders.

Iris wore a vibrant off-the-shoulder pink and white flamingo print caftan and purple, pom-pom fringed scarf, completed with bright red lips, loud gold bracelets and sandals to match. By contrast, Mum wore simple denim jeans, a navy T-shirt, flat white tennis shoes and minimal jewellery.

She was so unlike Iris, so conservative in outlook, in style, in dress. 'I'm a mother, Lily,' she'd say. 'I can't be gadding about in caftans and jangly earrings. What would people think?'

'Thank you, Daisy, darling. The cruise was *magnifique*. You must come along next time.'

Mum raised her eyebrows. But I couldn't concentrate because two more people came in. Hopefully customers who wanted to buy flowers. When Iris ushered Mum and Dad out onto the pavement, I almost wept with gratitude.

'We came by at ten, but you weren't open,' said one of the women as they looked around. A few minutes later, they decided on a bouquet of pink dahlias. Several other people wandered in. Eventually, I walked outside to find Mum, Dad and Iris at the café a couple of doors down.

'Goodness,' sniffed Mum, taking in my appearance. 'Is it this chaotic every day?'

I shook my head. 'Sundays aren't usually this busy.'

Mum continued as if she hadn't heard me. 'So many people and such a tiny shop.'

Really? I hadn't noticed.

'You've done a great job,' said Dad. 'It looks amazing.'

I smiled. 'I should get back.' I wasn't up for much chat today.

'No wonder Matt left,' said Mum.

'What?' I really didn't want to be interrogated or reminded about Matt. 'How did you know?'

Mum glared at me. 'What's not to know? You got it into your head you were moving down here after Matt got a job in Singapore. Now he's gone and you're all alone.'

'I'm not alone, Mother,' I said, irritated, but relieved I didn't have to explain Matt's visit. 'I'm making friends.'

Mum nodded. 'How will you ever keep a man?'

My headache roared back with a vengeance. I wanted to curl

up in bed and sleep for a week or at least numb my senses with several glasses of wine.

'What your mother is trying to say,' said Iris, 'is that if you're not careful, you'll end up like me, aren't you, Daisy?'

Mum glared at her. 'Don't be ridiculous.' She looked at me. 'Although—'

'Mum!'

My mother continued. 'Don't get me wrong, it's just that you have the potential to be doing so much more than this, Lily.'

Iris huffed, and I stared at my hands. Mum really believed that I'd peaked when I was dux of my primary school and the lead in the Christmas play. After such spectacular accomplishments, her constant refrain throughout high school was 'What happened? You had so much potential...' My entire high school experience, then university, was about trying to live up to my successes in Year Six. Tough gig. At twelve I was a big fish in a tiny pond. Hindsight. Truth is, there'd always be some bigger or louder fish than me ... and now I was living in Clearwater, I wasn't so much a big fish in a tiny pond, as a fish out of water, gasping to survive.

'I'm building a better life for myself, Mum.'

She looked around. 'I guess it depends on your definition of a *better life*.'

'I've got an idea.' Iris clapped her hands. 'Why don't I look after the shop, Lily. You take your parents on a tour of the town and the beach.'

I didn't argue.

I showed Mum and Dad the sights – the nearby blowhole, a rainforest and waterfall, and of course the beach. I even introduced them to Zena and Trish when we passed them in town.

'See, Mum,' I said gently. 'I know people. I'm almost a local.'

She smiled begrudgingly.

'I'm very proud of you,' said Dad, apropos of nothing. Dad was a dear, but he didn't used to be. The years had changed him.

Back at the shop, we spoke with Iris before going upstairs. I was torn. I didn't want to leave Iris alone too long. I could see she'd already rearranged several displays.

Thankfully, the apartment wasn't quite the bomb site I expected it to be. I must have buzzed around cleaning up on autopilot that morning as Matt packed his bag.

'I can see why you like it here so much, Lily,' said Dad, standing on the veranda, admiring the view.

Barely holding myself together, I said, 'I'm very happy here.' It was true, but that day? Not so much.

'Who are you trying to convince?' said Mum. 'You or us?'

Dad would understand if I told him about the Sydney crisis. Because I had no tenants. My beautiful cottage was idle. Probably a cat brothel by now. He'd also understand if I told him other things. The *other things* could wait. I seized my chance to talk as soon as Mum went to the bathroom.

'Dad, bombshell moment incoming,' I warned.

He saluted. 'Ready.'

'I have to sell the cottage.'

'What?'

'The family that was renting moved out and the real estate agent says I need to reduce my rent because there's a rental glut. That, combined with the costs here, I may need to sell.'

'Sell what?' Mum demanded.

Quickest toilet-stop ever!

'Nothing,' I shot back. 'Nothing.'

'Don't give me *nothing*, Lily Mason. What's going on?'

My forehead broke out in sweat. 'Don't get upset, but my renters have backed out.'

Mum raised her hand to her mouth. 'In Sydney? No! Surely not?'

'I could always sell—'

'But that's madness. It's madness, isn't it, Owen? You'll never get back into the Sydney property market, will she, Owen?' Mum was practically frothing.

'Your mother has a point, love,' said Dad.

'What does Matt think?' Mum continued.

'I've no idea,' I managed to say. 'It's not his property.'

'This is insane, Lily. You can't do it.'

Despite their comments, I wanted them to stay the night, however, Mum was eager to get home to Gary, the poodle. 'You know, he misses you,' she mused.

I loved Gary dearly, but he could get by without me. 'I'll try to come up soon,' I said, waving them goodbye.

Iris nodded as I walked back inside. 'Don't make promises you can't keep. Now then, how do you like what I've done with everything?'

Iris had rearranged my butcher's hooks, my knick knacks and cards. She'd also cleared my workbench. I'd never find anything.

I loved having her around. But sometimes...

After Iris left, I found my notepad and wrote my to-do list, starting with reorders. I needed to take my mind off the house and Matt. It was cathartic that he'd flown over to see me. That we'd formally broken up. We both needed to make fresh starts. That meant Singapore for him and Clearwater for me. Still, tears pressed at the back of my eyes.

CHAPTER 18

Weeks later, on a Friday afternoon I was practising my tap steps when Trish walked in. So far, Zena and I had endured four lessons.

'How's the *Shirley Temple* coming along?'

I winced. 'I'm determined to get it right. If Elsie and Betty can do it, so can I.'

'That's the spirit.' Trish grinned.

Two out of the class of six were the ladies from the retirement village. The other two were high school girls. They were more flexible than the rest of us, but Elsie and Betty kept up, unlike Zena and me.

'I had to endure ballet *and* tap lessons with my daughter,' said Trish.

'Ugh.'

'Led to much bickering.'

'I'm sure.'

Trish nodded. 'Dividing myself between soccer and ballet. There was only one of me. Even now, my daughter can be quite demanding. And my son, well, he wants a peaceful life, so he finds it quite stressful being around her. So much for twins having a cosmic connection.'

'As for sisters,' I added, 'I think the reason Mum's most upset is because I spend the odd day with Aunty Iris.'

'Siblings. There are certain blessings to being only children like us.'

'At least I didn't have to share my clothes.'

'And I didn't have to share my toys, not that I had many back in the day.'

I nodded. 'I think if Iris could have had children, she would have.'

'It's easier to be carefree and fun loving when you're the aunty. Mothers constantly fret about their children, regardless if they're four months, four years, or forty. Once a mum, always a mum.'

'Trish!' I said, almost shouting. 'That could be a chalkboard quote! *Once a mum, always a mum.*' I'd probably never be a mother because I didn't deserve to be.

Pulling me out of my melancholy, Trish said, 'Save it for Mother's Day. In the meantime, come up with your own quote that resonates with you.'

She left and I got on with the flap, heel, heel, brush, heel, toe, heel.

'Fuck,' I said as Zena walked through the door. 'It's going to take months to master this beginner step.'

'Yeah,' Zena agreed. 'I just call it *The Painful.*'

'Nice shoes though,' I said, yanking them off.

'That's one good thing about it.' After Zena had reluctantly agreed to lessons, she'd surprised me by buying us both red tap shoes. 'So,' she said. 'Busy day at the office?'

'Markets at 5am, then all day chatting to customers and passers-by. Henry at two, then Trish passed by. Oh, and Paula was here fifteen minutes ago. I'm knackered. You?'

Zena nodded. 'You bet. Paula's a piece of work, isn't she?'

'Bloody timewaster.'

'Yes, but people here have oodles of it to waste.'

'Love your outfit, by the way.'

Zena twirled in her black shift dress with pink and blue sequins. 'It offsets my tattoo rather fetchingly, don't you think?' She sat down. 'Nate came into the salon this afternoon, telling me he's changed and wants to give our relationship another try.'

'What did you say?'

'What I've been saying for months, "Fuck right off".' She laughed. 'Well that's what I wanted to say. Instead, I told him it was over and that if he really needed to, we'd talk about it at a more appropriate time. He came in because he knew I wouldn't make a scene, you know, like couples who break up at restaurants and other public places because it's safer. Annoyed the crap out of me.' She sighed. 'I still love him though.'

'Really?'

'Yar.'

'But you didn't say the end part out loud?'

'No!'

'What really happened?'

'Hung his head like a sad lost puppy and stood in the middle of the shop until I ignored him and he couldn't stand it any longer. I was in the middle of doing three sets. Friday afternoons are manic.'

'So, you're definitely not getting back together?'

'No!' she replied adamantly. 'I don't want to,' she added, less adamantly. 'It's just that I get lonely and it *is* getting cooler.'

'What about your July pledge, the six-month boyfriend hiatus?'

'Exactly. That's why I haven't succumbed. That, and I'm over him. Nate's never going to change.' Zena took a long sip. 'How's things with you?'

'Ticking along.' I dropped the bravado. 'Actually, I still haven't rented out my house in Sydney. I've dropped the rent by fifteen per cent but alas, no takers.'

'So, you'll drop it more?'

'I guess. I need income to cover some of my mortgage and rates. As it is, I have nothing.' My financial situation was deteriorating each day.

Zena nodded. 'You could always sell up and make this move permanent.'

I swiped at my tears and brightened. 'I know.' But Mum's words were ringing in my ears. *You'll never get back into the Sydney property market.*

'I'd like it,' Zena said, smiling. 'How's Taylor?'

I shrugged. 'She's coping. Just takes things as they come along. I admire her for that.'

'And Matt?'

'Not much. The occasional text. No doubt bonding with Sandy—'

'I thought her name was Sami?'

I nodded.

'Door's looking good,' she said, peering at my front door which was now vibrant green.

'Despite being painted at three in the morning. I touched up a few areas this morning after I got back from the markets. Amazing what can be achieved on adrenalin and fear.' I peered at Andy's painting, which hung on the wall beside my bench. 'Solid idea.'

'Speaking of which. Is he coming?'

'Assume so. Hasn't missed a Friday yet.'

'Have you thought any more about where he goes every Tuesday afternoon?' Every Tuesday, Andy closed up shop and disappeared. 'Where does he go?' she'd asked several times, expecting me to know.

I shrugged. 'How would I know? I've only been here a couple of months.'

'That makes you the *perfect* person to ask him. It wouldn't look suspicious. He's been keeping the same routine since I've been here, so I can't all of a sudden ask what he's up to.'

'And I can?'

'You could say something along the lines of, "I wish I could close up shop every Tuesday afternoon at two. Tell me, Andy, what's your secret?"'

I rolled my eyes. 'He's probably grocery shopping at that massive Woolies ten kilometres up the road.'

'Wouldn't that be a disappointment? No, I'm thinking along the lines of a secret wife and children. I could always follow and surprise him in the act.'

'I wouldn't. People always get more than they bargain for with surprises.'

'So, what do you think he's up to?'

'Music lessons?'

'Nah, I've never seen an instrument in his car.'

'Piano?' I sipped my drink and thought a bit. 'I reckon grocery shopping's your best bet.'

'Maybe. From what I've seen of Andy, he's very much a man of routine. Walk every morning—'

'Before buying his long black and opening the shop—'

'Then framing and stretching canvases. But I wonder...'

'Here's the man himself,' I said as Andy strolled through the door. 'We were just talking about you.'

Andy smiled. 'Good things I hope.'

Zena raised her glass. 'We were expecting you a bottle ago.'

'Actually,' I said, pouring him a glass of wine from the second bottle, 'Zena and I were wondering what you get up to every Tuesday afternoon.'

Zena glared daggers at me.

Andy examined his drink intently before taking a sip. 'What do you think I do?'

'If we knew that, Lily wouldn't be asking, would she?' snapped Zena. 'Anyway, she thinks you're grocery shopping.'

He looked at me. 'Good assumption. Veggies are pricy down here.'

'Ha,' said Zena. 'Try living on Norfolk. It's illegal to import fresh produce to the island.'

'That's a stupid rule. Who can live without tomatoes and lettuce?' I picked up Trouble and patted him. 'Or carrots?' Patted him some more.

'Okay, so we can rule that one out,' said Zena. 'And by the way, Andy, I'm not in the least bit curious. It's your snoopy friend here.'

Andy turned his attention to me. 'Why? Do you miss me?'

Thanks, Zena. 'Nope, but Tuesday afternoons are quiet. I have plenty of time to make up stories in my head.'

'Well there's no need.' Andy paused. 'Truth is, I attend support meetings.'

'You're sick?' I was crestfallen.

Andy shook his head. 'I'm fine, but need to keep focused, balanced and on the straight and narrow.' He noticed me eyeing the drink in his hand and held it up. 'Don't worry, I'm not an alcoholic.'

'That's a relief.' Zena drained her glass and reached for the bottle.

'It's not something I usually talk about, but a while back, I had a bout of depression. Ended up in hospital and now I go to a support group once a week.'

'No,' said Zena. 'You never had to wear a straitjacket, did you?'

I nearly spilt my drink. 'Zena!'

'No, Lil,' said Andy. 'She's right. I was confined to a straitjacket and left in a padded room.'

I sucked in a huge gulp of air and Zena's eyes widened in disbelief. 'Oh my God, Andy, that's appalling. I was trying to have a laugh. I'm so sorry.'

Andy grinned. 'And you succeeded. I'm joking. There were no padded rooms. But there was a straitjacket once or twice.'

I had no idea if what he was saying was true. 'Andy—'

'Joking. I wasn't even tortured.'

'Stop joking,' Zena said, getting uppity. 'What happened? Course, I have no right to ask, but—'

'I checked in voluntarily. It wasn't like I was committed.'

'I'm so sorry. I never knew,' said Zena.

'Don't be sorry,' Andy said. 'How could you have known? It's not something I go around shouting.' He paused. 'I kind of liked being there once I'd settled in. The routine, the regular morning walks, the creative arts program, painting, drawing, sculpting ... it was relaxing.'

I knew exactly what he was talking about. 'And were they all "we give you the opportunity to explore the negative thoughts and feelings that are causing conflict in your life, in a safe and non-judgemental environment"?'

Andy stared at me a moment. 'How did you guess?'

'I'm not just a pretty face.' Idiot Lily. I thought about my cousin, Elizabeth. 'I have family members who've been in therapy.'

Silence filled the air.

'So,' Zena said suddenly, 'apropos of nothing, I heard that Hannah Hayman—'

I squinted. 'Hannah Hayman. The name rings a bell.'

'The local kindergarten teacher,' said Andy. 'Remember the first Saturday when you said that guy—'

'Wanted to send flowers to his wife and flowers to—' Ah! The penny dropped. 'Hannah!'

'Bingo!' Zena licked her lips. 'Anyhoo, the cheaters have broken up. Apparently, Hannah hasn't been at school for days. On Monday, she was in the middle of reading *The Hungry Caterpillar* to eighteen four-year-olds and walked out ... just left. Poor little kids didn't know what was going on with the ravenous fellow who was chomping his way to obesity.'

Andy shook his head. 'Get on with the story.'

'*The Hungry Caterpillar* is the story!' Zena snorted. 'Okay, so the teacher's aide finished the story, but Hannah hasn't been spotted since. There's no way she's chomping herself to obesity. She was a waif to start with. Poor wretch. Men!'

'To be fair, she was having an affair with a married man.' Andy sipped his drink.

'What's this *to be fair* crap? Whom do we have to be fair to?'

Andy sighed. 'I'm just saying she knew what she was doing.'

'So now the guy gets off scot-free and she's left a sorry mess?'

'Who's Scott?' I asked.

Andy ignored me. 'Zena, shouldn't your sympathy be with his wife?'

'My sympathy is with both of them. Jason should be hung and quartered.'

'Boyfriend troubles?' asked Andy.

Zena drained her wine glass. 'Nope. I don't have a boyfriend.'

I picked up Trouble and nursed him on my lap. 'This is like watching a game of Ping Pong.'

'Actually,' said Zena. 'I'm weary. Need an early night, but before I go...' her words hung in the air as she fiddled around in her bag before pulling out a magazine clipping and thrusting it in front of me. 'I'm thinking this.'

I stared at a photo of an oversized burgundy floral headband. 'This what?'

'As a statement piece. Four large roses on top of a headband. The red's cool but it could be pink or any colour. Not yellow though.' She paused. 'Don't you think it's whimsical?'

'Makes a bold statement, that's for sure.'

'I know you don't have time now, but could you whip one up for me sometime? I'll pay you.'

I gazed at the photo. 'Sure. I'll try. It's definitely you. Special occasion?'

'Nah, I just think it'd be fun to wear on days when my hair isn't up to par. Clients can focus on my headband, rather than my hair.'

'What is it?' Andy said, peering at the photo.

'Lily's going to make one of these for me. You in?'

He stared at the photo another moment, pretending to think. 'Maybe not.'

Zena sucked in her cheeks. 'Your loss.'

'And on that note...' Andy stood. 'I should get going.'

'Me too,' Zena chimed in. She glanced at my wall clock. It was just after seven thirty. 'The three of us are ragers, aren't we?'

'Biggest ragers in town!' Andy replied.

Zena rolled her eyes. 'I can't afford to ruin Mrs Beattie's hair tomorrow morning or there'll be hell to pay.' She paused. 'You'll come to the fundraiser, Lil?'

I sighed. 'I'd almost forgotten about it.'

'Almost,' said Zena with a smile. 'It'll be fun. You'll meet all the locals.'

I turned to Andy. 'You going?'

He shook his head. 'To the surf club tomorrow night? Not my scene.'

'Your loss,' said Zena.

Andy smiled. 'You've told me before.'

'Yeah. Maybe I need a new catchphrase. Lily, I'll drop by around eight.'

The next night, Zena and I shared a bottle of wine while listening to ABBA and getting in the mood for the surf club do.

'Not sure I'm up for this tonight,' said Zena, sounding drained.

'Hey, you were the one who insisted we go.' I looked her up and down. She was dressed head to toe in black – tight fitting polo, jeans and boots. Her hair was a vivid green and the girl was a wiz with eye make-up. 'Looking great. Your eyes match your hair.'

Fifteen minutes later, when we walked in, the band, wedged in one corner, was pumping out Wham!'s 'Wake Me Up'. The floor flooded with dancers. Those who weren't dancing sang at the top of their voices, even those lined up at the bar, waiting to be served.

'This is going to be fun.' I handed her a drink. 'Let's dance!'

And we did for the first twenty minutes, before heading back to the bar.

'God, no,' said Zena moments later. 'Nate's here.'

I followed her eyes and spotted a group of surfer types standing by the exit that led down to the beach. 'Still not interested?'

Zena shook her head. 'No.'

We cranked it up on the dance floor, only stopping to refill our drinks.

An hour later, we were still dancing, often with several others in a large group.

Zena leant in and shouted, 'Feeling old and boring.'

'You? Never.' I motioned for her to follow outside where we could talk.

'All these lit surfer chicks. I'm never going to get laid again.'

'Hey, no downers, no frowners.' As I clinked glasses with her, a stranger bowled into me, took my hand and swung me round, knocking the drink out of my hand. 'Watch it.'

I managed to escape after several awkward moves but in that two minutes, Nate had manoeuvred Zena into a corner. 'I love ya, babe,' he was telling her, or rather, slurring at her.

'Am I interrupting?' I said.

'Nope.' Zena was breathless. 'Lil, have you met Nate?'

I shook my head. 'Hey.'

'Hey,' he replied, glassy-eyed.

Zena disentangled herself from him. 'I'm good to go.'

CHAPTER 19

Andy

A ndy was at his regular group session the following Tuesday, discussing his conversation with Lily and Zena.

'How did you feel talking about hospital?' asked his therapist, Joanne.

'Nervous. Worried that if I told them, they might be put off.'

'So you took a risk?'

Andy nodded.

'And what happened?'

Andy paused before speaking. 'I wanted to open up, to be less guarded. I've never spoken about my experience with anyone but you guys.' People nodded as he glanced around the room. 'It felt good to let Lily and Zena into my world. I was surprised I wasn't more self-conscious.'

'And?'

'The sky didn't fall in. They were both sympathetic.' Andy

briefly considered the conversation and Zena's comments. 'Well, to a point. Asked a lot of questions, of course.'

'And?' Joanne urged.

'Ever since, I've felt good. My spirit seems lighter.'

'You seem happy, Andy. Happier, at least.'

He smiled. 'I'm now wondering why I was so afraid.'

'We live in a world that encourages us to think less for ourselves and instead, simply follow others,' Joanne said calmly. 'But you need to trust yourself.' Her eyes scanned the room. 'You all do. Trust your instincts. Remember, you're on your own paths, no one else's.'

Afterwards, Andy drove back to Clearwater, parked his car at home, and walked to the beach. He usually walked Tuesday afternoons to process his sessions and clear his head. Group was always helpful but afterwards, judgements and recriminations crowded his mind. He still couldn't quite let go of his past. If he'd behaved this way, the outcome would have been X. If he'd acted that way, the result would have been Y.

Pacing, he repeated his mantra: *Let go of the past. I am enough. I do not need to prove anything to anybody.*

Decompress.

He was still ruminating when Lily walked towards him.

'Hey,' she said. 'Thought I might find you here.'

'You're in luck.'

'About the other night,' Lily said. 'Sorry we were being nosy. It was none of our business.'

'Not at all.' Andy sat on the sand. 'In fact, I feel more settled and at ease for having told you and Zena about my past.'

Lily sat beside him. 'I have a cousin who's schizophrenic. My dad's niece. For as long as I can remember, she's been in and out of hospitals and doped up on medication. She's only a couple of years older than me, but she doesn't drive and can barely look after herself.'

'I'm sorry.' Andy outlined some birds in the sand with his left forefinger. 'I've never been on medication except for when I was in hospital, and before that, I'd never had counselling.'

'How long did you stay?'

'Ten days. I could've left at any time. I chose to get help, plus the food was surprisingly good and the accommodation was comfortable.' Andy took a breath. 'I got hooked on music therapy, maybe because it reminded me of my childhood and simpler times.'

'Guitar?'

'Yeah. How'd you guess?' Andy liked opening up to Lily. He felt at peace. 'In primary school, it was piano. But when I was thirteen, my parents bought me a guitar.' He paused. 'I dabbled for a couple of years then started skipping lessons, so Mum cancelled them. I still loved playing though. But when I got to uni, I gave it up completely.'

'Why?'

Andy shrugged. 'The cool kids played guitar. I wasn't one of them. I didn't pick it up again until I was in hospital.' Andy's interest had reignited and he'd played ever since. Not that he'd played in front of anyone. Guitar was Andy's solace, his sanctuary. Whenever life seemed overwhelming or stressful, he picked up his instrument and strummed. It usually calmed him down.

'Anyway,' he shifted his feet in the sand, 'that's all in the past. I mainly go to therapy for the cupcakes and red frogs.' Andy checked his Fitbit. 'It's getting dark. I guess we should head back.' He stood up and offered Lily a hand. She accepted, and he pulled her up to her feet.

'Good chat,' Lily said at the top of the hill as they were about to part ways.

Andy beamed. 'Hope you don't think I'm prying...'

'After what we've spoken about, I'm not the one to be accusing you of anything. What's up?'

'I was wondering how things were with Matt these days? You never mention him, and I didn't want to ask.'

'Until now?'

'Until now.'

Lily smiled. 'It's over. We want different things.'

'I'm sorry to hear that.'

'Don't be. Clearwater is a new chapter in my life and I'm embracing it.'

'Life goals. I like it.'

Andy walked home, almost jogging, his head filled with hope and optimism. After an hour chatting with Lily, he felt more cheerful and light on his feet. He was looking forward to Friday already. Still, he hadn't told Lily everything. Not about Edie, or the darkness, the fear, the abuse. Lily didn't know he'd gotten so angry and desperate that he'd punched out a window and hurt himself.

Andy shuddered as the tape played in his mind, watching himself, like it wasn't really him. A person who looked a bit like him was bleeding. He remembered thinking, *I wonder how much blood I can lose before I fall unconscious, before I die.* Somehow, he'd snapped out of his funk and called an ambulance. Sometime later, he was in a psychiatric ward. He thought he'd be asked more questions; that it would be harder to get admitted. It wasn't. One moment he was punching out a window and the next he was bandaged and medicated, if only for a brief few days.

Andy shook his head at the memory. Life got dangerous when he couldn't control the voices, because that's what they were at the time, voices in his head. He didn't have a temper problem, rather, he'd been pissed off, unable to clearly express himself. His mind had been too loud and busy, filled with judgements and words careering maniacally around like dozens of balls in a pinball machine zinging from one target to the next, but mostly crashing into each other.

At home, Andy turned his attention to his easel and canvas. A beach scene. That's what he'd paint that night.

CHAPTER 20

Lily

It was Good Friday and despite being a long weekend, foot traffic in the village was virtually non-existent, maybe because it had rained for the past two days and locals were holed up at home with their heaters on. As for tourists, who'd visit the beach in this weather? The forecast was for rain and more rain. I was freezing, dressed in jeans and jumper, scarf, gloves and Ugg boots.

I still hadn't rented my Sydney house. Financially, my bank balance was looking grim. I needed to make some tough decisions, but the prospect was overwhelming. I stared at my flowers and smiled. Then, at the clogs. Argh.

In the afternoon, a stylish older woman in a leopard-print dress and serious high heels, pushed open the door and stepped inside. She fumbled with her umbrella before leaning it against the side of the door.

'Good afternoon,' I said.

She hesitated a moment before smiling tightly and turning, seemingly inspecting the blooming peonies and lilies.

My eyes drifted back to the counter and my never-ending to-do list. The plumbing was still causing me grief and I needed to buy food. I'd eaten most of Trouble's lettuce and carrots. The scowling woman looked at the small brightly coloured posies. She picked up two bunches and walked over.

'Gorgeous, aren't they?' I said when she handed them over to be wrapped.

'I guess,' she sniffed. 'I'm used to city florists. They have a much wider range.'

And a good day to you too. I ran through the mantra Iris had taught me with regard to winning over customers. *A florist needs to have a bright personality. She needs to portray herself as someone approachable.* Even in the cold. Even when the rain was torrential and everything felt damp and smelt musky.

A florist should also be able to read a customer's mind. You should know what to offer her. This woman had picked out posies. There was no need to read her mind, but I had complimented her.

Last but not least, the customer wants it NOW. I wrapped the flowers as quickly as I could.

This woman didn't do chit-chat. I didn't think she was a local, given I hadn't seen her before, but then again, I didn't know everyone in the village. She was probably a tourist.

I looked over to where Trouble was sleeping on a bale of hay. The woman's eyes followed me.

'Rodents, aren't they?' she said, staring at my darling.

I handed over the flowers. 'Are they a gift or for yourself?'

'My mother.'

'Nice. She'll love them.'

'She's in hospital. They're probably the last flowers I'll ever buy her.' Her voice caught and she steadied herself against a wall. 'Second last.'

When she'd walked out of the shop, I gulped for some air and picked up Trouble, patting behind his ridiculously long ears. I felt like I'd been holding my breath forever. 'You're not a rodent, are you, handsome.'

I was drifting off to sleep that evening when the florist landline buzzed. I looked at the clock. Nine thirty. My instinct was to answer – it was still a public holiday – even though I knew the person on the other end would be expecting an answering machine. I'd show 'em I was 'on' twenty-four hours a day.

'Lily's Little Flower Shop. Lily speaking. How can I help you?' The words rolled off my tongue.

'Oh,' said a voice at the other end of the line. 'I ... I wasn't expecting you to be in. It's Pamela Stevens. I was in this afternoon.'

My breath caught. 'Yes, I remember,' I said, trying to sound enthusiastic. 'How's—'

'Passed on ... I need bright flowers for the funeral.'

'Oh, okay. I'm sorry to hear that.' A surge of sympathy welled. Her mother had died. How awful.

'I want bright colours. Have I said that? Bright colours.'

We discussed her requirements for the next ten minutes. As she was about to hang up, I realised I didn't have her mother's particulars.

'I'm so sorry,' I said. 'I don't have your mother's name.'

'Of course you do. It's Patricia Foster.'

'Trish Foster,' I repeated to myself long after Pamela had hung up. No. My hands were shaking. Tears rolled down my cheeks. My heart felt like it was on fire.

Barely able to hold the phone to my ear, I called Iris with the news.

'I can't believe Trish is gone,' she said, her voice trembling.

'Neither can I,' I said through tears. 'I'm sorry I had to tell you over the phone Aunty Iris, but I needed to hear your voice.'

She sniffed. 'It's okay, dear girl.'

'Trish was so young, so full of life. What happened?' I started crying and couldn't stop.

'We'll find out soon enough, dear girl, I'm sure.'

I blew my nose. 'It's an awful shock when someone dies in the prime of life.'

'Yes, it is. Life is not a dress rehearsal.'

When the conversation ended, I climbed into bed and sobbed.

Somehow, I managed to sleep. By morning, the rain had cleared, so I placed several buckets of roses, dahlias and sunflowers outside the shop. But I couldn't stop thinking about Trish. The day was going to be a struggle.

Andy walked in around midday. 'Hey, how you doing?'

'Lots of orders to fill,' I said flatly.

'Mostly for Trish, I guess?'

I burst into tears. 'I can't believe it. Her daughter called me last night. She'd been in the shop earlier yesterday, but I had no idea.'

He raised his eyebrows. 'Pamela's been in?' Andy paused. 'It's awful news. I can't quite believe it.'

'Sorry,' I said wiping my eyes. 'I'm in shock. And now I have all these orders to fill. I've never done a funeral before. I feel...' I wiped my eyes again, 'gutted.'

Andy nodded and stared at the mess of papers on my workbench. 'Trish's funeral will be massive.'

'People have been ordering flowers for her all morning. I don't even know what happened. Didn't want to ask. She wasn't sick, was she?'

He shook his head. 'Car accident. Wednesday night. She was heading to a friend's for Easter, driving in torrential rain. Swerved to avoid a wallaby and hit the fox chasing it. In the slippery conditions, her car rolled several times, then hit a tree.'

I put my hand to my mouth. 'No.'

'Yeah. That's the story from the person in the car behind her.' Andy paused. 'Trish was as healthy as. She should have kicked on till she was ninety. And now you'll have to deal with Dragonzilla, her daughter.'

'I've had a glimpse of Pamela, but now that I know she's been in shock and grieving...'

'It's not just that. She's from the city. Thinks she knows everything.'

'I'm from the city.'

Andy smiled tightly. 'You'll see. Shout out if there's anything I can do to lighten the load.'

'Appreciate it.'

'And now, your smiling face is all we need to get us through these next few days.'

Thumbs up, Andy left, and as I was writing my to-do list, Pamela walked in.

'I'm so sorry about your mum. She was a lovely woman. We got along very well.'

Pamela shrugged. 'It's sad, but I need to be practical.' She stared around the shop grimacing. 'Maybe I should organise the

153

flowers from Sydney,' she said quietly, but loud enough for me to hear.

I coughed to get her attention. 'All of my flowers come from the Sydney markets. I can source anything you want.'

She glared at me. 'That's why I'm here. I want bright flowers for the funeral. Bright!'

I smiled and nodded. 'Of course.'

Pamela had specific instructions regarding the casket flowers and as she talked about other arrangements, I bluffed my way through. Pamela used botanical names I couldn't pronounce, let alone spell. I had no idea whether she was talking about daisies, dahlias, gerberas or hydrangeas. Not quite, I wasn't that unknowledgeable, but still.

'I hope I'm not making this difficult for you,' Pamela said, eyeing me as I scribbled on my notepad. If I didn't know better, I would have thought she was being condescending.

'Not at all.' I beamed. The last thing a grieving daughter needed was to have to deal with an incompetent florist.

It was an excruciating forty minutes.

I worked out that Pamela wanted a long low wreath to sit on top of the casket made up of miniature hydrangea, roses, Asiatic lilies, gerberas, gladioli, carnations and bells of Ireland. I could have all those blooms in stock Tuesday morning, assuming they were available, but as for putting them together? The whole town would be looking at my flower arrangements, examining them and judging me. The funeral was Thursday.

'I'll check in with you again Tuesday,' Pamela said as she walked out the door.

In a panic, I rang Iris and asked, 'How are you today?'

'Okay.' Iris paused. 'Trish was taken out by a fox? Can you imagine?'

'I'm trying not to. Pamela's just been in.' I explained to Iris about the wreath and other arrangements, then said, 'I don't think I can pull it off.'

'You'll be fine. Make sure you have plenty of stock in case you need to redo a wreath. Do you have oasis blocks?'

'I think so. I'm checking my order now.'

'Good. I'll send you a link to a couple of YouTube videos—'

'What? For wreath making?'

Iris chuckled. 'Yes, my dear. It's the twenty-first century.'

'I'm in way over my head.'

'You'll be fine,' she said again.

For the rest of the afternoon, as more orders flowed in, I googled botanical flower names, looked up funeral florist procedures, and drank Red Bull. Following Iris's instructions, I did a practice run and set about creating a framework made from eucalypt branches, for height and length. It took forever to get the greenery just right, so I could place the flowers. Between fielding calls and taking orders and making up on-the-spot bouquets, the arrangement took me the better part of three hours, but eventually it was done. Pretty good for the first time. I was relieved rather than pleased.

When I emailed Iris a photo, she phoned almost instantly.

'Looks great, Lily-Pily, but remember the flowers need to be positioned low, so when they sit on top of the casket in the hearse, they don't hit the roof and break.'

'I hadn't thought of that,' I said, sucking in air.

'Practice makes perfect. I'll come in Wednesday afternoon to help. Trish's flowers need to be perfect. It's the least we can do.'

After Iris rang off, I stared at the wreath. Even if I got the arrangement low enough, how was I supposed to attach it to the casket so it didn't slip off? I had visions of the flowers falling, perhaps hitting someone on the head, and then getting sued. Either that, or the stems breaking. I gulped my Red Bull. How was I going to fit the monstrosity into my mid-sized van to deliver it to the funeral home?

Ben walked into the shop. 'Hey.'

I smiled. He was as handsome as I remembered. A very bright spot in a very sad week. Fleetingly, I thought about Matt. I was a free woman so, if Ben asked me out to dinner again...

'Haven't seen you for ages.'

'Been back in Adelaide and then...' he paused. 'Now I'm back.'

I nodded. He seemed distant. Maybe distracted by the wreath that seemed to fill the space. 'How can I help?'

'I need flowers for my mum.'

'Forgot Mother's Day?'

'Something like that.' He picked up an arrangement of cream roses, lilies and lisianthas. 'I'll take these.'

'They're beautiful. I promise I won't overcharge you this time. Sixty dollars.'

He smiled, subdued, as he handed over the cash.

'See you soon,' I said to his back as he walked out the door. It was an odd encounter. There was no banter between us like on his previous visits.

I forced my thoughts back to the funeral. While I was talking to Ben, I'd received an email for a floral cross easel. It was similar to the casket wreath, but upright. How was I going to manage that one? I'd imposed on Iris enough. I'd have to google and wing it.

Two minutes later, I'd found a floral cross of white carnations and red roses. It was giving me head spins, though that could have been the Red Bulls, when I heard a ruckus outside. Ben and Pamela seemed to be having a disagreement in the street. She pointed at the flowers, gesticulating.

I edged closer to the front door. Ben looked like he was holding up the flowers in self-defence.

'I told you I didn't want those!' she yelled.

'What's wrong with them?'

I wanted to know too.

She threw her hands in the air and stormed off. He turned around. Embarrassingly, I was still staring.

He walked back into the shop. 'Sorry about that.'

'Not at all. Is something the matter with the flowers?'

He shook his head. 'My sister doesn't want any white in Mum's house. Says it's too funereal.'

'Pamela's your sister?'

He nodded. 'You've had the pleasure?'

I smiled. That must mean... 'I was very sorry to hear about Trish. I had no idea she was your mum. She is ... was a lovely lady. So kind.'

'Yeah,' he said, putting the flowers down on the front counter. 'You'd better take these.'

'What would you like instead?'

'Nothing. Pamela said she'd already ordered from you and requested bright colours.'

I stared at the beautiful flowers he had chosen. 'She did. But these are also beautiful. You could have both.'

'Not worth the hassle. Thanks, anyway.'

Poor bugger. 'If there's anything I can do, let me know. I'm really sorry.'

After he left, I unwrapped the flowers and placed them back where they'd been, near the front door. Then I remembered I'd forgotten to give Ben back his sixty dollars.

Ben was Trish's son? Why didn't anyone tell me? I knew she had two children but this? All three had different surnames. Questions bobbed around my head as I wrote my to-do list for the week. I didn't know what to make of Pamela, but I felt incredibly sorry for Ben. To lose his mum like that. I still couldn't quite believe it.

The rain started up again, and I needed a breather, so I closed the shop and wandered across to Zena's.

'Hey,' I said when I walked in. 'Don't mind me. I just need a break for a few minutes.' I sat down and flipped through a magazine.

Zena narrowed her eyes at me, nodded and focused her attention back on washing her client's hair.

Two minutes later, Pamela barrelled into the salon, shaking her wet umbrella against Zena's coffee table, spraying water all over me.

'Hello,' she said impatiently when Zena didn't immediately acknowledge her. 'I need my hair done. This weather's killing it.'

Poor choice of words.

'I was very sorry to hear about Trish,' Zena called from where she was standing. 'She was a lovely woman. I'll miss her.'

Pamela raised her eyebrows. 'Can you fit me in or not?'

Zena glanced at the wall clock. It had just gone three thirty. 'I'm afraid I'm fully booked this afternoon.' She dried her hands and walked over to the front desk where Pamela was hovering. 'The earliest I can do is Monday, eleven thirty.'

Pamela looked Zena up and down, unimpressed. 'For goodness' sake. What kind of business are you running here?'

'A busy one.'

'What do you have Thursday morning before the funeral? On second thoughts, Wednesday afternoon.'

'I can fit you in at four.'

Pamela gave a single brisk nod. 'Fine.' With that, she stalked out of the salon.

'She's in shock,' I offered.

Zena nodded. 'Maybe. But I've known Pamela four long years. She might be a big-wig in Sydney, but here in Clearwater, she needs to wait her turn like everybody else.'

I glanced over at my shop. 'I should get back to close up properly. Why didn't you tell me Ben was Trish's son?'

Zena was back doing her client's hair. 'I assumed you knew.'

I shook my head and blinked away tears. 'Also, why the different surnames?'

'Hello, Ms Twenty-First Century! Trish used her maiden name; Ben took his father's name; and Pamela still uses her first husband's name.'

'Does she have a second?'

Zena stuck out her tongue. 'Not that I know of, smarty pants.'

'Ah. I still can't believe Trish is gone.'

'No. Neither can I.'

CHAPTER 21

The next few days passed in a blur of wreath creating, posy making and people coming in to find out what had happened to Trish.

'Don't know why people think I'd know more than anyone else,' I said to Iris on Wednesday afternoon, as we filled final orders for the funeral.

'The florist is one of the first to hear about a death. Relatives are often too upset to order flowers themselves, so the funeral house orders for them.'

I hadn't thought about that, but Iris was right. Pamela had rung me on Friday night, within an hour of Trish's passing.

'When it's someone you know, it's hard to keep the information to yourself.' Iris gazed outside, lost in thought, then turned to me. 'But you learn to be professional.'

I nodded.

'Funerals are very hard, but the way I look at it, we're helping to make the service a little brighter.'

That was one way of looking at it.

That night I fell asleep at nine, only to wake in the early hours. I tried going back to sleep, but my panic was too intense.

The funeral was at eleven and I still had to finish the casket wreath. I got up and started work.

§⬥

Two hours later, I'd completed the wreath according to Iris's instructions. She wouldn't see the finished product until the service, and I didn't want to let her down. Then it was on with the other orders. Despite the cold, perspiration dripped down my back, but by seven thirty that morning (three Red Bulls down), I'd done what I needed to do for Trish.

Outside, the sun was shining. It was going to be a glorious autumn day, not too warm. Still, I had visions of my beautiful flowers wilting before the funeral got underway. I was also nervous that they would be scrutinised by everyone and I'd be run out of town for below-par service. But I only had a couple of minutes to torture myself before Andy arrived, coffees in hand. He'd offered to take the casket wreath and easel to the funeral home because his van was bigger than mine.

'How long have you been up?'

I yawned. 'Don't ask.'

It was a windy five-kilometre drive and the roads weren't the best, so every time we hit a bump, my heart lurched, and I reached out to hold the flowers in case they tumbled forward.

Sensing my panic, Andy shouted back to me in the rear seat, 'I'm going as slowly as I can.'

It was a relief to finally arrive and take them out and place them where we were directed by funeral staff. I didn't see Pamela or Ben. When pointed towards the cold room, I stopped a moment, a cold room where...

'It doesn't bear thinking about,' said Andy, clocking my reaction.

I kept walking, willing myself not to trip.

Ten minutes later, we were both back in the van, job accomplished and heading towards Clearwater, me sitting in the passenger seat beside Andy.

'Bet you feel like a stiff vodka,' he said.

I nodded.

'Relax,' he said, reaching over and squeezing my shoulder. 'The flowers are stunning.'

'I had a bad experience at my grandmother's funeral.'

He raised his eyebrows. 'You sang "My Way" and it was terribly inappropriate? And you didn't realise you're a bad singer.'

'No. "Always Look on the Bright Side of Life". And I'm a great singer.'

He smiled. 'Okay. Did the pall bearers accidentally drop the casket?'

I smiled.

'The lid didn't pop, did it?'

'Worse. I laughed all the way through the service,' I said, immediately laughing at the memory. 'You'd think my mum or dad would have taken me outside to calm me down, but they didn't. Mum just pinched my arm in the hope that I'd start crying.'

'Ouch.'

'She didn't hurt me, but God, it was awful. If I hadn't laughed, I'd have cried.'

'Hate to break it to you, but tears are generally expected at funerals.'

'Dad kept telling me we needed to celebrate Nanna's life, that she wanted it to be a joyous occasion. I guess I got nervous.'

I shuddered at the memory. I was eleven and hadn't been to another funeral since. Poor Nanna. I was so traumatised I feigned sickness to get out of going to Granddad's service.

Not long after I got back to the shop, Iris arrived, and I drove back up to the funeral home.

'You ready for this?' Iris asked, after I'd parked and we were walking towards a group of mourners.

I shook my head. 'No.'

Thankfully, the first people I spotted were Zena and Andy.

'Hey,' Zena said, walking over. 'The flowers are gorgeous, Lil. I had a sneak peek. You've made a big impression.'

'Absolutely,' said Andy. 'A funeral's certainly the way to get noticed.'

Iris smiled. 'See, Lily, I told you it'd be okay on the day.'

'Don't speak too soon,' I said, spotting Pamela, understated in a fitted pale blue jersey wrap dress. She was in deep conversation with Ben. He didn't look impressed, just kept nodding. I also saw Barry and Paula from the newsagency, baker Sally, and others.

The service got underway. As the celebrant spoke about Trish's life, her love for Ben, Pamela and her community, images appeared on the huge projection screen at the front of the room. There were photos of Trish as a young girl, cuddling a kitten; Trish as a school student; her wedding; photos of Ben and Pamela as babies and small children. I took a deep breath to stem the tears. But when Christmas photos of Trish, flanked by Ben and Pamela popped on to the screen, I cried.

After the celebrant had spoken, Ben stood up and walked to the podium. 'Mum would have been humbled by the community outpouring of love.'

People cried as Ben spoke of his mum and dad's love for each other, and how they were now reunited. Iris and I held hands, sniffing. There was no hysterical giggling.

Thirty minutes later, after Pamela and Henry each gave a reading and Trish's favourite song, "Stairway to Heaven", was played, Iris, Zena and I stood outside in the sunshine.

'How are you feeling?' I asked Iris.

'Tired. It was a beautiful service, but it's times like this when I think about Mike and all the time we didn't spend together.'

I hugged her.

An elderly lady approached us. 'I'd never have considered brightly coloured flowers for my funeral, but now that I've seen them, I'll definitely be requesting them. Thank you, young lady.'

'Your flowers are definitely a bright spot today,' Iris agreed.

'Very much so,' said the other lady before walking away.

I turned to Aunty Iris. 'Yeah, but I feel guilty that Trish's death has been profitable for me.'

'Nonsense. You're providing a service.'

§.

'Are you sure you won't come to The Fisherman's Club?' I asked Iris when we arrived back at the shop.

She shook her head. 'I'm an emotional wreck. I've paid my respects to Ben and Pamela. Now, I just want to go home, put my feet up and have a cuppa.'

I nodded.

'Plus, I need to pack for my road trip. The glorious outback. I wasn't planning to go, but what with Trish, well, I thought bugger it. So Mavis and I are off to Uluru for three weeks.'

'Thelma and Louise have got nothing on you two. Please drive safely.'

I kissed her goodbye and walked to The Fisherman's Club down the road. I caught up with Zena and Andy at the entrance.

§.

'It was a good funeral, if you can call a funeral good,' I said, minutes later, drinking my wine.

Zena nodded. 'Sad. Beautiful. But sad.' She raised her glass. 'Here's cheers to Trish!'

'Trish wanted her ashes scattered in the ocean,' said Andy. 'I might have the same done with mine.'

'Don't be morbid,' said Zena.

'I'm not, but given we've spent most of the day at a funeral, it's as good a time as any to talk about it. What do you want, Lily?'

I shook my head. 'I've never really thought about it.'

'Exactly,' agreed Zena. 'The fossil here,' she poked Andy in the ribs, 'needs to think about such matters because he's old, but you and I, we've got at least another sixty years.'

Andy smiled. 'Dream on.'

'I like the idea of her ashes being scattered. She grew up here, didn't she?'

'Close by, but Pamela's dead against it.' He gazed to where she had backed Ben into a corner.

I glanced over. 'Surely, they'll have to follow Trish's instructions?'

'Pamela can be quite persuasive.'

'Poor bloke,' I mused.

'He's actually quite wealthy,' said Andy.

'And single,' Zena chimed in.

'Got your eye on him, have you?' Andy asked Zena.

Zena snorted.

I sipped my drink, watching as Pamela made her way through the crowd and stood in front of us.

'I'm so sorry.' My words felt inadequate. I raised my glass to my mouth and noticed, too late, that it was empty.

She waved me away with her hand. 'Thanks. Your flowers were nice, by the way.'

I nodded. This day was no doubt one of the hardest of her life. Gratefully, I accepted more wine when the waiter offered.

'Pamela,' said Andy evenly, 'Trish will be much missed. I've never seen The Fisherman's Club so packed. Most of the town has turned out to bid her farewell.'

Ben joined the conversation. 'Yes, they have. Lily, your flowers were stunning.'

'Thank you.'

'The whole service was beautiful,' said Andy. 'Trish would have been touched.'

Pamela sighed. 'It took me five days to organise.'

'Job well done,' said Ben.

She cleared her throat and walked away.

Ben looked embarrassed. 'Sorry about that. My sister can be a little abrupt.'

I smiled. 'Not at all. She's grieving.'

'No, she's pretty much like that all the time.'

'She's actually quite mellow today,' said Andy.

Andy and Ben clinked glasses.

I gulped my drink. Why did they dislike Pamela so much? Yes, she was straightforward, but she'd lost her mum. There probably couldn't be a much worse time for her.

'Thanks again for coming today,' Ben said to the three of us. 'Mum would have been moved by everyone's kindness.'

Henry sidled up to Ben and hugged him. 'Mighty fine woman, that mother of yours.'

Ben returned the hug. 'Thanks, Henners. Sad day.'

They released each other and then 'Henners' shook hands with Andy. 'Mate, how you doing?'

Andy shrugged. 'Okay, chook.'

'Lily,' said Ben, 'Have you met Henners, my oldest and dearest buddy? His mob have been in the area since before time.'

Henry shot back with, 'Lily and I are firm friends.'

Ben looked surprised. 'How did I not know that?'

'Because you're never around, mate.'

'Henry's my accountant,' I said, hoping to lighten the mood.

Henry beamed. 'Please! Call me Hen. Though soon enough you'll be calling me chook, like everyone else.'

At that moment Barry passed by. 'Too right, chooky.'

'Small world,' said Ben. 'So you've had the pleasure of visiting his work abode?'

I nodded.

Henry smiled. 'Yep, I tell all my new clients, just look for the Aboriginal flag waving in the wind.'

'Can't miss it, can you?' said Ben.

Henry poked his shoulder. 'If I don't wave my flag, who will?'

'Here we go.' Ben grabbed Henry and held him in a headlock.

'And to think you're my best friend.' Henry shook himself free and gazed at a woman on the other side of the room. I recognised her from the photo on Henry's desk.

'Come on then.' Ben dragged him off.

After they walked away, Zena raised her glass. 'True gentlemen.'

I nodded, my eyes following them as they stopped to talk to the woman and a couple of others. 'Who's that?'

Zena sipped her drink. 'Sophie. Henry's fiancé. You'll love her. She's gorgeous, like you. By the way, you look so much more relaxed than when you first arrived. Not today necessarily, but you know what I mean. I'll shut up now.'

'I don't feel relaxed. I'm a total stress ball, but I'm slowly getting used to how casual coastal life is.' My vacant cottage flashed before my eyes. That and the overwhelming sadness I felt. Not just about Matt, but also about life choices I'd made. I didn't regret them but that didn't stop me thinking 'what if?'

'We just need to do something about your hair,' said Zena pulling me back into the moment. 'Lighten it, perhaps?'

'Maybe.' I wasn't sure. 'So, about Pamela, why don't you like her?'

'For starters,' said Zena. 'The way she maintains eye contact without blinking.'

'Predator stare,' Andy chimed in. 'It's like she's collecting a mental dossier on everyone. Doesn't bode well considering she might take over Trish's business.'

'Do you think she will?' I asked.

'Gossip at the salon,' said Zena, 'suggests she'll fly out as soon as this is wrapped up and leave Ben to deal with it.'

'I wouldn't count on it,' said Andy.

'But she hates Clearwater and the small-town vibe,' Zena argued.

He sighed. 'We'll see.'

I was starting to feel woozy and realised I hadn't eaten all day. My eyes drifted towards Ben. It was time to go. 'Either way,' I said, 'I'd better stay in good with the landlord, so I'll start by going home and tidying up. It's been a long few days.'

'Please stay,' said Zena.

Andy glared at me. 'Don't stop me now because I'm at a wake and having such a good time.'

I smiled but tears threatened. 'I'm having a ball.'

Zena stared. 'What?'

'Queen!' I replied. 'Anyhoo, I'm off.'

'They never wrote about a wake.'

I shook my head. If I stayed longer, I'd cry again. I was tired and the desire to curl up into a ball in my bedroom corner was never far away.

Whenever I was at a gathering, my mother's words always came to mind. *Arrive on time. Leave early. Don't disgrace yourself.* I'd successfully managed all three today.

I put my empty glass on a nearby table. 'You two have fun now.' As soon as I said it, I put my hand on my mouth. 'I can't believe I said that.'

Andy patted my back. 'We won't tell anyone.'

CHAPTER 22

The following Tuesday morning, Taylor insisted on meeting me at the flower market.

'It's bloody freezing,' she remarked. 'I must really be feeling sorry for you to venture out here. I almost got mowed down in the car park.'

I laughed. 'This isn't the place for politeness. I grab a spot wherever I can, then race around buying up all the flowers on my list so I can be back on the road by six thirty.'

Taylor glanced at her watch. 'Except when you're meeting your bestie for coffee. Seriously, Lil, who else would meet you at six fifteen for a skinny latte?'

'True, but look at the place. Flowers stretching as far as the eye can see.' I admired the growers who'd been awake since one am, loading their trucks, arriving, and then unloading before buyers like me piled in. They didn't seem to mind whether it was warm and muggy or cold, dark and stormy. Everyone at the flower market was family. Italian and Greek growers downed coffee shots while hassling each other, telling rude jokes and frantically shouting to tell clientele their 'best' flower prices and flirt with them.

'Yeah, yeah. Pretty and stinky. I get it.' She stifled a yawn. 'How are you feeling after the funeral?'

'Sad, obviously. I still can't quite believe it. I keep expecting Trish to walk into the shop.'

'You're still in shock,' said Taylor kindly.

'I've never had a friend die before. Death happens to other people, not people I know. Not Trish.' I blinked fast, struggling to swallow. 'Everyone's going about their business, but it's like there's a gaping hole.' I struggled to hold back tears. 'Every time I walk past the real estate office...'

Taylor cleared her throat. 'I'm sorry I never got the chance to meet her.' She ruffled my already messy hair and sipped her coffee. 'What else is happening? Are you talking to Matt?'

'Nah. With the wisdom of hindsight, I realise that it's about much more than distance. We have fundamentally conflicting views about what we want from life.'

'Fair point.' Taylor sipped her coffee. 'What about Banging Ben?'

'What about him?'

'Anything going on there?'

'Taylor! His mother's just died and no! Talk about insensitive.'

Taylor put her hands up. 'Sorry, that was a dumb-arse question.'

'I'm barely keeping my head above water with this.' I gestured to the flowers that surrounded us. 'That's my entire focus. Making the flower shop a success.'

'How can it not be? Once you set your mind to something, you give it your all. Your dedication knows no bounds. But you need to have fun as well.'

'Fun is making sure my numbers balance at the end of every day. Fun is spending time curled up with Trouble. I don't have time for anything else.'

'You need to make time, girlfriend.'

'Stop it.' I threw my napkin at her. 'How are things with Gabe?'

Taylor rolled her eyes. 'Over before it started. Such is life. Guess what? I have news to cheer you up.'

'I'm listening,' I said, half-listening, distracted by the four men downing ouzo shots nearby.

'Word on the wire is that Glenn is skating on precariously thin ice.'

'Hookers and strip joints?'

'I don't know the ins and outs, but I do know most of his female clients aren't happy. Neither is Alastair.'

I raised my eyebrows. 'It's not as if he wasn't warned. The board should have known better.'

I was back on the road an hour later than normal, but it was worth it for the catch-up with Taylor. I really missed her. Missed the ease with which we could talk about any and everything. Though she'd never admit it, I think she was impressed with the market's vastness and how well I knew my way around.

❦

At the shop, I wrote on my chalkboard. *May flowers always line your path and sunshine light your day.*

A new baby had been born overnight, so I was swamped with phone orders. It always surprised me that callers continued to spell out words like *congratulations* and *celebration* as if I was a complete idiot. I was a fool about some things but prided myself on my ability to spell.

Henry walked into my shop mid-afternoon. 'Hi.' I swear he did a double-take, probably because I was dishevelled and in need of a decent night's sleep. 'Everything okay?'

I nodded, stretched and rubbed my eyes. 'Yeah. A bit shattered after the market run this morning.'

He waved some printed pages in front of me. 'Thanks for emailing me these figures last week.' I nodded again. 'It's my professional opinion that instead of driving to the markets twice a week, you find a supplier and get your flowers delivered. It'll prolong your life. You really do look tired.'

'Cheers.'

'I'm serious. What time did you get up this morning?'

'Three.'

'This is what I'm talking about. When you add up your time, petrol costs, entry fee. Plus...'

'What?'

'You say you don't overspend, but—'

'Okay, sometimes I do.'

'If you give your supplier a list, you'll only get the flowers on that list, which you can add to on special occasions. Costs will be contained.'

'What's the point of having my fabulous van if I don't drive to the markets?'

He smiled and shook his head. 'You still need the van for deliveries.'

'True. And I've raised my prices like you suggested.'

Henry turned his head to one side. 'Probably not enough. Your overheads are very high.' He took a moment. 'Business has significantly dropped since Valentine's Day. You need to rein in your expenditure. Especially now that you need to make up the shortfall from your non-existent city rent.'

'Thanks. I'd almost forgotten.' (As if!)

'Speaking of which, what's going on with your Sydney house?'

'Jake says I need to drop the rent by at least twenty per cent. Preferably twenty-five.'

'And?'

I sighed. 'If I do that, the rent won't cover my mortgage.'

'But not renting it out means you're not getting any money. At all.'

'I know that!'

'You need to make some hard decisions.' Henry shuffled some papers. 'Paying a mortgage, starting up a new business. Something's gotta give.'

I couldn't bear the thought of selling my home, however, it was becoming increasingly obvious that I needed to do that if I was to stay in Clearwater. I couldn't have it both ways.

'You need to be practical, Lily. Please give it some thought.'

I nodded, feeling tears prick the back of my eyes.

'Okay,' he said pivoting. 'About getting a supplier?'

'Yeah. I *am* really tired of getting up so early. It's cold and dark.'

'Case settled. Do you have one in mind?'

'Maybe.' Tony, Iris's friend, the guy I bought ninety per cent of my flowers from, was a possibility. He'd been badgering me for a while to have my flowers delivered. My shoulders sagged with relief. It felt like the weight of the world lifting. Henry had given me permission to employ a supplier and I suddenly felt a lot less tired. I'd miss the markets, but not the early morning wake-ups.

'There's something else I want to discuss,' said Henry. 'Sophie and I have set our wedding date.'

I smiled. 'Congratulations.' I'd met Sophie briefly at Trish's wake.

'August twenty-sixth.' Henry beamed.

'Almost spring!'

'Almost. We're having it at Ben's winery, and obviously, as my best friend, he'll be best man. Don't tell him but I only chose his venue because of him.'

'Smart thinking.'

'I'm joking.' Henry was almost giddy with happiness, like he had the most amazing secret and was bursting to tell the world. 'Lily, we'd like you to do the flowers.'

'Wow. Really? You don't have to.'

Henry waved his arms in the air. 'We do. Anyway, we have heaps of time, but Soph's already panicking. I'll leave you two to sort out the details. But, Lily, one thing?'

'Yes?'

'For God's sake, charge us the going rate. You need to turn a profit.'

I shook my head. 'I couldn't possibly.'

'You can, and you will.'

Henry left and I paced around the shop. A wedding!

Five minutes later, panic kicked in. What if Henry only chose me to do his wedding flowers because he felt sorry for me? This would be my first wedding. What if I wasn't good enough?

I pushed the thought from my mind. At least I had a few months ... and Iris! I'd have to tell her now so she didn't organise a holiday to Egypt or Alaska.

CHAPTER 23

Andy

At home on Tuesday evening after therapy, Andy tried to master a new piece of guitar music. His fingers were red and sore. He played a mournful tune, grieving Trish. As he played, his thoughts turned to how kind she'd been when he'd moved to Clearwater eight years earlier after his mother died.

Trish had found him a great rental residential property close to the town centre, and had introduced him to Henry, who was looking for a new shop tenant. Seemingly, everything had fallen into place when Andy moved to Clearwater. Then he met Pamela, Trish's daughter, and Pamela's best friend, Edie. He and Edie fell in love and Edie moved in. Perfect. They married. He moved out when their relationship fell apart.

Trish found him his second rental, not quite as nice, but by then, Andy was saving for a home deposit. Then it was Trish again, who sold him this beautiful home. It had been love at first sight; the huge garden, the view, the privacy, so much more affordable than Melbourne real estate.

Andy stopped strumming his guitar and shook his head. He didn't want to think about Edie. Or Pamela. When he considered that Pamela might stick around, he felt physically ill. Possibly the worst scenario would be Pamela taking over Trish's business. Trish? Why, of all people? Her death had knocked Andy more than he cared to admit. He walked into the kitchen to refill his water glass and thought about his conversation with Zena at the wake.

'I'm so upset,' Zena had said. 'At the unfairness. The randomness of life. If anyone was going to get taken out by a fox, why couldn't it have been Pamela?'

Andy smiled. 'Evil.'

'I never said I was Snow White.' Zena was teary. 'Being here, it makes you wonder, doesn't it?'

Andy had taken her hand. 'You're not going to die any time soon, Zeen.'

Zena had looked down at their entwined hands. 'Is this weird?'

Andy squeezed her hand again before slowly taking it away. 'I've been thinking—'

Barry interrupted them, and the moment was lost. Whatever that moment had been.

Andy wondered what he would have said to Zena had Barry not joined them.

A knock at the door interrupted his thoughts. He glanced at the wall clock. It was just after 6pm.

'Pamela!' Andy said when he opened the door. 'What are you doing here?'

'You're a cheat,' she barked.

Andy glared at her. 'Pardon?'

Pamela swayed slightly. 'You heard me. I saw you holding

hands with Zena at my mother's funeral. Have you no shame? What about Edie?'

Was Pamela slurring her words? No way was he letting her into his house.

'In the first place, Edie and I are divorced. And in the second place, what I do with my life is none of your business.' He went to push her out so he could close the door.

'Don't touch me,' she screamed. 'You're disgusting.'

He noticed a neighbour peering over a side fence and lowered his voice. 'I understand you're upset about Trish. It's been a difficult time. You're clearly exhausted. You need to rest.'

Pamela leaned into him and pointed at his beard. 'Still sporting that growth on your face, I see.'

'Again, I'm very sorry about Trish. She was much loved.'

Pamela glared at him. 'As opposed to me?'

'I'm just saying I'll miss her, as will everyone in town.'

She screwed up her face. 'I know what I saw. You and that hairdresser! Wait till Edie finds out.'

With that, Pamela walked away and Andy shut the door. His hands were shaking. That woman's only purpose was to stir trouble. Zena and he were friends. Nothing more.

Seeing Pamela triggered memories Andy didn't want resurfacing.

His body shivering and forehead sweating, he lay down on his bed. His heart thumped. He couldn't play guitar now. The thought of Pamela telling his ex-wife about Zena gave him the urge to vomit, even though he had no food in his stomach.

He wished Edie would stop texting him. He'd blocked her number, but she always found a way to contact him, either by using a burner phone, calling from a public telephone or sending him a letter or email. The thought of Pamela and Edie in the same room together was enough to make him ill. He could sense the growing panic, his heart pounding and blood pressure rising.

Andy closed his eyes. He had to stop worrying about the past. He couldn't let Edie back into his life. He was a grown man. He was divorced. He could hold any damn woman's hand he wanted to.

CHAPTER 24

Lily

As we moved closer to Mother's Day, the days grew cooler, the air crisper. The leaves changed colour, curling and crinkling, and fell from the trees along the promenade, making a vibrant carpet of burnt orange every morning. Life at the flower shop took on a calmer vibe even though I had to learn a host of new autumn flower names. I kept busy, but still mourned Trish.

Zena had been right about trade falling off. Even though I was supplying weekly flowers to Zena, baker Sally, the newsagent, and the Surf and Fisherman's clubs' functions, some days I barely sold enough to pay the rent. My shop appeared busy because locals wandered in to gossip. There was talk about Pamela taking over Trish's business permanently, but Pamela hadn't contacted me, thankfully, so I had no knowledge to impart.

Given the slowing trade, I tried to close early most Sunday

afternoons so I could call into the retirement village before walking along the beach. But that just gave me more thinking time.

As if reading my mind, Jake, my Sydney real estate agent, called.

'Good news, I hope?' I said.

'I've managed to secure tenants but at seventy per cent of what you were after.'

'Faark! That's not good news.'

'It's better than having no tenants which you've had for almost three months.'

After I'd hung up, I did some mental calculations. More calculations. This couldn't continue. I had a to make a choice: Sydney or Clearwater.

❧

Monday morning, Larry Downey, the funeral director, rang to compliment me on the flowers at Trish's service. 'Sorry I haven't rung before this, but we've been run off our feet.'

'That's good, I guess,' I said, not knowing how else to comment.

'We haven't had a local florist since I've been in the business, over fifteen years. All of our arrangements come from up the coast or inland country. Now that you're here, how would you feel about being our preferred supplier?'

I didn't have a clue what he meant, so I was terrified and thrilled at the same time. 'Yes, I think.'

Larry chuckled. 'Henry's one of my mob. He reckons you're okay, so...'

I smiled to myself. 'Thank you.' I hesitated. 'What does preferred supplier actually mean?'

'It means that when mourners choose flowers for their loved

181

one's service, I'll order from you, unless they have a specific florist in mind, which I can tell you, they won't. They have enough on their plate, ordering coffins, preparing eulogies and selecting songs and photos for the slide show.'

After the conversation, I felt a bit queasy. I had no desire to go back to Larry's funeral home, let alone prepare wreaths and other death flowers.

Soon after, Ben strolled into the shop and I brightened.

'Larry's solid. Henry's cousin. You're getting in good with the family,' he said when I told Ben about my conversation. 'Seriously, you'll like doing business with him.'

'As long as I stay on the side of the living.'

Ben smiled. 'That would be the plan. Thanks again for doing a great job with Mum's flowers.'

I took a deep breath. Though it seemed superficial given the circumstances, I was proud I'd pulled it off – with huge input from Aunty Iris. 'I missed you afterwards.'

Ben shifted on his feet. 'Yeah, I hightailed it back to Adelaide. Speaking of Mum, Pamela's going to take care of the business for now.'

'O...kay.'

'If I didn't need to be in Adelaide, it'd be easier to sort out Mum's estate, her house and the real estate company. I'm also expanding Ravenstone Winery here. I'm getting pulled in all directions.'

'Is Henry's wedding reception part of the expansion?'

Ben smiled. 'The ratbag talked me into it. It'll be the winery's first wedding, so if something goes wrong...'

'I know what you mean. I'm doing the flowers. My first wedding too.'

'A first for both of us. We can muddle through together.' He checked his watch. 'I need to get going, but how about you, me, Henners and Soph have dinner together soon?'

'I'd like that.'

'Leave it with me.'

Soon after he left, my phone pinged.

How are you placed for dinner with Henners and Soph Wednesday night?

Wednesday night? *I replied.* I'll have to check my social calendar, but I think I'm free.

Great, I'll pick you up at seven.

❦

By six forty-five Wednesday evening, I was practically hyperventilating. Perspiring, even though it was seventeen degrees. My trembling fingers could barely apply my mascara. I bothered with what to wear, how to blow-dry my hair. Should I use a straightener or curl it into soft waves? I couldn't control my hands so it ended up a combination of the two.

'Don't give me that look,' I said to Trouble as I changed shoes for the fourth time. 'There's a fine line between sexy and impractical.'

I put my hair up, put my hair down. I fussed with a different lipstick and gloss. It was a relief when I heard a knock on the flower shop door and walked downstairs.

When I saw Ben, my heart did a little skip. He looked handsome in beige chinos and a navy button-down shirt. Relaxed. 'Right on time.'

'Looking lovely,' he said, kissing my cheek.

As he leaned closer, I took in his scent, fresh, like the ocean. I blushed.

'We're meeting Henners and Sophie at Thai-One-On,' he said, as we walked out into the street. 'Have you been before?'

I smiled. 'Only for takeaway.'

'Hope you like it,' he said, taking my hand.

Goosebumps.

Henry and Sophie were waiting when we arrived. I soon found out that Sophie taught at the local primary school and she asked about my life before coming to Clearwater.

'It was crazy,' I told her. 'I'm much more laid-back here.'

'That's a big move by yourself,' Sophie said. 'Brave.'

I nodded. 'I was ready for a big change.' I deliberately didn't mention Matt. 'I'm confident the business will work out. I'm happy here.'

Sophie nodded. 'I'm happy too, and now my guy and I are getting hitched, it looks like Clearwater will be my home for many years to come.'

Henry leaned over and kissed her. 'I won the jackpot, that's for sure.'

I felt a pang of longing for a close loving relationship like theirs.

We moved on to the business of flowers.

'I'll come in soon to show you some pictures,' Sophie enthused.

'Be prepared, Lily,' said Henry. 'She has a scrapbook full of them.'

I smiled. 'It's good to be organised and know what you want. Yours will be my first wedding. I'm really excited.'

'The first of many, I'm sure,' said Ben.

'It'll be perfect,' said Sophie. 'We want something simple, elegant and fun, don't we, Hen?'

Henry nodded. 'Just like you, darling.'

'Have you told Henners your other news, Lily?' Ben chimed in.

It took a moment to realise what he was talking about before I spoke. 'I don't want this to put a downer on things, but Larry, the funeral director, rang. Lily's Little Flower Shop is now his preferred florist.'

The other three cheered and raised their glasses.

I laughed. 'Isn't it a bit inappropriate we're cheering?'

'No,' said Henry. 'It's a business. Do you think Larry's making a profit? Don't answer that. He is. And so should you. People die. It's a fact of life.'

Sophie slapped him on his arm. 'Henry!'

He glanced at Ben. 'Sorry, mate. That was insensitive of me.'

'Not at all,' said Ben. 'You're quite right.'

Profits ... I wasn't making much extra, but, still, I took my weekly bunches to the retirement village. I wasn't a baker and I couldn't sew to save myself, but was determined to contribute to the community, if only in a small way, by brightening up the retirement villagers' lives with flowers. Elsie, the sherry connoisseur, Betty, who liked all sweet treats, and April, the flirt, would never forgive me if I stopped dropping in, delivering flowers, and chatting over glasses of sherry.

'Sophie is gorgeous,' I said, as we walked back to the shop after dinner. 'She and Henry clearly adore each other. I want to be like them when I grow up.'

Ben stopped at my door.

'I'd invite you in but—'

'Your boyfriend's home and he'll get pissed off.'

'What?'

Ben smiled. 'Relax. I was joking. I had a great night.' He pulled me in close and kissed me. 'How did I manage to score a date with the hottest-looking woman in Clearwater?'

I laughed. 'You know all the lines.'

'No, I don't. But right now, I'm thinking life needs to be lived.' He leaned in to kiss me again, his arms snaking around my waist.

I didn't resist. I liked being held in his arms and the kiss was even better the second time.

He pulled back and smiled. 'Can I see you again?'

'I'm sure you will. It's a small town.'

'You know what I mean.'

'That would be lovely.' Butterflies swarmed in my stomach.

He kissed me one last time before he walked to his car. I liked Ben. He was charming, funny, easy to talk to. I definitely wanted to see him again, but part of me was holding back just like I had with Matt.

Still, I wanted to give it a shot.

'Would you like dinner, sometime,' I blurted. 'Here? I can't cook. In fact, I'm lousy—'

He turned around. 'Gee, with an offer like that, how can I refuse? Yes, I'd love to.'

'Tomorrow? Six thirty?'

Ben nodded. 'Until then.'

'Wait,' I said as he was climbing into his car. 'Better make it seven.'

I felt giddy watching him drive away. Was I mad inviting him over to dinner? I could barely scramble an egg.

Back inside, I opened Trouble's hutch door and scooped him into my arms. He could sleep in my bed again tonight. This was becoming a habit, a good habit. Just as well he was toilet trained. Now, if only I could stop him from chewing my hair to wake me up in the mornings.

I lay in bed thinking about Ben – his voice, the way he threw his head back when he laughed, the goosebumps. Still weird though, kissing someone new after being with Matt so long. Part of me felt guilty and part of me felt free, like I'd suddenly been released. I was my own person again, able to make choices and mistakes without Matt beside me.

§&.

The next night, I closed the shop an hour early, showered, picked out the floaty dress Ben had admired previously, and teamed it with my new denim jacket and strappy nude-coloured sandals. I dashed around, tidying the flat, and placing flowers in the bathroom, lounge and bedroom. To set the mood, I played some classical music, lit several candles and prepared an antipasti platter. I'd also made a lasagne for dinner, pretty much the only dish I could make without getting stressed.

Standing back to examine the living area, I decided I'd lit too many candles and had piled too many cushions on the sofa. But I had no time to do anything because the shop door buzzed.

Taking a lungful of air, I breathed into my hand. How was my breath? Confident it was fresh, I skipped down the stairs.

'Perfect timing,' I said, greeting Ben with a hug.

'Looking beautiful, as always.' He handed over two bottles of his signature wine.

I blushed, my heart rate rocketing.

I led him upstairs – the first time he'd been inside my apartment. Was this cheesy? Had I tried too hard with my clothes and make-up? My thoughts about what we'd talk about? I'd looked up his home state in South Australia and the Adelaide Hills, so I could always fall back on that. I poured us both a glass of the wine he'd brought and led him out on the balcony. Too many cushions and candles!

'I like what you've done with the place.' He took a sip before putting his drink on the table and looking at Trouble, who'd hopped outside with us. Ben nudged him away with his foot.

'Not an animal person?' I remarked.

'I prefer dogs.' He picked up his drink. 'Now, what was I saying?'

'That you like what I've done with the place.' I made a point of picking up Trouble and patting him. 'It's compact but I love it and you can't beat the view.'

We admired our surroundings before walking back inside to prepare dinner in my tiny kitchen.

'This is only the third time I've used the oven.'

'Third time lucky. I'm honoured.'

We shared the space but didn't bump into each other. I caught him looking at me and brushed stray strands of hair from my face, did I have carrot in my hair? 'What's up?'

He leant over and kissed me, long and hard. I tasted wine on his tongue. I tried to forget that he wasn't enamoured with Trouble.

'I've been wanting to do that since last night.' Ben put his drink down and kissed me again. I didn't want the kiss to end.

'So,' I said, fussing with cutlery, 'Henry and Sophie are a great couple. I can't believe they've asked me to do their wedding flowers.'

'Why not? I can't wait to see what you come up with.'

'You're so sweet.'

'No, I'm not, at least not all the time. I love what you've done with the old butcher's shop.'

'It certainly smells a lot better.'

He nodded. 'Bit different from your previous job. You doing okay?'

I thought about it a moment. 'Honestly? I'd like to be earning more, but I like what I'm doing.' I grinned. 'Sometimes I even love it. Obviously not the past few weeks so much.'

Ben clinked his wine glass with mine. 'Here's to Mum.'

'To Trish,' I said before taking a sip. 'I wonder what she'd have thought about this?'

Ben raised his eyebrows and I suddenly felt sick. That I'd overstepped the mark. 'Us having dinner?'

'I guess,' I replied, wanting to kick myself.

'Mum would have loved it and asked why it took us so long.' Ben leant against the kitchen bench, looking incredibly fetching. 'It must feel very special making up flowers for new babies, birthdays, anniversaries...'

'Weddings!' we said together.

I smiled. 'It really is.'

'Even funerals,' said Ben. 'Flowers are the centrepiece of people's lives at the most special and important times of their lives.'

'Wow,' I said, punching him in the arm. 'Can I employ you as my PR rep?'

'Of course.' He leant over and kissed me. 'I'm cheap.' He kissed me again. 'You're making people feel good about themselves, Lily Mason.'

I smiled. 'Well, right now, you're making me feel rather good about myself.'

It was on the tip of my tongue to tell him about the weekly deliveries I made to the retirement village, because they were so special to me, but that night was special enough. There'd be plenty of time to tell him. Hopefully.

Ben and I kissed again after dinner, but that's as far as things went.

'I like where this is heading,' he said.

'But—'

'But nothing. I like where this is heading.' He frowned. 'Okay, there is a but. I'm flying again to Adelaide tomorrow. I should have told you at the beginning of the night, but I didn't want to ruin the evening.'

'That's fine,' I said, toes wiggling, fingers shaky, feeling anything but fine. I didn't want him to leave. 'For how long?'

'Not sure. I need to wrap things up so I can come back and focus on Mum's estate and the winery. I'm sure Pam will be okay unsupervised.'

I smiled half-heartedly. 'To be honest, I wish it were Pamela leaving.'

Ben kissed me lightly on the lips. 'I feel the same way. I'm sure she means well. I know she can be difficult but...' He paused a moment. 'After Dad died, Pam felt lost. Mum was grieving. I threw myself into sport. Pam didn't have much to help push through the sadness. She coped the best she could.'

'And now?'

He picked up his keys. 'She is who she is. I'll call you.'

CHAPTER 25

Mother's Day weekend, and I'd slept in. Faarrk!
Thank God Tony was delivering my flowers. Or
rather, Tony's transport guy. I'd received a couple of deliveries
from him already. All good. But the day would really test him.
What if the delivery was made up of half-dead flowers? What if I
got all the ugly, unloved, unsellable flowers? What if...?

I was close to hyperventilating when Mum phoned.

'I'm very upset we won't be seeing you tomorrow, Lil,' she
said.

'It's the busiest weekend of the year.'

'That's what you said about Valentine's Day. You haven't been
home once. Gary misses you.'

That's right. Gary, the dog, missed me, but Mum couldn't
bring herself to say she did.

'Mum, I can't go AWOL on the biggest flower day of the
year.'

It was the truth. Not everyone had a lover or was into the
schmaltz of Valentine's Day, but everyone had a mother, used to
have a mother or was a mother. And the term 'mother' was
broad. There were grandmothers, godmothers, stepmothers,

expectant mothers, pet-mothers. The list went on. I'd already taken several orders to be delivered to the local cemetery, retirement village and hospital. Then there were people like me, the never mothers.

A delivery truck pulled up in front of my shop.

'Mum, the flowers are here. Gotta go. I'll be home for a visit as soon as I can. Promise.'

Minutes later, my shop was blooming with the most gorgeous flowers. I texted Tony straight away.

Thank you. I love them! I love you! Why didn't I do this sooner?

His reply was immediate.

I wish all my customers were as easy to please. Glad to be of service.

Henry was right. Ordering through Tony meant I'd stick to a practical list. I wouldn't overbuy (unless I placed my request after a few wines with Zena and Andy). And the best part? There'd be no more waking up at 3am and fumbling around for clean clothes.

Today's delivery had been triple what I'd normally have purchased, and, in addition to flowers, I bought balloons, vials and oasis blocks.

I was dethorning roses when Taylor rang. I put her on speaker and continued working.

'Hey, stranger,' I said. 'How've you been?'

'Sorry. Lots of work hassles. Listen to this. You'll never guess but Glenn was suspended yesterday pending an investigation.'

I almost gagged. 'You're kidding me? Golden Boy?'

'Yep. Credit card fraud.'

This news warranted stopping dethorning for a moment while it sunk in. 'Shit. Really?'

'Yeah.' She took a breath. 'So, Mother's Day, hey? Sorry I can't be there to help.'

'No worries. You have your own mother to attend to.'

'Don't I know it. What a drama queen. We're going to some fancy restaurant in the city with the brothers and their kids. Ugh!'

'You'll love it.'

'I won't, but Mum will. So, being the good spinster daughter...'

'Any news on the romance front?' I said, stabbing myself in the finger with a thorn.

'My well is still dry. You?'

'Nah. Although—' I was going to tell her about the dinner with Ben but held back. Since being in Adelaide, we'd spoken a couple of times and texted, but he had no idea when he'd be coming back to Clearwater, so it was best I put him out of my mind.

'Although what?'

'Mother's Day has got me thinking, will I ever be a mum? Have I left it too late? Will I always be working?'

What if ... How different would my life had been if I'd gone through with the pregnancy? A one-night stand. I was a virgin. Inwardly, I choked back tears. At least when I found out, I was staying with Aunty Iris. Ashamed, guilty and sad.

'Sweetie, you need your mother,' Iris had said, trying to convince me to tell Mum what had happened.

'I can't. Please don't tell her,' I'd begged in between sobs.

Clearly conflicted, Iris said, 'I don't feel comfortable keeping something this big from Daisy.'

'I'll run away.' I was maniacal. 'You'll never see me again.'

'Lily!'

'I will. You can't tell Mum. She'd never understand.'

Aunty Iris had wrapped herself around me. She kissed my forehead. 'I don't agree, but it's your decision. There are several clinics in Wollongong.'

Years later, I'd wanted to tell Matt, but after I accidentally discovered his views, I could never bring myself to spit the words out.

'That's just you,' said Taylor, pulling me back into the present as my inner dialogue raged. 'You might never slow down. It's not in your nature.' She paused. 'But Lil, you're only thirty...'

'Thirty-one!'

'Okay, thirty-one, there's plenty of time. If you want a kid so badly, you should've gone to Singapore with Matt. You'd probably be knocked up by now.'

If only she knew. I couldn't share. It was too late. 'Well that conversation escalated.'

'You started it.'

'Maybe. Anyway, today isn't the time to think about slowing down or being a barren spinster, not when I have more than thirty bouquets to create.'

'Wow. Go you.'

'Thanks. Give Peggy a kiss for me. Hope she has a lovely Mother's Day.'

'Sell those flowers, and Lil, we should have our kids together.'

'Say that again?'

Taylor laughed. 'Not in that way, obviously. But when the time's right, I'll be cool with being a single mum, even if I don't have a wife. I've got time. So have you.'

I hung up wondering how I could have children if my life was wrapped up in a business that kept me tied up seven days a week? I wanted this flower shop, but was it forever? And after what I'd done to my body, could I have a child even if I wanted to? I had to brush those thoughts away otherwise I became too sad pining for what might have, could have been.

When Aunty Iris called, I put her on speaker, and continued dethorning roses.

'You're back! How was Uluru?'

'Incredible, the spiritual heart of this great land. And it really does glow red at sunset and dawn. Like nothing I've ever seen or will see again.' She sighed wistfully. 'You have to go, Lil. You have to.'

I yawned. 'Will add it on my to-do list.'

'Everything okay, dear? All under control for Sunday?'

'Of course.'

'Confidence. I like that. Mother's Day is a happy time, but you'll also get calls and walk-ins from people who are having their first Mother's Day without their mum, or those mothers who lost a child in the past year.' She took a breath. 'Then there are those wanting to be mothers and trying for a child ... Some people will come into the shop just to talk.'

I thought about Trish. The next day would be hell for Ben and Pamela.

'I don't really have time for that, Aunty Iris.'

'You can't afford not to have time for that. It's far more emotionally charged than any of the other days. I'll be in first thing.'

'Thanks. You always put customers at ease.'

'There's a lot of sadness in people's lives, and unless you know them personally, or have some direct knowledge of their heartache, it's easy to make them feel worse. Being empathetic helps.'

By the time my thirtieth bouquet was finished, I had blisters on my blisters and several empty Red Bull cans littered my workspace.

I glanced at the clock. How had it gotten to six already? I peered outside. It was well after dark and the street lights blazed.

❧

On Sunday morning, Damien, the uni student, and Iris were due at eight. But by seven, several dads and children had already lined up outside.

'Good morning,' I said brightly, opening the door and letting them in. 'I hadn't expected customers so early.'

'We left Mummy in bed, didn't we, boys?' said one very tired-looking dad, struggling with twin boys who seemed about two.

'So did we,' said another father, who had a baby strapped to his chest and was carrying a newspaper and two coffees.

I handed over blooms as quickly as I could to let more people in. It wasn't 7.30am yet and my shop had never been so busy. Just as I thought I might be able to breathe, the ninth dad came in and bought a gorgeous pink hydrangea plant.

I smiled. 'Great choice.' I'd placed several potted hydrangeas and peace lilies out the front and happily, they were selling well.

He handed over thirty-five dollars. 'Yeah, my wife said she didn't want flowers this year, simply for me to take the three kids out for the day.' He pointed to three young children outside who were running in circles around a small furry dog. 'She made it clear that the best gift we could give her today was our absence, but I'll buy her some flowers anyway.'

He walked off just as Iris and Damien arrived.

'Thank goodness you're here. It's been crazy.'

Iris clocked my chalkboard, which said: *I cry at random things, like holding a flower, snuggling my pet rabbit, and hugging my mum. Happy Mother's Day.*

She smiled at me. 'You haven't mentioned the author.'

I smiled back at her. Iris knew me too well.

After putting down her bag, Iris got to work replenishing stock from the cold room while I helped load her station wagon with the first-round of deliveries.

'I'm giving you the easy ones,' I said when I handed Damien the address list. 'I'm not sending you to the cemetery or hospital.'

He grimaced. 'Thanks.'

'Get back here as soon as you can for round two.' Given he was covering a distance of thirty kilometres north-west, and had fifteen deliveries, I'd be lucky to see him in under two hours.

'Looking good,' I said to Iris when I stepped back inside the shop.

'Get ready for another influx,' she said as two new customers came in.

It felt like a few minutes later when I turned around and Damien was standing in front of me. 'Signed, sealed, and delivered,' he said, triumphantly.

I loaded him up with another eleven bouquets and sent him south. It was almost ten thirty.

'Iris, would you be okay if I delivered these,' I said, pointing to several bunches in the cold room. 'To the hospital and cemeteries.' She knew what I meant.

She nodded. 'It should start to ease off soon. Should, darl. Should!'

First up, Verna and I stopped at the cemetery overlooking the ocean. Prime real estate. Several families, couples and singles walked around or sat on the perimeter, staring out to sea. Little posies dotted the gravesites. I distributed three similar flower arrangements.

First up, 'Maria Press, forty-nine, beloved mum to Miranda and Patrick'. Next, Greer Strong, followed by Noni Franks. After I'd placed the three bunches, I took a moment to think about all the people buried here. For a small country town, the cemetery was vast.

Next was the Anglican Church graveyard, then, five deliveries at the hospital, two for the maternity ward and three for general admissions. I didn't realise I'd spent so long with the deceased, so was thankful when the hospital's receptionist said I could leave the flowers with her.

Good. On to the retirement village.

'Hey, Kristi,' I said, as I bowled through the door carrying three large bouquets.

'Goodness, how many more do you have?'

'Two.' I sat them on the welcome table, walked back outside and returned a couple of minutes later. 'Here you go.'

Several ladies came rushing in. I knew most of them by sight. 'Mrs Porter, these are for you,' I said, handing her a huge bunch of chrysanthemums. 'And for you too, Elsie.'

'Ooh, all the way from Queensland! How thoughtful,' she trilled.

Minutes later, they'd all disappeared except for Mrs Porter. 'Everything okay?' I asked.

She nodded, her eyes filling with tears. 'Jacqui only lives down the road. Why couldn't she come and see me?'

I looked at Kristi. She shook her head.

'I haven't seen her for months.'

'Now, now, Mrs Porter,' said Kristi, glancing at me. 'Jacqui visited a couple of weeks ago.'

Poor dear Mrs Porter. I bit my lip. Then thought about my own mother. 'Mrs Porter, maybe Jacqui is working today, or—'

'There's always some excuse. Thank you for my flowers, dear,' she said, patting my arm. 'They're beautiful.'

Just then, Elsie reappeared. 'Come on, Ports, gorgeous flowers, you lucky gal. But it's time for Scrabble. You're on my team today.'

I winked at Elsie. She smiled and said, 'See you tomorrow night at graduation.'

'I'll be up all night rehearsing my steps,' I said. 'I don't want to trip or do something silly.'

With that, they disappeared down the hallway.

☙

By the time I got back, it was close to one o'clock. 'How's it going?' I asked Iris, as she wrapped more posies. 'I see we've sold out of the hydrangeas and lilies.'

She looked up. 'I don't think you'll have much stock left, darl.'

I gazed about the shop. 'Good.'

'Damien's been and gone. I paid him for five hours.'

I took a deep breath. 'Thanks, Iris. I don't know what I would've done without you. I didn't realise the deliveries would take so long or be quite so sad.'

'Emotionally draining, isn't it? But sweetie, you gave yourself the rough end of the stick – cemeteries, hospital and retirement home.'

'That was definitely the saddest. Speaking of which, I still haven't called Mum.'

'The first thing that pops into your mind after the words, retirement home, is your mother? Daisy will skin you alive.'

'It's just that one old lady got upset because her daughter had sent her flowers instead of visiting.'

Iris nodded. 'Happens all the time. You'd better hurry up and call her or you'll never hear the end of it.'

'Mum,' I said, moments later when she answered. 'Happy Mother's Day!'

'Thank you, Lily. I thought you'd forgotten.'

'How could I forget? I'm sorry I couldn't ring earlier. I've been on the go since dawn. Are you having a lovely day?'

'It would be better if you were here.'

I sighed. 'Did you get the flowers I sent?'

'The bunch was so enormous I had to break it into three parts.' She took a moment. 'They're very beautiful.'

'Thanks. I'm sorry I'm not there today. I love and miss you very much.'

At the other end, I could hear Mum catching her breath, as if she might cry. Mum rarely cried; we weren't an overly emotional family. I swallowed, willing her to speak.

Finally she whispered, 'I miss you too, Lil.'

୫

By mid-afternoon the shop was quiet, so Iris and I started tidying up.

'What a day,' I said. 'Good mostly, but also sad and lonely.'

'Mother's Day is a tough one.'

'Yeah,' I said, sweeping the floor. 'I think I did okay with the ordering.'

'You sure did. There's not a lot left over. Thankfully, not many chrysanthemums anyway. A few days into those and the odour starts getting to me.'

'Do you ever regret not becoming a mum?'

Iris stopped mid-way through the cold room entrance. 'Sometimes. It's only natural for a woman to think about such things. But I have so much joy in my life. Good friends, travel, you. There's so much to be thankful for and I choose to focus on that, rather than be angry because I'm not someone's mother. I rather like my life.' She paused a moment. 'And my freedom.'

I wondered whether I'd be so gracious if I didn't end up having children. When I was at university, the thought of having kids was horrifying and even through my late twenties, I was certain I'd be a career lifer. But recently I'd started thinking 'what if?' What if I hadn't had the abortion at sixteen?

'Why, Lily-Pily?' Iris asked. 'Mother's Day throwing up all sorts of questions you'd rather not think about?'

'Something like that. My baby would be almost fifteen.'

'It wasn't the right time, Lil. You were still a baby yourself.'

I wiped at some tears. 'I don't think I'll get the chance now. I blew it.'

'Nonsense. Once you find the right bloke, and the timing's right, those clucky instincts will kick in.'

'You think?'

'Yes.'

'But karma—'

Iris grabbed me, pulling her close to her chest. 'Stop punishing yourself.'

I dried my eyes. 'I did a bad thing.'

'No, you didn't. Please forgive yourself.'

'But—'

'Is this about Matt?'

'What? No. He made a flying visit just after Valentine's, but no.'

'I knew it.'

'How?'

'Who do you think tidied up your apartment before you showed your parents? I could tell something was up. You were completely flustered when we arrived.'

'You? I assumed I'd cleaned up on autopilot that day...' I paused. 'Thank you. Anyway, we're just friends now.'

'They all start out as *just friends*.'

'Well, this time, it's how it's ended. Matt's a city boy.' I fought back tears again. 'And I don't want that life anymore.'

Iris sighed. 'Fair enough, sweetheart. It's your life.'

'Back to you,' I said, sniffing. 'Did your clucky instincts ever kick in?'

'Sure. Several times over several years. Lily...'

'What?'

Iris wiped away tears. 'Women make decisions for all sorts of reasons. Difficult decisions. Try not to judge.'

'I'm not.'

'If we could go back to those moments...'

'Why? What do you think would have happened—'

'If you'd have had that child? Your mum would have gone nuts. And me? I was too afraid at one time, and too old at another.'

When Mike came along, Iris was forty-five. 'It took me a while to find the love of my life and even then, it was only for a while.'

Mike succumbed to lung cancer nine years later and Iris had never re-partnered, not seriously, at least.

We hugged and she blinked away a tear. 'I loved Mike. He would have been an amazing father, but it wasn't meant to be. I have you. And, as I said, my life is full in other ways and I live it to the hilt. Did I tell you I've booked an Alaskan cruise?'

I raised my eyebrows. 'No! Do you ever stop?'

'Plenty of time to rest when I'm dead.'

'I know I'm being selfish here, Aunty Iris, but you had better not be away on Henry and Sophie's wedding day.'

'Of course not. October fourteen. I asked Daisy to join me, but she said she couldn't leave Gary! She can leave your dad, she said, but not the poodle!'

Once old Gary died, Mum would be in for a struggle. I didn't want to think about that day.

'I'm not too late, am I?' said a young man, rushing in. 'Mum's gonna kill me.'

Iris stepped aside, while I sorted out the agitated customer.

'Are you sure you won't stay for dinner?' I asked Iris, when we'd finally closed the door. 'We could go to The Fisherman's Club?'

'Thanks, but I'd better get going,' she said, putting on her coat. 'My eyesight's not what it used to be. I don't like driving at night.'

❧

Not long after Iris left, Zena and Andy turned up. We were all feeling maudlin.

'Mother's Day was a success,' Andy said.

'Yeah, but I haven't visited Mum since I moved here. She's not happy and now I feel really guilty.' I looked at Andy. 'What about you?'

'Mum passed away years ago. That's one of the reasons I moved to Clearwater. I have few ties in Melbourne now.'

'I'm sorry,' I said.

'Hey Mum, dead Mum,' Andy replied.

'What?' asked Zena.

I shook my head. '*Beetlejuice*. Obscure reference.'

He gave me the thumbs up. Zena looked confused.

'Yar,' said Andy. 'Though it was a long time ago, I think about her a lot. I miss her.'

'True, I'm glad my mum is around.'

'My mum was cranky with me too,' said Zena.

I sighed. 'Bit harder for you to fly to Norfolk than for me to drive to Sydney.'

'Yeah, but I haven't been back for over a year.'

We swallowed our drinks in silence.

'Well, this is a bit depressing,' I said to no one in particular. More silence. I was so sad. I'd fucked up my life years ago. I didn't deserve to be a parent. 'I'll add to the pity party by

203

saying that sometimes I wonder if I'll only ever be Trouble's mother.'

Zena nodded. 'I feel the same way. I'd like to have a family one day, but I need a relationship first.' We clinked glasses.

'Tell you the truth,' I said. 'I've always been a bit intimidated by my mother, ever since I was about two. Growing up, the refrain "don't underestimate me, young lady" was something I heard time and time again.'

Zena perked up. 'God, my mum's the same. I swear she has eyes in the back of her head.'

I grinned. 'It's like a sixth sense. I could never outwit my mum. She always knew when I was sneaking extra chocolate biscuits, feeding the dog sausages under the table or silently cursing her.'

'One of my mum's favourites was "Wake up to yourself",' said Zena. 'I thought that was odd.'

Andy smiled. 'Motherisms. When I was four, Mum smacked me and said, "friends don't bite friends".'

I laughed. 'She was right about that. We weren't allowed to say we were bored. Mum would freak out and say, "Bored? I was never bored at your age".'

Zena said, '"If you think you're getting a belly piercing?" or "If you think you're going out with blue nails?" Followed with, "Think again. Over my dead body".' She drained her drink and put the empty glass on my bench. 'I wonder what she'd think if she saw my blue hair?'

'And your dragon,' said Andy.

CHAPTER 26

Taylor turned up to watch Zena and me graduate from tap class.

We were chatting in the dance studio when Zena arrived sporting a hot pink shoe-string flapper dress with a silver sequin trim at the neckline and sparkling silver sequins that peaked through five rows of fringing.

'Wow! You're really aiming to dance and dazzle tonight,' Taylor said.

Zena's smile broadened. 'Hello, stranger! Why are you here?'

Taylor exhaled noisily. 'Why are you both so surprised?'

'It's Monday night for one,' Zena deadpanned.

'To complete your outfit,' I said, once Taylor and Zena had embraced, 'I've got a surprise for you.' I handed her a box. 'Here.'

Zena's eyes widened and she pinched Taylor's arm. 'I thought Taylor was my surprise.' Fumbling, she focused on the box and opened it. 'Oh. My. God! The headpiece. I assumed you thought it was a dumb idea and decided to ignore me.'

'Ignore you, Zena? How could anyone? No, I haven't been feeling creative recently.'

'You could have fooled me.' She squealed, positioning it on her head of blue hair. 'It's divine!'

I adjusted it and Zena looked at herself in the full-length hall mirror before clapping. 'I. Love. It.'

'You certainly look the part, Zena,' said Betty, as she and Elsie sidled up beside us.

Zena giggled. 'That's the aim. Don't you just love the flower crown Lily made for me?'

'It's perfect,' said Elsie. 'I want one.'

I beamed. 'I'll see what I can do. Can you believe we've been coming here these past three months?'

'We've had a ball, haven't we, Betty?' said Elsie.

'I feel bad that April didn't join,' said Betty, 'but her knee's been hurting and she's having heart palpitations.'

'Doesn't sound good,' said Zena.

'You'll both be staying on for Tap Two, won't you?' Elsie smiled.

I cleared my throat and looked at Zena.

'Sure. Why not?' said Zena, happily. 'I'm surprised how much I've enjoyed it. Besides, we've got a month's break before the next course begins.'

'Let's wait and see if we pass this exam,' I said as Miss Liz walked in and "Uptown Funk" started playing. Taylor sat at a bench seat on the side.

She clapped. 'Positions, ladies. We'll start with an easy paradiddle and stomp.'

Miss Liz walked around examining us one at a time. 'Dig, spank, tap, heel. That's right, Betty. Now try it faster.' Miss Liz stood for a moment to observe before moving on to me. 'Remember, loose ankles. Let your knees do the work.' She turned to Zena. 'Nice. Relax your upper body. Natural and loose. That's the way.'

I glanced at Zena and rolled my eyes. Taylor quietly giggled.

An hour later, my feet were killing me. 'Miss Liz, you're one tough tap teacher.'

Miss Liz nodded. 'I am, but you all passed with flying colours. I'm very proud. I hope you'll all sign up for Tap Two.'

Elsie and Betty immediately put up their hands. I groaned.

'Come on, Lil,' said Zena. 'We can't be tap shamed by these two!' She grabbed my hand and raised it in the air. 'We're in.'

'How about we hit the pub to celebrate?' I said as Zena and I left the hall.

Zena looked down at herself. 'In this?'

'Why not? It's not too different from your everyday attire.'

Zena carefully removed her headpiece and examined it. 'Looks like my gorgeous crown will survive to see another day.'

'I'm not sure how long it'll last.'

'Do I need to spray it or something?'

I shrugged. 'Maybe. This is all new to me, but make sure you keep it somewhere cool tonight.'

Settled at a table ten minutes later, Taylor asked how we were getting on after Trish's death.

'Getting better,' said Zena quietly. 'One of the differences here I've noticed, is how after a death, people pull together. In the city, you might get a couple of neighbours offering condolences. Most people are so busy, they forget about the tragedy five minutes later. Not so in Clearwater.'

'I agree,' I said, nodding. 'I think that's partly why I'm so exhausted. All day people come into the shop just to talk. If anything, Trish's death has made me realise I need a mind shift about how I regard people, especially here.'

'How do you mean?' asked Taylor.

'In the city, I'd have been immediately suspicious if a local, say a neighbour, or someone I vaguely knew, had started a conversation with "Just passing..." But in Clearwater, it seems many are just passing and so, drop in.'

'You're wising up,' said Zena. 'I felt a bit like that in the beginning too, then realised that this was my life now and I needed to embrace it and move forward, not keep looking back.'

'I'm trying. People come in to chat, not necessarily to buy flowers. People are always up for a yarn ... all the time, because time has little currency here.'

'I'm used to it,' said Zena. 'On Norfolk, that's all anyone does. Talk, talk, talk. Generally, they're not after anything but companionship. Sometimes sex.' She thought a moment. 'Probably mostly sex.'

'It's so far out of my comfort zone,' said Taylor. 'For me, work in Sydney is the opposite of companionship and chit-chat.'

'So,' said Zena, after a few moments. 'I've been having a few one-on-one conversations with Andy.'

'Do tell,' said Taylor, wide-eyed.

She fiddled with her glass. 'He's easy to talk to.'

'Go for it,' said Taylor. 'What have you got to lose?'

Zena hesitated. 'Not sure.'

I took a deep breath. 'Do you want to be more than friends?' I quizzed.

Zena shook her head. 'I don't know. I haven't got a great track record. Besides, I know.'

'What?'

Zena glared at me. 'You like him. Come on, it's obvious.'

'I've never thought about Andy like that,' I said confidently. Okay, so perhaps fleetingly when he said something mildly amusing and did that thing where his nose twitched. That was endearing.

Zena fiddled with the salt shaker in front of her. 'Besides, he has a beard.'

I sighed. 'Don't be looksist.'

'Or beardist,' Taylor chipped in.

I thought for a moment. 'I do think he's lovely.'

'Yeah well...' Zena said, gulping her wine.

'Ask him out,' I pushed, thinking about Ben, trying to make us work. Inwardly, I cursed myself. 'You have to eat. Or a movie? That's non-threatening.'

'Maybe he's not your type,' Taylor mused.

'Exactly,' Zena agreed. 'And say we did have dinner? What next? What if it didn't work out? Then where would I be? Humiliated, again.'

'Who's to say he'd be the one in charge?' I said, pouring more wine. 'The one calling the shots.'

'Because that's what men do. Also, he works across the road from me.'

'Beside the point,' I said. 'What if Andy falls head over heels and you don't?'

Zena shook her head.

'It's entirely possible. You're loveable.'

'Yes,' Taylor concurred. 'Totally loveable.'

Zena shook her head. 'Dial it down, girlfriends. I couldn't imagine Andy falling *head over heels*. In fact, the idea's ludicrous.'

'So, you're going to do nothing?' I asked.

'Correct. If you think I'm going to offer myself to him, I'm not.'

'How will you know if you don't give it a go?' I pressed.

'She said no, Lil,' Taylor said matter of factly.

'Exactly. I'm seriously not having this conversation.' Zena dusted her hands together, thus putting an end to the conversation.

'Okay,' I agreed, rubbing my ankles. 'Your life.'

CHAPTER 27

The following Friday, even though my feet had aged twenty years, I was still smiling. Until Pamela walked in.

She glanced at Trouble. 'Still got the mangy rodent, I see.'

Trouble twitched and ran underneath his hutch.

I forced myself to smile. 'How are you this bright autumn day, Pamela?'

'Sorting through rental contracts.'

I gulped. 'Ah, well you don't have to worry about mine. It's fixed for twelve months with an option to sign for another year.'

She handed me a letter. 'For the foreseeable future, I'll be looking after Mum's business. You're now my tenant.'

I nodded. 'Great.'

Pamela stared around the shop. 'You're on a very good rate.'

'Which I appreciate, and one which the owners of this building agreed to,' I said quickly. 'Starting a new business, I need all the breaks I can get.'

'My mother was generous. Too generous with the terms. The office hasn't made a profit for years. But that's all about to change. I've been in contact with the owners. They're happy for me to charge more rent where I see fit.'

I calmed myself before I spoke. 'What do you mean?'

'There's a clause that allows amendments when real estate ownership changes.'

'But it hasn't, has it? Not yet?'

Pamela looked me up and down. 'You forget, Lily, I'm city through and through, just like you. I work in the corporate world, like you did. I know how to work the system.'

My hands trembled, but I stood my ground. 'While you're here, could I get a plumber in to check my toilet? It's been temperamental since I moved in. Maybe we need to get it replaced. There are several other issues as well—'

'I'll look into it.' Pamela walked out, leaving me stunned and angry.

What a first-class bitch. I wanted to throw something. My phone rang, and I answered it without looking at the number.

'Lily, Lily, Lily.'

'Taylor, Taylor, Taylor. Why don't you just move down here and be done with it. You know you want to.'

'You jest, but I call bearing good news. Glenn was sacked an hour ago.'

'No!'

'Yep. The credit card thing. He tried to blame it on his wife by saying his personal and corporate card were both the same colour and that the bulk of the expenses claimed were accidentally placed on the corporate card rather than his personal card.'

'No way!'

'Way. Alastair kind of bought that, but coupled with growing complaints from clients, the board was forced and Alastair happily agreed.'

'So Golden Boy turned out to be faux gold?' Yes! I smiled, breathing deeply. My instincts had been right all along. 'What are they going to do?'

'Who knows? It's a huge mess. I'm sure if you called—'

'I have a flower shop,' I said in a sing-song voice. 'Why don't you city folk get that?'

'I do, but you mentioned before that you were worried about money, so—'

'I'm happy here, as you well know. Let some other sucker get gobbled up by a greedy corporation.'

'Hey, careful. I'm one of those suckers.'

'There's always room for you down here, Taylor. The Clearwater pizzeria's for sale.'

'I'll keep it in mind. I do love it down there, a world away from Sydney.'

'Ha! Your mother would never forgive me if you moved here.'

'Yeah, but imagine the bitch sessions Mum and Daisy could have?' She took a moment. 'How's it going?'

'Not much since you saw me Tuesday morning, except that Ben's sister, The Bitch, wants to put my rent up.'

'She can't do that, can she?'

'I don't think so, so I'm going to try not to let it worry me. In other news, I've spent the better part of the week investigating the floral headband market.'

Taylor giggled.

'Don't laugh. It's a thing, besides, you liked the one I made for Zena.'

'I did actually. Not for me, but it suited Zena's quirkiness.' She paused.

'You have a thing for her.'

'What? No. Definitely not.'

'Right.'

'Please come home,' Taylor said, changing the subject.

'You sound like my mother.'

'Yes, well your mum, me and corporate Sydney need you.'

'Why, yes, of course. Thirty seconds ago, you did a perfect

sell job. I'd be crazy not to come back.' I laughed. 'I've grown my hair. It's wild and free, like me. I'll never wear a charcoal or navy suit again. Probably never even a suit!'

After the phone call, I thought more about Taylor's suggestion and shook my head. I really did love my shop and Clearwater. I was proud to have created the business by myself, as opposed to running someone else's business for them. Also, did Taylor have a thing for Zena?

'Friday evening greetings,' Zena said, strolling through the door with Andy on the nose of 6pm. She held up a bottle of white wine, as a dozen or more colourful bracelets rattled on her wrist. 'Courtesy of Steve at the Bottle-O.'

I smiled. 'Where would you be without your contra deals?'

'Sober?' said Andy without missing a beat.

'Exactly.'

'Don't knock it,' said Zena. 'Just because Steve doesn't want your flowers.'

'Whatever.' I grabbed three glasses and Zena opened the bottle and poured us each a glass while I told them about Pamela's visit. 'She can't really put the rents up, can she?' I asked.

Zena shook her head. 'I don't know why she's intent on causing mayhem.'

'Because she's a greedy unscrupulous bitch,' said Andy.

'Well, she's not going to bully me. I signed a contract,' I said.

'Exactly,' said Zena. 'Still, I'm glad I have a rental agreement directly with the owner and not with her.'

'Same,' said Andy.

Zena sipped her drink. 'I've been meaning to tell you, Lil, my headband was a huge hit! The salon ladies have been asking when I'm going to wear another one. Not to mention all the high school girls.'

'I know.' I pointed to a stack of half completed headpieces on my bench. 'I've had a dozen requests from giggling girls

"desperate" for them for their school dance this Saturday night.
Tiaras, crowns, and hair clips, and everything from fairy themed
and daisy chains, to rose ones like yours. So ... guess what I'll be
doing for the rest of the night.'

Zena smiled. 'You're welcome.'

'Yeah, they're great for special events like the dance, but if
people want them as keepsakes or to wear them regularly as
statement pieces—'

'Like me.'

'They'll need to be sturdier. I've sourced some silk flowers
online.'

'Are they a bit...' Zena hesitated, 'tacky?'

I shook my head. 'You can be the judge when I present you
with my next creation.'

'Goody,' Zena trilled.

'But for now,' I said, taking empty glasses from Zena and
Andy's hands, 'I need to get on with making the real thing.'

'Are you trying to get rid of us?' Andy asked.

'Not at all, but I'm way behind. Why don't you two go out to
dinner? I'll only drag you down, hanging around here.' I
practically pushed them out the door. 'Have fun, kids.'

An hour later, nine headbands completed, and another glass
of wine down, I was still feeling unsettled. I called Henry. 'I'm
sorry to call on a Friday night.'

'No problem, Lily. What's up?' Henry's friendship put me at
ease.

'Pamela came into the shop a couple of hours ago. I'm
worried she's going to hike up my rent.'

'I've been hearing stories about this all over town.' He
waited. 'But I truly believe Pamela's all bluster. Out to make a
point. Trish was a good businesswoman. I'm sure her contracts
are tight, both with renters like yourself and with property

owners. But if you need a good lawyer, I can point you in the direction of my cousin—'

'How many relatives do you have around here?'

Henry chuckled. 'You'd be surprised.'

'It's hard to believe Ben is Pamela's brother. He's so nice and normal and she's—'

'Difficult?'

'Something like that.'

'Seriously, if Pamela does anything more than threaten, call Teddy. I'll text you his details.'

I hung up feeling slightly better. If all the shopkeepers banded together, surely we could take her on. Strength in numbers and all that. Then there was Ben. We'd been regularly texting and he'd sent several photos of his South Australian winery. He hadn't mentioned Pamela but I wondered if he knew what she was up to.

CHAPTER 28

Andy

'Lily threw us out,' Andy said to Zena as they stood on the pavement outside Lily's shop.

'She's very rude,' Zena agreed. 'Should we grab something to eat?'

'Sure. Though I'm not up for the pub—'

'Another night, perhaps?'

Andy hesitated, not sure what to do. 'You could come back to mine. I have plenty of food ... and wine.'

Zena smiled. 'Thought you'd never ask.'

They walked in happy companionship for fifteen minutes, chatting about their respective days.

'What do you think of Ben?' Zena asked.

Andy stopped walking and turned to her. 'Why? You fancy him?'

Zena threw her head back. 'No, but maybe Lily does. She had dinner with him.'

Andy took a moment. 'And?'

'He's Pamela's brother.'

'We shouldn't judge people by their relatives.'

'I guess not. He seems cool.'

They stopped at Andy's front gate. 'I can't believe you've never invited me over before,' Zena said, staring into the massive front yard.

'I thought you'd assume I had ulterior motives.'

'Do you?'

Andy shook his head and held the gate open as Zena walked through. He showed her around his garden. Camellias, lemon trees, azaleas.

'It's like an estate. So grown-up.' She laughed. 'And the view!'

'Yeah, can't complain.' He guided her around the side. 'The back garden leads to a reserve and then down to the beach.'

Zena whistled. 'Wow. This is amazing. I'm impressed and a little overwhelmed.'

'This is my pride and joy.' Andy stopped walking and pointed at his vegetable patch. The moonlight shone on spinach, lettuce and tomatoes.

'Quite the green thumb, aren't you?' she said.

Short of breath, Andy replied, 'Full-time job keeping the rabbits away.'

She laughed. 'Trouble would love this.'

Andy took her hand. 'Be careful,' he said by way of an explanation. 'The outside light bulb has blown. It's easy to trip in the dark.' He led her inside the house.

Andy enjoyed being close to Zena, the intake of her perfume, her candour. He wasn't sure how it happened, but suddenly they were inside the doorway kissing. Pulling back, he switched the light on.

Zena sighed. 'Way to kill the mood.'

'I can turn it off again if you prefer,' he said, hesitating in the middle of the hall. Though his mind was on Lily, he wrapped his arms around Zena's waist and nuzzled her ears.

Moments later, they were on Andy's bed with Zena straddling him, both still fully clothed, as they kissed. Andy enjoyed the spontaneity and unexpected passion, but it didn't feel right. Zena was a friend first and foremost, and he liked it that way. He stopped kissing and pulled back. Immediately, Andy felt her body stiffen as she rolled off and to the other side of the bed, her back to him.

Andy wasn't sure how long he'd been quiet when Zena spoke. 'Everything okay?'

He swallowed hard. 'I like you, Zena, but—'

'Your heart is elsewhere?'

'I'm not sure.' Andy was sure. He liked Lily. 'I like you as a friend.'

She sat upright on the edge of the bed, and twisted her torso towards him. 'Worst thing ever you can say to a girl who's in your bed.'

Andy moved closer to her and stroked her cheek. 'Not if he means it and intends said girl to be his long-term, lifetime friend.'

'If we're being honest,' said Zena, 'I still have a few issues with Nate.'

Andy nodded. 'What are you going to do about him?'

'Truthfully, I want it to be over once and for all. But he keeps turning up.'

'You need to lock your doors.'

Zena hugged her arms. 'I should go before it gets awkward.'

'Let me at least make you dinner.'

Thirty minutes along, they were eating fresh prawn pasta with spicy chilli tomato sauce.

'If I'd have known earlier that this was the kind of friendship we could have,' said Zena, sucking up a spaghetti strand, 'I would have wrangled an invite a long time ago.'

'Are we okay?'

Zena nodded. 'I don't regret kissing you, if that's what you're asking.'

Andy grinned. 'I don't regret it either.' He didn't feel uncomfortable. Well, maybe a little awkward. More importantly, their friendship had moved to a new level of trust and comfort.

'I hope this isn't the equivalent of a walk of shame,' Zena said as they arrived at her cottage at 9pm.

Andy shook his head and brushed Zena's cheek with the side of his hand. 'No. I drove you home, so if anything, it's the drive of shame.'

She punched him on the shoulder. 'Not remotely funny. You sure we're good? You're not going to blank me in the street, are you?'

'Never.'

'The girl who snags you is a lucky one,' said Zena.

As Zena got out of his car, Andy noticed Pamela drive past. 'The wicked witch of Clearwater.'

'That's putting it kindly.'

He nodded. 'Still good for Friday night drinks?'

Zena giggled. 'Naked or clothed?'

'You choose,' Andy said, before driving home. No awkwardness, just banter, the way it should be.

❦

In his shop the following day, Andy absent-mindedly sketched a winter beach scene. When he put down his pencil, he decided to check in with Zena to make sure she really was okay after the previous night. He needed a strong black and he'd buy her a soy latte.

'Here you go,' he said as he walked into her salon and handed Zena a coffee. 'You scrub up well.'

Zena twirled. 'Why thank you. Bit haphazard,' she said, touching her hair, 'but I couldn't be late for Mrs Beattie.' She raised her eyebrows. 'You were already waiting before I opened the salon, weren't you?'

'Morning, Mrs Beattie.' Andy beamed.

'Morning, love.' Mrs Beattie settled in at the basin for her regular wash and eyed Zena thoughtfully. 'You've a spring in your step today, my girl.'

Zena turned to face her. 'Have I?'

'You know you do. I see your hair's still blue.' Clearly, Mrs Beattie wasn't overly enthusiastic about Zena's colour.

Zena laughed. 'Is it? I haven't noticed.'

Andy was enjoying their camaraderie when Pamela strode in. What on earth was she wearing? It resembled the black rubber of inner tyre lining.

'You were up and about late last night,' Pamela said, marching up to Andy with Edie beside her, smoking a cigarette.

Andy bristled. Pamela smiled.

Zena continued washing Mrs Beattie's hair. 'Can I help you with anything?'

'Have you met my friend, Edie?' Pamela said to Zena, gesturing to Edie. 'She's here for the weekend, tying up loose ends.'

Edie laughed. 'You're the famous Zena?'

'You shouldn't be smoking in here.' Zena turned back to Mrs Beattie.

'Always a pleasure being in Clearwater.' Edie smirked,

cigarette ash falling on the salon floor. 'You definitely weren't around when I was here.'

Andy was horrified.

Zena looked up. 'You lived here?'

Edie nodded as she fingered the flower display, before picking off a leaf and stubbing out her cigarette on it. 'Biggest mistake of my life.'

'I have to get back to the shop.' Andy made a move to leave.

Pamela rubbed Edie's arm. 'Zena, about Andy, he's a bit old for you, isn't he? I'm sure you could find a local labourer or mechanic to amuse yourself with.'

'Yes,' said Edie. 'What do you really know about Andy?'

Zena glanced at her client before speaking. 'I really don't think this is the time or place, so if you'll excuse me—'

'Don't mind me,' Mrs Beattie chimed in. 'No problems here.'

'No, no,' said Pamela sweetly. 'I don't mean to intrude. Just looking out for you, Zena. I'd hate to see you get hurt.'

Zena scowled. 'You don't know me.' She directed Mrs Beattie to a chair in readiness for her blow-dry.

Through the mirror, Andy watched as Pamela and Edie walked out of the salon. He imagined hurling Zena's sharp and pointy scissors into Pamela's back and seeing her collapse.

Zena glared at him. 'What was that about?'

Andy shook his head. 'Long story. Tell you later.' With that, Andy and his half-empty and cold coffee left the salon. Wavering on the pavement, he came face to face with Edie. Again.

'She's too young for you, Andy. What were you thinking? You're an embarrassment, a lech. You should be run out of town.'

Andy's mind blanked. He was back inside their bleak marital home with Edie abusing him. His arms shook.

'You're pathetic!' Edie screamed. 'Look at yourself.'

Andy glanced at his crumpled shirt and jeans. He felt like an orphan being berated by the headmistress. Try as he might, his counsellor's advice wasn't doing him any favours. A small crowd gathered to witness his mortification and terror.

Zena strode towards them. 'Hey! What do you think you're doing?'

'As for you,' said Edie, wheeling around. 'You should be ashamed of yourself.'

'Who are you?' Zena said, looking to Andy for support. 'Andy?'

Andy shook his head. 'It's nothing.'

'You know exactly what's going on, Andy.' Pamela was clearly enjoying the spectacle.

'What *is* going on?' Zena demanded.

'None of your business,' Edie growled. 'You have no idea what this man is capable of!' she shouted, pointing at Andy. 'He's a monster who takes advantage of vulnerable women.' She stared straight at Andy. 'They should never have let you out.'

Lily came out from her flower shop and put her arm around Zena.

'You're an adulterer, Andy!' Edie screeched. 'You're married to me!'

Andy dropped his coffee and it splattered on the ground around him. He couldn't believe what he'd just heard. 'We're not! Don't be ridiculous.'

'No!' said Zena, gasping for breath.

'Yes,' said Edie, triumphantly. 'I have the papers to prove it. You're a married man, Andy Peterson.'

Edie marched down the road with Pamela, leaving Andy fuming with rage and humiliation. What game were Edie and Pamela playing? Why were they doing this and what the hell was Edie on about? They were divorced and had been for over four years. Still, his feet tapped the pavement and nausea welled in his stomach.

'Andy?' said Zena, her voice shaking. 'Are you okay? Can I do anything to help?'

'I'm so sorry,' he said, walking away. 'I can't talk about this right now. I have to get it sorted.'

If he didn't leave immediately, he felt sure he'd vomit or worse. Once the nausea subsided and his heart rate returned to a manageable level, the rage would build. He needed to make sure that didn't happen.

CHAPTER 29

Lily

I stood on the pavement, hugging Zena, numb and lost for words. 'You okay?' I finally managed.

She stared at me, red-faced with bloodshot eyes. She shook her head. 'Andy's married. I can't believe it.'

'He said he wasn't,' I said, shocked.

Andy was talking to Barry. Or Barry was talking to Andy. They had their backs turned, which made it difficult to tell.

'Can I get you something?' I asked. 'Coffee? Vodka?'

'No,' Zena answered slowly. 'I...' she paused, looking towards her salon.

'Crap!' I said. 'The shop.' Zena and I darted in opposite directions.

Before I walked back inside, I saw Barry put Andy in his car and drive away. That strange woman and Andy ... married? So many questions, starting with what was going on between Andy and Zena?

Zena walked in mid-afternoon. 'I couldn't stay at the salon any longer. I closed up. My hands are shaking. Pamela and that Edie woman are terrifying. Poor Andy.'

Zena looked even worse than she had on the street.

'Still, I've brought wine,' she said, cry-smiling, and plonking down on a rickety wooden stool beside the bench. 'I had a disaster colouring Sally's hair. It looked horrendous. Instead of putting in ten vols of peroxide, I used forty.'

I handed Zena a glass of wine. 'Ouch.'

'Ouch exactly. Sally was on target to leave the salon with coarse hair the colour of an orangutan, instead of a luscious shade of caramel brown.'

'I rushed her to the basin and it went green.' Zena gulped her wine. 'I had head spins, heart palpitations. I even silently prayed.'

'A big call for a devout atheist.'

'Yeah. Anyway, I toned and treated her hair. Fifteen minutes later, Sally's hair was on the floor and she was bald.'

I almost spat out my drink. 'What?'

'Not really, but after a hell of a lot of toner, her hair looked normalish. Not great, but not completely frightening. I got her out the door as quick as I could and offered her a free colour touch up and blow-dry, next week.'

Zena sniffed. 'How could I have been so careless? I can't afford to make mistakes like that.' She wiped away tears. 'Have you seen him?'

I shook my head. 'Andy and Barry drove off, just afterwards, but not since then. He might have gone home. I don't think he's been back at his shop.'

'Do you really think he's married?' Zena was staring at the floor.

'I don't know,' I answered truthfully. 'That woman certainly thinks so. But maybe she's some whacko stalker. Who knows?'

Zena shook her head. 'She's Pamela's friend. Said she used to live here.'

'And?'

'For someone so set in his routine, so seemingly predictable ... I just...' Zena started crying. 'Men. I don't get them.'

I wrapped my arms around her. I agreed but knew saying so wouldn't be helpful.

'And, after last night...' Zena said.

'Yes,' I said, remembering Edie's words. 'What about last night?'

Zena wiped her nose on her shirt sleeve. 'God, I'm pathetic.'

I fossicked under the bench and produced a box of tissues. 'No, you're not. What's going on?'

Zena took a deep breath and sipped her wine.

I stared, unblinking.

'You were the one who pushed us together by throwing us out onto the street.' Zena was being melodramatic, but I let it go. 'My head's throbbing. I want to throw up. I'm an idiot.'

I handed her two Panadol and a glass of water. 'Drink!'

She did as she was told. 'Thanks. I don't know why I'm so worked up. Andy and I are just friends.'

I wanted to quiz her, but before I could, she started talking again.

'I keep checking my phone for messages. Nothing.' She shook her head.

I turned on my chair. 'There must be an explanation. It doesn't make sense.' I dialled his number, but it went straight to voicemail.

'I want to throw things. I'm so confused.'

I spied Trouble sleeping underneath his hutch, well out of harm's way. 'Why don't you spend the night here? I'll whip up some pasta, we'll watch *The Notebook*, cry, drink wine, cry more and then sleep. Tomorrow is another day.'

Zena drained her drink. 'Thanks, but—'

'*Beaches*?'

Zena shook her head. 'Again, thanks, but I didn't get much sleep last night so...'

'Lucky you. I'm sure Andy has a logical explanation, like he's separated and just hasn't told anyone.'

'It's not like that. Andy doesn't want to go out with me. Then again, why would he want to be with a blue-haired hairdresser? Look what happened with Nate and my other disasters. Perhaps all I deserve are surfer pot-heads.' Zena was rambling. In shock.

I dialled his number again. 'No answer.' I rubbed her back. 'A good night's sleep will make all the difference.'

'Yeah, you're probably right.'

As Zena was about to leave, my phone rang. I glanced at the caller I.D. 'It's Andy.'

'Quick, answer it.'

'Oh, Andy ... Are you okay?' I said. Pause. 'Aha ...Yes ... Okay ... Okay ... Bye.' After a moment I said, 'He's at some sort of medical clinic.'

'What? Like a hospital? Is he okay? Did he have an accident?'

'No accident. I think it's like a hospital but a private one. He promised he'll call and explain everything when he can. Said it was too hard to talk now. But his tone was dull and distant. Clinical, like he could have been talking to his therapist or a nurse.'

Zena left and, I texted Andy, R U OK?

A Mormon just believes.

Okay, Elder Price. *Running with the theme.* Are you a Mormon?

No, I'm not.

I wiped my brow. Just an idiot? I hope you're okay.

Yeah. Talk to you when I get back.

As I was throwing together a Greek salad, my phone buzzed. I hoped it would be Zena, but it was a text message from Ben.

Hey Lily, bloody boiling in Adelaide. Miss your smiling face. Back in C soon. Would like to see you. X

I felt a rush of happiness. Then guilt. Zena and Andy were miserable, and I was giddy, but confused. I was happy about seeing Ben, but in my heart, I wanted to see Andy.

CHAPTER 30

Andy

Andy's roommate at the clinic, Justin, had a T-shirt featuring a cat's head and the words *Ceiling Cat Is Watching You.* Underneath, he wore only briefs. Some shorts would have been nice.

'You like?' Justin stepped back so Andy could climb out of bed.

'Yeah, sure,' Andy said. 'What's new pussycat?'

'Cats are everywhere,' Justin continued, ignoring Andy. 'They're watching us. You know that, right? You like cats?' Yesterday, Justin had worn a shirt with a bubble coming out of the cat's head, sprouting the words *'Resistance Is Feline'*.

'I love cats. Who doesn't?' Andy could have gone on about *Cats, the Musical* but chose to be kind.

'Exactly, my man. Exactly.' Justin nodded.

The wall beside Justin's bed was covered in posters of cats – Egyptian cats, Roman cats. Interesting. He couldn't add value to the conversation. He hadn't known the difference between a Birman and a Burmese until Justin gave him *the talk* the previous night ... a solid one-hour lecture.

How had it come to this? Again? One moment, Andy had been happily going about his business, glad that he and Zena were friends after their night together, and the next, he was in the middle of a street war, being abused by Edie.

Afterwards, he'd been a shaking furious mess. Unsafe thoughts raged through his mind. He'd wanted to a punch a wall or worse. Why couldn't those women leave him alone? Knowing where this could lead, he rang Joanne, his therapist, and two hours later, checked out of Clearwater and into a private clinic.

This morning, Andy felt surprisingly calm. He showered, dressed and walked to the communal hall for breakfast. Joanne was coming in to see him that afternoon. Before that, he had to endure a compulsory group session.

An hour later, he sat in a meeting room waiting for the session to begin. Four others played cards. A lot of patients seemed to have an addiction to cards ... okay, so they weren't allowed to use the word *addiction*, but many played cards for hours at a time.

A booming voice called out, 'Cheat!'

Andy rolled his eyes.

'Who you calling a cheater?'

'I'm calling you a cheater! Cheater!'

It was the kind of exchange that would be hilarious on YouTube, if it weren't so sad.

'Hey, hey,' said a guy walking into the room. He looked about Andy's age, had a slicked back ponytail and wore dark jeans and a chequered navy shirt. 'What's going on?'

Someone mumbled something about 'duplicitous double-dealing'. Another mentioned 'dishonest, deceitful fraud', but the ruckus quickly settled.

He walked over to Andy and held out his hand. 'Nick Morris, I'll be taking this morning's session.'

Andy stood up and shook his hand. 'Andy Peterson.'

Minutes later, the group of eight sat in a semicircle, asking questions, mostly directed to the new guy. Andy.

He wiggled his toes and squeezed his hands together, all calmness evaporated. He shook his head to relieve his looming headache. He would have been better staying at home. Andy glanced at the scars on his left hand and arm, his constant reminder of a pain he never wanted to feel again.

Excruciating memories of Edie's tantrums exploded in his head – Edie yelling at him, hurling vile abuse. When he shut down and refused to participate in her outbursts, which he had resorted to late in their marriage, she scratched him and pulled his hair. His neck hurt just as it had when Edie grabbed him by the throat and dug her nails into his flesh. Horrible. The times he had to wear turtlenecks or scarves to disguise his injuries were countless. Then there was the hair pulling. Hair pulling didn't leave visible scars.

She'd finally sent him over the edge when she stubbed out a cigarette on the back of his hand. It took all of his self-control not to hit her. There was no excuse for hitting another person. Ever. But he still hadn't gotten over the feeling of wanting to punch her and keep going until she was dead. Instead, he'd thrown his coffee cup at her and fled, locking himself in their bathroom where he'd punched out a window. Yes, she'd had a hard life. Yes, as a child, she'd been abused. But understanding her behaviour didn't excuse it.

He'd admitted himself to hospital and two weeks later, told Edie their marriage was over. He moved out of their home that same day. Andy wanted a divorce. Edie was ropable because her control over him had come to an end, or so he thought. He vividly remembered that horrible final meeting where he'd signed the divorce papers and she'd insisted she deal with the solicitors from there because she was 'a professional'. What had gone wrong? How could he still be married to her?

Back in the semicircle, people kept throwing questions at him.

'Are you thinking about suicide?'

'Do you want to shoot yourself in the heart?'

'Stab yourself in your throat?'

'Cut your wrists?'

'Slash your balls?'

'Overeat?'

'Okay, guys,' said Nick, 'that's enough. Let's talk.' He searched the room. 'Who wants to start?'

Definitely not Andy.

The guy beside Andy turned to him. 'Do you remember *Get Smart*?'

Andy nodded.

Justin sighed theatrically.

'It's just like that, the cone of silence,' his neighbour explained.

'Except there is no cone,' said Justin.

'I said it's *like* the cone, Catwoman.'

Nick Morris looked towards the ceiling, seemingly for divine guidance, then back down at the group. 'What Ian's trying to say, is that what's said here in the group, goes no further.'

Andy made sure it went no further by saying very little.

By the time he'd been for a short walk and eaten a salad and egg sandwich for lunch, Joanne, his psychologist, had arrived.

'Thanks for coming, Jo.' They sat down at a table in the sunshine where they couldn't be overheard.

'What happened?'

'My ex-wife happened.'

Joanne raised her eyebrows. 'Edie?'

'How many ex-wives do you think I have? Yes, Edie.'

'You knew there might come a time when she'd reappear.'

'That's not the worst of it. She said we're still married.'

'Is that true?'

Andy shook his head. 'I signed the papers. I don't know what she's on about. She attacked me in the middle of the street. Zena was there. Then Lily appeared, along with the rest of Clearwater. I rang you, and, well, here we are.'

'Do you think you overreacted?'

Andy shrugged. 'Really? Overreacted? Yes. I could have stayed and confronted Edie. Explained to the township. But I ran away.' He thought for a moment. 'At the very least I should have taken the time to really speak to Zena and Lily and explain the situation to them.'

'You did what you needed to do at the time, and there was a spare bed here. You can go home tomorrow if you like.'

'Not today?'

'Afraid not. It's a two-night minimum.'

Andy nodded. 'Quite the B & B.'

'Funny. We need to discuss strategies. You need to talk to Edie. Do you have a copy of the divorce papers?'

'I'm not sure. I thought I did, but I can't think where I put them. I think they're with my property deeds, so am assuming my solicitor has them.'

Joanne nodded. 'You can't move forward with your future happiness without confronting Edie and putting the past behind you.'

Andy winced.

'Sorry, but that's the way it's got to be.'

Andy sighed. 'I want to get back to normal. A normal I'm used to and can manage.'

'Andy World?'

'What's wrong with Andy World?'

He liked Joanne. She was a straight-shooter. He never felt judged. Everyone was going through crap, and whilst everyone's crap was different, it was still crap. Joanne never made Andy feel like he was the only crazy person on the block.

'Let's keep things in perspective, Andy,' she continued. 'You're not having a bad life, you're just having a bad few days. You know what, or rather *who*, has caused them. Yes, you need to deal with Edie, but you also need to live your life one day at a time, not live in the past or worry too much about the future.'

Andy nodded. He knew the drill. Depression was all about dwelling on the past; anxiety centred around future worries and expectations. He was despondent. Teary. Heart palpitations. A grave sense of foreboding. Really he just wanted to curl up into a ball and cry.

He hated Edie, but where had hate ever got him? Just more angst and fear. Edie and Pamela were destructive people who were only ever happy when making others miserable.

'Let's talk about Edie.'

He sighed. 'Let's not. Once, there was a time when I loved Edie, or thought I did.

Back in the day, when she wasn't on the war path, she was a wonderful companion. Warm, funny, empathetic. It didn't last long, probably ran out of steam even before we were married.'

Joanne nodded, drawing him back into the conversation. 'Let's be proactive. Confront Edie. If she won't listen, hire a lawyer and find out what's the story with the divorce. Next, talk to your friends. Trust them. Explain what's going on, once you find out. But most importantly, you need to take care of yourself.'

'I want to go home. I'll talk to Edie. If we're not legally divorced, I'll make it happen.'

Didn't everyone come with a certain amount of baggage? Andy's suitcases were stuffed to capacity but with a bit of help, he could cast off the past and move forward. He had to believe it was possible.

§❧

Andy walked into Lily's shop late Monday afternoon, soon after he checked out of the clinic. Zena was also there but refused to look at him. After less than five hours' sleep, he was running on empty. He'd had about ten hours sleep in the last two nights. But the sooner he explained to Lily and Zena, the stronger he'd feel. He hoped.

'Andy.' Lily hugged him. 'How are you?'

'Okay. I don't want to interrupt, but I just wanted to talk about—'

'Of course,' Lily replied, cutting him off. 'Zena and I wanted to see you too.'

Thirty minutes later, Andy, Zena and Lily were at The Fisherman's Club drinking beer while Andy ate steak and chips. It had been a long time since he'd eaten red meat.

Zena looked away most times they made eye contact. Lily seemed more forgiving.

Zena speared a piece of salt and pepper squid, put it in her mouth and chewed. 'We were really worried about you.'

'I'm sorry I lost it. I had to go somewhere where I could ... centre myself. Regroup. You saw what happened.'

'Yes, Edie.' Lily paused. 'I know you're going through shit now—'

'It's more than shit.'

'I know,' Lily said. 'How can we help?'

Andy shook his head. 'If I knew the answer to that...'

'I get it.' Zena rolled her eyes and waved her hands in the air. 'You're emotionally fragile. Well, you know what, Andy? So are a lot of us. We're all fragile.'

LISA DARCY

'You don't understand. I didn't know I was still married. I signed divorce papers, for God's sake. If you'll let me explain—'

Zena stood up out of her chair. 'I'm going to stop you right there. I don't want to know any more. I know enough.' She grabbed her bag. 'No wonder you didn't want to pursue a relationship with me. You're already married.'

Lily reached out to Zena. 'Let him explain.'

Andy shrugged. 'I didn't question that I wasn't divorced. Why would I? I assumed I was. I've been spending time focusing on my own mental health and well-being.'

'I've got a full day tomorrow, Andy. I'm tired and I've got a headache.' She shook her head and wiped tears from her cheeks. 'I need time to process. I've got to go.'

Andy and Lily watched as Zena walked out the door.

'I should go after her.' Andy went to stand but Lily spoke.

'Let her go. She needs time to cool off and you need to eat.' Lily pointed to his half-eaten meal.

But Andy had no appetite.

'We don't have to talk about what's going on between you and Zena. Is there anything you do want to talk about?'

Andy forked a couple of chips. 'I know you're shocked, but I thought I was divorced. So Edie telling me that we aren't ... well, I'm having difficulty processing that information.'

'Understatement,' said Lily.

Andy nodded. 'Until two days ago, I had no idea I could still be married. But I guess that's what I got for trusting her.'

'Instead, she ambushed you on the street and accused you of adultery.'

Andy drained his beer. 'Something like that.'

CHAPTER 31

Lily

Zena was wrapped in a navy towel, red eyes, puffy face, and dishevelled hair when she answered the door an hour later.

I hugged her. 'Given your state when you left the club, I wanted to check in. How are you?'

Nate wandered up the hall with a bottle of red wine. He had a matching towel draped around his torso. 'Babe, who is it?'

'Sorry,' I stammered. 'I should've called.'

Zena turned around to face him. 'Go away, Nate. I'll be back in a minute.' She turned back to me. 'I can explain.'

'I don't need an explanation. Just wanted to make sure you're okay. *Are* you okay?'

'Not really. But...' She paused. 'It's not what it looks like.'

'Zena, it's all right. I'm not your mother. As long as you're fine.'

'When I got back, Nate was here, a man with no strings, no

history, and no wife.' She half smiled. 'I guess I'm not sticking to my celibacy-until-July plan.'

৫৯

Tuesday morning at work, Sophie stepped through the doorway carting a book labelled *Weddings*. 'Bet you thought I'd forgotten about coming in.'

I could barely remember our dinner. So much had happened since then, the evening was almost a blur.

'For the next few weeks, my afternoons are going to be taken up rehearsing the infants' musical item for this term,' she said. 'From experience, I can tell you how difficult it is to wrangle twenty six-year-olds. Why did I agree? I can barely sing a note or play the piano, but I got lumbered with it.' Sophie pretended to pull her hair out. 'So I thought I'd see you before madness descends. Is now a good time to discuss flowers?'

I laughed. The shop was near to overflowing with flowers. 'Yep. You've come to the right place.'

She showed me photos she'd torn from bridal magazines. Simple cream rose arrangements for side and banquet tables, pink rose posies for the tables, and blood-red roses for her bridal bouquet. They were fancier than some of the arrangements I'd created before, but nowhere near as daunting as the ones for Trish's funeral.

'I can do these,' I said confidently. 'They'll look stunning.'

'I knew you could. I promise I'll try not to change my mind too often between now and the wedding. Have you heard from Ben?'

'A little. He's good at texting.'

Sophie squeezed my arm. 'I'm so pleased. It would be nice to see you both again when he gets back.'

'Whenever that might be.'

Sophie smiled. 'Hope you don't mind me saying, but I think you and Ben make a great pair. He's generally so cautious.'

'About?'

'Girlfriends.'

'I'm not his girlfriend.'

'Not yet. And after what happened with his last one...'

'What happened?'

'I really shouldn't say. Adele's a friend. Was a friend.'

'And?'

'She cheated on him. Ben took it very hard. Cheating is...'

'Unacceptable?'

'Anyway, he's met you now, and Hen and I have high hopes. Ben deserves to be happy, especially after his mum...' Sophie sniffed. 'Enough of being maudlin, these look cute.' She pointed at a couple of headpieces I'd been fiddling with.

'Just experimenting,' I explained. 'I've had schoolgirls, uni students and mums request them, so I thought I'd make a few.'

She picked one up and examined it. 'Maybe I could have one for my wedding.'

'They're trending on social media.'

Sophie checked her watch. 'Leave it with me. Now, as I have the morning off, I'm going to surprise my man at his office.'

I shuddered at the memory.

The mail guy wandered in and handed over a couple of letters. The first was from a pest company advertising their winter specials. The second looked official. I ripped it open. The contract rumours were true. It was a letter from Pamela informing me that my rent was going up by fifteen per cent the next month. My financial situation was going from bad to untenable.

Thank goodness for Henry's cousin the solicitor.

I rang Teddy for an appointment. The last thing I needed was a rent hike, especially as I'd factored a set amount into the budget for the twelve-month contract. Ironic given I'd dropped my tenants' rent in Sydney by thirty per cent to secure tenants, yet here was Pamela trying to put up mine by fifteen. I couldn't afford it.

Two hours later, I'd closed my shop and sat in Teddy's office showing him Pamela's letter and explaining my situation.

He nodded. 'I see. We'll send Ms Stevens a letter, reminding her that you have a fixed rental agreement for twelve months, and that the contract still has over six months to run.'

I was doubtful. 'Do you think she'll back off?'

'She has to, it's the law.'

Teddy wasn't much of a talker, but I left his office feeling hopeful. I walked past Andy's shop on the way back to mine, but it was closed. Ah, Tuesday afternoon, of course. I thought about going to Zena's salon but decided against it.

Friday night, just after closing, I waited expectantly for one or both of them to show up, but neither did. I texted but got no reply. Maybe they were out together somewhere. Part of me was disappointed. I looked forward to our Friday evening chat session.

On Sunday morning, just before opening, Andy knocked.

I rushed around the flower buckets to open the door and hug him. 'How are you?'

'I'm doing okay. Haven't been up to work though. Been taking long swims and even longer walks. Haven't been up to chatting either, but thanks for your messages.'

'No need to apologise, you're here now. I've been worried,

especially after how things ended the other night at dinner. Have you seen Zena?'

Andy shook his head. 'Nah, I'd say I'm pretty much *persona non grata.*'

Yikes. What a mess. 'Give her time. Zena won't stay mad at you forever.'

He sat on one of my rickety stools. 'So...'

'So ... what's happening?'

'I've hired a lawyer and we're looking into Edie's claim. She almost destroyed my life and still she doesn't seem to have had enough.'

'She can only hurt you if you let her.'

'Which I won't.' He stared at the wall. 'Compared to me, everyone seems so normal.'

'Don't you know the first rule of life? Don't compare yourself to others. I think it was Theodore Roosevelt who said, "Comparison is the thief of joy".'

'True. No one really knows what's going on in other people's lives.' Andy kissed my cheek. 'Thanks. See you later.'

I followed him to the front door. 'Don't be a stranger, or strange,' I said and stuck my head out, shivering as the cold air hit my face.

Clearwater village was bustling. The little town was getting back to normal after Trish's death, and doing what it did best, enticing the tourists and locals into town to buy fresh apple pies from the bakery, and sip cappuccinos in the beachside cafés as they read the weekend papers and enjoyed the crisp winter sunshine. A few doors down from me, the surf shop had an outdoor stall selling tickets to an upcoming concert at The Fisherman's Club.

In the spirit of all things positive, my chalkboard words of wisdom were: *Just living is not enough ... one must have sunshine, freedom, and a little flower.* Hans Christian Andersen.

Happy couples wandered along the promenade, holding hands and reading real estate brochures promising waterfront views at a fraction of the price of those in Sydney. Occasionally, someone walked in, admired the glorious blooms and patted Trouble. They often walked out without buying anything.

Every time that happened, my worries about money, or lack thereof, escalated. I still wasn't earning a living wage and my savings were dwindling. To take my mind off my worries, I rang Taylor.

Less than a minute into our conversation, I managed to moan. 'The costs are killing me. And on top of that, I have to pay for a lawyer to fight Pamela.'

Taylor was sympathetic. To a point. 'Look on the bright side, you're living in paradise...'

'Yeah, but it's winter and no one's buying flowers.'

'That bad?'

I stared around my beautiful fully stocked shop. 'Maybe not, but it's been a slow weekend.'

Taylor laughed. 'What? No one died?'

'No babies were born either.'

'Which leads me to talk to you about the firm. How about you come into the city for the day. Eat lunch. Talk to Alastair?'

I picked up Trouble, pulled his ears, ruffled his fur and thoroughly annoyed him. 'Taylor, I don't want to go back to that life, the pace of the city, the hassle, everyone busy, always going somewhere. Rushing.'

'Aren't you always rushing down there too?'

'It's different.' Trouble bit me. I yelped and put him down.

'Okey doke.' Taylor sighed on the other end. 'Next week, sales will boom. It's winter, I predict a couple of flu-related deaths ... and in nine months, so many births, you'll be run off your feet.'

After the call, I felt flat. Flatter. I called Jake, the real estate agent. 'Can I see you tomorrow morning, say around eleven?'

'Sounds ominous. I'll clear my schedule.'

'Thanks. I'm thinking about selling.'

Jake took a sharp intake of breath. 'The tenants have signed a six-month lease which they're only two months into.'

'That's fine. By then it will be mid-spring and...' My voice caught. 'I don't have another option.' What could I do to boost sales? I couldn't randomly poison people. Although...

I rang off, closed the shop and bundled up several flower bunches for the retirement home. The residents always made me feel welcome and happy. Even on the days when I said, 'I'm only popping in to deliver flowers', or 'just passing through', or 'has anyone died lately?' I got roped into drinking sherry and/or playing Scrabble. I was genuinely happy there.

❦

'What have you got for us this week?' Elsie, Betty and April chirped when I walked through the door. I swear it was as if Santa had arrived. Their happiness was infectious, and their enthusiasm immediately cheered me.

'Roses! My favourite,' said Betty, when she saw them.

'Betts, every flower is your favourite,' said Elsie, good-naturedly.

I smiled. 'Every flower is my favourite too.'

'I don't much care for natives,' April piped up. 'I know I should, but I just don't.'

'I've got something else for you today,' I said, presenting them each with a box that contained a crown. They took them, giggling.

'Oh my!' Betty squealed, quickly putting hers on her head. For Betty, I'd created a garland of red roses.

'You look like a princess,' I said.

'I've never seen anything so pretty.' April, her face fully made-up, admired her headband of yellow daisies.

'Thank you so much,' said Elsie, as she put on her white gardenia headpiece. 'You've made my year. I feel as grand as the Queen. 'Betts, we can wear them to tap.'

Betty smiled. 'Grand!'

April stared out the window. 'Wish I could go to the classes with you.'

'Hey,' said Elsie, taking her by the arm. 'While we've been tapping, you've become a champion Scrabble player. Lily, did you know that April's been the top scorer for over a month now.'

I shook my head. 'Congratulations!'

April beamed. '*Dishevelled* and *unrequited* took me straight to the top.'

'Well done,' I said, taking a seat on a sofa in the common room. 'So, what else is news?'

'Well,' said Elsie, voice lowered, as she poured four sherries and offered me one, which I accepted, wishing my glass was bigger. 'Our resident man-about-town, Trevor, appears to have a new leading lady.'

'Remind me who Trevor is.' I scanned the room. 'The guy in the blue jumper over there? Holding court?'

'That's him, the Lothario,' Betty chimed in, sipping her drink.

He looked like a typical grey-haired eighty-year-old grandfather.

'He's got three of them on the run now,' continued Elsie. 'Including...' she paused for dramatic effect, 'our own April.'

April blushed. 'Elsie! Stop.'

'I will not! Lily, he sat at our table last night. Bold as brass. I don't for one minute believe he accidentally dropped his fork under your chair, April.'

244

'Elsie's right,' said Betty to April. 'Trevor was giving you the eye.'

I smiled. 'Sounds serious.'

'Yes,' said Elsie. 'All the time Betts and I were worried about leaving April alone on Monday tap nights, Trevor's been calling on her. Playing Scrabble and wooing her.'

I smiled. 'Is that right, April?'

April nodded.

'What do you think will happen next?' I asked.

'We already know.' Elsie chortled. 'He's asked April to join him for tonight's movie, *On Golden Pond*.'

I clapped. 'Sweet. But how do his other two ladies feel?'

April looked sideways before speaking. 'I don't think they're impressed.'

Betty laughed. 'He's bad news.'

I left the retirement village feeling better than I had all week. I didn't want my good mood to evaporate, so instead of going straight home, I detoured to the beach. It was high tide. I took off my shoes and walked along the sand barefoot, enjoying the cool, gritty sensation between my toes. Several people were swimming. The water felt like ice.

'Hello,' a voice called out.

Fifteen metres up the beach, Zena waved at me, wet and wrapped in a towel.

I walked up to her. 'How long have you been doing this?'

'Since I woke up to myself about Nate. I've had the locks changed.'

'Good to hear. Sorry I haven't been over. I was giving you space.'

She nodded. 'Thanks, but I should be apologising to you.'

I shuddered. 'All good. Aren't you freezing?'

She laughed. 'Keeps me young and my skin tight. You should try it.'

I admired her stamina. 'I'll think about it. Let's get back to normal again by going to tap tomorrow night and then dinner at the pub. I'm going to Sydney to see my real estate agent, but I should be back in time.' I needed to see my parents too.

'I'd like that, but I have an evening training session on hair colouring, and given how I butchered Sally's hair, I really need to go.'

We parted ways and I walked for a further thirty minutes before returning home. I picked up Trouble and we sat on the veranda. I drank beer and he ate carrots. He wasn't in a chatty mood.

Homesick, I rang Mum. 'So, you're still alive?' she said, serious voice.

'Yes, Mum. But what are you doing tomorrow for lunch?'

'Hopefully eating with you.'

I smiled. Mum could be a dragon, but she was my dragon. 'I'm a two-hour drive away. It's not like I'm living in London.'

Mum sniffed. 'You may as well be. We never see you.'

'I just said I'll come tomorrow. How's Dad?'

'Gout's still attacking him at every turn.'

'And Gary?'

'On his last legs. I'm glad you're making the effort.'

Why did I call?

'How's Matt?'

'Mum, Matt and I broke up, remember?'

'I was hoping it was just a passing phase. He loves you.'

I distracted myself with Trouble.

'Lily, are you listening to a word I'm saying?'

'Yes, I'll see you tomorrow.'

After that successful phone call, I drank another two beers and watched the sun set before switching on my computer and finding an email from Matt. I shouldn't have read it. Why couldn't he accept that our relationship was over? Why make this so much harder than it had to be?

§.

Monday morning, I drove up to Sydney and parked in front of my home. I'd fallen in love with it the first time I'd seen it advertised. I'd been so excited to place the winning auction bid, then move into my very own house. Matt and I had shared good times there.

I strolled around my neighbourhood. Loud with blaring horns, trucks rumbling up the roads and barking dogs. Lots of new construction – old homes being pulled down to make way for designer apartments, funky cafés and shops. I stopped by the beautiful park and sat at my favourite bench where I'd drunk too many cappuccinos to count. Then there were the pubs, practically one on every corner. I loved this area.

§.

'Lily,' Jake said when I walked into his office. 'I gather from yesterday's conversation this isn't a social call.'

'I need to sell the cottage,' I said, cutting through the niceties. 'I understand the tenants have another four months, but after that, we need to put it on the market.'

Jake was all business. 'Can do. Auction?'

'Yeah.' My heart was breaking. I loved my home.

Jake nodded. 'Plans in place. We need to take photos, dress it up—'

'I thought it was dressed.'

'Tenants don't look after it the way you have, Lil.'

§.

I arrived at Mum and Dad's an hour later, having cried all the way.

'I don't understand,' said Mum, clutching at Gary. 'Your house, your job. Matt.'

'Give it a rest, love,' said Dad. 'Lily doesn't want to live and work in the city and she doesn't love Matt. It's her life, not yours.'

'Matt's a great guy, but that's not enough. I don't want him to be the father of my children.'

Mum snorted. 'Fat chance you'll have any children now.'

That hurt. If only she knew.

'Daisy,' Dad protested. 'Lily's still young.'

'Not in reproductive years,' Mum barked.

'Can't you be happy for me?' I pushed back tears, my anger rising. 'I'm pursuing my dream.'

'A dream none of us knew existed this time last year.'

'Get used to it. Your spinster daughter lives in Clearwater and runs a flower shop. I'm selling the cottage.'

'Dear Lord!' said Mum. 'No!'

Dad placed his hand on my shoulder. 'Are you sure, love? It's a big decision.'

I nodded. 'And I'm a big girl. If I'm going to do this business properly, it needs a cash injection and I want cash in the bank. I can't have a mortgage as well.'

'You put your heart into the cottage,' Mum reminded me.

'Yes, I did. Now I'm putting my heart into Lily's Little Flower Shop. Is that so bad?'

Mum burst into tears. 'It's not that it's bad. But I miss you. Instead of living fifteen minutes away, you're two hours' drive from here. All you do is work. When are you ever going to meet someone? With Ma—'

'Forget about Matt,' I said, my voice strained with frustration. 'It's over.'

'Yes, you've made that clear.' Mum wiped her eyes and blew her nose. 'I worry about you. Look at Iris.'

'Look at Iris, what? She's perfectly happy.'

'She would've liked children.' Mum exhaled.

'I know, Mum, but we can't always get what we want.'

'Ask yourself if the sacrifices you're making are worth it in the long run.'

'I do, Mum, every day.' I got up, kissed her cheek, hugged her, walked out the door and set off for the flower markets, not sure if any of the sellers would still be there.

Who was I kidding? The car park was nearly full and the market floor was as crowded with flowers and people as it had been months earlier. The only difference was that it was colder. I wandered the aisles looking at pink daphnias, polyanthus, snowdrops and pretty primroses, before walking over to Tony.

'Lily,' he said, hugging me like a long-lost friend. 'How happy I am to see you.' Then, just as quickly, 'You're not cancelling on me, are you?'

I laughed. 'No, I'm used to my sleep-ins. I was in Sydney, so thought I'd come in for old time's sake. What are these?' I said, spying a bucket of striking deep purple climbers.

'Hardenbergia. More commonly known as the Happy Wanderer.'

'Nice. And this one?' I pointed to several clusters of small rosy-pink flowers.

'Luculia. Temperamental bastards.' Tony also had potted flowers like lavender and cyclamen. 'Can I interest you in anything to take with you today?'

I shook my head. 'No, but I've got a wedding coming up—'

'Congratulations!'

I slapped his arm. 'Not mine! A client's, and I'm after some amazing roses.'

He nodded. 'You've come to the right place.' I gave him the

date and he assured me he'd send plenty of stock. 'Hydrangeas, magnolias, dahlias,' he said, pointing to each flower, 'orchids, lisianthus ... they're all popular wedding choices.'

'She wants to keep it simple, understated. Roses, daisies, obviously plenty of green foliage for the bigger arrangements...'

'But of course. Ferns, camellia, eucalyptus—'

'Maybe not eucalyptus. She doesn't like the smell...'

I arrived in Clearwater as the sun was setting. 'Welcome home, Lily,' I said out loud as I stepped out of my van and opened the front door. Tony had persuaded me to buy several pots of paper daisies and lavenders. And I had not one ounce of buyer's regret.

CHAPTER 32

Despite the uncomfortable conversations with Mum and Dad the previous day, Tuesday morning I played some boppy music and tap danced around the shop. My shop. Sometimes I still couldn't believe it was all mine. I was happy and feeling okay about selling the cottage. Sad but okayish.

Unfortunately, Pamela strode in at eleven. Eye-popping was the only word to describe her look: a blood-red knitted corset dress, boobs out front and blonde hair flowing.

'Lily,' she said, all smiles. 'I got your letter.'

I nodded. 'I'm concerned—'

'I really don't care,' she said, cutting me off. 'My interest level in your concerns sits below zero.'

I took a step back. 'I think—'

'As I said, I don't care,' she replied, with a wave of her hand. 'My mother's terms were too generous.'

'Trish's terms were fair.' I was determined not to let Pamela see that she'd rattled me.

'What's fair? What Andy put Edie through? The way he's taking advantage of Zena?'

I put my hand up. 'None of my business, Pamela. Now, about my contract?'

'Andy's sick. I doubt he can cope without his medication.'

'Hey!' I said, my cheeks red and flaming. 'That's slanderous.'

Pamela smiled, showing her perfectly white straight teeth. 'Is it? You have a lot to learn.'

I took a deep breath. 'Pamela, my solicitor has replied to you. I hope this can be resolved amicably.'

'I'm sure it will ... if anyone's going to be breaking their contract, it will be you.'

I shook my head. 'I don't think so.'

Pamela smiled. 'Let's see, shall we?' She turned to walk out of the shop. 'Toodles.'

My good mood had evaporated but two baby boys had been born overnight, so I contented myself making bouquets for their mothers. I loved delivering flowers to the maternity ward. It had such a happy vibe, the brand-new babies and their overwhelmed, but thrilled, parents and proud, excited grandparents. And the odd one who wasn't excited about it at all.

My beef? Not many people called their children regular names. I was always having to ask the spellings – Skylah, Ebonney – and then repeat them because they never looked right to me. Double-barrelled surnames were also tricky. Lily Mason sounded positively pedestrian.

Today, however, the names were simple. Jackson and Hugh.

I really hadn't done anything except work since I'd opened the shop. And I still wasn't making any real money.

In the afternoon, at our meeting, I vented my frustrations to Henry.

'At least you're making a tidy sum from the funeral business,' said Henry, enthusiastically.

I stared at him. 'People around here do seem to make a habit of dying.' After the talk with Larry, the funeral director, business had started rolling in. Since Trish's death, I'd done four more.

He grimaced. 'Sorry, that didn't come out right.'

'I know what you mean and I'm slowly getting used to it. As you say, it's all part of the business.'

∗

A couple of hours later, Larry called to tell me that April had passed away. 'She was walking to her room when she slipped and had a fatal heart attack.'

'But I only saw her Sunday. She was going to watch *On Golden Pond*.' I started to cry.

'I'm sorry,' he said. 'It's not an easy business.'

'Elsie and Betty will be shattered. All the village residents will be.'

'Yes.' Larry paused. 'They don't know yet. Only April's relatives have been notified.'

'Of course.' That meant that my grief had to be contained until the village and townspeople had been informed. 'She didn't like native flowers.'

'I have that written in my notes,' he confirmed. He explained the arrangements April's family wanted. 'Bright colours ... roses, lilyanthus, gerberas...'

∗

The following Friday, I delivered April's flowers to the funeral home and sought out Elsie and Betty at the service.

'Ladies, I'm so sorry,' I said, hugging them both. 'I know how close you were with April.'

'The Golden Girls,' said Elsie quietly. 'And now...'

'There's just us,' said Betty, tears threatening. 'Just the two of us.'

'April will be pleased you've done her flowers, Lily. We all are,' said Elsie, inspecting them. 'They're bright, just like April wanted.'

I clocked Elsie's yellow dress and Betty's pink pant-suit. 'I take it the dress code also called for bright.'

They nodded.

'The three of us have stipulated loud and bright for our funeral parties too,' said Elsie, half-laughing. 'April would love this.'

I'd never get used to grieving relatives ringing to organise funeral flowers, but I was getting better at handling the inquiries, at knowing what to say and which arrangements to offer. Funerals were hard, but the way I looked at it, I was helping to make the service a little brighter. Today, I smiled a little.

§.

The following Monday at five fifty, I walked into Zena's salon. 'It's week three! Grab your tap shoes.'

'I can't,' Zena protested. 'I'm dead on my feet.'

'You can and you will. You've missed the first two weeks and I let it slide.'

Ten minutes later, Zena and I were pulling on our shoes at the school hall.

'I hate you,' said Zena.

I smiled. 'Yeah, I hate you too. But it'll take your mind off your troubles for an hour. Don't you want to win an award at the end of term?'

Zena pulled a face.

Moments later, Miss Liz walked in to the room and welcomed the group. 'Zena, you have some catching up to do. Elsie and Betty, I'm sorry for your loss. Now let's begin.'

Zena nudged me. 'What happened to the teenagers from last term and who are these?' She pointed to three tweens.

'The teenagers quit and those three are...' I thought for a moment. All colours, I knew that much. 'Ruby, Scarlett, and another, I can't quite remember. Blue?'

'Ladies!' Miss Liz snapped her fingers. 'Concentrate!'

I tried to focus on Miss Liz's feet as she demonstrated. 'You remember the Bell Heel from last term. Ball Change. Shuffle. Heel Step. Who wants to show me their *Shirley Temple*?'

Elsie raised her hand and with a nod from Miss Liz, performed the move.

Miss Liz clapped. 'Excellent. Now let's move on. Positions, ladies.'

ا&

'Pink!' I loud whispered to Zena, during a break. 'Named after the pop star.'

After class, Zena took me aside after failing yet again to master the *Shirley Temple* from first term. 'I am not about to be taken down by a girl named Pink. We have to nail the moves this term.'

'I know.'

Zena smirked. 'Or, we could just leave them to it and go to the pub?'

'And order Shirley Temples.'

❦

The next morning, I was practising travelling wing-steps and scissor-steps in my limited floor space, when Ben walked in and said, 'Broadway, get ready.'

'What an unexpected surprise,' I said, blushing. 'I thought you were in Adelaide.'

He smiled. 'I'm back. All good? You look like you're on *42nd Street*.'

'I have two left feet, but it's fun.'

'Any other news?'

'Getting to grips with winter flowers. Trouble's being Trouble.' There was no way I was talking about Zena and Andy. Or Pamela, for that matter.

Ben bent down and patted Trouble. 'I hear Pamela's causing pain around town.'

'Something like that.'

'Like what?'

'Bumping up the rents...'

'Sounds like my sister. Let me know if she persists. She can't hike up your rent mid-contract. She's continuingly trying to prove herself. It doesn't always work out. But enough about her. When can I see you again?'

'Other than right now?'

'Can I cook you dinner tonight? My place?'

I grinned.

'Great. How about you come over around six thirty? Rabbit stew?'

'What?'

'Steak?'

'Better.'

'Excellent. See you then.'

'Could we make it seven?'

Ben had his back to me and was walking out the door. 'As you wish, m'lady.'

§∙

Late afternoon, I made my deliveries to my contra businesses. In return, I got magazines from the newsagent, pastries from baker Sally, and fresh fruit and veggies from Darren, the greengrocer. But sadly, no cash.

Darren complained about Pamela attempting to hike rents. It turned out I wasn't the only one being threatened. 'Is she trying it on with you too?' he asked.

'Yes, but I'm hoping my contract is tight. My lawyer has written to Pamela telling her that the increase would be illegal.'

'I hope he's right.'

'I'll keep you in the loop,' I said, before dashing into the Bottle-O.

'Can I interest you in a bunch of flowers?' I asked Steve, like I did every week.

'I admire your determination. Can I interest you in a Shiraz?'

'Just a six pack of Peroni.'

He took my money. 'If Pamela puts my rent up, I'll go out of business.'

I repeated to him what I'd told Darren and then felt awkward that I was looking forward to a date with Pamela's brother.

§∙

Ben stood in his stylish large kitchen – any kitchen was large compared to mine – laying out the ingredients for a ragu steak with red wine sauce. He reached into his enormous stainless-steel fridge and pulled out a Sav Blanc, then retrieved two glasses from the cupboard above my head. He set the glasses down beside me, then unexpectedly reached around my waist and kissed me. Silently, I reached for his hand and he led me into his bedroom.

He beamed. 'The steak can wait.'

Kissing, we fell on the bed and grinned as we lay side by side, his hands cupping my face to kiss me again. I hadn't had sex for so long, my whole body was shaking with a combination of lust and nerves. Could I get involved with a guy who didn't live in Clearwater? Was I ready for another relationship? I didn't know Ben the way I knew Andy but pushed those thoughts aside. I liked Ben. I liked Andy. Andy and I were friends...

A minute later, Ben and I were naked and exploring each other's bodies.

Afterwards, we snuggled into each other. I was content. I wouldn't say the sex was mind-blowing. In fact, it had felt a bit awkward. Then again, I was so used to Matt. It would take time to adjust to a new lover's moves and quirks.

The next morning, he said, 'Can I see you tonight?'

I nodded as I rolled into him, stroking his stomach. 'That was some enchanted evening.'

'What?'

'Someone may be laughing ... you know?'

He shook his head. 'I have no idea.'

'Sorry. *South Pacific*, the musical? It's just a thing.' Andy would have got it.

He grimaced. 'Do you know who Luke Skywalker is?'

'*Guys and Dolls*?'

'No. *Star Wars*.'

'No?'

'Exactly.'

Okay. This wasn't working. Time to change speed. 'How do you think Pamela will feel when we tell her?'

He sat up but remained silent. 'Well, it's none of her business,' he said finally. 'But for now, I'd rather this remained between us.'

I nodded awkwardly. 'Yes, our secret.'

'Just until we're sure.'

Fair point. We'd been together less than two days. Eventually, we'd have to tell Pamela and of course Zena and Andy, but for now, it was just Ben and me. I couldn't wipe the smile off my face.

'I'll call you,' Ben said, and kissed me again before I left.

CHAPTER 33

For a week, Ben and I spent almost every night together.
Most days, if he was staying with me, like that morning, he
slipped out before nine with a promise to return in the evening.
That day was no exception. I was operating on autopilot, smiling
at customers, preparing bouquets, blissful in my bubble. I didn't
even mind when Trouble completely destroyed several reams of
coloured ribbon and straw. I hated to think what the inside of
his stomach looked like.

As I watched schoolkids on the way home drag their bags
along the pavement, sucking back milkshakes and eating hot
chips, wishing I could do the same without putting on ten kilos,
Ben surprised me with a massive bunch of gerberas. My
favourite. I could hardly breathe.

'I wanted to buy you something special.' He kissed me softly
on the lips before handing them over.

'They're beautiful. Stunning. How? Where?'

He smiled. 'You're not the only one who knows where the
flower markets are.'

'Really? You did that for me?'

'I did, so don't even think about reselling them!'

'Never. They'll be front and centre upstairs on my bedside table. I love them.'

'I'm glad. So, tonight?'

I smiled. 'Yes.'

'I'll drop by at seven.'

'I'll be waiting.'

Ben left and I had a definite skip in my step. It might have been winter outside but my heart was full of sunshine, hopefulness and gratitude.

As I marvelled at the gerberas, I heard footsteps behind me and arms wrapped around me. I turned, eager to kiss him again.

'Hey, hey, hey. Who's the prettiest girl this side of the equator?'

'Matt?' The flowers fell from my hands onto the floor.

'Surprise!'

I nodded, unable to breathe.

'It's been four months and I miss you. I miss us.' Matt put down an overnight bag and hugged me.

I pulled away. 'We're not together anymore.'

Shit. Shit. I couldn't think straight. I took a deep breath. 'Why don't you go upstairs while I finish up down here.'

Matt hesitated. 'You don't seem happy to see me.'

'It's not that...' I was lost for words as the two of us stood in the middle of the shop. 'I'm shocked, Matt. Really shocked. What are you doing here? We've broken up.'

'That's what I'm here to talk to you about.'

He went upstairs. I closed the front door and rang Ben, not having a clue what to say. Thankfully, I got his voicemail.

Ben, hi it's ... um ... Lily. I'm sorry but a friend has just arrived unexpectedly. Can we take a raincheck tonight? See you tomorrow? Sorry about this. It's Lily. Have I mentioned that? Okay. Bye.

I hung up and promptly forgot what I'd just said. Did I mention the friend was Matt? What the hell did he want to talk to me about? And why couldn't he have just picked up the phone?

My phone beeped. A text from Ben.

Lil, no problem re tonight. Shame though, I'm going to miss you. See you tomorrow. B xx

Trembling, I texted Taylor.

Shit. Matt's here, as in here in Clearwater. What do I do?

I picked up Ben's beautiful gerberas, placed them in a vase, and, five minutes later, when there'd been no response from Taylor, I composed myself and walked upstairs. Matt had made himself at home, drinking Ben's Ravenstone wine and eating the leftover Thai beef salad that Ben had made.

I placed the vase on the kitchen bench, and accepted the champagne Matt had poured.

'Babe, it's been so hard without you,' Matt said. 'I've missed you so much.'

We were sitting on the sofa and I drank way too fast as I tried to take in what he was saying.

'I've been so lonely, Lil—'

I resisted the urge to mention Sami. 'But it must be amazing living in a city like Singapore?'

'I guess. It's huge, so many people, but I have no real friends.'

'Work colleagues? Other ex-pats?'

'Yeah.' Matt sipped his champagne. 'But I really miss you, Lil.'

All I could think about was Ben. Sophie's words about how

he'd been hurt before rang in my ears. The last thing I wanted to do was hurt him.

§

After the second glass, Matt kissed me. I pulled away, made an excuse and went to the bathroom. I felt ill. Matt and I were finished. I didn't want to start anything with him, didn't want to give him false hope. I was with Ben now, and I was happy.

I stayed in there for a good ten minutes, washing my flushed face.

When I came out, Matt had opened another bottle of Verve.

'Come, sit,' he said.

I shook my head. 'I don't want any more to drink.'

'I've been bursting trying to hold it in, but—' Matt went down on knee '—Lily Mason, I love you. Will you marry me?' He had tears in his eyes. 'Please? I love you so much. I can't live without you.'

My eyes widened in disbelief. 'I don't know what to say, Matt.'

'Say yes.' He produced a ring box and said again, 'Will you marry me?'

My heart stopped beating. Tears streamed as I reached for his shoulder, grabbing at his jumper. 'Please stand up. Please.'

This couldn't be happening. I was so sad for him, for me, for us.

'It's all right, sweetie.' He stood to cuddle me. 'I know this is what you've wanted the whole time. But it's taken me a while to realise.'

'No, Matt.' I wiped my eyes and composed myself. 'Please stop.'

'We don't have to live in Singapore. I have a job offer coming up for Paris. How about that? A bit more romantic than Singapore, hey?'

'Please stop.' I could feel my voice getting higher, louder.

Matt shook his head. 'Why?' His voice sharpened. 'Either you want to marry me and spend the rest of your life with me or you don't.'

'I loved you. But it's over. It was over when you came back in February, and it's still over. I'm sorry, but I can't marry you. I'm not in love with you.'

At last I'd said the words. I'd turned down Matt, the guy who had been my best friend, my confidant, my lover. But it was true. Our time together had passed.

'You're not thinking straight. You, Lily Mason, are the love of my life. I want you by my side.'

I shook my head. 'Stop saying that. Matty, you're a great guy, but you're no longer my guy. My life is here in Clearwater, while yours is a constant adventure. Singapore, Paris. Who knows where to next? Tokyo? New York? That's great for you, but it's not for me.'

'But it's all sorted. I've spoken with Pamela.'

'Pamela?' Alarm bells rang in my head.

'Yeah. I thought about it for months, and the more I thought about it, the more I realised my mistake. I should have proposed to you the first time I came here. You wanted a commitment, a true commitment.'

'No, I didn't. You have your life and I have mine. I'm not going to marry you.'

He shook his head. 'I don't believe you. Once you've had time to think about it, you'll see. I've taken the lead. It's all arranged. We can leave as soon as you're packed and sorted out the finer details about your lease. Your mum said she'll take care of Trouble.' He smiled. 'I've thought of everything, babe.'

I shook my head. 'Wait. Back up. Pamela? When did you meet her?'

Matt laughed. 'You'll love this. I was sneaky, as you know I can be. I set up a meeting with her last week, then met with her this afternoon before I saw you.'

'I don't believe it.'

'I knew you wouldn't. Cool, hey? Smart detective work. But I found your real estate agent. We talked, and she said there won't be any early-exit penalty fee. Great news, hey?'

I struggled to comprehend what he was saying. 'No, it's not great news. You had no right to talk to her.' Pamela of all people. 'Your name isn't on the contract. You have no legal right to negotiate on my behalf.'

'I know that. I've just started the ball rolling. You can meet with her tomorrow. The main thing is that there'll be no early-exit fee.'

'No! I'm sorry if I gave you the wrong impression, but I'm not going to Singapore and I'm not marrying you.'

'But your emails? Your texts ... Don't you love me anymore?'

'I did. But this is where I'm at now...' Matt was my past. 'We want different things. I didn't want to go to Singapore six months ago, so why would I want to go now?'

'Because I didn't make the ultimate commitment to you and now I have. I miss you. Us. And we can travel anywhere together if we're married.'

I held his hand, feeling myself tearing up. 'Matt, it's not going to work. I'm not giving up my lease or my flower shop.'

'I'm not going to ask you again.'

'I know.'

'Lily, do you know how frustrating you can be?'

'Me? You're the one who ambushed me,' I snapped.

'How else could I see you? I was worried if I called, you'd tell me not to come and I couldn't handle that. I had to see you.'

'I'm sorry.'

'Not as sorry as I am. Is there any way I can get you to change your mind or at least consider it?'

'No. I'm sorry, Matt. It's over.'

'I was hoping that when you saw me—'

'I'd change my mind?'

'Something like that.' Matt glanced away for a moment. 'What happens now?'

'I guess you fly back to Singapore, serve out your time, then head to Paris.'

'I'm lonely.'

I spied the gerberas on the kitchen bench. 'That's no reason for us to stay together.'

'So, I guess I should get a room somewhere?' he said.

It was late in the night. We were both wrung out and shattered. I was sad. Matt was devastated.

'It's too late. Stay here.'

Matt brightened. 'Really?'

'In the guest room.'

☙

When I woke the next morning, Matt was sitting on the edge of my bed. 'I made you a tea.' He pointed to a cup on my bedside table. As I moved to get up, Matt reached for me. 'Please say you'll reconsider. I love you. Marry me.'

'No. I'm sorry.'

I got up and walked into the bathroom to shower, sniffing and dabbing at my eyes. Matt was a good guy, but it was too late for us. I considered telling him about Ben, but there was no need; it would be unnecessarily hurtful and humiliating after he'd just proposed. It would be kinder to wait until he'd gone back to Singapore before breaking the news.

I was drying myself when I heard voices. Maybe Matt was on speakerphone? I wrapped a towel around myself and walked into the lounge room to see Matt and Ben facing each other.

'I bought coffee and pastries for you.' Ben pointed to the kitchen bench. 'Thought I'd surprise you, but it looks like I'm the one who got surprised. I thought it was over between you and your boyfriend! Isn't that what you told me?'

I stared at Matt's boxer shorts and shook my head. 'It's not what it looks like.'

'Who's this?' Matt asked.

Ben frowned. 'I thought I was Lily's boyfriend.'

'So all that time we were reminiscing, drinking champagne and I was telling you how much I loved you, you never thought to mention him?' Matt glared at me. 'For fuck's sake, I got down on one knee and proposed to you, Lily. You told me you loved me.'

'You're getting married?' Ben shouted.

'No. You've got it wrong. I didn't say that.' I was practically hyperventilating and my towel felt too small.

'He's the reason you won't marry me?' Matt shouted. 'We drink champagne all night, we kiss, you tell me you love me, and somehow forget to tell me you have a new boyfriend?'

'I never said I loved you!'

Ben threw his hands up in the air. 'Count me out. Enjoy your croissants. I hope you have a happy life together.' He turned to walk down the stairs.

'Wait!' I rushed forward to grab his arm.

He shrugged me off.

'Ben, I told you about Matt. We used to go out. We don't anymore.'

'So why is he in your apartment? You told him you love him, and today, he wants to marry you. Must have been some night.'

'For crying out loud, will you just sit down and let me talk to you!'

Ben ran downstairs, opened the front door and stormed out.

'Don't bother.'

I followed him to the door, but I only had a towel on. I went back upstairs to find Matt dressed, bag packed.

'It makes perfect sense now,' he said.

'Matt, it's over between us. It has been for some time.'

'Sorry, I didn't get that memo.'

'Stop being a dick! I never gave you the impression I was going to marry you or move to Singapore! I'd said no all along!'

He walked down the stairs and slammed the front door.

I checked my phone. Three missed calls from Taylor and several text messages including:

Tell me what's going on??? Don't make me come down because you know I will. Lily Mason, I will get in my car and hunt you down!!

Shaking, I called Ben. It went straight to voicemail. 'Ben, nothing happened between me and Matt last night. Will you please talk to me? Matt misunderstood—' the message cut out.

I called again. 'Matt and I are finished. Nothing happened last—' The message cut out again.

I got dressed, then sat on the floor and cried.

Minutes later, my phone rang. I hoped it would be Ben or at least Taylor. But it was Mum.

'Darling,' she trilled when I answered. 'Tell me all your wonderful news. I knew it was only a matter of time before you came to your senses. Took you long enough, but that's all in the past now.'

'Mum, stop. Matt had no right—'

'Don't be silly, he's practically family.' She cackled. 'And soon, he will be. You're getting married. Can you believe he convinced me to take care of your rat?'

'I'm not getting married and I'm not leaving Clearwater. And you're certainly not having Trouble.' Rat indeed.

Mum gasped. 'What do you mean?'

'Matt's going back to Singapore and I'm staying here.'

'But why?'

'Do you really need to ask? Matt and I aren't together. We haven't been for months.'

Silence. I wasn't sure what to expect next. Tears? Anger?

'Lily, you're not thinking straight.'

I rolled my eyes and gritted my teeth. 'Mum, I am.' As I said the words I saw Ben heading towards the shop. 'Gotta go. Talk soon.'

I hung up to her spluttering, 'Lily Mason, don't you d—'

'So,' said Ben, striding in. 'What's happening?'

My heart almost leapt out of my chest. 'Nothing.'

'Nothing? Ha. Pamela told me that your friend, Matt, had a meeting with her and you're leaving Clearwater, getting married, and moving to Singap—'

'That's not true. Matt flew in from Singapore to surprise me and took it upon himself to meet with Pamela. It's not what I want.'

'But still, he did it. Why didn't you tell him about me?'

'Because he asked me to marry him, and even though I wanted to tell him about you right then and there, it seemed unkind. I thought I'd let him go back to Singapore and then tell him. Besides, you told me to keep it between our selves until we were sure. I did that.'

'You told him you loved him?' Ben looked upstairs. 'Is he still here?'

269

I shook my head. 'I said I used to love him, and he left straight after you.'

'But he stayed last night?'

I nodded. 'Yes, b—'

'You don't owe me anything. But I thought you were different. I thought ... well, whatever I thought was wrong.' He turned to leave.

'Ben, for crying out loud! Matt stayed in the spare room. It was late. He was tired. We're still friends. Where was he supposed to go?'

He turned back. 'This is what I think. Matt arrived, love, love, kiss, kiss, proposed, stayed the night.'

I shook my head, exasperated. 'I want to be with you, Ben.'

He shook his head. 'I don't think so. Lily, I want an uncomplicated life. The baggage between you and Matt is too difficult to deal with right now. I'm grieving for Mum and I don't need any more angst. Besides, I won't be living in Clearwater permanently. It's for the best.'

I felt myself shrink. 'Nothing happened.'

'Really. Champagne, kissing, falling asleep in each other's arms, you in a towel, Matt in his underwear?'

I shook my head. 'It wasn't like that at all. You're making things up.'

'I don't care, and I don't want to know. I'm sorry, Lil, it was fun but it's not going to work between us.'

He left, and I sat at my bench, too exhausted to cry anymore. The last twenty-four hours were a blur.

I looked up to see Pamela walking in. The very last person I wanted to deal with.

'Hope I'm not interrupting.' She smiled brightly, waving papers in the air. I swear that woman's mouth grew wider every time I saw her. 'Lily, we'll be sorry to see you go. It was fun having a flower shop in town, but onward and upward as they say.'

'Pamela, I really don't think...'

She laughed. 'You don't say? Ben was a bit taken aback, when I told him, almost like they were the last words he expected to hear.' She offered a sour smile. 'Whatever. All in the past. I told him your knight in shining armour had come to rescue you – because that's what Matt called himself. Your *knight in shining armour*. Cute.'

I was too exasperated to speak.

'But Ben? Gee, he must have quizzed me for a good twenty minutes about your beau. You have a looker there. No wonder you're giving up paradise to be with him.'

I put my hand up in the air. 'That's enough,' I said, a little too loudly for such a small space.

She barged on. 'Yes, down to business. Now, despite what I said to Matt, there will be a slight penalty, given you've only been here six months, but at least I can put the rent up for the next tenant.'

'I'm not leaving. It's a mistake.'

'But—'

'I'm sorry for the bother, but I'm staying. Matt had no right to talk to you.'

'You're not going to Singapore?'

'No.'

'You're staying on?'

'Yes.'

She raised her eyebrows. 'Well, that's a wasted morning of paperwork.'

'Why? The lease is in my name. Legally, Matt couldn't have terminated it.'

She waved her arms in the air. 'For goodness' sake, make up your mind.'

'I was never going to leave.' I took a breath. 'Did he bribe you?'

Her eyes narrowed. 'Don't be ridiculous and don't go causing me any more grief. Or you'll be getting a letter from *my* solicitor!'

She flounced out of the shop.

I called Taylor, but it went straight to her voicemail. 'I'm the biggest loser ever. Call me.'

I didn't want to see anybody so I closed the shop, slunk back upstairs, and wept.

CHAPTER 34

I wallowed in my flat, not even pretending I was going to re-open the shop that afternoon. Still, I didn't want to spend the entire day moping, so I visited Zena.

'Hello, stranger,' Zena said when I walked into her salon. She squeezed my arm, then peered down the road. 'What are you doing here? Why is your shop closed midweek at midday? I'm sure the old biddies wanting baby's breath are beside themselves.'

'How long have you got?'

Zena checked her watch. 'A good ten minutes before my next client. Spill.'

'I really like Ben.'

'That's great.'

'I slept with him. Several times.'

Zena's eyes widened. 'That's even better. I can't believe you haven't told me. How long's it been going on?'

'A bit over a week.'

Her eyes widened, and she flicked water at me. 'I thought we were friends.'

'I didn't want to jinx it. It was really good, but—'

'Was? But what?'

'Matt arrived from Singapore last night.'

'I thought you two broke up.'

'We did, but he came back and got it into his head to propose.'

'Matt? Shit! Seriously? What did you say?'

I blinked. 'No, of course.'

'Did you sleep with him?'

'No, but he stayed over. It's complicated, Zena. It was late, and he was tired, and there was nowhere else to go. But Ben turned up this morning and caught Matt in his underwear.'

'Shit.'

'Ben left. Told me it's too difficult and that I come with too much baggage and he's not up for it.'

'Harsh.' Zena checked her watch. 'I'm sorry, but I need to clean myself up.'

'I haven't even asked about you? It's been weeks. What's happening?'

'Nothing. All good.'

'Really? You look tired. Everything okay?' The more I studied Zena, the paler and more run down she looked. The stress with Andy was taking its toll. 'You don't look so good. Are you feeling all right?'

Zena started crying. 'Not really.' She blew her nose. 'I'm pregnant.'

'You're what?'

'Pregnant. And before you say anything, I've checked with the pink stick jury three times. Calculating from the start of my last period, I'm about seven weeks.'

'Holy. Fuck!' Confused and a little jealous, I said, 'Have you told Andy?'

'In time, I guess. The news is only just sinking in. Why the rush?'

'Because Andy's the father.'

'No, Nate is. If only it was Andy's. At least the kid would have a decent dad.'

'I'm confused. I thought you spent a night with Andy.'

'No, I didn't and no, we didn't, er, go all the way.'

'So, Nate?'

'Yep. He's the only guy I've been with in recent memory.'

'Lordy. Have you told him?'

'No. After that horrible night at the club and then finding Nate at home, I kicked him out the next day.'

'Why didn't you call? Or say something?' I caught my breath. 'What can I do? How can I help? What happens now?'

Zena half smiled. 'So many questions, all of which I have asked myself and can't answer. Part of me wants to run back to Norfolk.' Zena grimaced. 'But that's not an option. There's no maternity ward on the fucking island. I guess I could get an abortion and pretend it never happened.'

'Do you want that?'

'I don't know what I want.'

'Can I get you something? Coffee? Cake?'

She shook her head. 'I can't stomach food. If I'd sworn off men like I said I would, this wouldn't have happened.'

'It might help if you spoke to him.'

Zena's bravado faded away. 'I can't. Can't tell him how stupid I am.'

'It takes two.'

'It's over between Nate and me. Besides, I haven't come to terms with it myself. You're the only person who knows. If you can't support me and my decisions...'

'I do. I just think if you told Nate—'

'Pink unicorns will appear, and my life will suddenly become magical? No.'

I nodded. 'Okay, but please talk to me. I might say dumb

275

things, but you're my friend and I love you. Somehow, we'll work this out.'

Zena wiped a tear from her eye. 'I know. I still have time.'

I breathed deeply. 'I'm going to tell you something nobody else knows ... only Iris. I never even told Matt. But ... when I was sixteen, I got pregnant. A one night stand. The guy wore a condom, but ... I was working at Aunty Iris's shop when I found out.'

Zena was shaking her head. 'You poor thing.'

'She organised my abortion. It was incredibly difficult.'

'What are you saying?'

'I'm just telling you my story in case it helps. At the time, I felt relief. It was only later that the sadness and guilt kicked in. I hated myself. It was awful. I've stopped crying for that child now, but it took the longest time.'

I left Zena's salon struggling to process the news and push away the demons from invading. Zena was pregnant. By Nate. Back inside my shop, I distracted myself with cleaning and ordering flowers, patting Trouble and gulping a stiff gin and tonic. I downed it in one and dialled Ben's number, knowing he probably wouldn't pick up.

He did.

'Ben, before you say anything, yes, Matt did stay the night, but nothing happened and it didn't mean anything.'

'What a cop out. How could it not mean anything? He proposed. You told him you loved him.'

'I didn't.'

'Did you have sex?'

'No!'

'No kissing, no intimacy?'

'It's not like I kissed Matt back when he kissed me. I did my best to keep him at a distance.'

'Why didn't you kick him out?'

'I let him stay in the spare room because he is an old friend, that's all, and tired, and had nowhere to go.'

'How could you do that to me? To us? You took your ex-boyfriend to bed hours after you and I...?' He took a deep breath.

'I didn't sleep with Matt. Either you believe it or you don't. But I'm not saying it again.'

'Lily, I don't want to know, and I don't care. Just stay away from me. Please.'

My anger evaporated. I was desperately sad. 'Ben, please, I know you've been hurt...'

'You don't know anything about me, Lily.' The line went dead.

Instead of drinking an entire bottle of gin, I headed to the beach, determined to throw myself into the freezing water and drown. Or maybe just clear my head.

As I tried to build up the courage to dive into the charging waves, I spotted Andy.

'Hello,' I said. 'You look as miserable as I feel.'

He smiled. 'Miserable and frustrated.'

'Still no word about the divorce?'

Andy shook his head. 'I don't want to pester Teddy, but I need to see him. I want this to be over. Edie's leaving me messages—'

'I hope you're keeping them as a record?'

He nodded. 'They're not threatening. Just annoying. I keep blocking her. And Zena still isn't talking to me.'

I wished I could explain about Zena, but it wasn't my place.

We continued walking a few minutes more before Andy

spoke again. 'What's new with you? Haven't seen you for a while.'

'Ex-boyfriend arrived in town, proposed, current boyfriend walked out. Doesn't want anything to do with me.'

We stared out at the sea.

'I said no, by the way.'

'Yeah. You going in?'

I shook my head. 'I want to but the water's freezing.'

He laughed. 'It's winter, Sherlock. Did you bring your wetsuit?'

❧

'Finally,' said Taylor when we spoke that night. 'What's going on?'

I didn't draw breath for five minutes as I relayed the whole sorry saga.

'So that's it?' she said.

'Pretty much. Ben hates me. Never wants to see me again.'

'What the hell were you thinking? I mean, clearly it was fun at the time, but both of them?'

I walked out to the veranda and took a seat. 'It wasn't like that. I told you I didn't sleep with Matt.'

'I know, but to us mere mortals—'

'Stop it.'

'I'm sure once Ben calms down—'

'You don't understand. He's been deceived before. Now he thinks I've cheated and cheating isn't acceptable.'

'Reality check. You and Banging Ben had a few nights together.'

I moaned. 'But...'

'Whatever!'

'How could my world have been turned upside down so dramatically in such a short time? It doesn't make sense.'

'Deal with it. I'm not letting you carry on anymore. Pull yourself together. Yes, you fucked up royally, but you have to move on.'

'I know.' I walked back inside, not knowing if I wanted to sit or stand. Instead, I paced.

'Have you ever thought Ben might have been a rebound fuck to finally get over Matt? Dare I ask about him?'

'Matt's my past.'

'As you've said. But he still stayed the night.'

'We slept in separate rooms.'

'Because you were sensible. Who knows what happened, or would have happened had you been more inebriated?'

'I do! We kissed. That's all. It's not like I had sex with him for old time's sake.'

'Blessed are the small mercies.' She sighed. 'Honey, I'm really sorry. What can I do?'

'Nothing. I'll feel better tomorrow.' I took a breath. 'I haven't even asked about you. How goes it?'

'We still don't have a replacement for Glenn so most people, including me, are running around like headless chooks, plugging leaks where we see them. I've got ulcers on my ulcers. Sometimes I wish I could pack it all in and give up, run away...'

Her words hung in the air.

'Like I did?'

'You know what I mean. City living, corporate life. At least you're your own boss and you have the beach to entertain you.'

'Yeah, but I'm not earning a wage and any savings I had have dwindled to non-existent.' The worry about money was giving me stomach cramps. 'I live with constant fear that Pamela is going to raise my rent, even though my solicitor says she can't. I have a legally binding contract.'

'That's hopeful at least, but I'm sorry about the ongoing worries. What can you do?'

I groaned wearily. 'I'm selling up in Sydney.'

'No! You've really decided?'

'If I'm going to stay in Clearwater and give the shop any chance of survival, I have to.'

'No!'

'Taylor, I don't have a choice. I met with Jake. It's over. It'll be up for auction in the spring. I can sell the cottage, pay off my mortgage and have a tidy sum left over.'

'But you'll never get back into the Sydney property market.'

'Yes, Mother. So people say.' I paused. 'Changing the subject, any love interests I should know about?'

'I wish. But how would I get the chance to meet anyone? Last night, I worked till almost midnight. I was so wired when I got home, I couldn't sleep. Drank a bottle of Shiraz. It's not healthy.'

I clicked my tongue. 'You okay?'

She laughed. 'Probably not, but who is? We're all damaged one way or another. I'm working crazy hours, don't have a social life, and most of the time I'm running on fear and Coke Zero.'

'Sounds like me except Red Bull is my drug of choice.'

I hung up, grabbed Trouble and climbed into bed, wrapping the two of us in my blanket. So, a replacement for Glenn still hadn't been found. In many ways, it would be easy to pack up the shop, return to Sydney and slot straight back into the life I'd lived for years. I knew the job, the staff and was sure I'd make a more effective team leader than Glenn.

CHAPTER 35

By Sunday I still hadn't spoken to Ben. My eyes were forty per cent on the shop and sixty per cent on the pavement, wishing he'd walk by. I'd made up endless scenarios imagining myself nonchalantly opening the front door and shouting out 'Hey, Ben, saw you standing outside' and starting up a 'friends-only' chat. Other times, I pictured him walking by, and me rushing out and running up behind him, grabbing him around the waist and saying, 'Where have you been, you handsome devil? I've missed you.'

I stood outside my shop and stared down at the real estate office – the words 'we're local, like you!' mocking me. I wasn't a local. I was an outsider. Pamela was the only person who'd know what was going on with Ben, but I couldn't ask her.

On a whim, I closed up early and bought a wetsuit from the surf shop. I tried on three, not realising how tight they had to be in order to be effective. Because of my indecision – they all looked dreadful – the assistant chose the one that most stuck to my skin. I could wear this under a cocktail dress and still look slim. I couldn't feel my hands or feet.

❧

At six thirty Monday morning, after three hours of restless sleep, I headed to the beach, determined to dive in. I tugged on my wetsuit, relieved that only surfers were out – and they were far out, focusing on their next big ride. Without checking the water temperature, I dived into a wave and screamed. My head, hands and feet felt like ice. Proud, I dived under again and spent a full fifteen minutes in the water. To my surprise, I enjoyed it, especially when I was back home taking a warm shower. I felt alive for the rest of the day with the smell of salt in my hair and on my skin. My body tingled.

❧

Seven days later, I'd swum seven mornings in a row. But my life was still a mess. In the shop on Tuesday morning, I didn't bother listening to the voice messages left by Mum, Aunty Iris, and Taylor, doubtless reminders about what a terrible person I was.

On top of that, my shop was crap. I'd forgotten to place my order with Tony. He'd emailed, but I'd forgotten to email back. It was eleven before I realised the flowers hadn't arrived. My shop looked even sadder than I was.

I emailed Tony and he replied immediately. 'I wondered where you were. Thought you might have skipped off to the Maldives. Will get the delivery to you tomorrow morning.'

Dark clouds shifted restlessly and rumbled. More rain was coming. My hands were frozen as I swept the floor, tears leaking down my face. Very few customers walked in. None of them bought anything.

'Lily!' It was Aunty Iris. She squeezed me, then stood back, eyeing me intensely. 'How are you, darl, because you look terrible.' She glanced about the shop, shaking her head and sighing. 'You haven't returned any of my calls. What's going on?'

'Nothing.'

'That's bulltwang and you know it. Tell me.'

We stood in silence a moment.

'Actually, your mother's filled me in, but I can't help thinking—'

I sniffed, then blew my nose. 'Whatever she's told you—'

'She said Matt came over from Singapore. Proposed. Wanted to take you back with him. Correct?'

I nodded.

'You said you couldn't go because you love Clearwater and your shop, and you're selling your Sydney home.'

'I have no choice.'

'You don't look like you're loving anything right now.' Aunty Iris examined me closely. 'What am I missing? There's more to the story.'

'Iris, I can't—'

'Has this got something to do with Ben?'

I looked up. 'How did you know?'

'Because when you mentioned his name weeks ago, you got all starry-eyed. So?'

I waved my hand in the air. 'It doesn't matter now.'

'Ah, Lily-Pily.' She wrapped me in her arms. 'You'll tell me in your own good time. And you'll tell me about Andy.'

I raised my eyebrows.

She raised her brows back at me. 'Yes. But right now, we need to get this place looking brighter. The few flowers you've got are wilting. When's your next delivery?'

'Tomorrow.'

'Good! Otherwise your run into the weekend will be dismal. In the meantime, let's put some bunches out the front. We'll offer a special price, just for today. Give yourself an early mark,

I'll tidy up while you go for a walk along the beach. Or sleep. Did I mention you look a wreck?'

'I've started swimming.'

'What? At the beach? In the middle of winter?'

'Yep.'

'You're crazy.'

'That's the point. If I didn't do it, I think I *would* go crazy.'

'Is this some self-flagellation thing you've got going?'

'Something like that.'

I left Iris and walked to the beach. On the sand, I removed my shoes and shivered as the cold grains worked their way between my toes. Then I stripped down to my swimmers and tugged on my wetsuit, still damp from my morning swim. I watched the sea as it raged. I'd forgotten it was a king tide. Huge waves crashed against the sand. As for the waves hitting the rocks? Spectacular. Angry white froth battered the rocks. Eagles circled overhead with sea gulls keeping a safe distance. Pelicans ambled along the beach, seemingly having not a care in the world. Surfers waited to catch the perfect wave. I stood on the water's edge, wiping away tears.

I hesitated, but this was about me forcing myself into a healthy routine. I plunged in and went under, bobbed up and floated, the waves crashing against my body. Sometimes, like now, I thought I might drown because I was so frigid with cold, and helpless against the fierce pounding waves.

The good news was that I was unable to think about anything other than saving myself and swimming safely back to shore. If my mind wandered to Ben, Andy or keeping the shop afloat, it would be mere seconds before another wave pulled me under water and I'd be gasping for breath. There was no time to feel sorry for myself when survival was at stake.

CHAPTER 36

Andy

In Teddy's office, Andy told him the whole sorry saga.

'So, four years ago, you served a divorce petition on Edie,' Teddy said. 'Was it a joint application?'

'No.'

'But you both signed the divorce papers?'

Andy nodded.

'You say Edie lodged them in court on behalf of both of you. Right?'

'Yes. I assumed—'

'Never assume anything, Andy. I can see your mistake straight away. You served the divorce petition, a sole application, which means you had to lodge it with the court. Did you do that?'

'No. I told you, Edie said she would.'

'Do you have a certificate of divorce to prove you're free?'

'No.'

'Mate,' Teddy was shaking his head, 'you're not divorced. You didn't follow procedure.'

The words rang in Andy's ears. 'But I found a copy of the divorce papers.' He pulled out crumpled sheets from his backpack.

Teddy raised his eyebrows and reached across the table to grab them. 'Why the hell didn't you say so?'

Andy watched as Teddy silently scanned the papers. 'This doesn't have Edie's signature.'

'I took a copy before giving her the original.'

'For a smart man, you can be quite naïve, Andy.'

Andy nodded. 'Tell me about it.'

'Leave it with me. I'll make some inquiries.'

'So that's it? There's nothing more I can do?'

'No, I have what I need. I'll be in touch.'

'Thank you.'

'Don't thank me just yet, but I think this will prove to be a storm in a teacup.'

৯

Andy saw Lily staggering up the beach. 'I thought it was you. What the hell are you doing?'

She stumbled toward him. 'Trying to get fit.'

He grimaced. 'I can think of warmer ways.'

'True. The water's so bitter, my fingers and toes are numb. It takes hours to get the circulation back.'

'Bloody hell,' Andy said, staring at Lily intensely. 'I was only joking the other week when I asked if you were going swimming.'

She shrugged off the top half of her wetsuit revealing a black one-piece swimsuit.

Andy gulped but couldn't look away.

Lily wrapped a towel around herself. 'I've missed you.'

He nodded. 'It's nothing personal. I've been working shorter hours, trying to get my shit together. Going to counselling. Trying to get over the feeling that I've fucked up my life.'

'It's not that dire, surely?'

'I can't move forward until I sort out things with Edie. The good news is that I finally met with Teddy. He hopes it'll turn out to be a storm in a teacup.'

Andy and Lily walked along the beach.

'Excellent.' Lily grinned. 'If it makes you feel better, my life's still fucked too.'

'Still?'

She rolled her eyes. 'If only Matt hadn't come to Clearwater. If only I hadn't invited him up to my apartment. If only we hadn't opened the second bottle of champagne. The only person to blame is me.'

'It's definitely over with Matt and Ben?'

Lily nodded. 'Yep. Both of them have left the building.'

'I'm sorry, Lil. When do ties get cut?'

'Why can't exes remain exes?'

Andy laughed. 'They always hang on.'

'Yes they do. Not Ben, obviously. I thought I might have something with him, but it was clearly a rebound hiccup.'

'And now we're both single.'

'What happened between you and Zena? I thought there was a spark.'

Andy contemplated the question. 'I thought there might be too, but we're much better suited being friends. If she ever stops being angry with me.'

'It was a misunderstanding. It'll blow over.' Lily stopped walking and her eyes filled with tears.

'Hey, what's up?' Andy asked, looking at her. 'Have I upset you?'

Lily shook her head. 'I love it here, but...'

'What? Why?'

'The shop. It's costing more money to run than I'm earning. If I want to continue, I need to sell my Sydney cottage. In fact, I *am* selling my cottage.'

'You've made a choice? I'd hate you to leave. I didn't realise the situation was so bad.'

'So many things here have bought me great joy. Clearwater, my shop, owning my own business, the glorious coastal vibe, the beach, my new-found love of winter ocean swimming—'

'Of course,' Andy deadpanned.

She touched his shoulder. 'True. I'm really glad you suggested the idea.'

'I wasn't serious.'

'You should try it. We can do it together.'

'Mental health and all that.'

Lily sniffed. 'Something like that. Anyway, I really like hanging out with you and Zena. In many ways, it's been the best experience of my life.'

'But? Girlfriend in a coma?' Would she get the reference?

'I know, it's serious,' said Lily.

She did. Andy was chuffed. 'Who doesn't love The Smiths?'

'You'll never defeat me, Andy,' Lily said, smiling. 'But it is serious. The cottage, the money. Mum and Dad getting older and living in Sydney. And honestly, sometimes I feel a bit lonely and lost here.'

He pulled Lily close, before releasing her. 'You have me and you're only two hours' drive from civilisation. Please don't rush into anything.'

Lily wiped her eyes. 'I'm not crying. It's the wind.'

'You won't always feel like this,' Andy persisted. 'Give it time. There's no quick fix. Believe me, I know. One day you'll wake and you'll feel brighter. Time is a great healer.' And Andy believed every word he was saying.

'I feel better just talking to you.' Lily brightened.

They stared out to sea a bit longer. Watching the fading sun, the surf and the surfers, before the wind became icy.

'I don't know how surfers do it day after day in the freezing water,' Lily said, as they turned to walk into town.

'What are you talking about? You've just been out there.'

'For fifteen minutes, not three hours.'

'How do any of us do it, Lil? Surfers spend hours paddling and treading water waiting for the perfect wave. The rest of us are probably searching for solid ground. I know I am.'

CHAPTER 37

Lily

The night after I saw Andy at the beach, Zena dragged me to the pub. When I say dragged, I mean I eagerly obliged.

'Seven days in a row?' she said when I told her I'd been swimming every morning.

'Eight!'

'I'm impressed.' She paused and stared at our meals. 'Still. Look at us. Two fucked-up messes eating a house salad and fries and drinking mineral water.'

'At least we might win the meat tray.'

We clinked glasses and laughed.

'So, what's happening?' I asked.

Zena shook her head. 'I don't know. Am I fit to be a single mum? I have blue hair, a dragon tatt and dubious dress sense.'

I checked out her red and white striped knitted dress and patent leather black boots. 'Red suits you. You'll be an amazing parent.'

'Thanks. I'd have to change my whole way of living.'

I stared at our glasses. 'You already have.'

'I don't even know if I want to keep the baby. If I want to be a mother.'

I poked at my salad. 'No one can answer that question except you, and probably Nate. Have you seen him? Spoken to him?'

Zena shook her head. 'No.'

'I regret my abortion, but at the same time I didn't want to be a mum at sixteen. It would've been a disaster. Now I worry if karma will decide for me. I want children. One child at least.' I took a breath. 'Who knows what I'll do if the right guy doesn't come along. I might have a baby on my own, if I'm capable.' I stared around the pub. 'But then, how would I do it? Sperm bank? Friend?' I shook my head. 'You're running out of time to decide.'

'I never envisioned being a single mum. I wanted the whole deal.' Zena's eyes welled.

'Prince Charming?'

'Something like that. I'm so confused.' She wiped her eyes. 'Enough about my sordid life, let's talk about the clusterfuck that is *your* life. Have you spoken with Ben?'

I shook my head. 'Nope. He's wiped me from his life. Completely disappeared. It's totally my fault, but I've rung. I've texted. Emailed. He's not responding. It's over.'

'Cause and effect. You were naughty, but I apologise for suggesting your whole life's a clusterfuck. Remember the disaster with the cold room thermometer? Now, *that* was a clusterfuck! Completely ruined several hundred dollars' worth of flowers.'

Zena smiled, so I smiled back. We raised our glasses.

'Chin up, Lil.'

Winter on the coast was beautiful but harsh. The days were shorter and darker. Temperatures dropped to freezing, the bitter winds bit hard. To keep warm inside the shop, I wore jeans, a jumper, scarf, leather gloves and two pairs of socks with my boots. There were fewer tourists and the town's people didn't seem to buy flowers, even though most blooms were looking their best in winter. But people kept dying, babies kept being born and couples still celebrated anniversaries. I also had my standing weekly orders with a couple of restaurants and local businesses.

I wasn't sleeping much, so at odd hours, I watched and listened for the dark dwellers. Lights came on at one when Sally's boss, baker senior, baked bread for the morning; and Barry the newsagent, at four, rolled up newspapers in readiness for delivery. Street cleaners arrived every morning promptly at five, along with the dawn milk deliveries to cafés. Truck drivers, nurses, plumbers, builders hit the roads at first light. Dog-walkers came out about the same time. Most city commuters caught the five-forty train to Sydney. They dashed for the station, wearing their corporate navy, grey or black uniforms. I didn't miss the mad scramble to make it to the bus or train on time, or the battle for a seat.

Because I was up half the night, during the day, I went through the motions and tried to avoid falling asleep. Every day bar Friday and Monday, I swam in the ocean, despite the maximum temperature for the last four days being twelve degrees. The sea temp was fifteen, so it was warmer in the water than out.

❧

On Friday morning, there was little foot traffic, so to amuse myself, I strung up fairy lights around the walls and front door. I also made silk floral headbands, steady sellers. The rest were on display.

'Greetings,' said Henry, walking in. 'The shop's looking great.'

I smiled. 'Thanks.' Embarrassed, my lips quivered. 'About the only thing that does.'

Henry scratched his chin. 'Yeah. Shit happens.'

'It shouldn't.'

'Nothing's so bad it can't be sorted. But please don't have a screaming match at my wedding.'

I blinked away a couple of rogue tears. 'I'll understand if you don't want me doing your flowers.'

Henry looked startled. 'I was joking. I don't know exactly what happened between you and Ben, but you'll work it out.' Henry took a deep breath. 'Though, if push comes to shove, you understand I'll have to choose Ben. He is my best man, after all.'

'Of course.'

'But you'll have it sorted by then. Think positive.'

'Have you seen him?'

Henry shook his head. 'Not since he went back to Adelaide.'

I coughed. 'Adelaide?'

'Sorry, Lil. I thought you knew.'

'It's okay. Do you have any idea for how long?'

Henry shook his head.

'In more positive news, Teddy called. Pamela's caved. He received a letter from her confirming that my current contract is valid.'

'That's great news.'

'I know. A huge relief.'

'Now then, about this,' Henry said, handing me a folder with my recent financials. 'Do you have a moment?'

The shop was empty. 'Sure.'

'Good news. Your figures are looking slightly better.'

'Really?'

'I said, *slightly*. I'd hold off on buying the Ferrari for a little bit longer.'

Boys and their toys.

'The headband venture saved you this winter.'

I beamed. 'Who'd have thought?'

'Well, clearly you did, Lily. You have an eye for the innovative. Go with your gut. It's working.'

'Not when it comes to gardening clogs.'

'No, but you were a novice when you bought those. However, you could be doing better.'

'But I don't spend any money except on the shop. I'm not doing anything but living, breathing, sleeping and existing as Lily's Little Flower Shop.'

'You're still not pulling a minimum wage.'

I shrugged. 'I don't need more than a minimum life. I wake up, sell flowers, feed Trouble, sleep. Repeat. I'm selling the cottage in the spring so that will help.'

'It certainly will and then you can focus solely on this business, but is this what you want?'

'It's what I have to do.'

'Only if you truly love it. You could always pack up and move back to Sydney.'

'And do what exactly?'

'Corporate life and suits?' Henry thought a moment. 'Are you still delivering flowers for free?'

I nodded.

'Wrong answer. You should charge a minimum of ten dollars per delivery, depending on distance. Don't give away your services free of charge. There's petrol to consider, your time. No one gets anything for free.' He took a breath. 'Is your supplier the cheapest and the best?'

'I think so.'

'You think? You should have more than one supplier anyway, to keep business competitive. And try to secure more standing orders for cafés and other local businesses. At least with those, you're guaranteed weekly sales.' Henry looked around the shop. 'I know the clogs weren't a success, but you're selling floral headbands at a great pace. How about candles and chocolates?'

'As in, "Here are your flowers; would you also like a box of chocolates?"'

'Why not? Upselling is the name of the game, and it could mean the difference between just scraping by and making a profit, especially in the slower months.'

'So, you're okay with me buying chocolates and candles?'

Henry smiled. 'Within reason. You could have chocolates by the cash register—'

'And candles in the front window.'

He left and I sat alone in my shop with Trouble, drinking tap water and sourcing chocolates and candles. I placed a couple of small orders. That task completed, my fingers itched to call Ben's number. Rather than put myself through the misery, I deleted it. There was no way I could text or phone him on impulse now.

'Good morning, Lily's Little Flower Shop,' I answered when the phone rang.

'Lily Mason? It's Zac Berry from AustIn, Human Resources. Hope I'm not interrupting.'

My old company. 'Well, actually—'

'I won't take up much of your time. You may have heard that Glenn Kelly has left. I'm letting you know in case you'd like to interview for the position.'

I almost laughed out loud. 'Thank you but no.'

Back to business. Normally, baker Sally was in first thing Friday for her standing weekly order. But it was after midday and there was still no sight of her. I decided to take the flowers to the bakery myself and stuck a *back in ten minutes* sign on my front door.

'Sally, hi. Here's your order for the week. Gorgeous, aren't they?'

As soon as she saw me, I realised I'd made a terrible mistake.

'I must have forgotten to tell you, Lily, I won't be ordering any more flowers from you.' She said it without a trace of emotion.

'Pardon?'

'I don't want your flowers.'

'But ... why?'

'Do you really need to ask? I'm surprised you can still show your face, let alone walk into my shop. Ben didn't deserve to be treated like that.'

'I don't know what you've heard—'

'I've heard all I need to know from Pamela. Please leave.'

'You don't want the flowers?'

Sally shook her head. 'Maybe you can buy city people off, but it's not the way we do things around here.'

Dazed, I slumped into Zena's salon and plonked the flowers on her front desk. 'Here! Take these. You have to come over after work. It's Friday and I need you.'

'What happened?'

'Sally's cancelled her weekly order. Says Ben didn't deserve how I treated him.'

'Harsh, but then, Sally's a bitch.'

'I'll miss her croissants.'

She sighed. 'I'll share mine. See you at six.'

I walked back to my shop and wrote on my chalkboard. *Time for a cocktail? It's always five o'clock somewhere in the world.* Anonymous.

I texted Andy.

Please come over for a drink after work. I miss you.

At five forty, fed up and having had enough of the day, I was about to close when the front door swung open and a guy walked in carrying an enormous bunch of red roses.

'Not often I deliver flowers to a flower shop,' he chuckled. 'Lily Mason?'

'That's me.'

'These are for you.'

He handed them to me and left just as quickly.

My hands were shaking as I opened the card, hoping it was from Ben. The flowers were from Matt.

Lils, I'm sorry I couldn't keep you. I'll love you forever. Take care. M xxx

CHAPTER 38

Z ena turned up just after the flowers arrived. 'Here,' she said, handing me a bottle of wine. 'I can't drink, but that doesn't mean you have to suffer too. Feeling any better?'

'I can't afford to lose any more standing orders,' I sighed wistfully, 'but on the bright side, I've got candles and chocolates arriving on Monday.'

'Why more merchandise?'

'I've got to improve profit. You sell shampoos.'

Zena spied the roses. 'These are gorgeous.'

'Matt.'

Zena raised her eyebrows. 'I won't ask.'

'I can always resell them.'

'No!'

I smiled. 'Now, about you. Any more thoughts?'

'I have no idea—'

'Andy!'

'Lily, I told you—'

'Andy and Zena in my flower shop.' I beamed. 'Just like old times.'

'Hey, Zena.' Andy politely kissed her on the cheek.

She flinched. 'Hi.'

There was a long pause before I spoke through the silence. 'About time you saw each other. This is ridiculous.'

Zena and Andy stared blankly at me.

'Right then,' I continued. 'The reason I've gathered you here this evening is because Teddy called telling me that Pamela has accepted that she can't raise my rent until my contract expires.'

'Woo hoo.' Zena smiled. 'That's great news.'

'I'll spread the word,' said Andy. 'Well done, Lil. I'll make sure that everyone knows. Your win will encourage others to fight Pamela's rent hike.'

'Indeed,' I agreed. 'And now, enough of this stilted polite conversation—'

'What?' Zena quizzed.

I ignored her. 'I don't care that I'm being an interfering friend, but we're the three musketeers—'

Andy and Zena both groaned. Then laughed.

'Sorry I was a dick about Edie,' said Zena, spinning toward Andy. 'I was being pouty and petulant. Because it happened straight after our night, I thought you'd been using me like so many other men I've been with.'

Andy shrugged. 'How can you say that? Never.'

'Should I leave the room?' I said.

They shook their heads.

'No,' said Andy. 'Stay.' He turned to Zena. 'What I told you that night still holds. I've grown to love you as a friend. I thought we were all good when I dropped you home that night.'

'We were.' Zena wiped away tears. 'But then Edie happened. I was so stunned. Next thing I know, you're in hospital. I was thinking about myself when I should have been reaching out and being a real friend.'

'I told you both at the club, I had no idea we were still

married, and as it turns out,' he waved some papers in front of us, 'Edie and I are officially divorced.'

'That's fantastic, Andy.' I pulled him into a bear hug. 'Congratulations.'

Was Andy blushing? I handed him a glass of wine. 'This calls for a celebration.'

'Thanks,' he said, reaching for it, 'but let me explain. When I first met Edie, she was charming and confident. It took me a while to realise she had a huge ego and was manipulating me. In the beginning, I was under her spell. Edie had, or rather *has* no "off" switch. She has no natural sense of boundaries that normal people have. She always pushes to the max. But at first, she was mesmerising—'

'You don't have to explain.'

'Please, Lil. I know I don't, but I want to. Talking about it helps me too.' He gulped his wine. 'Edie was great back then. Funny, bright. I fell in love with her.'

'We know that, dummy,' Zena said, punching Andy in the arm. 'You did marry her.'

He winced. 'About that, by the time we married, I was having real doubts. The fights had started, the yelling, her obsessive behaviour.'

'So why propose?' I asked, frustrated.

Andy shook his head. 'I didn't. She did. I was so taken by the gesture and the fact she loved me, I said yes. We married two months later. By the time the date came around, I was too far into it to express my doubts, which were mounting daily.'

'But you still did it?' Zena said.

'Marrying Edie was an act of self-loathing.'

I knew all about that. 'So how did it get so bad?' I asked. Then regretted it. 'Sorry. We're giving you the third degree.'

'It's fine. Could I please have more wine?' I did as requested. 'Where was I?'

'How did it get so bad?' Zena asked.

'She liked to be in control and when I say control, I mean down to the tiniest detail of my life. The minute I left work, she'd ring. Every day it was the same. As if she couldn't stand for me to have time to myself. What was I doing? Who was I seeing? She told me it stemmed from childhood. Edie's dad walked out when she was seven and it was like she was trying to punish me for her father abandoning her all those years ago.

'I didn't realise until I was too entrenched, that even Edie's relationship with Pamela and other close friends, was screwed. Edie blamed her mother for her dad leaving. Looking back, I can see that every friendship and relationship she's had, turned toxic. Like King George's relationship with America.'

'I will kill your friends and family to remind you of my love.' Andy smiled. 'Oceans rise, empires fall—'

'What?' Zena asked, confused.

'Don't worry.' I smiled at Andy. '*Hamilton*. What about Pamela?'

'Nice segue way. They fight. But Pamela always has her own agenda. It suited her for Edie to come back and stir up trouble. Perhaps to deflect what Pamela's been trying to do with the rents since Trish died.'

Zena and I nodded. 'Makes sense,' I said. 'What comes next?'

'The papers are signed and I've got a copy, so can leave Edie behind. As angry as I am about how she pretended to submit the divorce papers and abused me, I have to move on and take the next step. Maybe even forgive.'

'Nice,' I said.

He gave me a thumbs up. Andy was a gem.

'You don't need to forgive,' Zena said heatedly. 'Why do you have to forgive Edie?'

Andy swallowed. 'I'm not interested in living the next forty years enslaved to anger and bitterness. Life's too short to put up with being unhappy.'

Zena nodded. 'You're quite together for someone who's seemingly—'

'A loon?'

'I didn't say that.'

'Other skeletons?' I asked, swallowing my drink.

'Other than the marriage and hospital stints?' He paused. 'None that I can think of. And I don't want there to be any. I'm learning from my past behaviour and trying not to repeat it.' Andy's voice was soft. 'I checked into the clinic as a precaution. I needed a zero-stress environment to get my head together. Trish's death really knocked me, and then Edie...'

'Yeah. A lot of info to take in,' I said.

'I'm sorry I freaked out,' said Zena.

Andy laughed. *'You freaked out!'*

'Me three,' I added.

'Okay. All three musketeers were officially freaked out.' Zena half smiled. 'Speaking of being freaked out...'

'Who's freaked out and what have I missed?' Taylor bellowed, bounding through the door. 'Come on, guys, spill.'

There was a crazy four-way hug and then we stepped back to our respective seats. I dragged over a wooden box for Taylor.

'More importantly,' I said, facing Taylor. 'What are you doing here?'

'You sounded like such a sad sack on the phone the other night, I thought I'd come down and surprise you. I was under the impression that Friday night drinks had ceased, but clearly I was wrong.'

She enthusiastically accepted a drink. 'Here's cheers,' she said, taking a large swig. 'Walked in just as Zena was taking the stage.' She looked directly at her. 'What's going on?'

I held my breath. 'Maybe now's not the time,' I suggested.

Zena waved me away. 'Tell one, tell all. Taylor, we're in the midst of baring our souls so I thought I'd throw in my own news—'

'You're pregnant,' Andy blurted.

I gasped.

Zena looked shell-shocked. 'Am I showing?'

'Joking,' Andy replied. 'Zena, I'm joking, aren't I?' He turned a whiter shade than my walls.

'What?' said Taylor. 'You're pregnant?'

Taylor fell silent and my tongue was tied.

'And the baby is...' Andy put a finger up to his lips. 'Nate's?'

Zena burst into tears. 'I'm so bloody stupid. I'm eight weeks, give or take. In some ways, it seems like yesterday and in others, so much has happened since then.'

Taylor and I were crying.

'So you've decided...' I started.

'Yes, keeping the baby. I'll tell Nate when I find him. He's taken off up the coast.'

'I'm confused,' said Taylor. 'Are you two back together?'

'No way!' Zena yelled. 'No,' she repeated more calmly.

I reached over and wrapped my arms around her. 'It'll be okay.'

'Of course it will,' said Andy. 'We're the three musketeers, four counting Taylor, five, if you count bub. We'll help, won't we, gals?'

'Aunty Lil?' I said. 'I like it.'

'Bloody hell,' said Taylor. 'Bombshell. Nate's baby. Well, blow me.'

Zena sniffed to stem the tears. 'Long story.'

'We've got all night,' said Taylor. 'Who's up for the pub?'

'I'm in,' said Zena. 'Only just got my appetite back. According to the experts, I'll lose it again, but right now I'm famished.'

'Thanks,' said Andy, 'but I'll take a raincheck. It's been quite the night already.'

'Why don't you two go,' I encouraged. 'I might come down when I finish my paperwork. If not, I'll see you when you get back.'

'You sure?' Taylor asked.

'Yes, shoo. Zena can fill you in on everything. I've heard it all before.' I squeezed Zena's hand. 'Love you.'

CHAPTER 39

'Come on, Taylor.' I pulled up the blinds late Saturday afternoon after I closed the shop. 'You've slept long enough.'

'I've been working hard,' she whined. 'I needed a decent sleep.'

'How's the hangover?'

'What hangover?' she croaked.

'I hope you didn't lead Zena astray.'

'Mineral water all the way. For her. Bourbon for me. And we played pool. It was fun.'

Much to Taylor's horror, ten minutes later, we were at the beach and I was rolling on my wetsuit.

'You're really going in there. To swim?'

'Indeed.'

She took in my appearance as if noticing me for the first time since she'd arrived. 'Darling, you're all skin and bone and bloody pale. You need a holiday.'

'Shut up.'

'No, seriously, a quick trip to Hawaii.'

'Having you here is as good as a holiday. See you in fifteen.'

I wandered down the sand, found my spot, took a deep breath and plunged in. I'd never get used to the shock of ice water hitting my face and scalp. Invigorating was not the word I was screaming. I paddled around for the obligatory fifteen minutes before I could stand it no longer. It was a relief to step onto dry land.

'You were really loving it out there.' Taylor rolled her eyes and greeted me with a towel.

'Absolutely,' I agreed.

'Now that the bracing, nay, freezing wind has cured me of my headache and tiredness, tell me what's going on?' she demanded as we walked back to the shop.

'You know everything—'

'Tell me again. And, after we've exhausted all conversation, let's watch *Titanic*.'

I groaned.

'See, your life could be much worse.'

'Yeah, though I'm firmly entrenched in feeling sorry for myself and moments away from an all-consuming depression. Not only that, but my financial situation hasn't improved. Well, not much. Although, thanks to my lawyer, my rent will remain the same until the end of the contract. Still, I had to pay for his services. But after I sell my cottage, finances will improve.'

'How's the market?'

'You'd know better than me, but I'll take what I can get. Again,' I said, almost talking to myself, 'I don't have much choice.'

'You really are doing an amazing job with the shop, Lil,' she said after we walked inside, picked up a crown and tried it on. 'How's the headband business?'

'Thriving.'

'Clogs?'

I pointed to Trouble's hutch. 'Still got seven pairs.'

'Ouch, you should offer a free pair with every purchase over one-hundred and fifty dollars.'

'That's not a bad idea. I've also ordered chocolates and candles to diversify.'

'Always the entrepreneur.'

'Except I'm going bankrupt while doing it.'

'As sad as it is, I think you're making the right decision re your house ... unless of course you want to give this up and move back to Sydney?'

'No, I'll keep moving forward. Spring's around the corner and the wedding season will be upon us.'

'Maybe you should have heard Zac out when he called. I bet the company's offering a good deal.'

I snorted. 'He asked me to interview for a position I'd essentially held six months ago. No way.'

'No way? You won't consider taking the promotion that was rightly yours?'

'He wanted me to interview. Besides, I don't want the job. However amazing the salary might be. Come on,' I grabbed Trouble, 'let's sit on the veranda.'

Taylor followed me upstairs. I had a quick shower, while Taylor busied herself pouring wine and laying out cheese, olives, smoked salmon and crackers on a platter.

'Okay, change of topic,' said Taylor, once we were settled outside. 'How about we do some online shopping? Or window shopping, at least? I've found some great websites to stalk. But I need to be careful. After a few too many of these,' she held up her glass, 'I tend to make poor decisions. My cupboard is littered with clothes and shoes I don't wear.'

I gulped my drink. 'No danger of me overspending. My

credit cards are maxed out. I might just retire to my bed for the foreseeable future.'

'Stop being so dramatic. Here!' Taylor pushed a bowl of green olives under my nose. 'Suck on one of these.'

I pushed them away, then relented and took a couple.

Taylor leant back on her chair, taking in the view. She looked quite pleased with herself. 'You're not still mooning over Ben? Daydreaming about a guy who's not even in the same state as you is a bloody waste of time. I'd understand if he was around the corner and we could spy on him, maybe follow him to the shops and stuff, but we can't even do that, so what's the point?' She popped an olive into her mouth.

'I'm not. As I said to Andy, Ben was a bounce-back affair. I can see that now.'

'Bounce Back Ben! I like it. Speaking of Andy, did he stay long last night?'

'No. He helped me tidy up. We chatted, both worried about Zena, and how she'll manage the pregnancy, but agreed we'll be there for her.'

'Are you blushing?'

I felt my face. 'Just flushed from the swim. Enough about me. What's going on with you?'

'You know me, Lil. I'm a slave to the office. Though...'

'Though, what?'

'Nothing.'

Taylor had just popped *Titanic* into the DVD when Mum phoned.

She was crying. 'Gary died.'

My heart wrenched. As for my guilt at not being with her? Priceless. 'I'm so sorry. When?'

'This morning.'

I motioned for Taylor to pour me a wine. 'What can I do?'

'Nothing. He's dead. My baby.'

'I'll come up and see you, I promise.'

'Poor Gary,' I said to Taylor ten minutes later as I patted Trouble. 'Very sad.'

'He was old though,' Taylor soothed.

'The heart doesn't care about age. He was her companion.'

CHAPTER 40

Monday afternoon, Taylor was back in Sydney and I was in my shop when Alastair Briggs, the AustIn CEO, phoned. I almost fell over.

'Hello, Lily, long time, no see.' He paused. 'Yes, I still have the lamest lines. Don't say I told you so, but I'd love to talk to you about new opportunities within the company.'

'Thanks, but—'

'Before you say anything, you won't have to formally interview for the job. Zac got a bollocking over that.'

'I'm sure he was just following orders from the board.'

'Salary's negotiable,' Alastair said, as if I hadn't spoken. 'But it will be substantially higher than your previous, somewhere in the one hundred and fifty thousand range. Starting date is also negotiable.' He sucked in some air and breathed out. 'In addition, you'll have a bigger office, larger support and sales team to manage, autonomy of your own projects—'

'That's a lot for me to take in, in under a minute. Plus, I have a flower business. And what about the board?'

'I'll pretend I didn't hear that. All I'm asking is that you have lunch with me in Sydney to discuss the offer.'

'Thanks, but I'm very busy.'

'I'll make it worth your while. Not to put any pressure on you, but can you do midday tomorrow? Spice Market?'

'You remember my favourite restaurant?' What would it take for me to move back to the city, live in my beautiful cottage and resume work at AustIn?

'Let's make it Wednesday.'

'Okay. Wednesday it is.'

After Alastair hung up, I thought about the salary. It would be nice not to have to keep an eye on petrol prices. I entertained the idea of commuting from Clearwater and employing someone full-time to run the shop. Sometimes I felt isolated living down here. But if I were to commute, I'd be exhausted and miss my swims. Still, for one hundred and fifty thousand dollars, plus bonuses, it was tempting. More than tempting.

I rang Iris and confided in her, but not before telling her about Gary.

'Your poor mother must be devastated.'

'She is.' I sighed. 'I've been offered a promotion at AustIn.'

Iris clicked her tongue. '*The* promotion?' She stopped briefly. 'And?'

'I haven't made up my mind. I'm meeting my old boss in Sydney Wednesday for lunch.'

'A couple of weeks ago you declared your undying love for Clearwater—'

'I know, but money—'

'Money isn't everything. Remember what I said at the beginning of this venture, about how the life you choose to live may not make you rich, but will reward you in many other ways?' Iris cleared her throat. 'Lily, are you really going to run back to Sydney because you've hit a speed bump?'

'I'm considering my future. And I'm financially strapped. Returning to Sydney, I could slot back into my old life and with the salary increase, could pay off my mortgage in seven years, not seventy.'

'I understand it's tempting, but even so, ask yourself, what makes you happy? That's what you need to decide. What does Lily Mason want?'

'Money,' I answered quickly. 'Financial security.'

'Honey, you've been there. Done that. Focus on the now. On what is. Put one foot in front of the other—'

'I'm trying, Aunty Iris. I really am.'

'Don't keep looking in the rear-vision mirror. Move forward.'

'It's hard and I'm really tired.'

'That's life. Get used to it.'

Wednesday morning, I was excited to meet with Alastair, intrigued. I hadn't slept in anticipation. Maybe even hope. I arrived at the restaurant bang on midday.

Alastair met me at the entrance. 'You always were punctual.'

I smiled. 'I don't like mucking people around. Time is money.'

'Spoken like a true capitalist.'

'I'm not so sure anymore.'

Once shown to our table and seated, Alastair began talking. 'So, you've heard about Glenn.'

'I tried to tell you.'

Alastair nodded. 'The board thought they were acting in the best interests of the company.'

I didn't respond.

'I'm here to make you an offer. I know you'll be brilliant at this job. As I mentioned over the phone, an increased sales team, autonomy, One hundred and fifty thousand—'

'Make it two and I'll consider it.'

His eyes gleamed the way they always did when he was in the heat of negotiation. 'One hundred and seventy-five thousand. And a new car. I'll give you as long as you need to wrap things up down south.'

'It's tempting.' I wasn't lying. It was more money than I could ever imagine earning at the flower shop. 'I'd have my own clients and the board wouldn't interfere?'

'To a point.'

'What does that mean?'

'You'd still have to answer to them like you did before.'

I sipped my mineral water and thought back to my years with AustIn. The endless meetings, the compromises. The bullshit. 'Yes, I would,' I said finally. 'I would have to answer to the board.'

Having my own business, I only had to answer to myself. Could I give it up?

We ordered lunch, including my favourite Peking duck pancakes, and chatted about market conditions, rival companies and changing personnel.

After we'd eaten, Alastair got back to the point. 'Last year, you'd have killed to be offered this job. You had fire, determination—'

'But you still chose Glenn over me. In your words, "the company feels you'd be wasted in management".'

'I was wrong.' Alastair sighed. 'The company has made several missteps. Regrettably, we can't go back, but we can move forward and with you being at the front of the team, we can do that.'

'Alast—'

'Hear me out. The company shafted you.' He drank some water. 'I know that. The board knows that. We want you back. Glenn is gone.'

I shook my head. 'There will always be others. The boys club always wins.'

He scratched his head. 'We need you.'

There were many reasons to go back. The salary. Sydney. My cottage. But... 'I have my own business now.'

'Selling flowers?'

'I love it. I'm my own boss.'

'But is it financially viable?'

'It will be once I sell my cottage.' I took several moments to think about it. 'I appreciate the offer. I really do.'

Alastair read my expression. 'But?'

'Now that I've experienced being in charge of my career, I don't think I can go back. I want to stay in Clearwater and focus on my business.'

'Is there anything I can do to change your mind?' Alastair seemed sincere. 'Think of what you're giving up. The money—'

'My independence. I don't want to move back to the city. I'm sorry. I've thought about it. I've considered the costs and benefits, but my heart won't allow me to give up what I have now.'

Alastair went to speak, but I stopped him. 'Thanks, but no. Last year I'd have jumped through hoops. That position was a long-held ambition, but once I let it go—'

Alastair sighed. 'You let it go. I understand, but if you change your mind—'

'I'll let you know.'

We parted amicably and on the drive back to Clearwater, I felt relieved.

'In my heart I know it's the right decision,' I said to Taylor when I called her.

She sighed. 'I didn't think you would. Despite the ups and downs of your love life and the shop, I've never seen you looking so animated and engaged.'

'Yeah. I realised the only reason I wanted to go back was for the money. The job didn't make me happy. It's not creative. It's actually kind of dull.'

'Thanks. I won't take it personally.'

'You know what I mean.'

'For what it's worth, Lil, I think you *have* made the right decision.'

CHAPTER 41

The following Monday evening I arrived at Zena's salon to find her chatting to Andy. 'Glad you guys have made up.' Zena giggled. 'I'm trying to convince Andy to dye his hair.'

I shook my head. 'Please no.'

Andy grimaced. 'Sorry, Zeen. Two against one.'

Zena pretended to sulk. 'I don't care. Maybe I can convince someone from tap. Miss Liz, perhaps.'

'Fat chance,' I replied. 'Come on, we have an exam to get to.'

Zena pointed at her tap shoes. 'I know. Nine long weeks.'

'I'd love to come along.' Andy glanced at Zena's stomach. 'Although, do you think you should?'

'Andy,' Zena rolled her eyes, 'it's amateur tap, I'm not shooting for an equestrian gold medal.' She paused. 'So, you're in?'

Andy grinned. 'Sure. Why not?'

'Fine.' I tapped my Fitbit. 'Could we get a move on? There are certificates to be handed out.'

'Can't wait,' said Andy.

'We're pretty shit,' said Zena.

Andy laughed.

'Zena speaks the truth, Andy. But if you have an hour to kill, you may as well watch our excruciating routine.'

❦

'Don't laugh.' Zena was pulling on her tap shoes at the school hall.

'I'm not here to judge,' Andy replied.

For the next hour, Zena and I twirled and tapped our hearts out, Zena especially. So much so that Miss Liz gave her the certificate for *Most Improved*.

'I was sure I'd win it,' said Betty, after the awards were handed out. 'I've been dancing with bunions.'

'Aw, Betts, pay the young ones their due,' said Elsie.

I turned to look at Ruby, Scarlett and Pink, who were standing in a corner, giggling and on their phones, before realising she was talking about Zena and me. 'I got *Most Persistent*,' I stated. 'Not sure I'm happy about that.'

'Tell you what,' said Zena, clearly on a high. 'Elsie and Betty, this week, your washes and sets are on the house. Okay?'

Betty smiled. 'Okay.'

'Could I interest you in a green colour as well?' Zena asked.

Elsie and Betty laughed.

'Always the card,' said Betty.

'Can you believe we've been doing these classes all these months?' I said.

'Maybe I can't,' agreed Betty, 'but my feet can.'

'Will you all be back next term?' Miss Liz asked as we were leaving.

'Yes.' Zena hesitated. 'Maybe.'

'I'll definitely be back,' I said.

'So will we,' Betty and Elsie chimed in.

'Those old girls are dynamite,' said Andy as we walked out of the hall.

'Yeah.' Zena giggled. 'I'm going to miss them and the class.'

'You're not dying,' I said as we ambled along the street. 'I'm sure you could squeeze in another term.'

'Squeeze being the operative word.' Zena patted her stomach.

After discussing whether to have dinner, Zena opted out, so I dropped her home, ready to drop off Andy as well.

'We should hang out together more often,' Andy said as I pulled into his driveway. 'Come in for a bit?'

'Sure, but we hang out a lot, Andy.'

'You've got to eat. I've got tons of French onion soup. *Be my guest. Put my service to the test.*'

I laughed. 'How can I resist such an outrageous accent?' I turned off the engine and followed him inside.

He opened the front door and paused, but not for long. 'I'm in love with you, Lily Mason. Have been since you first arrived in town. How could I not be?'

I was stunned. Speechless.

'Anytime you want to step in and say something would be great,' he said.

Wordlessly, I walked over and touched his cheek. He took my hand and kissed it, then took my face in his hands and kissed me on the lips. 'Is this okay?'

I nodded. 'I think so. I'm just surprised. Also, you promised me soup?'

'We can stop if you like.'

'Let's not be hasty.' I kissed him again. 'What happens next?'

He grinned. 'I could show you my secret love dungeon.'

I took his hand. 'Wonders never cease. Lead the way.'

We started kissing on his bed but then he pulled back. 'Lil, before this goes any further, what's really happening with Ben? And Matt for that matter?'

'It's completely over with both of them.'

'You sure? I don't want to start something and have my heart broken.'

'Me neither.'

He kissed me again. 'We can take it slowly.'

'Or not. Kiss me again.'

It was a kiss full of warmth, passion and promise. I kissed him back, my arms pulling him in to my chest. His hands travelled up my body, cupping my neck as his mouth kissed mine, more urgently this time.

'This is very forward of you, Miss Lily,' he said, as I pushed him down on his bed.

He smiled as I moved on top, my upper body bending lower to kiss him. At first, we were slow and tentative, his hands travelling the length of my body.

'Have I mentioned you're a good kisser?' he said, when we took a breather.

I smiled.

'Well, you are. But I think we're both wearing too many clothes.'

I was melting. This felt different to the times I'd been with Ben, maybe because I'd gotten to know Andy as a friend first. Of course, I still had no idea what I was doing. My stomach wobbled, my upper arms were pale, and as for my hands and fingernails? They were a mess.

Andy kissed me on the lips, then stared into my eyes. 'Hey, beautiful, where have you gone?'

I shook my head. 'Nowhere. I'm just...' *Don't fuck this up, Lil. Just don't.* I took a deep breath, sat up and pulled my navy jersey dress up over my head and threw it to the floor. Now, I was only wearing a bra, pants and sheer black cami.

Andy pulled me back down on top of him and kissed me, his hands venturing under my camisole. His warm hands sent shivers down my spine.

A few seconds later, I took off his shirt and jeans and could feel his erection through his boxers. Breathily, he whispered, 'I think we need to lose all the clothes.'

He removed my camisole and bra. I felt vulnerable, but safe at the same time. The anticipation totally exquisite. I wanted him. All of him – I never wanted this moment – these moments to end.

Us making love, having sex, fucking ... skin to skin. This was what I wanted. I was determined to leave my insecurities with my discarded bra. In this moment, as we explored each other's bodies, I'd never felt so alive, so wanted and so sexy.

Forty-five minutes later we were both flat on our backs, hot, sweaty, exhausted ... and I couldn't wait to do it all over again. 'I liked that.'

He pushed me away. 'You liked it? Is that all? You *liked* it?'

I bit my bottom lip, suppressing a giggle. 'Very much.'

He pulled me in close, wrapping me in a bear hug. 'Must admit I was hoping for more than *I liked that*. I have my work cut out for me.'

I sighed, completely satisfied. 'We have all night.'

He hugged me tighter. 'Yeah, but I'm a bloke. I need to recuperate. Plus, I'm starving.'

I masked my disappointment. The last thing I wanted was for Andy to get out of bed. I wanted him here, to caress him and run my hands over his handsome naked body. I hadn't realised how handsome he was until now. I wanted his undivided attention. I'd liked being with Ben, but this was unique, exciting and new but also comfortable. Being friends first made all the difference. 'Yeah, well I'm still waiting for that soup.'

'Have you seen my underwear? I only cook in the nude on a second date.'

'Promise?'

He left to potter in his kitchen. A few minutes later when I heard him singing, I dragged myself out of bed, hastily dressed, then walked into his en-suite bathroom. I looked in the mirror. I was a mess. Hair that screamed I'd just been fucked, exclamation mark, was only the beginning. I fixed my hair, rubbed some toothpaste over my teeth, sprayed some perfume that I carried in my bag, and wandered into the kitchen.

Andy smiled. 'Finally!' he said, kissing me on the lips and handing me a full glass of wine. 'You look gorgeous.'

I blushed a hundred times over.

'The good thing about soup and salad is that it takes practically no time to prepare. We should be back in bed within minutes.' He paused. 'That is if you want to stay.'

'Stay? But I haven't brought my pyjamas.'

'Exactly.'

Thirty minutes later we were back in bed.

I only drank two glasses of wine, but the night seemed to disappear. Every time I thought we'd completely exhausted ourselves, one of us touched the other and we'd start up again. Sometimes, it might be half an hour that I'd run my fingers ever so lightly over his stomach and chest and then, just when I was drifting to sleep, thinking he too was asleep, Andy would say, 'Don't stop. I'm not asleep, just resting my eyes.'

'I don't want this night to end.'

He cradled me in his arms. 'Why? We have endless nights like this ahead of us.'

Those words made me happy. I rolled into him, spooning him and nuzzling his shoulder. Moments later, we were making love again.

ॐ

'What a night,' I said in the morning, as Andy and I lay in bed kissing.

'No regrets?'

I smiled and kissed his belly. 'None.'

He pulled me up by my arms and kissed my lips. 'I really like you, Lily Mason.'

I kissed him back. 'I really like you, Andy Peterson.'

We kissed again, for a long time.

'I don't want you to go,' he said as I was getting dressed.

'I don't want to leave either,' I whispered. Just the thought of him on top of me made me tingle with ecstasy. Letting Andy into my life felt so right.

'No regrets about not moving back to Sydney?'

I shook my head. 'None. I want this—'

'You mean me, of course.'

'Of course, but I also want something that means something to me—'

'Not quite sure how to take that.'

'I want you,' I said, whacking his arm. 'And I want something more than money.' I grinned. 'That is, once I sell my house. I want my flower shop. Mine. Mine and Trouble's.'

Andy and I kissed again.

'I do have one concern though,' I said. 'I hope us being together won't make things awkward with Zena.'

'If I know Zena, she'll be positively giddy for us.'

CHAPTER 42

Sophie sprang through my door later that morning with her wedding scrapbook. 'Hello!'

I checked my watch. Eleven thirty. 'Skipping school?'

Sophie laughed. 'Not quite. Extended "little lunch" period.'

'So, eleven days to the wedding!'

'That's what I'm here to talk to you about. Sorry I haven't been in for a while. But I must say, you're glowing. I was worried about you after Ben went back to Adelaide.'

'I'm fine, really, Sophie.' I smiled. 'Before you say anything, I understand if you want someone else to do your flowers.'

Sophie looked confused. 'What are you saying?'

'The flowers. Ben.'

'Lily, that's none of my business. But if you want to talk about it—'

I shook my head. 'No.'

'Okay, so let's discuss wedding crowns. Can I have a real one and also a replica as a keepsake? Same for my bridesmaids?'

I beamed. 'Of course.'

Sophie examined the four on display. 'They're amazing, Lil.' She looked more closely at the tiara with four huge cream roses, then one with magenta roses. She picked it up. 'This one's definitely the most striking.'

'I agree.'

'But this is cute and simple.' She replaced the magenta one and picked up another, decorated with white daisies. 'You know,' Sophie said, as if thinking aloud. 'Could I have a simple daisy tiara? And I think my two bridesmaids will look stunning wearing the magnificent magenta ones.'

I nodded. Sophie: understated and beautiful. 'I was at the flower markets the other morning and spoke with my supplier. Your wedding will be overrun with magnificent roses.'

She smiled. 'I can't wait.'

'Though if your bridesmaids are wearing magenta roses, maybe you should be carrying them as well?' I added. 'Instead of blood-red ones?'

Sophie paused for a moment. 'You're right.'

After arranging to meet at Ben's winery the next morning, she left and I got to researching unknown flowers, wedding bouquets, and other things floristry. My mind drifted back to Andy. I wanted to go and sit in his shop and hang out.

As for Ben, I hoped I'd see him before the wedding. What was he up to? Was he going out with someone? Was he happy? Part of me saw the wedding as my opportunity to make amends, and scenarios raced through my mind. What would I say when I met up with him face to face? And what would his response be?

The next morning, I set off early to meet Sophie at the winery to discuss where to position the flowers. For the entire fifteen-minute drive, I had heart palpitations, terrified I'd run into Ben. I saw the 'Ravenstone' sign and turned left down a dirt road. Vineyards intersected with rose bushes. Rolling green hills stood out in the distance. The scenery was breathtaking. A kilometre later, when I pulled up in the car park, Sophie was waiting for me.

'Perfect timing,' she said brightly.

'This place is amazing.' I stepped out of the car and took in the extraordinary view. 'Such a romantic setting.'

Sophie smiled. 'Wait till you see the Ravenstone Dining Room.'

So many reminders of Ben, but I didn't feel melancholy. As soon as I entered the restaurant, I was overwhelmed by the simple luxury of the space, an elegantly refined venue with lofty timber-beamed ceilings, sandstone walls and two enormous open fires.

'Ta da!' Sophie was practically hyperventilating.

I was in awe. 'Wow doesn't begin to describe it.'

She nodded. 'I'm going for understated elegance.'

'Exactly, so we're thinking masses of huge cream roses. Posies for the tables and taller arrangements for the fireplaces and side tables?'

Sophie clapped. 'Yes!'

I took notes and photos as we walked around examining the restaurant and discussing where the arrangements would go.

We walked outside to an adjacent undercover deck that had sweeping views over cow-filled fields, down to the ocean in the distance.

'What do you think?' she asked. 'This is where we'll have the ceremony.'

'Breathtaking. Magical.' I tried to imagine the forty guest-filled chairs, Sophie, Henry, the celebrant... 'Will you have a table set up for where you'll sign your marriage licence?'

She nodded.

'How about a more intricate bouquet for that? It'll come up great in photos? And we can scatter rose petals down the aisle?'

'A mix of pink, magenta and white?'

'Sure.' I took in the amazing views again. 'Sophie, your wedding is going to be spectacular.'

'You feeling okay about seeing Ben?'

'Of course, we're both adults.'

꙳

Thirty minutes later, I stood in the newsagency, mulling over a *PEOPLE* magazine, when my heart did a double flip. Ben was in the shop. His back was towards me, but I recognised his stance, his hair – longer than it had been – and his voice, especially his voice.

In that split second, Ben turned and our eyes locked. Clutching his newspaper, he brushed my arm, close enough that I could smell his aftershave.

He raised his free hand. 'Hey,' he said, smiling curtly and continued walking out to the pavement.

I wanted to flee to my apartment, lock myself in and hide. Or at least go and see Andy. Unsteadily, I picked up a magazine and walked to the counter knowing several pairs of eyes were staring at me.

Behind the counter, Barry smiled. 'You okay, Lily?'

I nodded, distractedly. Outside, I could hear Pamela's familiar voice. 'I heard you were back.'

I couldn't hear Ben's reply, but I could certainly hear Pamela. 'Were you going to tell me?'

The shop was eerily quiet. I wanted to leave but they stood facing each other blocking the path.

'I don't need this now,' Ben said. 'I've been dealing with tenants' complaints since I got back last night. What the hell are you trying to do?'

'Mum wasn't making enough money. I'm doing this for us, Ben.'

'No.' Ben's voice was loud. 'You're doing this for yourself, Pamela. You're being greedy, and in the process, making me very unpopular. What's wrong with you?'

'The rents are too low—'

'Too bad. I'm not letting you destroy these people's businesses.'

Pamela glanced inside and caught my eye. 'Is it because of her?' Pamela pointed at me and Ben followed her gaze.

'What? No.' His voice grew louder, sharper. 'You can't put up people's rents. It's illegal. And wrong. I won't let you do it. I'm going into each shop we manage and reassuring them. I'm surprised the owners of these buildings haven't sacked us, what with you giving them the run around and promising things you can't deliver.'

Pamela was defiant. 'You'll regret it.'

Ben shook his head. 'I'm amazed you haven't been run out of town. I'll be at the office later to go over the accounts, then I'm giving the contracts to Henry to manage.'

'You can't—'

'Actually, Pam, I can. If you'd read Mum's instructions about ensuring the integrity of her business, you'd know that. Now, if you'll excuse me.'

Ben walked away, leaving Pamela standing in the street. She strode inside the shop towards me.

'What a bloody troublemaker you are,' she snapped. 'I might have known you'd get in Ben's ear, though why he'd listen to a slut like you!'

Several people in the shop gasped.

'I- I haven't spoken to him,' I stammered. 'I didn't even know he was back in Clearwater.' I raised my head so I felt a few centimetres taller. 'And don't you dare call me a slut.'

'Pamela,' Barry said, 'you're suggesting a fifteen per cent hike in rents. It's grossly unfair.'

A couple of people in the shop nodded.

'And,' said a lady I vaguely recognised, 'if you put up the rents at the cafés and the flower shop, then shopkeepers will have to put their prices up, and no one will be able to afford their services.'

'You're running the risk of killing the town with these antics,' said Barry. He turned to me. 'Thanks in part to Lily's efforts, we know you can't change the rental agreements mid-contract.'

Pamela glared at me, before turning around and stalking off.

'Thank you,' I said to Barry.

'No problem.'

I hurried out of the newsagent's in a daze and headed towards my shop. I almost tripped over the pavement in my rush, but as I approached, I saw Ben and Pamela near my shop, still arguing. I ducked into Zena's.

I croaked, 'He's back.' I didn't care that she had a salon full of clients.

Zena nodded. 'I saw him a little while ago. I wanted to ring but was with a client. Sorry.'

'That's okay, but what am I going to do?'

'You're going to create the most spectacular wedding flowers Clearwater has ever seen.'

'I've just come back from the winery. It's stunning, a beautiful property. I don't think I can do it.'

Zena put down her comb and scissors and grabbed me by the shoulders. 'You can, and you will. But first, let's make you an appointment for Saturday. Your hair needs to be perfect.'

'I won't have time.'

Zena put her palm up to my face and checked her appointment book. 'I can schedule you for 8am.'

'What about Mrs Beattie?'

'Mrs Beattie will be bumped. She'll have to deal with it.'

❦

When Iris rang to check that I hadn't changed my mind about returning to the city, I updated her on the wedding plans. 'I'm nervous.'

'But why? The arrangements sound simple, and you've ordered enough of everything, haven't you? And you've got ribbons, rubber bands, raffia palms, clippers, etcetera—' she paused. 'Because you don't want to run out on the day. Imagine if you can't find your scissors or clippers?'

'All under control. And the flowers are being delivered on Thursday.'

'Lils, I've done a few weddings in my time. I'll meet you at Ravenstone first thing Saturday and we'll place the flowers together, if you like?'

'I'd like that very much.'

'Good. 8am sharp.'

I rang Zena and told her I'd have to reschedule.

'Fine, but ten at the latest. Mrs Beattie need never know.'

❦

'Hey, Lily,' said Ben, when I emerged from the cold room with a bucket full of yellow roses. 'Thought I might find you here,' he said, straight-faced. 'How have you been?'

'Not bad.' I plonked the bucket down on my bench. 'You?'

'Fine,' he replied, distractedly. 'I owe you an apology.'

I shook my head. 'No, I'm the one who's sorry. It was a horrible situation and I know how bad it looked.'

'Yes, it did. But I jumped to conclusions. I've been hurt

before and assumed it was history repeating. I didn't want to go through it again.'

'I understand.' My hands were clammy and a pain in my neck was on the verge of paralysing me. 'But Matt and I were definitely over. And we were over before you and I started going out. He turned up uninvited and proposed—'

'Can we leave the past in the past?' Ben asked, his voice serious.

I nodded.

'I got jealous and bent out of shape. I should have listened to you. I'm sorry.'

'Apology accepted.'

'I wanted to let you know that I'll be here for the next few months.'

I raised my eyebrows. 'The winery needs your full-time attention?'

'That, and Mum's real estate business. I need to salvage it after Pam's recklessness.'

'But what about her?'

'Pam's life is in Sydney. She was only ever supposed to stay a few weeks to help sort out the business. Instead, she's created havoc. I'm in the process of hiring a manager—'

'Taylor would be great for that job.'

'What? Is she thinking of moving here? I know she's your best friend...'

'Yeah. Probably not. Not sure why I said that. Wishful thinking.' But I missed Taylor and did wish she was closer by. 'So Pamela's agreed?'

'Not in so many words, but I can be pretty convincing when I need to be.' He leant against the bench. 'I'm seeing someone,' he blurted. 'Early days but it's going well. Uncomplicated.'

I smiled. 'She doesn't have an ex-boyfriend who pesters her?'

He crossed his fingers. 'So far, so good.'

'I'm really happy for you.' And I was. Genuinely.

'No hard feelings?'

'Of course not. We had fun, didn't we?'

He nodded. 'We certainly did. So, are you seeing anyone?'

I nodded. 'I think so, but like you, it's early days.'

As he turned to leave, I said, 'I'm really happy for you and I'm looking forward to meeting your new friend.'

CHAPTER 43

Andy

After work, Andy met Lily and drove her back to his house feeling happier than he had in months. In the not too distant future, he imagined the two of them playing happy families, tending a robust vegetable garden, with a kid or three. Definitely a chook run. A simple country life.

Lily reached across and squeezed his thigh. 'What are you smiling about?'

Andy turned slightly. 'I could ask the same of you.' He paused. 'I'm smiling because of you, us. Suddenly, my world seems a lot brighter. I've been looking for you all my life.'

Lily nodded. 'No pressure then.'

He pulled into his driveway, parked the car, and leaned across to kiss her. 'Stay here a moment.'

Lily looked confused. 'Why?'

'Patience.' Andy climbed out of his car, walked along the path to his front door, unlocked it, and then came back to the car. He opened the front passenger door and held out his hand for Lily to take, which she did. When Lily stepped out, he bent down and picked her up in his arms.

She giggled. 'Andy, what are you doing?'

He carried her through the front door. 'And over the threshold, we go.' But instead of putting her down, Andy continued walking into his bedroom where he laid her on the bed, smothering her in kisses. Tenderly at first and then more forcefully and passionately.

Lily sat up when they took a break.

'Are you okay?' Andy asked. 'Too much?'

Lily laughed, ripping off her clothes. 'Are you kidding? You might not be in any hurry to get naked, but I am.'

Andy didn't need to be told twice. Moments later, they were between the sheets and skin to skin.

❧

After they'd made love and were lying together entwined, Andy felt safe, stable and calm. 'Lil, there's no better feeling than having my arms around you.'

She looked up and kissed his lips. 'Really? I can think of a couple of things.' She kissed him again.

Andy hugged her tighter. 'This feels right.'

'You say that now—'

Andy kissed Lily's lips, silencing her. 'I'm so in love with you.'

CHAPTER 44

Lily

The next morning when we were lying in each other's
arms, I thought back to Matt and the secret I'd kept from
him. If Andy and I were going to be together, we couldn't have
secrets. Taboo subjects. I was done with that. He'd been brave
enough to tell me about his past. I needed to tell him about
mine. If I told Andy and he couldn't accept it, so be it. I couldn't
live with my grief and shame any longer. It was time.

'Good morning, beautiful,' he said, holding me tight and
kissing my neck. 'I didn't dream last night. You're really here?'

'Hmm.' I moved away slightly.

'What's wrong? Have I upset you?'

'No,' I said, pausing. 'But I need to tell you something.'

Andy released me and sat up. 'You have another boyfriend?
Husband?'

Tears trickled down my cheeks.

'Please don't cry, Lil. I'm listening.'

'Okay. Here goes.' I took a deep breath. 'I had an abortion when I was sixteen. I mightn't be able to fall pregnant again, so if you can't handle that—'

He stroked my arm. 'Have you tried?'

'No.'

'So we'll cross that bridge. We're together now. You're safe. Do you remember what I told you last night?'

I paused. 'That you loved me?'

'No. I said I was *in* love with you. There's a big difference.'

'And my abortion? Do you forgive me?'

He took me into his arms again. 'There's nothing for me to forgive. And it's way past time to forgive yourself.'

Tears fell. I cried and cried.

At last, I sniffed and said, 'Thank you.'

'What for? We're human. We make mistakes. We learn and hopefully move on. It's time, my Lily, to move on.' He smiled. 'Now, don't go breaking my heart.'

'I couldn't if I tried, Elton.'

'Nobody knows it,' we sang together.

I sniffed back my tears and smiled wider than I'd ever smiled. 'But when I was down—'

'I was your clown.'

Yep. Andy was the one for me.

❦

Over the next couple of days, Sophie visited the shop and examined the mock-up arrangements of her wedding flowers, tweaking here and there.

'They're beautiful, Lily,' she said Friday afternoon, when she saw the final bouquets and posies. 'And the headpieces and my tiara are out of this world.'

I smiled. 'Glad you're happy.'

Sophie beamed. 'I'm so happy. My wedding day is finally here.' She paused. 'Lily, you're definitely coming to the wedding, aren't you? As a guest? I've you seated next to Zena and Andy.'

Andy! We hadn't told anyone about our fledgling romance, but the secret would be out the next day. I didn't want to hide it from Zena.

I hesitated, then nodded. 'I want to, but I don't want to make it awkward for you.'

'Nonsense. But tell you what, I'm going to give Ben a talking to. He's a bloody idiot.'

'Please don't. It was my fault. And we've both moved on.'

'Really?' she quizzed. 'Both of you?'

I smiled. 'Ben told me he's seeing someone. I'm really happy for him.'

She tilted her head. 'You sure?'

'Definitely.' It was almost six o'clock. 'Don't you have a rehearsal dinner to get to?'

Sophie checked her watch. 'Aww. Late as usual.'

'Before you go, I have a little something for you.' I ducked into the cold room and came out with a delicate cream gardenia wrist corsage. 'Here,' I said, tying the ribbon around her wrist. 'For luck.'

Sophie examined it, eyes widening. 'It's beautiful,' she said, getting teary.

I kissed her on the cheek. 'Go on, get outta here.'

I was putting the bouquets into the cold room when Zena and Taylor appeared.

'Surprise!' Zena beamed.

'It certainly is.' I blinked.

'We're here to make sure you dazzle everyone tomorrow.' Taylor held up a suitcase. 'Zena rang and said you might need extra moral support, so here I am.'

Zena was carrying her mini sewing machine under one arm,

and in her other, she held champagne. 'I can't drink it, but I can watch while you two do.'

They walked inside, and I closed the door, eying Taylor suspiciously.

'Aren't you happy to see me?' she said, all hugs.

'Come on,' said Zena, walking upstairs to my apartment. 'We don't have a lot of time.'

I trailed behind them. 'For what?'

'You told me you didn't have anything to wear to the wedding, and no time to shop, so I knew you were in trouble.' Taylor opened her suitcase. 'I raided my wardrobe for my online shopping disasters. I've bought so many things that don't fit me.' She laid out several dresses and pairs of shoes. 'You're slimmer and taller than me. One of these will do.'

'These clothes are divine,' I said. 'And the shoes.' I picked up a pair of silver sparkly sandals. 'Gorgeous.'

'You're going to be the belle of the ball,' Taylor chirped.

'Or at least the wedding,' Zena added.

'I love them all, but I couldn't—'

'Fine!' said Taylor, throwing up her arms. 'Show us what you're planning to wear.'

I sighed and retrieved a beige sleeveless knee-length shift from my bedroom.

Taylor shook her head. 'Boring.'

'Dull,' added Zena.

'Lifeless,' said Taylor.

Zena seized a pink silk dress with white silk flower embellishments on the neckline and hem. 'This one is perfect.'

Taylor nodded. 'It's probably a bit big but it's still too small for me. If Lily wants it, it's hers.'

I stared in disbelief at the beautiful dress. 'Taylor, I couldn't—'

Zena interrupted. 'Shush. This is the one. How could it not be? Flowers! Now, try it on so we can get to work.'

Minutes later, I was wearing the dress and Zena had her pins out, pulling and tugging on all sides. After she'd pinned me, Zena stood back. 'Not bad. This won't take long to adjust.'

I stared at myself in the mirror. Suddenly, I didn't feel tired and anxious. I was feeling hopeful. The dress really was stunning.

'Oy.' Zena clicked her fingers. 'We don't have all night. Take it off, woman.'

I did as I was told and Zena got to work making the adjustments.

'I can't believe this is happening,' I said as Taylor and I drank champagne and watched Zena expertly handle the dress with her nimble fingers.

'I should have been a fashion designer,' said Zena, her mouth full of pins.

'You still can be,' Taylor replied.

Zena pointed to her stomach. She was barely showing. No one would guess she was pregnant.

'Baby clothes?' Taylor suggested.

'Maybe. I'm still coming to terms with being pregnant.'

'It's very grown-up,' agreed Taylor.

Zena nodded. 'Speaking of being a grown-up, Taylor has something to tell you, don't you Tay Tay?'

Taylor feigned shock. 'Why do I have to?'

'Because I'm pregnant and hormonal.'

'What is it?' I asked. 'Nate being difficult?'

Zena shook her head. 'He's MIA, so all quiet on that front. Fine, Taylor. I'll tell her. Taylor and I pashed and we're—'

'No way!'

'Way,' said Taylor. 'We got to talking. Talking led to kissing, kissing led to—'

I put my hand up. 'I get it, so when did this happen?'

'It's been brewing a little while,' said Zena sheepishly.

Taylor swung Zena around and kissed her. 'We're having fun.'

Zena raised her eyebrows. 'Fun? Is that what this is?'

'No...' Taylor said, genuinely worried.

'Congratulations.' I was truly happy for them. Andy and my news could wait.

'Yes, well enough of that. Focus, Lily,' said Zena, all business. 'Take off your robe and try the dress on again.'

I did as I was told and stood in front of the mirror.

Taylor raised her glass. 'Perfection.'

'Not bad at all.' Zena admired her handiwork before picking up some scraps of fabric and packing her machine back in its box. 'Tight schedule tomorrow. I want you showered and on my doorstep at 10am.'

'Then straight back here,' said Taylor. 'I'm doing your make-up.'

I nodded. 'And I'm meeting Iris at Ravenstone at eight.' I stared at myself in the mirror again. 'I'm really nervous.'

'We know,' said Zena, 'but I'll be by your side. It'll be okay.'

CHAPTER 45

I didn't think I'd be able, but by 11pm, I was asleep and, soon enough, I woke to Taylor tapping me on the shoulder. 'Sleeping beauty, it's after six. Shower time.'

I sat up, dazed. 'I don't think—'

She handed me a coffee. 'Drink this and hop in the shower. Today is not a day for thinking. It's a day for doing. Hustle.'

Before I knew it, I was outside the shop and staring at my chalkboard which said: *Love is the answer, and you know that for sure; Love is a flower, you've got to let it grow.* John Lennon.

We loaded the flowers into my van and arrived at Ravenstone just before eight.

Taylor took in the view. 'Wow, this is some place.'

The sun was shining and there was a gentle breeze. The day was picture perfect. Even the cows had come up to watch the spectacle.

Iris arrived soon after and greeted me with a salute. 'Reporting in, captain.' She glanced inside at the van. 'You've done good, girl.'

While I went in search of the manager, Taylor and Iris started unloading.

Later, the three of us were inside the dining room, placing posies and then, the larger arrangements on the fireplace mantles and side tables.

'Lily,' Iris was tweaking petals, 'these flowers are stunning.'

I smiled. 'Let's hope Sophie thinks so.'

Taylor tapped me on the shoulder. 'It's almost nine thirty, we should be getting back.'

I turned to Aunty Iris. 'Are you sure you're okay with delivering the bridal bouquets and crowns to Sophie's and then coming back here to scatter the rose petals? I feel bad—'

'Nonsense. Anyone would think I was an amateur. You take my car and I'll take your van. Now skedaddle, kids.'

'Your aunt's a good old stick, isn't she,' said Taylor as we drove back into town.

'Enough about Iris. What about you and Zena?'

'Yeah.' She beamed. 'I like her a lot.'

'But a baby? How's all this going to work?'

'I've taken two weeks' leave so am going to stay with Zeen, if that's okay? I don't want you thinking I'm ditching you.'

'Not at all. It's wonderful.'

'And we'll play it by ear. I'll commute most weekends because of Zena's Saturday workload, but if it works out, we'll look at something more permanent.'

'Here?'

Maybe, but Zena's open to taking a sabbatical in Sydney for six months after the baby's born. We'll see.'

'Ben's looking for an office manager for the real estate office.'

Taylor raised her eyebrows. 'Interesting, but I don't know the first thing about real estate.'

'Hasn't stopped others. Think about it.'

❦

Just before ten, I was at Zena's being ushered to the basin.

'I'm thinking loose and light, a few curls,' said Zena. 'Au naturale.'

'Sounds good.' I grabbed Zena's arm. 'I'm nervous.'

She hugged me. 'I know. Now pop your head under the tap and let's do this.'

Three quarters of an hour later, I wouldn't have recognised my hair. 'It looks amazing.' I couldn't wipe the smile off my face.

'I aim to please. Now get out of here. I have to check on Sophie and her bridesmaids. See you in a couple of hours.'

I walked inside my shop, hoping Iris would be back by eleven to open up.

Upstairs, Taylor was waiting with what looked like a full shop of make-up, laid out on my bathroom vanity. 'I don't think—'

'That's right,' she said, directing me to a stool in front of the mirror. 'There's no thinking today. Here, if you feel like talking, munch on these.'

I stared at the fruit salad, then sat as instructed and tried to keep my mouth shut. Taylor carefully pinned my hair back and got to work on my face.

'I'm not used to wearing foundation during the day.'

Five minutes later, 'Do you think black eyeliner is aging?'

Another few minutes passed before I said, 'Taylor, I draw the line at deep plum lipstick.'

Taylor sighed heavily. 'You'll wear what I'm applying. Also, it's not plum, it's *Passion* and it's perfect. Could you keep still? You're starting to annoy me.'

'I think I have diarrhoea.'

'Nice try. You're not escaping. Eat a grape.'

I squirmed. I wasn't used to people fiddling with my face. I even found eyebrow waxing a chore.

'For the love of God, would you please sit still.'

It was another few tortuous minutes before Taylor let me look in the mirror.

I was lost for words.

'Let's get you dressed.'

We walked into my bedroom where Taylor's dress was hanging. 'Thank you,' I said as she helped me into it.

Taylor stepped back and looked at me. 'You look beautiful, Lils.'

'Okay.' I looked in the mirror. 'Anyone would think it was my wedding.'

Taylor was stroking my shoulder. 'Let's do this.'

Iris had also appeared. 'Lily, you look exquisite.'

'Thank you.' I had tears in my eyes.

'No tears, Lily,' Taylor's voice echoed. 'You'll ruin your make-up.'

Composing myself, I turned to Iris. 'Everything okay?'

She smiled. 'Clockwork. Sophie looks almost as dazzling as you. She's thrilled with her bouquet, and the three crowns look perfect. You'll see for yourself soon enough.'

'Did you scatter the petals?'

She nodded.

'The wind's not going to blow them away, is it?'

'No. Lily, relax. Ravenstone is all set for a glorious day, and, if you're finished interrogating me, I need to get back downstairs. I left the shop unattended.'

While we waited for Zena and Andy, Taylor and I ate the rest of the fruit salad. I did my best to remain calm, though my hands were clammy. Thirty minutes later, they arrived at the shop – Zena looking exotic in deep purple and Andy, ravishing in a tux.

As soon as he saw me, he swept me into his arms and kissed me lovingly.

Iris, Zena and Taylor looked on, stunned.

I grinned. 'You're not the only ones who have secrets.'

'Apparently not,' said Taylor, clearly itching to ask more.

I took Zena aside as best I could in my little flower shop. 'Are you okay? I'm sorry I didn't tell you earlier, but it's very new. And then when you told me your big news last night, I didn't want to rain on your very happy parade.'

She squeezed me tight. 'I'm so happy for you. You make a gorgeous couple.'

'Now, you kids have fun,' Iris said, as we were leaving. She kissed my cheek, before standing back.

I nodded. 'Thank you.'

'And don't worry about Trouble and me. We won't get up to mischief.'

I gave Trouble a quick pat. 'Of course not.'

'Remember to breathe.'

Butterflies swirled in my stomach. My first wedding! I focused on putting one foot in front of the other and breathing. Always breathing.

'It's good of you to drive us, Taylor,' said Andy, when the four of us were in my van.

'No problem. I'm going to have a lovely afternoon with Iris, and I expect a full debrief tomorrow morning at Lily's apartment, 10am.'

'Can we make it ten thirty?' I said, feeling my voice falter. Andy held my hand and kissed it.

We pulled up at the winery and piled out.

'Thanks again, Taylor,' I said. 'For everything.'

She hugged me gently. 'Have fun. Leave me and Iris alone to gossip about you and totally rearrange your shop.'

Taylor drove away and I walked in, arm in arm with Andy,

Zena on my other side, towards Ravenstone Dining Room and the huge deck, where I could see bunting, fairy lights and my flowers. Cream silk bows decorated forty white wooden chairs, and rose petals were sprinkled the length of the aisle.

'I'm going to check on the flowers,' I said, as we got closer. 'I need to focus.'

As I said the words, I saw Ben talking to Henry. I waved before turning my attention to the flowers.

Now that the tables were dressed, the posies looked even more stunning, as did the bouquets dotted about. I nipped into the restaurant kitchen where I'd left my spritzing bottle and filled it with tap water, then gently sprayed the larger arrangements. They looked as good as they had the previous day.

Outside on the deck, I inspected the arrangement on the registry table. The sun was shining but it was still cool. I doubted I needed to worry about wilting flowers today, but I gave them a spray and picked off a browning camellia leaf. Perfect.

I put the spray bottle in a nearby cabinet and turned round to see Elsie and Betty standing nearby. I walked over and hugged them both. 'What a lovely surprise.'

'Betty is Sophie's great aunt,' said Elsie.

'I didn't know that.'

'You look very beautiful,' said Betty.

I blushed.

'And look at all the pretty flowers,' said Elsie, happily.

Zena tapped me on the shoulder. 'Hello, ladies, how are we all?'

'Very excited,' said Betty.

Zena nodded. 'Me too. We should take our seats.'

Henry and Ben stood to one side of a podium. Henry tapped

his foot, watching for Sophie. Ben patted his back and whispered something in his ear and they both laughed.

Moments later, Sophie appeared – a vision of a 1920s flapper bride, all cream satin and lace, strands of pearls hanging from her neck, and her delicate daisy tiara framing her face. In a word, stunning.

'She looks beautiful, doesn't she,' Zena whispered. 'The headpiece completes her outfit.'

'You're only saying that because it's true,' I whispered back.

'When the orders start rushing in, I want you to remember whose idea the headpieces were.'

'What do you mean, *when*? They already are.'

Zena winced. 'The baby!' She guided my hand to her belly, then rested her hand on mine. 'It might be my imagination but I think the baby wants to say hello.'

After the celebrant announced Sophie and Henry 'wife and husband' everyone clapped and whooped to the sound of Smash Mouth's, 'I'm A Believer'. All around, people laughed and drank champagne, basking in our friends' marital happiness.

'Congratulations,' I said to Sophie. 'Dazzling doesn't begin to describe how stunning you look.'

Sophie smiled widely. 'I feel like a princess.'

'I'm very proud of you, dear Sophie,' said Betty, her eyes filled with happy tears.

Sophie beamed. 'Lily, have you met my Aunty Betty and her dearest friend Elsie?'

'She certainly has,' said Betty, cutting in. 'Our sweet Lily comes to the retirement home most Sunday afternoons to bring us flowers. She's never too busy to stop and natter.'

'Even though we know she could be swimming at the beach or seeing friends,' said Elsie. 'Lily always brightens our day. She even adjudicates our Scrabble games.'

Sophie laughed. 'Really?'

I nodded. 'Not as easy as it sounds. There are some obscure

two-letter words.' I could see Andy standing nearby talking to the photographer and my heart danced. 'Did you know that Zo are Himalayan cattle?'

'That was dear April's favourite word. God rest her soul,' said Betty, getting misty-eyed.

Elsie nodded and held her close. 'Maximum score, thirty-three. On a triple-word square. April's other favourite was Qat.'

Sophie looked confused.

'Hallucinogenic drug,' I said. 'Maximum thirty-six.'

Sophie grinned. 'You have your work cut out for you, Lil.'

'And,' I added, 'Zena, Elsie, Betty and I do tap together.'

'Indeed we do,' said Elsie. 'You should join us next term, Sophie, dear.'

Sophie was saved from answering as Henry walked up and kissed her cheek. 'You ladies look very pleased with yourselves.'

'We were just telling Sophie how we know Lily,' Betty said, excitedly.

'Yes,' continued Elsie. 'We first met her when she stopped by the Sunday after Valentine's Day with flowers, but then quickly became a regular Sunday afternoon visitor—'

'Drinking sherry and adjudicating our Scrabble games,' Betty added. 'Sophie, darling, we have to find Lily a lovely young man, like your Henry.'

Sophie's eyes sparkled. 'I have done rather well for myself, haven't I?'

I nodded. 'You have. You both have. Congratulations, again. I'm so happy for you.'

'You regularly donate flowers to the retirement home, Lil?' Henry asked, knowingly.

'It's, er, not what you think,' I said. 'It's not like I'm being frivolous.'

'No! Indeed not,' agreed Betty. 'Our Lily is so hard-working, she's no time for fun.'

'Betty, I have fun every Sunday afternoon,' I playfully scolded.

Henry winked. 'I think it's marvellous that you give to charities, Lil. We'll discuss this in more detail *after* I get back from my honeymoon.'

'Exactly.' Sophie kissed him on the lips. 'No work talk today.'

'You're looking rather dashing,' said Betty, to Andy, who had drifted towards us with the photographer hovering beside him. 'I saw you canoodling by the rose vines with Lily. Please tell me you'll make an honest woman of her.'

'Betty!' I protested, trying to distract myself by listening to the Beatles' 'All You Need Is Love'.

Andy beamed and put his hand on his heart. 'I'll try. Isn't she beautiful?'

Sophie moved between Andy and me and linked arms with us both. 'Aunty Betty, they make a dashing couple, don't you think?'

Betty smiled. 'As good as you and Henry?'

Sophie glowed. 'I think so.'

'Hey,' said the photographer, tapping Henry on the shoulder. 'Can I steal you and Sophie, please? I've scoped out a setting down there, overlooking the valley and the ocean.' He pointed. 'The lighting's perfect.'

'Say no more,' said Sophie, as she and Henry followed him.

Elsie and Betty giggled as they chattered with other guests and called a waiter for champagne.

Ben appeared beside us.

'The best man,' said Betty. 'Elsie, Ben owns this winery.'

Elsie swooned.

Ben and Andy shook hands. Ben turned to me. 'Ah, your new guy. I definitely approve.'

'Thanks, mate.' Andy leant in and kissed me. 'I feel very fortunate.'

'Come with me,' Ben said to both of us. Together, we walked over to the vineyards. He pointed to several buds. 'Spring has sprung. It's going to be a bumper season.'

'How can you tell?'

'I can feel it.' He looked over several vines that had started shooting along trellises. 'I'm thinking of planting more roses.'

Among the thorny rose bushes, I could see tiny pink buds. 'They're going to look spectacular in a couple of months.'

Ben nodded. 'Roses and grapes in full bloom are a striking sight.'

'I've always wanted to know why roses are planted at the end of the rows. In addition to looking pretty,' I said.

'In the old days, rose bushes were good indicators of potential problems in the vineyard with mildew, soil, and insects, but now with all the modern treatments, they're no longer as important, but you're right, they look fantastic.' He halted. 'Now, it's more tradition than anything.'

'Definitely a tradition you should keep,' said Andy.

Ben smiled. 'There's someone I'd like you both to meet.' He walked up to an elegant blonde and slipped his arms around her waist. 'Andy and Lily, meet Nina.'

I felt instantly relieved. Ben was all smiles.

'Another champagne?' said Andy after they'd walked away, Nina's head resting on Ben's arm. I stared into my empty glass. 'Why not?'

Andy took my hand again, grabbed two champagnes from a passing waiter and led me further away from the crowd. 'Where are you taking me?'

'For a little privacy.'

I giggled. 'I'm not complaining.'

He backed me into a private alcove of rose bushes and kissed me.

Five minutes later, we were both hot and bothered.

'My hair's a mess,' I said, feeling it fall on my face.

'It's beautiful.' He stroked my cheek.

'You're just too good to be true,' we sang together and broke into laughter.

'We're both lunatics,' said Andy.

'But I just may be the lunatic you're looking for. Come on.' I took his hand and pulled him back towards the party. 'Everyone will wonder where we are.'

He swung me around and kissed me again. 'Can we take up from here later?'

I smiled. 'We can.'

Together, we walked back onto the deck, where guests cheerfully chatted, sipping champagne and eating canapés. American Authors' 'Best Day of My Life' was blaring and all I wanted to do was dance. I was delirious with joy.

'Hello, lovebirds,' said Zena appearing beside us. 'You two—'

'Yes, us two.' Andy chuckled.

Zena clapped. 'Woo hoo!'

'Finally,' I said, turning to Zena, my face flushed from the sun and champagne, 'I feel like part of the town.'

'Good. Don't ever leave,' she said, radiant and rubbing her stomach.

'No. Don't leave.' Andy wrapped his arm around my waist and took a sip of his beer. 'And what?' he said, turning to Zena. 'About your baby, are we going to be godparents?'

Zena smiled. 'You bet.'

'Thank you.' I turned to Andy, eyes wide. 'I didn't know what I was looking for until I found Clearwater.'

The three of us held our drinks up high and clinked.

'Here's to the future,' I said. 'Our future. Together.'

THE END

351

ACKNOWLEDGEMENTS

Dearest Lou, we had some awesome chats at your little flower shop in Wentworth Falls, NSW, Australia. You pushed me to write this book and I'm so glad you did.

Thank you, Michael Cybulski, at NAC for taking me on. After six published books, I thought no agent would want me. Thank you. Big shout out to Ros Harvey and Dennis Fisher too.

Massive kisses to Andrea Barton, my editor at NAC. When COVID ends, I owe you a big drink. Thank you for everything, including talking me down when I wanted to jump.

A huge thanks to everyone at Bloodhound for seeing this book's potential, especially Betsy Reavley. My editor Morgen Bailey, editorial manager Tara Lyons and publicist Maria Slocombe. Thank you.

Nicola O'Shea, thank you. You've been with me since the beginning.

To Lis Mamari, thanks for all of the hairdressing do's and don'ts. X

Squad: Susannah Hardy, Dianne Riminton-Johns, Annarosa Berman, James Worner, Shelley Kenigsberg, Desney King. I apologise if I've left anyone out.

Best friend reading group: Valerie Blackford, Bozena Gawart, Jane McLeod, Janette McLeod, Libby Sherrard, Fiona Truskett. It's almost 20 years.

My beautiful children, Josh, Noah and Mia. Thank you for putting up with me.

Parents, love you xx

My gorgeous partner, Chris. I adore you. I always loved Hi-5, but you made it real. XX

To Louise's husband, Anthony, and my best friend Lou, love you both.

Lou, you better be waiting for me on the other side.

A NOTE FROM THE PUBLISHER

Thank you for reading this book. If you enjoyed it please do consider leaving a review on Amazon to help others find it too.

We hate typos. All of our books have been rigorously edited and proofread, but sometimes mistakes do slip through. If you have spotted a typo, please do let us know and we can get it amended within hours.

info@bloodhoundbooks.com

Made in the USA
Monee, IL
26 September 2021